HE WILL
FIND YOU

An absolutely gripping crime thriller with a massive twist

CHARLIE GALLAGHER

First published 2019
Joffe Books, London
www.joffebooks.com

Please join our mailing list for free Kindle crime thriller, detective, mystery, and romance books and new releases.
http://www.joffebooks.com/contact/

ISBN: 978-1-78931-151-8

AUTHOR'S NOTE

I am inspired by what I do and see in my day job as a front-line police detective, though my books are entirely fictional. I am aware that the police officers in my novels are not always shown positively. They are human and they make mistakes. This is sometimes the case in real life too, but the vast majority of officers are honest and do a good job in trying circumstances. From what I see on a daily basis, the men and women who wear the uniform are among the very finest, and I am proud to be part of one of the best police forces in the world.

Charlie Gallagher

CHAPTER 1

Sunday

Diane Cummings heard the brakes squeal and felt the car lurch at the same time. It rocked her forwards gently. Her head had been back against the headrest, her eyelids fluttering closed. The early morning daze still hadn't worn off.

'What the hell . . .' her husband muttered next to her. She opened her eyes. They were just a few metres from the entrance to the car park where John would drop her off. She was due at work, already running late. Her eyes were dragged to movement across the front of their car — a small boy, ten or eleven years old maybe. He looked slight, his walk more of a stumble. He was in a grey top with a purple hood, his hair a dirty brown. She could make out freckles on a filthy face. His bottoms matched his top, they were grey too, but the purple detail was ad-hoc, like a splatter pattern. As he moved to the other side she could see he was barefooted.

'Jesus, John, that's blood!' She pushed open her door. The crossing in front of their car was raised and she stumbled a little as she made her way around. Light raindrops combined with a chilly breeze snapped her fully awake. 'Hey! You okay?' she called out. The face that turned to her was wide-eyed and

1

terrified. She raised her hands, palms out and slowed her walk. He looked like he was poised to run. 'Are you hurt?'

Her husband's door popped open. 'He okay, Di?'

She ignored him. The boy had stopped but he had only half turned. He looked like he was waiting for a starting gun to sprint away. She had edged a little further along the front of the car and could feel the heat from the idling engine. The blood on the boy was thick, she could see that now, but it was dry too. The staining was darkest on his head. It looked as if someone had tipped up a bucket of the stuff and it had splashed down his body, flattening his hair against his head. She could see dried streaks where he had swept it off his forehead and his hands were stained too. His hood was one big stain and even his feet had smatterings of the stuff.

'Are you hurt?' she said again. She smiled and nodded, as if it was okay for him to tell her. He looked at her, his eyes still wide but it wasn't fear that filled them now; they seemed to well up with moisture. His lips quivered. Maybe he was trying to form words? Di was patient, still standing in front of the car as the fan clicked on to cool the engine. The boy's eyes snapped towards the sound. It was the starting signal he had been waiting for. He darted away and broke into a sprint.

'John, call the police!' she called out. She took off after the boy. There was the shriek of brakes and a beeping horn as cars pulled up behind theirs. This was Canterbury's central shopping district, but it was early on a Sunday morning and the impatience was likely to be from shop staff running late. Diane pursued the boy along a route that led to the High Street. The main bus station was immediately on their right, the rear entrance to some shops on their left. The path was sheltered by a roof, held up by concrete pillars. At its end, the pavement turned sharp right where it met with a window display then cut back left. The boy was nearly at this point. She slowed to a walk as she struggled to get her breath back. The boy had stopped too at a window into Fenwick's department store. The display featured a male mannequin embracing a female version in a glitzy dress. Now there was a little boy sat in front of them, squatting on his heels. He looked even smaller than he had just a few moments before. He lifted his head as she approached. She hung back.

'Hey! You don't have to run from me, lad. I'm not going to hurt you, okay?' She was still trying to catch her breath. 'You're a lot faster!' she breathed, 'I'm no threat to you.'

The boy looked up at her but said nothing.

'Are you English? Do you speak English?' she asked. A bus pulled into the station and its doors hissed open. A couple of bored-looking passengers stepped out onto the pavement. They wore headphones and their faces were down. They split and filed away without casting her or the boy a glance. Diane looked back towards John and the car. It was closer; he had pulled it forward and parked in an area marked for taxis and set the hazard lights flashing. He was out on the pavement with his phone against his head. She could see that he was talking into it.

She turned back to the boy squatting with his back against the window. His legs were bent, stretching the fabric of his clothes over bony knees that pointed towards her. She was certain the staining was blood; nothing else looked like it — wet or dry. She'd seen enough of it as a retired midwife now happy to top up her pension with a simple retail job. She didn't think the blood was his, though. There was too much of it and it didn't seem to be leaking from any wound that she could see. The boy's expression was a rigid mask of fear that didn't look like it was going to drop away any time soon. His chest rose and fell fast enough for her to know that he was panicking, clutching for breath. His muscles would be saturated in oxygen, ready to propel him away at any moment. She didn't move any closer. She would wait for the police to arrive. There wasn't much else she could do.

A loud thud snatched her attention towards a black wooden pod that had blended into the early morning shadows. The boy noticed it, too, and his eyes sprung even wider. A man walked calmly around to where the front of the kiosk had fallen open to form a serving hatch. On the

3

side was daubed *Lost Sheep Coffee*. He wore a fleece with a matching slogan and he sent her a smile that dropped away quickly. He looked from her to the little boy squatted against the window and frowned.

'He okay?' The man walked over. He never took his eyes off the boy.

'He won't speak. I've asked him. I just found him like this, he walked from Dane John Gardens, just crossed the road in front of us.'

'That's blood though, right?' The man moved beyond her, closer to the boy, who now stood up, his hands reached back to lie flat against the window, like he was ready to use it to push off and away. He stared at the man, every inch of him tense. The man must have sensed the latent panic and took a step back. 'You okay little mate? That blood yours? We just want to know you're okay.' The boy bit down on his bottom lip. His head snatched to the noise of another bus that settled like a spitting cat. 'Just stay there, okay? You hungry?'

The boy's eyes followed the man as he walked back to his pod. He was back just a few seconds later, unwrapping a muffin and with a bottle of water tucked under his arm. He put the items on the pavement a few metres from where frightened eyes still followed his every movement. Then he backed away and he stopped next to Diane. The boy's focus flicked from the food and drink to the two adults. He scurried forward and snatched the items before backing up again to the window so sharply that it flexed as he bumped off it. He tore at the remainder of the packet like something feral and then froze as the window behind him pulsed suddenly to reflect the blue strobe lights of an arriving police car.

Diane breathed a sigh of relief.

CHAPTER 2

Detective Sergeant Maddie Ives had decided that walking from Canterbury Police Station was by far the quicker way to get to the location of the call. Much quicker than trying to take a car out in the traffic, something she had come to detest even in her short time working the area. It was before 8 a.m. on a Sunday morning and the cars were already at a crawl between the roundabouts at the top of the town. The medieval city had hardly been designed with modern-day traffic in mind.

Maddie walked through a damp subway that led under the bumper-to-bumper traffic. The draught seemed stronger down here, colder too. She pulled her jacket in closer and lifted the collar. Halfway along the tunnel was a bundle of homelessness with a cup next to it. Someone was wrapped in tight. She dropped a couple of coins into the cup and a dog's head lifted from under part of the cover. She met its bright eyes. 'You're welcome,' she smiled.

Her feet scuffed, as the walkway became an incline and the sound echoed off the tiled walls. Once she emerged back into the early morning light she discovered that although her method might be the quickest, it would not be the driest. Winter was dragging its heels. The emergence of spring was only hinted at in a subtle changing of colour and the appearance of some hardy shoots in Dane John Gardens that she now passed to her right. The rain was sudden and the freezing wind behind it enough to fool anyone into thinking it was still mid-winter, not the middle of March.

She turned left into the bus station to find a parked police car and a gaggle of people at the far end. She'd taken a short phone call to summon her to this point, the sort of call that started with a uniform sergeant apologising for making it in the first place and then saying that he didn't know if he should have called at all. Since her move to Major Crime, she had quickly become used to taking calls from sergeants who were at something they didn't like the feel of and had no idea what to do next. This particular incident concerned a young boy. He was barefoot, mute, and covered in blood. She could understand why it had immediately felt wrong. It being a Sunday, she was the most senior officer for the east side of the county and had been asked to attend in the first instance. The Duty Inspector was not yet summoned. For that to happen would typically involve a dead body, or at least a good likelihood of one, and nobody could guarantee that yet. Today she just happened to have been in a police station that was hardly five hundred metres from the boy in question; she could hardly complain, and the description had certainly piqued her interest.

She recognised the same uniform sergeant who had handed over a rape case a few weeks before. 'Hey, Joe.' She proffered her hand. Joe's handshake was firm but freezing cold.

'Morning, Maddie. Again, sorry to call you lot out on a Sunday morning.'

'Don't be. What have you got?'

'Pretty much as I said on the phone. A shop worker saw a boy covered in blood, walking barefoot towards the town. He came from the Dane John Gardens area. He hasn't said a word to anyone. He was hungry, though. Some fella runs a coffee pod over there and he's given him something to eat

6

and drink. I've tried to talk to our boy but he's not having any of it. He looks terrified.'

'Covered in blood?'

'It certainly looks like blood. A lot of it, too — like the kid's been bathing in the stuff. I don't think it's his. He won't let me get close enough to see if he's injured, but if it were his I don't reckon he'd be standing. It looks dry, too.'

'Okay. Did you get the actions done we talked about on the phone?'

'Yeah. The park's taped off best we can, it's not an easy scene to hold though — it's massive. I called CSI and they're on their way. I also spoke to the FCR and we've got no child mispers in the county at all at the moment. They did say they'd check further afield for us. With regard to violent disturbances, we had two in the city overnight involving blood, both night-time economy calls. Both at pubs. No kids involved as you would expect and not enough claret to be linked to our boy.'

'And RTCs?'

'A fatal on the A2. A long way from here. Car versus motorway bridge. All passengers have been accounted for. Did you want us to consider a media appeal?'

Maddie looked beyond the sergeant to where the group of people at the far end of the pavement had already swelled in number. 'No. Let's see if we can get him to give us a clue first. Contact the inspector at the FCR though, make sure he has every detail so he can let us know if anything comes in that might be linked.'

Joe nodded.

'In the meantime, I'll go and introduce myself.'

The group of people included a couple of women in the uniform of a chain of chemists. Their place of work had a rear entrance that Maddie could see as she approached. They had been so desperate to come out for a look they had left their coats, but still stayed to gawp at the small boy, scared that they might miss something in the thirty seconds it would take to go back and get them. Instead they shivered as they talked among themselves, their attention flicking between the uniform cops and the small boy backed against a glass window.

'We need everyone to back off,' Maddie announced. 'He's scared enough, don't you think?' She was careful not to raise her voice beyond the level necessary to address them all. All eyes turned to her. There was hesitation and some dirty looks, but she stared right back until they got the message. They did move back, some as far as the chemist's rear door. One disappeared only to come back with a handful of coats. Maddie turned back to the boy. The two uniform officers stepped back too. She wiped the rain from her brow. Her hair was tied up but she could feel the water running down the back of her neck. It was uncomfortable and it was cold. She noted the boy's bare feet sticking out from under him as he squatted against the window. He had to be freezing.

Maddie squatted down herself, close enough not to have to raise her voice but not so close for him to fear she might reach out and grab him.

'I'm a police officer. My name's Maddie.' She made a show of looking around. 'It's cold out here. Wet too. I've asked someone to get you some new clothes. Is that okay?'

The boy stared back. The rain seemed heavier and dripped from the overhang just a few steps behind. She heard a bus pull up, sloshing through standing water as it came to a halt. The boy still didn't react. Maddie studied the blood for herself. It looked like it was centred on his hair, as if a bowlful had been tipped on him from above and it had cascaded down, splashing on his clothes and feet. He had been bare foot when it had happened, she could see that. He was slight in build and he held himself like a boy rather than a young man. On the phone, the sergeant had guessed him at ten to twelve years old. She felt that was about right. On first impressions she fancied him as a witness rather than an offender, but she was keeping an open mind.

'Can you understand me okay? We're here to help you. That's what we do. That's why I'm here. I'd like to make you warm and to take you somewhere safe. Will you come with me?' Maddie was still squatting. She wrung her hands, careful not to reach out towards him. Her thighs were starting to burn a little but she wanted to stay low and in the least threatening posture she could manage. The boy tried to back away a little further. Maddie thought he had understood her. She assumed he didn't want to go anywhere with her. For now, at least.

'It's okay. You don't have to talk to me. I have an idea . . . you see that bottle?' She gestured at the empty water bottle beside him. The boy looked down at it. 'I'm going to ask you a question. If you touch that bottle then I'll take it you are saying *yes*. If you want to say *no* to me, you push that bottle right over, okay? You don't have to do anything you don't want to. I'm not here to hurt you.' She did her best to give a reassuring smile. The boy looked down at the bottle again. He reached out and pulled it closer and more central so it sat on the floor in front of him. Maddie could see a food wrapper there too.

'Can I get you some more water? And maybe something more to eat?' The boy's eyes dropped to the bottle. They lifted back to Maddie. He looked to be chewing on his lip. Maddie nodded. 'I'll take that as a yes! Give me one second, okay?'

She got up and walked to the coffee pod where a young man in a black fleece was leaning forward onto a serving hatch. 'I gave him a muffin earlier and the water. He ate it like he was hungry. Does he want another?'

'I think he does. They must be good muffins.' Maddie took out some money but the man held up his hands.

'No need. Can I get you a coffee too?'

'That's very kind. White with one. Thanks.'

'I just hope you sort the lad out. He looks like he's had a bad night.'

Maddie peered back over. The boy was staring straight at her, maybe even craning his neck slightly. Maddie couldn't tell if it was hunger or interest.

'I'll be right back with you, okay?' She called out then she looked around. The throng of onlookers was larger still, but at least they were staying back, positioned further up the pavement and under the protection of the canopy. Most were still, some shuffled on the spot while breathing into their hands. Towards the back, a taller man in a dark jacket with a hood up over a woollen hat stood out by his movement. He walked the length of the crowd before turning to retrace his steps. He was half-turned the whole time, his hands thrust deep into jacket pockets.

'Hey, Joe?' Maddie called out. The sergeant walked over. 'Can you get the details of the people stood watching the show for me?'

'Okay. Are you thinking they might be witnesses? The CAD said there was nobody here but the woman who called it in and her husband. They're being spoken to at the nick?' He sounded unsure.

'I get that. But if we assume this boy is a witness to something that covered him in blood, whoever was responsible might have unfinished business with him.'

The sergeant turned to the crowd. 'And you think that *someone* might be here?'

'We should consider it.'

'I'll get on it.'

'Thanks.' Maddie turned back to the pod. Her items were on the counter. She walked the few steps back to where she had squatted before. This time she put a white coffee on the ground, marking out her intention to move back there. She stepped over it with the bottle of water and the muffin to hand them to the boy. The hand that snatched out was stained with dry blood. It was a darker tone on the back than the front. Maddie had seen large bloodstains on skin before: the greater the volume of blood, the darker the tone. She lingered long enough to nod and smile, then stepped back to her coffee. As she sipped, a woman approached whom Maddie recognised immediately. She had been unsure who was on shift for CSI when she made the request, but she was always happy to see Charley Mace, no matter what the job. Maddie moved closer to Charley and further from the boy so they could talk freely.

'This is unusual,' Charley said. Her smile was subtle and quickly hid behind a coffee cup branded with the *Lost Sheep* logo. Her attention was focussed beyond Maddie to the seated boy.

'Unusual?'

'Are Major Crime branching out into the living? I can't remember the last time you lot called me to work on someone who could answer back.'

'Well, he hasn't so far. And I guess the assumption is that there might be someone dead somewhere. There's certainly a lot of blood.'

'You sound like you're living in hope!'

'Major Crime will do that to you, even after three months. It's no problem for you is it? Working with the living, I mean? You certainly don't need to worry about making small talk.'

'Well, you tell me. I've been told no one can get near him and we know nothing. That does make a CSI tasking a little more difficult.'

'Well, he hasn't ran away yet. We're taking it slow is all. In an ideal world, what would you need?'

'Depends. What are we trying to achieve here, Maddie?'

'Identity — his and the blood donor's. Assuming it is blood and that it's human, of course.'

'Well, I can tell you that quite quickly. The rest depends on a lot of things. What we hold on our databases for comparison for one, having something to compare it against for another.'

'So then . . . ideal world . . . hit me with it.'

Charley shrugged. 'I can't say I've seen this too many times, but, seeing as how there's a lot of claret and he's not speaking, I'd have to treat him like a dead body. I won't mention that to him of course. So I'd want photos of him as he is and where he is, then I'd want swabs from his clothes and hands, and scrapings from under his nails as well as swabs from his mouth. I'd take an indent of his teeth, too, and comb his hair while he was lying down on my sheet. I'd want his clothes, obviously — the outer ones will do for a start. I'd also want to measure and photograph any wounds — a full body map. This whole area is a scene, too. Even now he'll be shedding contact evidence, let alone when we go to move him.'

'So not much then.'

'That's assuming there's nothing that needs further investigation from those initial checks. This is why I prefer working with the dead.'

Maddie turned back to where the boy was already finishing his second muffin and water like a ravenous animal. 'Maybe I shouldn't have gone with the muffins so soon. How much of that would you do here?'

'Here?' Charley scanned her surroundings. She looked less than impressed. 'The photo of him *in situ*. Other than that, I would bag up his hands and feet and get him moved as soon as possible. I don't want to be doing much more out in public and I'm damned sure he doesn't either.'

'I thought you'd say that. Do me a favour would you and get your suit on. The sooner he sees you in it, the sooner he gets used to the idea.' Maddie went back to her coffee and squatted to pick it up, she sucked the liquid through the lid. The boy was looking over at her. He looked a little more relaxed, a little less like he was waiting for his opportunity to run at least. He pulled the empty bottle closer.

'I need your help,' Maddie said to him. 'I really want to know how I can help you the best. That means I need to know who you are and maybe what happened. I can see you have blood on you. Are you hurt?'

He hesitated. His eyes were still wide but now he looked upset, like he was holding himself together. The bottle toppled over. His hands snatched back from it like it was scalding hot. His movements were slower as he reached back out to pick it up. Maddie took her time.

12

'Okay, is it blood?'

The boy's nostrils flared; his face shook like he was fighting a sob. He rested his hand on top of the bottle. It didn't fall. He moved his hand back. Maddie took that as a *yes*.

'A person's blood?'

Again the boy hesitated, but his hand did eventually rest on top of the bottle.

'Do you know this person?' Maddie's thigh muscles burned so bad she changed her position to sit with her legs crossed in front of her.

He tapped the top of the bottle again. This time he was quicker.

'And this person . . . is it a boy?'

His hand shot out to tap the bottle top.

'And is he okay now?'

The bottle tipped over. The boy's head dropped as if he was studying the ground. He sniffed sharply and this caught her out; since he wasn't talking, she had begun to wonder if he was capable of making any noise. He had pushed out harder this time; the bottle rolled towards her and she stopped it with her hand. She leaned forward to stand it back up, close enough for the boy to reach. His sniffs had become a cry, he was doing his best to conceal it by wrapping his hands around his legs to cuddle them tight and pushing his face down into his chest. His shaking shoulders gave him away.

There was a rustling behind Maddie. Charley was in full forensic gear and hanging a few steps back. Beyond her was a uniform police officer with a carrier bag branded by one of the local department stores. CSI were ready and the change of clothes she had asked for was here. She turned back to the boy.

'I want to help you and I want to help that boy, okay? Or at least I want to find the bad people that hurt him. Was he a boy like you, or a grown-up?'

The boy looked over at her but he made no other movement.

Maddie tutted. 'Sorry! Let's try something you can answer. Was he a grown-up?'

The boy reached out. Maddie realised she was holding her breath. He rested his palm on the top of the bottle then moved it away again. Maddie finally took a breath. A seriously injured or dead man she could cope with; she wouldn't have known where to start if the victim had been a child.

'Someone in your family?' She leant forward, her voice softer. She was holding her breath again.

The boy's hand moved slowly towards the bottle but he stopped short, his eyes meeting hers, as if he wasn't sure what to do next.

'Your dad?' Maddie chanced, thinking he may need a prompt.

Now he tapped the top of the bottle. It was a quick but definite movement and then he buried his head between his knees.

'Did someone hurt him?'

The boy's movement to tap the bottle was quicker still.

Maddie felt a surge of anger, enough to make her sit straight. 'Listen to me . . .' Her voice carried her emotion and the boy looked up instantly, as if he might have thought her anger directed at him. 'I want to find the bad people that hurt him, but you need to help me. You don't need to speak to me, not if you don't want to, but you need to help me. Can you do that?'

Charley must have recognised her cue, and moved closer. The boy's eyes lifted to take her in. She was in a full white suit with her hood up, her shoes covered in bright blue plastic, her hands the same colour in forensic gloves. The elastic pocket of material that would cover her mouth was slung around her neck, ready to pull up. A large camera hung down and stuck out from her chest.

The boy took his time. His eyes moved down Charley until they rested back on Maddie. He reached out for the bottle and tapped it gently.

Maddie exhaled and gave her best warm smile. 'Thank you. This is Charley. She isn't a police officer. She's just here to get the information we need and she's going to ask you to help her. Some of it might seem strange, but I promise you it's all so we can find the bad people. Okay?'

He tapped the bottle.

'We just need to get a picture of you, that's all. Then I want to take you to the police station so we can stop all of these people looking at you. Is that okay?'

The boy pushed the bottle over then backed away from it, pushing himself against the window, using it to get to his feet. His body tensed again and he looked around anxiously. He was looking for a way out, for somewhere to run. She lifted her hands, showed her palms, and took a step back.

'Stay calm, okay? I'm not going to make you do anything you don't want to. Just like we said, okay?' The bottle was too far out of reach. Maddie picked it up, slowly and gently. She stood it back up — not too close; he would just have to take a step. She edged away. 'Can we at least change your clothes? You look cold and wet?'

He was still looking around and his gaze fell finally on the bottle. He leaned forward to tap the top.

'Thank you,' Maddie said. 'Just a minute . . .' She turned back to Charley. 'It's going to have to be here. All of it.'

'You want me to do a full forensic exam here? A juvenile? In public and with a crowd?'

'I don't think we have any other choice.'

'He's a kid. What about appropriate adults? We need permission from someone! And just the thought of stripping off a boy in public! I don't think it's a good idea.'

'It isn't. It's a terrible idea. But it's also the only option. You can list me as giving you the permission. It will be far worse if he runs. Then my options are to let him go or to wrestle him to the ground in front of all these people and all their camera-phones. If that happens, permission will be the least of my problems. Do you have a forensic tent that we could use maybe?'

Charley exhaled. 'Well, I've never used it on a live person before. I'm not sure it sends the right message. But I take your point. The thought of you grabbing hold of him — shaking off all the contact evidence. It's enough to make a CSI officer shudder.'

Maddie flashed a smile. 'I wish I'd thought of that! You'd have crumbled immediately.'

'I would have.'

Maddie stepped back over to the boy. He was lower again now but still pushed up against the window. He looked at her expectantly. She squatted down to his level. 'I know you don't want to go to the police station and we can't leave you here. So I'm going to sort somewhere more comfortable for you to go. Just for a short time. We'll get you changed first, but we'll do that here. You don't want to go anywhere just yet, but we can't stay here. So we get you changed. My friend'll do a few bits and pieces to make sure we get the information we need and then we'll go somewhere else. Is that okay?'

The boy hesitated but finally he did reach out to tap the bottle.

'Okay then. I'll need to go and make a phone call. I want somewhere warm and safe ready for you. Is it okay if I walk over there for just a minute?' Maddie stood up. The boy pushed the bottle so it rolled into her feet. She met Charley's gaze and he shrugged. 'Okay then little friend, let's do this together shall we? I'll stay right here.' She did manage one step away as Charley moved in closer. The boy stood up as her CSI colleague stepped in awkwardly. Later, Maddie would tease her about how she might have been doing this job too long — she was definitely more comfortable working with the dead.

'Maddie . . .' This time it was the uniform sergeant's voice in her ear. She turned away to speak with him.

'What's up, Joe?'

'We got details for the onlookers — all except one. I couldn't get to him in time. The bastard made off after he took a picture on his phone! I was talking to someone else and I heard the click go off. Some people are pretty sick.'

'They are. That will be on his social media by now. Nothing we can do about that.'

'I know. I've never understood that. Is there anything else you need from us here?'

Maddie considered this for a second. 'I don't think so. I need to start making some calls for somewhere to go. There are emergency foster placements that Social Services can sometimes sort.

'There are. I never have too much luck with Social Services.'

'They're just strapped — like everyone else, really. I hope they can help. I'm not sure what I can do with him if they don't.'

Joe nodded. 'They have to help. I reckon that lad's been through enough for one day.'

CHAPTER 3

Harry Blaker's daughter, Melissa, pulled her coat tighter and folded her arms over her lap. She knew he had noticed, too. She caught his eye and smiled awkwardly. It was a cold morning. Harry didn't normally feel it, but even he was aware of the cold wood of the park bench seeping through the back of his waxed coat. The early morning rain had now stopped but the trees lining the banks still shed droplets that made dimples in the slow-moving river.

'We should have gone to a coffee shop,' he said.

'I know you don't like them.'

Harry was stuck for a reply. Stuck for anything to say if he was honest. He didn't mind cafés; it was other people he didn't like and he would usually spend his rest days as far away from them as he could. His daughter hadn't wanted to come up to his house. He could understand that. The last time she had been there they had argued, almost to the point of no return. Maybe that was why she had suggested a park bench. There were still people around, a few runners and dog-walkers mostly, but they would be noticed if they made a scene. As it was, nobody was paying any attention to them, and Harry had no intention of making a scene today. Today was about building bridges, not fanning embers.

'You would be warm at least,' Harry said.

'But you would be uncomfortable. Not that you look massively relaxed out here.' Melissa wrapped herself up tighter.

He smiled and waited for her to turn and notice.

'What?' she said.

'I fancy a coffee.' He stood up. A large drip bounced off his closely shaven head and he flinched.

His daughter giggled.

'You need a hat, Dad.'

'Not in a nice warm coffee shop I don't!'

There was a coffee shop a short walk across a footbridge. Melissa led the way. It was one of the major chains and clung to the side of a superstore like an afterthought. It was busy. He could tell his daughter was conscious of him as they joined the back of a lengthy queue.

'How about you grab that table, Dad? I'll sort this.' She pointed at a table that was being vacated by a couple with a young family. The surface was a mess of dirty coffee cups and empty crisp packets. It was close enough for him to put his jacket over the chair. He tried to pass her a ten-pound note. She refused, firmly enough for him to know not to try again. She was so like her mother.

Harry picked at a discarded newspaper. There was a time when he read them every day — he'd even had them delivered for a spell. He never read them anymore and didn't watch the news either. What wasn't depressing was either entirely sensationalised or entirely made-up. The problem with twenty-four-hour news channels was the need to fill twenty-four hours. Melissa returned. They waited for a spotty youth with an ill-fitting uniform to clear the mess from their table.

'Coffee, black, two shots,' she said.

He scowled. 'Shots?'

'That's what you get when you ask for *strong*.' She sat down, still with her coat on. It was warm. The tall windows were condensed, highlighting the contrasting warmth with

19

outside. Either she didn't plan to stay long or she'd been chilled to the bone. He reckoned on the first one.

'How have you been?' he said.

'Good.' She sipped at her coffee. It looked like it was far too hot for her. It dawned on him that she was rushing, like she didn't want to be there at all. With the grief and desperation of losing his wife, Melissa's mother, had come some stark realisations. The first was that he now faced the world alone, that the retirement they had planned, that was within sight, had been taken away. But one he hadn't seen coming was just how important his wife had been in managing his relationship with his daughters. Suddenly he didn't have her around to soften his questions, to communicate on his behalf, to explain that sometimes he said things that could be misconstrued, that could come across as harsh.

Ignore your father! That's just his way!

Thinking back, Harry realised that this was something Robin had said a lot. He was a police detective; his whole life had been about finding the truth from people who would seek to deflect it. You didn't just walk through your front door and switch that off. His daughters had often been the subject of his questioning: boyfriends, living status, study — for him it was all about knowing the truth so he could keep them safe. It was because he cared. But neither of his children wanted to be sat down with a light shone in their eyes and questioned about their day-to-day lives. Without Robin, his relationship with both daughters had quickly deteriorated. They were all that he had left and he was more terrified of losing them than he could even comprehend. They pushed back. Harry wasn't used to that. When their mother died they were both studying at university and they lived away. It was easy enough to cut him off and he didn't chase them. He didn't know how.

Today, on a cold park bench and now in a crammed coffee shop he hoped that he could at least make a start — with one of them at least. Mel had finished university early. Officially she was 'taking a year out', but that had already run into two and she wasn't showing any signs of wanting to go back. The university was accommodating: in the circumstances, they had told her that her place was there when she wanted to finish the course. But Harry was no longer sure she wanted to. At first, he was disappointed and angry, but he had quickly come to realise that she was suffering, that she simply wasn't able to finish her studies right now and that this was his opportunity to show understanding of his daughters' needs.

'You speak to your sister?'

'Of course,' Melissa snapped, as if it was a stupid question. It was too. There was twenty-two months between them and they had always been close. When they lost their mum, they had become closer still.

'She okay?'

'She's Faye. She'll always be okay.'

'Did you tell her you were meeting me today?'

'Yeah. We got together actually, to sort your birthday. Half each.' She reached down to her bag and lifted out a small box wrapped in brown paper, impossibly neat with string tied off in a bow. Robin had always loved a traditional wrap; it was just like how she would have done it. She'd always spent a lot of time and effort getting it just right. Melissa pushed the box towards him. He rested his palm gently on the top and ran the rough string between his fingers. He didn't want to unwrap it.

'You didn't need to bother,' he said.

'It's your birthday, Dad. Of course we needed to bother. Open it!'

He felt the string for the last time before pulling it apart. The paper followed. The white box underneath had a picture of a watch on the front.

'A watch?' He hoped he had hidden his disappointment. He had a watch. Robin had bought it for him, twenty years or more since. It looked a little worn out but it was simple and functional. It suited him.

'A smartwatch. It links to your phone, so when we send you a message you'll get an alert. When me and Faye talked, it was the only thing we could think you needed. It might mean you actually respond to us!'

'I forget to check it. I'm not a fan of the things.'

'I know that. This way you only need to check it for the important stuff. Like when me or Faye call or text!'

Harry nodded. He recognised the symbolic nature. At least it showed that they wanted to speak to him. Just a month ago that wouldn't have been the case. 'Well, okay then . . .'

'Just give it a try, okay? The instructions are in there, but it's easy. I've got one, too!' She pulled up her sleeve to show a sleek-looking black watch. It didn't look at all simple or functional.

'Thanks,' he said.

'No problem. But you might need to work on that fake gratitude!' She chuckled but she eyed him closely.

'I'll bear that in mind! I am grateful. You know me and new things. I'm happy that you want to be talking to me though. I'm just happy to see you, that's enough.'

'Well, now you have a watch, too.'

Harry sat back. He tried to form words but abandoned the attempt in favour of a swig of his coffee. He couldn't think how to start. Melissa picked up on it.

'What's the matter? It's okay, you know, if you want to take it back. I won't take offence.'

'No! It's not that at all.'

'There is something then.'

Harry licked his lips. He put his drink back on the saucer and fixed on the dirty brown liquid that picked up the light as the surface rippled. He had always been fine with breaking news, good or bad. You learned it quick in policing — just get the news out, hard and fast, then deal with the aftermath gentle and slow. Delaying only made it worse. But this was new to him. This was his own family.

'He's getting out.' He had to force the words, but finally they came. It was out in the open. He almost felt a little relief.

'What? Who?'

'The man who . . . the man who was driving the car. He's getting out.'

'He's getting out? How can he be getting out? It's four years — not *even* four years! He got twelve!' Her chest was heaving.

'I know . . .' Harry hesitated. 'Good behaviour.' He knew it was a mistake the second the sentence fell from his lips. He knew how it had made him feel when DCI Julian Lowe had told him. If finding out the man who killed your wife is getting out of prison after just four years was a blow enough to knock you to the floor, the phrase *good behaviour* could kick any remaining oxygen from your lungs. Melissa couldn't even repeat it.

'Good . . .'

'I know.'

Her chair scraped and she stood up. It was as if her own reaction caught her by surprise and now she didn't know what to do. She dropped back into her seat, her face flushed. She wiped a hand over her eyes and sniffed.

'I wasn't going to tell you at first — I mean it changes nothing. But I thought you'd want to know.'

She jerked a nod and sniffed again. 'Yeah. I guess we should know. Better that than just bump into him one day, eh?'

'I guess so. And for all I know it might appear in the media.'

She looked at him intently. 'How do you feel about it?'

'Well, I can't say I'm delighted. I was told on Friday. My first reaction wasn't good, but I've had some time. Whether he's in prison or not, it changes nothing. It doesn't bring your mother back.'

'Or take her further away.' Melissa's voice broke. A thick tear ran down her cheek and she wiped it away. She looked around to check that nobody was watching.

'No, it doesn't do that either.'

'Good behaviour!' She snorted a laugh. 'Fuck!' Her eyes flicked up, they were ringed-red and watery. 'Sorry . . .'

He waved her away. She could have that one.

23

'Will you get to know where he is?'

Harry stalled with a sip of his coffee. 'They haven't told me.'

'But you could find out?'

'I could.'

'Are you going to?'

He paused. 'No.'

'You had to think about that! I remember what you said when he was sentenced. I can't have you doing anything stupid, Dad. I can't lose you too.'

'Don't be silly. It was an emotional time.'

'And now isn't?' She wiped a fresh tear.

'We've had some time. Even if I found him, what would I do? He was a junkie. He was the getaway driver for another junkie who was also a petty shoplifter. His life was nothing. *He* was nothing. So he comes out of jail? He'll still be nothing. A bottom-feeding scumbag spending every moment trying to get his fix. Not a life any of us would choose. He's got what he deserves.'

'Has he?'

Harry shrugged. 'I can't worry about him. All I care about is you — you and Faye. We need to make sure we're alright.'

'The Blakers against the world, hey?'

'Something like that.'

'Those of us that are left.' She eyed him closely again.

'I guess so. I suppose what I'm really worried about is that . . . that this might set you back.'

'Set me back?' Melissa's cheeks dimpled when she bit down on her jaw. It was something her father had come to recognise as a warning. 'You mean what with me self-harming an' all that?'

Harry raised his palms and bowed his head. He wasn't here to have a go at her. Not this time.

'Yes. I know how this has made me feel. I just don't want . . .' He ran out of words. He'd practiced this, too. He'd reckoned he knew just about what to say but the words had gone now. All that was left was a lopsided smile and a guttural sound as he tried to find a word that worked.

'I'm fine, Dad. I told you, I'm getting over it. I haven't had a down day for a little while now.'

A down day. Harry almost smirked. That was just about the understatement of the century. Harry had seen depression come and go in colleagues, or at least he had seen them come and go from the workplace with it. What he had never seen, what he had never really understood, was just what it was like to be around someone under its dark blanket. To love someone who was so down and listless it was as if death itself was quietly and silently consuming them. Harry could still remember the terror every time he had turned up at her house. He'd had his own key and would let himself in. He'd find her in bed and would take her a cup of tea. Every day for weeks, he'd just prayed that he'd find her still breathing. The self-harming part he had coped with better. But the depression . . . Robin had kept the worst of that from him, but with her gone he was aware of it constantly.

Melissa stood up, smiling. It looked like she was doing her best to be reassuring. It was the sort of smile he should be giving her. Harry leaned back to peer up at her. He couldn't remember just when the roles had switched in this relationship, when she had become the one protecting him from the harsh realities of the world, buying him watches so she knew he was safe.

'I need to get back to it. It was nice to see you, Dad.'

Harry rose to his feet and pecked her on the cheek. 'You too.'

'We'll do this again soon. I think Faye will come along. She's back for Easter.'

'That would be great.'

'Okay then. I'll send you a text.'

Harry lifted the box with his new watch, 'And I'll see it straight away.'

Melissa smiled. He watched her leave. He remained standing, stock still among the bustle of the coffee shop, even after she was out of sight.

CHAPTER 4

Rain had been a feature of the day but it seemed to have come on stronger for the night. The windscreen wipers did their best but the deluge was too much. Oncoming vehicles were just blobs of distorted lights in the film of running water and he held his breath as he turned right, across the fast-moving carriageway and onto the hardstanding that made up the car park for the Ports Café. He was more than a little relieved to feel the terrain change under his wheels as he made it across. The Ports Café was situated between the towns of Langthorne and Ashford and it doubled as a truck stop, providing a place to park and twenty-four-seven services for lorry drivers. It was ideally situated and aptly titled, being just off the M20 motorway and twenty minutes from the main ferry port that linked the UK with mainland Europe. The Channel Tunnel was closer still at just a five-minute drive.

The hardstanding was a large area, but the torrential rain made everything blur together so it looked like almost every inch was covered in dark outlines of HGV's resting in silent formation. Some had interior lights visible under pulled curtains where their occupants were still up and awake, others lay in darkness. It was late, nearly midnight. He was right on time for his meeting.

His car bounced and lurched over the rutted surface and filthy, black water burst from the potholes when his wheels dropped into them. The terrain was made up of grey grit, but the forty tonne lorries and their slow manoeuvres had churned it up, gouging out holes and scars for the rain to dance in. He found a space of sorts and turned off the engine. The sound of the rain was suddenly louder and, with the wipers stopped, the windscreen had become a slow-moving blur. He pushed up the hood of his top.

As he stepped out, the rain was so hard he could feel the strikes against his head and shoulders despite his layers. The water bounced off the ground all around. He was drenched almost instantly. He locked the car and ran across the hard standing. The rain blew into his face and he could barely see the café entrance. A heater blew searing air at him the second he stepped through the door. He dropped his hood and wiped his feet, taking a moment to scan the interior. He didn't know who he was looking for. The message had just said that he should order the pancakes with a coffee and he would be *found* — whatever that meant. He stayed at the door. He could feel his excitement increasing. It was mixed with a little anxiety but overall he felt alive, adventurous. He was about to pass the point of no return. Up to this point, it had been a bit of a game, but once he sat down and uttered his order, things would get a lot more real. It had been hard work getting this point but it had been worth it. Finally he felt like he was a significant part of the world. He had worth, value; he was *part* of something — or on the cusp of it at least. He just needed to sit down and make his order.

'In for a penny . . .' he muttered aloud.

'You okay?' The woman's voice from behind him made him jump. He turned to see a thirty-something waitress looking him up and down with her hands on her hips. She gave him a smile but it looked a little empty. He thought it might be a pretty smile when she meant it. 'Can I get you anything?'

'I er . . . I just wanted some pancakes . . . and a coffee,' he blurted out. He had been practicing it in the mirror ever since he had seen the message. It had seemed cooler in his bedroom, more natural. He scolded himself; he needed to be calmer. These people were the real deal. They would see right through him.

'Okay then. Did you want to find somewhere to sit? You should find somewhere!' The smile was more of a flicker now as she gestured at the interior of a café that was largely empty. Three tables were occupied by single, male occupants, all of whom looked like lorry drivers. He chose the table furthest away from any of them in the opposite corner to where he had entered. The café had windows on three sides and the counter was to his right. He sat facing the door with the parking area beyond. He had to strain to see through the swathes of rainwater. He was trying to see a car — some movement . . . anything at all.

He jerked to the noise of the door opening. A man in a long, black coat stepped in. He wore it open and a black hood rose out the back and over his head. His pale skin was emphasised by the harsh lighting on a face made reflective by a layer of moisture, and there were bags under his eyes that seemed to almost glow red. He was looking down, shaking his jacket free of loose water. His eyes snatched up suddenly.

The coffee arrived and he was glad of the excuse to look away. The woman seemed to linger on him. He waited for a question. It didn't come. When she moved away the man in the long, black coat was closer. He took the seat opposite.

'I'm J-Jack,' he spluttered. He was caught out, a little panicked, the intensity in the man's stare making him feel intensely uncomfortable. He stood up to shake hands and cursed himself for the nervous enthusiasm in his voice. He had knocked his coffee, too, enough for it to slop over the sides.

The man ignored his hand. 'Your name means nothing. We don't use given names. You will earn your name.' His voice was a low hiss, his teeth clenched. Jack slowly sunk back into his seat and swallowed. The man glanced around the café and then returned his gaze to Jack. He had a tired-looking face, like someone who hadn't slept for days, but the eyes that beamed out from it were a bright blue and it was a struggle to break away from them. Up close, Jack could see that the man's skin was pitted and around his mouth was a red rash, as if he might have shaved with a blunt razor. He had a small tattoo on the side of his neck: three curious symbols in a row, maybe four; it was partially hidden by his chin most of the time but Jack could see it all now that the man had his jaw jutted towards him, doing nothing to conceal his disgust. His hood had fallen back a little, enough to reveal red hair that was shaved close and receding in a V shape. His forehead was slick with moisture, and he wiped it away with a hand that was tightly bandaged. Jack saw a flash of red on the palm side, as if it still covered a fresh wound. He tried not to stare.

Jack cleared his throat, which suddenly felt a little dry. It had all been a bit of game to this point, an adventure, something he could stop. This had been the point of no return. Suddenly he wished he hadn't crossed it.

'Sorry. I . . . I guess I need to get used to the rules, right?'

The woman returned and pushed the pancakes in front of him. The movement made him jump again. He sat back and thanked her. She moved away without asking his guest if he wanted anything. Jack watched her.

'Do you know why you're here?' the man said.

'Yeah. Well, I think so. I know that I'll be matched, that though I've proved myself with the solo challenges, there are now tasks I have to complete with someone else—'

'With me.' The man leaned forward and his eyes seemed to increase in intensity. 'This is a test. We have tasks to complete. We pass or we fail — together. You understand what I am saying?'

'I . . . Yeah, I mean, I know that bit. I saw that on the—'

'I have been failed once. The fact that the cause of the failure was not mine is the only reason I get a second chance. I will not get a third. I will not fail again. Do you understand?'

'I understand, yeah. No worries.'

The man licked his lips. 'No worries?' The lips curled at the edges; it was a long way from a smile. He took a phone from his pocket and Jack could see the Apple logo on the back. The phone made a sound like a camera shutter, then a few seconds later a sound like someone had blown into the top of a bottle — a message had been sent. 'I will not fail again.' He stood up and Jack leaned back to look up at him.

'Okay then.'

'Our journey starts tomorrow.' He strode to the door. The white noise of rainfall pushed its way in for the moment it took for him to step through. Jack watched as he lingered for a few seconds outside. When he moved away Jack strained to follow his direction and found himself rising to his feet.

'Are you leaving already?' The woman who had served him was back and standing close enough to block his view.

'Yes . . . it's . . . er . . . it's getting late.'

'You don't like my pancakes?'

He looked down. He hadn't touched them. 'Eyes bigger than my belly. Sorry. I'll try and do better tomorrow!'

'Tomorrow?'

'Yes, so it seems. Oh! I didn't pay!' He scrabbled in his pockets but she was shaking her head.

'Tomorrow's fine.' She walked away across the floor and through a door behind the counter. Jack looked around. None of the other occupants were paying him any attention. He shrugged and gathered up his car keys. When he pushed open the main door it looked like the rain had worsened if anything. He bent his head and made for his car.

CHAPTER 5

Monday

'Why are you just telling me this now?' Maddie had been in full flow but she was stopped abruptly by the question. Detective Inspector Harry Blaker always growled when he spoke but she was learning to differentiate — and this was a more upset growl than standard. It was first thing Monday morning and she was bringing him up to date on the weekend. She was just a few points in.

'Do you want me to tell you the rest?'

'Does it get any better?'

'Depends what you mean by better.'

'So far it can only get better. You've got a boy covered in enough blood for you to think somebody came to some serious harm in front of him, who can't communicate, and was walking through a town centre barefoot. Why am I only hearing about this now?'

'Give me some credit, Harry. You were off-duty. I appreciate you were on-call for emergencies and major incidents, but this didn't fit with either. The kid's safe. He was when I got to him. It was basically processing a crime scene and we did that. I was just going to explain the rest, calling you out would have achieved nothing more. I did everything you would have done.'

'No, you didn't. I would have called my inspector.'

'I made sure the FCR inspector was fully aware.'

'He doesn't run the Major Crime department for your area.'

'I take it your weekend off was not a restful one?' Maddie huffed. 'Whatever your problem is, you don't need to be taking it out on me.'

Harry's lips flickered. Whatever his reaction was going to be, he had stifled it. 'This thing you have . . . where you don't ask — where you don't *want* to ask. I can't work out if it's because you still feel that you've got something to prove or if it's just plain arrogance.'

'I've got nothing to prove. Not to you, not to anyone,' Maddie spat.

'So it's plain arrogance then?' Harry said.

'I don't like being micro-managed.'

'There's a rank structure. It's been around for a hundred years or more, so it's pretty well tested. You report upwards, that's just how it works.'

'And don't you like to remind me? I've sent you a full report from the weekend, there's nothing more I can tell you anyway.' Maddie made for the door that would take her out of Harry's office. She left it swinging open. She threw her daybook onto her desk as she passed and continued on. She needed some fresh air. Maybe some fresh coffee too.

* * *

When Harry found her, Maddie was a little calmer. The red mist had cleared enough for her to see the situation with a little more clarity. Harry might even have had a point, but it was the way he had got it across that had upset her. When they had first started working together he had made her feel like that a lot, but she felt like they had moved past that now. Most of the time if he was upset with her these days it would

32

be a conversation rather than a one-way rant. She was pretty sure that the difference today was not the circumstances, but his mood. He had to be carefully managed. If there was any suggestion that she was actually in the wrong then she would need to be the one to apologise. Digging her heels in would be pointless.

Maddie was aware of movement in her peripheral vision. She lifted her head enough to see Harry's midriff as he sat down at her table. He was directly opposite. She kept her eyes down and could just see his hands. They were interlocked and resting on the scuffed, wooden surface of the table, almost touching the two coffees she had purchased a few minutes earlier. She pushed one towards him.

'Black, no sugar, extra strong,' she said. Harry didn't react. She lifted her head. No one had ever had the ability to make her feel like this. She was desperate for him to talk, to give her a sign that she wasn't in trouble. She hated that he could make her feel like that. 'It's a sort of apology.'

'No, it isn't. It's a hot drink.'

'You want me to say it? You want me to feel like some scolded child?'

'That's how you're acting.'

'So well done, job done, then.'

'What does that tell you?'

Maddie huffed. She took a moment. 'I'm sorry, okay?'

'For what?'

'You don't have to make this more difficult for me. Point taken.'

'This is important. For what?'

Maddie huffed again. 'You were right, okay? I should have called the Major Crime inspector. It fit the criteria. But I didn't.' She finally made eye contact. Harry was still fixed on her with his back straight. He wanted more. 'And I shouldn't talk to you like I did, even when you are being a miserable old git!' She chanced a smile; it got no reaction. 'I'm still not great with working with people. I was working covert for a long time and spent long periods not really reporting to anyone, having to make my own decisions, decisions that ultimately kept me alive. I had to manage myself and I learnt to trust my own instincts. I know I'm struggling a little to adapt, but I will. When I was working CID I was told more than once that I needed to get over myself. Maybe they had a point.' Maddie had a second go at a chuckle. Harry finally reached for his coffee, a sign that she had said enough perhaps. He pushed the lid off.

'You're a fine detective — sharp and brave. But it doesn't matter how good you are, we're all better when we bounce ideas off other people. The rank thing, that is important, but I'm more upset that you didn't call me to get my opinion, not my instruction. We work together or we don't work. I wouldn't have come out and taken it over — I know you're capable — but there's more to it than that. It's about knowing that you respect my opinion, that you want a discussion at all. I would have called you.'

Maddie felt a little stung. She hadn't considered that angle at all. He was upset that he didn't think she trusted him enough to call.

'Point taken. I guess I saw you as the next rank up and I can have problems admitting that I might need some support. Everything got done, that's the important thing.'

'We'll see about that.'

'I'm sorry. I respect your opinion — more than I care to admit. And in the future I will look for it. As long as I can get over myself, that is!'

She still didn't get a smile from him but he sat back and seemed to relax a little. She took a sip of her coffee; it was still scalding hot. 'How was your weekend? I assume you didn't do anything you wouldn't want to be disturbed from?'

'No.'

'Okay then. So what made your weekend so terrible?'

'It was my birthday.'

'Your birthday! I had no idea. You know, for most people that's a *good* thing. Some people even celebrate it.'

'Some do.'

'But not you.

'Not me. What were your fast-track actions?' Harry snapped back into work mode. Maddie huffed to show her frustration at the closing down of small talk. She'd raised the point before: it was a basic courtesy among colleagues. She knew she was wasting her time.

'I asked for the FCR to review all the calls that had come on the box up to twenty-four hours before. Anything with blood in it. I looked at assaults, night-time economy, domestics and RTC's. There was nothing that matched. I had DC's reviewing for any missing children, just in case I wasn't aware — I know it's unlikely. I also asked the FCR to put news out to bordering forces in case there was something that matched from further afield. I had resources out doing house-to-house and CCTV reviews, commercial and private. I was hoping to see where he came from but nothing yet. The boy had a full forensic examination. The only thing we couldn't get was the scrape from his mouth, but Charley's happy she can get DNA from his hair. Oh and I had a search team do the park and area as a whole — there wasn't a blood dog in the whole county on a Sunday.'

'Anything else?'

'What did I miss?'

'He was barefoot, right?'

'Yeah.'

'So he hasn't come from far. We could start with the theory that he lives in the area. Your report says he looks thin, malnourished even, and his clothes were cheap. He sounds like he might be known to Social Services. No harm in circulating his image among all the children's services that cover Canterbury. See if anyone recognises him. All police officers too, for the same reason. And hotels . . . is anyone checking in Canterbury hotels for disturbances they didn't report, or asking the question as to whether they have anyone in with a boy around ten to twelve years old. We might get lucky.'

'Okay . . . No, I haven't had anyone at hotels and I didn't consider Social Services. So maybe I didn't think of everything. We wouldn't have got through to Social on a Sunday anyway.'

'You might not,' Harry conceded. But Maddie knew what he was really saying.

'Like I said . . . point taken.'

'I'm not trying to make a point, Maddie. Not anymore. We are where we are. The ports, too. The ferry port and the Channel Tunnel . . . they have their own system for recording calls. It's worth checking with them what calls they've had, also finding out if any kids missed their boat or train.'

'Okay. I'll make sure that happens.'

'When is Charley expecting results from her assessment?'

'She's going to try and fast-track the DNA. She said three to five days. We were able to ascertain that the blood wasn't his at least — and it *is* human. The boy seemed to indicate that it was his dad's, but we can't be sure. He had a few bruises, but nothing more than you might expect on a ten-year-old boy. He was in good health. Just thin.'

'The boy's still the key, then. What did he have on him?'

'Nothing. Empty pockets. And I mean *completely* — not even pocket litter.'

'Okay. It's all very odd.'

'It is. I'm heading out to see him this morning. We put him in an emergency foster home. Somewhere Rhiannon Davies knew. The local police have used it as an emergency provision in the past. I think she's retired now — we were lucky Rhiannon had a relationship there. I made sure there was a patrol there all night. They took a plain car. We can't be sure if he's in danger.' Rhiannon Davies, a detective working in CID, was someone Maddie trusted implicitly and Harry knew it. She didn't expect him to question her faith in her. He didn't.

'It's right to be cautious.' Harry said. He sipped at his own drink. 'I read the report. Not a word said, but he reacted okay to the forensic examination?'

'That's right. He just sat still and looked terrified. He understands well enough, though. He was definitely responding to my questions.'

'And you got yes and no answers only?'

'In a fashion. It certainly wouldn't be evidential. We came up with a way of communicating between us. The kid touched a plastic bottle for *yes* or pushed it over for a *no*. It was the best I could manage.'

'That's where the dad ID came from?'

'Yes. His reaction seemed to back it up, too. He got very upset.'

'What are we doing around psyche assessments? Maybe getting him some help with the talking?'

'I have a forensic psychiatrist meeting me at the home. She's also an expert in trauma in children, which includes those that present as mute. They go hand in hand it would seem. I didn't have a choice about that . . . the Control Room inspector called her direct. Apparently he's used her before when he worked counter-terrorism. He spoke with her and then had me call her to give a summary.'

'Do you think she can help?'

'She didn't give me much on the phone. Struck me as the sort who wasn't going to commit to anything until she had more of the facts. Makes sense, I suppose. I sent her a sanitised version of the report I sent you.'

'Sanitised?'

'Yeah, I redacted the address details. I wasn't sure I should give it to her to be honest. The fewer people that know where this kid is, the better for me.'

'Okay, makes sense.'

'It does and it doesn't. Turns out she's vetted to a higher level than you or me. She's one of the few people in the country with her specialist skills. She's based in the West Midlands and a lot of forces use her for migrant children. I guess they get a lot that have seen some pretty nasty stuff. You hear about it . . . kids fleeing the Taliban or the war in Syria. She must be trusted, to work in counter-terrorism at all.'

'So we can trust her, that's what you're saying?'

Maddie shrugged. 'Her vetting level says so. And she's based a long way from here. If we can trust anyone . . .'

'But you didn't trust her enough to give her the kid's address.'

'I was being over-cautious. I don't like not knowing anything about what happened here. I'll send her the address details and have her meet us there. Best we don't unsettle the kid any more than we have to.'

'Okay then, I agree with you.' Harry's face softened. It might have been the beginning of a grin. 'And it's so nice to be given the chance.'

* * *

The elderly man counted out the last of his pocket change to match the bill exactly. Jack puffed his cheeks out. The man lifted his head and pushed back his thick-lensed glasses. His nose scrunched up like he was worried about losing them again.

'I think that's about right lad.'

It was Jack's turn to count it, to make sure that it married up with the seventeen pounds, twenty-seven pence that showed on his screen. He was due a break; it was two hours into a shift that had started at 7 a.m. and he hadn't stopped yet. There were several people queuing for his checkout behind the old man. He took his time counting it all out. Then he broke the news that his till was closing down for fifteen minutes. Inwardly, he beamed at their upset. He ignored the tutting and eye rolling as he walked across the floor and thumped through the double doors at the back of the supermarket that led to the break area. He needed a cigarette. His shoes scuffed and caught on the brown-edged floor tiles as he walked through the staff area. On the shop floor the same tiles would squeak under his sole where they were polished to within an inch of their life. Not back here. The staff, it seemed, were not as important as the customers.

His coat was on a hanger in the locker room that doubled as the boiler room. It smelt musty and close. He didn't stay in there long. He pulled on his coat and moved through a fire door that took him out to the rear of the shop. They were supposed to leave the site completely for a smoke. Nobody did. A small patch of grey concrete greeted him, it overlooked the loading area and was raised enough to meet with the back of a lorry. The floor underneath was littered with cigarette ends. A lot of them would be his. He sat on the edge, his legs dangling against the cold concrete. The nip in the air though, was pleasant and fresh. The rain clouds of the night before had scarpered to leave a clear sky and a ground frost in the parts that still lay in the shade. The door thumped again. Alyssa followed him out.

He had liked Alyssa Mills immediately. Not necessarily for her looks. He thought her rather plain looking, especially when she came in some mornings and you could tell that she was running late and hadn't had time to do much with her hair. He liked her attitude more. She was a lot like him. The job was a pain in the arse, a way to get some cash for the weekend. It didn't mean shit to him and it didn't mean shit to her either. She smiled and sat next to him. He lifted his carton of cigarettes. She had her own in her hand but she took up the offer.

'Am I seeing you tonight?' she said. It seemed she had been up in plenty of time that morning; her black hair was straight and the blonde roots that had started to show were gone. Her eyebrows were dark and lengthened onto her cheek with a flourish, her lipstick and nails bright red against her pale skin. This despite warnings at work that she needed to *tone down the goth*. Jack had been there when one of the bosses had used that expression to her and they had shared a rolling of eyes and a humoured smile. No one said *goth* anymore — no one relevant at least.

Jack sucked on his cigarette, narrowed his eyes and shaped his mouth to blow the smoke out as a thick clump. 'Sure. We can do something early on if you like. I gotta get an early night, though. I've got an early start tomorrow.'

She reached out for his thigh and slid her hand up it. 'I was thinking the same thing!' She giggled. That was another reason why Jack liked her. She was an easy lay. 'And since when did you care about a late night and early starts?'

'I've just been knackered recently.'

'Fine then. We'll get a movie or something. You can buy me a pizza and I'll make it worth your while. I'll be gone in plenty of time for your precious beauty sleep. Fuck knows you need it, right!' She bumped his shoulder playfully.

He giggled, expelling another lungful of smoke, then bumped her back. 'Sounds like a perfect night.'

The door behind them thumped and Jack heard feet scuff behind him. He was staring out over the yard, his thoughts elsewhere.

'Time's up people!' The nasal voice of Jamie, their shift supervisor, cut through the haze. Jack bit down hard; how he hated that voice.

'We just got here,' Alyssa replied. Jack stayed looking out, refusing to even acknowledge him.

'You get fifteen minutes. I saw you both go. I started my watch. It's fifteen minutes now and you're not even back at your station. I suggest you get going. You get two paid breaks. I won't pay you for a minute more.' The shoes scuffed again and the door made a slamming sound. Jack checked his watch. Alyssa looked over at it too.

'Is it really fifteen minutes already?' she said. 'I swear, it's ten minutes of walking there and back. We only get a few minutes off.'

Jack threw his spent cigarette to the floor in front and watched its trail. He liked to imagine it as a shot down plane, passengers pressed up against the window to watch their doom arrive. He straightened his arms by his side, ready to push himself back to his feet. He glanced at Alyssa. 'You know what,' he said, 'when I'm in charge, that fucker will be the first to die!'

She chuckled and held out her cigarette carton towards him. 'Fuck him! Another?'

Jack grinned. Yet more reasons to like her.

* * *

Hythe Road was one of the arterial routes into Ashford. At most times of the day it was choked with traffic but rush hour had brought it to a standstill. Maddie was looking out at the faces of the other people in their cars. There was nothing better to do. Conversation had been stilted. She had long accepted that Harry was not the sort of man to make small talk, but today it was even more noticeable. She was sure his foul mood wasn't all her doing, but she wouldn't ask; she knew better than to waste her time. In the early days, she had felt awkward around him, human nature perhaps — the need to fill the silent void. Not anymore. She was turned away, staring out of the passenger window while Harry stared forwards at the rows of brake lights. She liked to people watch. It had been a big part of her life as an undercover police officer and she had learned quickly that you needed to be tuned in to people: how they were feeling; what their intentions were; what they wanted and whether they presented a threat. It was surprising how much information you could get about someone with a quick glance. Looking around today she was sensing a lot of frustration: people checking watches and leaning out to try and see what the hold-up was. It was just after 9 a.m. and a lot of these people were probably late for work. Maddie was late too. She had called ahead and agreed to be there for nine. Their meeting was at an address that was less than a hundred metres from where they were sat, just off a roundabout at the end of the M20 slip road.

It would be another twenty minutes before they were able to park outside. It was a large detached property, a typical 1930s house, big and square with bay windows top and bottom and a front door with a porch, off to the left side. The door was answered almost immediately.

'You must be Sergeant Ives?' An older woman with a beaming smile greeted them. She wore loose-looking blue jeans and a fleece top zipped up under her chin. Her hair was tied back; it had a brunette base but the grey looked to be taking over. She stepped back and gestured them inside.

'Maddie.' They shook hands. Harry introduced himself with his full rank and they shook hands, too.

'Nice to meet you both. I'm Rose. I run the house here. I know you're here to see my new guest. He's in his room.'

'How has he been?' Maddie said.

Rose pushed the door shut behind them and puffed out her cheeks. Her smile dropped away a little. 'Quiet.'

'He's not said anything then?' Harry cut in.

'No. He won't even look at me, love. He's closed all the curtains on the top floor. It's as a dark as night up there. He was under the covers last I saw him. He would only take the smallest room, too — it's like a box, really. I think if there was a dark hole up there, he would happily crawl in. But it's early doors. I've had a lot of young people here through the years and there's not much I haven't seen before. A lot of them just need time. Time and a loving heart. That's all any of us want, really!' Rose beamed enthusiastically at Harry, whose attempt to mirror it looked like it had caused him pain. 'The poor love's been through something mighty terrible from what I hear. I know you'll get to the bottom of it. These kids . . . some of the stories you hear . . .' She was shaking her head. 'Everyone deserves a childhood.'

'They do. Is my colleague here yet?' Maddie said.

'No, but she called. She said she was running a little late. Stuck in the traffic. I got the impression she's had quite a journey. Is she not local?'

'She's not. Her skills are not that common, unfortunately. She's come down from the Midlands somewhere.'

'You don't work together often, then?'

'We haven't worked with her before. She works with . . . well, with another department usually. But she's the right person to help us with our friend upstairs I'm sure.'

'Well, okay then. She gave me very clear instructions on the phone. She said to leave the boy alone until she got here. She said that if anyone arrived before her, I was to keep them away from him. I guess she means you!' Rose chuckled, but it was uncertain.

42

'Don't worry,' Harry said. 'I'll let her know that you passed on her message. But we'll need to speak with him now.'

Rose shrugged. 'Not for me to tell you what to do. I said I'd let you know. She was very insistent on the phone, though. I wouldn't say she sounded too . . . well, friendly.'

'You direct her to me,' Harry said. He made for the stairs. Maddie flashed her best reassuring smile at Rose then followed him.

Every one of the steps creaked, which seemed to be in keeping with the house in general. The walls were painted plainly in a light tone at the top and a slightly darker tone under a worn dado rail. The furniture was an assortment of different types and shades of wood, and the carpet faded lighter the higher they went — Maddie put it down to years of sunshine being allowed to pour through a large window at the top. Today it was covered over. A cabinet at the foot of the stairs had one door that wasn't quite closed. The whole house had the serendipitous feel that came with misshapen carpentry, and of odd furniture and décor that might have been rejected elsewhere. But here, among similar pieces, everything made sense. Maddie considered that this was not unlike children who had passed through these doors; they were all uniquely different and therefore the same. She was glad of the creaking steps; each one would announce their approach. She could still picture the terrified expression that the boy had worn like a mask when they'd first met. She couldn't imagine the impact of sneaking up on him now.

The light dimmed the further up the stairs they went. The large window was covered by a thick roller blind. The doors on the landing were shut too. All bar one.

'He's in there,' said Rose, a few steps behind them. 'One of my rules is that they don't close their doors. I'll leave you to it. I'll put the kettle on for when you're ready.' Rose headed back towards the light of the ground floor. Soon the stairs gave their last creak and she was out of sight. Still ahead of Maddie, Harry stepped onto the landing, but stopped halfway to the open door. Maddie stayed still. She had one foot on the landing, the other still taking her weight on the next step down. She leant forward.

'Hey.' Harry's gruff voice cut through the silence. 'My name's Harry. I'm a police officer. I'm here to help you out, lad. Will you help us?' Harry paused. Maddie couldn't see into the room so she just bent her head and tried to listen. Her eyes focussed on a piece of carpet that was frayed where it butted up against the banister. There was no response. No sign of any movement either.

'We want to help you. And if someone else needs help then we want to help them too. But you need to let us know what happened. Can you do that, lad?'

They waited . . . still nothing. Harry looked back at Maddie. Even in the low light, she could see he was frustrated. She edged forward a little.

'I want you to know that I'm here too. I'm Maddie, remember? I was with you yesterday.'

There was a sound. Just a small sound, like someone moving a duvet or a cover, but movement all the same. Harry beckoned for her to come closer and stepped back so she was in front of him. She was close enough to see into the open room. It was small. There was a window at the back where hints of daylight leaked out from behind another blind. It was a miserable day and, even with the blind wide open, it would hardly have been bright. She took a step to the left, enough to make out a bed. The covers were gathered up from the edge into a pyramid, the shape of a small boy sitting up.

'You must be hot under there!' Maddie said, genially. She waited a few more seconds. There was no more movement. 'I'm not going to come any closer, okay? I'm not coming in. I'm just here to talk to you, to make sure you're okay. Just like yesterday. You remember that?' There was still no movement. 'I need to be sure you're okay. Can I see you at least?' She waited, longer this time, determined to coax a reaction. Eventually the cover moved and a spindly arm appeared. It pulled the cover away from a face that still wore the same terrified expression.

'Okay, good!' Maddie said. The boy's eyes caught the poor light behind her but only enough to give a clue when they moved. They moved now, from her to the inspector stood behind her shoulder. 'I brought a friend. Harry here wants to help you just the same as I do. He's a good friend. He *can* help you, too. But you need to let him. Is it okay if he stays? I will, too. I promise.' The glint moved back to her. The boy had wrapped the bedsheet round his shoulders like a cloak and his legs were crossed in front of him. Maddie's eyes were becoming a little more accustomed to the poor light and she could pick out some details. He wore a white vest and tracksuit bottoms that rode high up his shins. To his right was a bedside cabinet. The boy groped for something under the duvet then pulled out a battered-looking water bottle. Maddie beamed as he placed it down on the cabinet.

'Is that the water bottle from yesterday?'

He looked right at her then reached out to touch the top of the bottle.

'Well, that was really good thinking!'

He tapped the bottle again.

'What would really help is if I knew what to call you. Do you have a name?' Maddie was still smiling. She was sure that she would be better lit than he was. He should be able to see her facial expressions. He tapped the bottle.

'Can you write it down maybe?'

The bottle toppled over. It rolled off the edge and fell onto the carpet beside the bed.

'Okay . . .' Maddie tried to think. 'Is there any way we might be able to find out your name?'

The boy moved off the bed and took the duvet with him to sit on the floor. His arms and legs were so desperately thin, even for a young boy. He pulled the duvet tighter round his shoulders and set the bottle up in front of him, only to push it over. He looked up at her expectantly.

'I tell you what, the first time I heard about you, I was told you were seen coming out of Dane John Gardens. That's the park near where I found you. Now, you don't look much like a *John* to me, so how about Dane? Is it okay if I call you Dane? For now at least.'

The boy took a moment, maybe considering her question. When he reached out, he picked the bottle back up and tapped the top.

'Good! Dane it is. So, Dane, are you hurt anywhere?'

The boy pushed the bottle over. Maddie already knew from the forensic examination that he had some bruises on his back and legs — small ones, the sort that a boy his age picked up easily. Charley had still taken pictures as part of her assessment and documented each one diligently on a body diagram. Maddie had wanted to get the boy checked out by a doctor but that had proven a step too far. He had been okay with Charley, but just the suggestion of going to a hospital was met with a very obvious reaction. A medical assessment would still need to happen, but it would have to be when they had a little more trust.

He stood the bottle back up. His eyes lifted expectantly.

'Do you take any medicine regularly, Dane? Like every day?'

He pushed the bottle back over.

'So you don't have asthma or anything that I should know about?'

The same reaction. He picked the bottle straight back up and looked at her, it was becoming routine now and his expression had softened a little. They were getting somewhere.

The doorbell punctured her concentration — the boy's too. The glint in his eyes suddenly moved away from her, trying to see beyond her as he anticipated a threat. His body shifted and he brought his legs up tight to look even smaller.

Maddie held up her hands. 'It's okay. You're safe here, okay? I have a friend coming here who wants to help us both. That might be her.'

His eyes still searched. He pulled the duvet tighter. Maddie heard the front door being pulled open. Soon after, there was a shrill voice. Maddie couldn't make out words at first, then it got louder. *What do you mean? I asked you specifically not to let them up there before I got here!'* From the corner of her eye, Maddie saw Harry turn and then she heard the stairs creaking as he moved quickly down them. The boy scrambled back onto his bed and buried himself in the duvet. The bottle still stood in the middle of the floor.

Maddie raised her voice a little to be heard. 'Tell you what, Dane . . . I'm going to go and talk to my friend. I'm going to tell her that we need to give you a few minutes, okay? But then I am going to come back up. It will be me that comes back up to talk again. I'll bring my friend up to say hello, so you know that she's just here to help. Is that okay?'

Maddie got no reaction. She gave it a few more seconds then turned for the stairs herself.

She made it to the ground floor and found Rose in the kitchen, which was dominated by a large table. Rose smiled at her as she felt the side of a big teapot on the stove. 'I'll make a fresh pot, then,' she announced.

A woman was on the other side of the room. She stood tall and slim in a smart grey skirt and matching jacket as she scrolled through her phone. She glanced up at Maddie before dropping her eyes to her phone again.

'Anna?' Maddie prompted.

The woman raised her eyes and lowered her phone a little. 'Yes. And you are?'

'DS Ives . . . Maddie. We spoke on the phone briefly yesterday. And this is Inspector Harry Blaker.'

'Well, okay then. So you'll remember the description I gave of my role?' She was curt and it felt instantly like a telling off.

Maddie didn't appreciate being told off once in a day, much less twice. She bit down on her lip. 'Yes, I remember we spoke about—'

'What we spoke about was the need for me to assess the young person ahead of any other professionals. I said specifically that this would include police officers. What I *told you* was how important that would be.'

Maddie took a breath before she replied. 'I seem to have built a little rapport with the lad. I was the first person on scene and—'

'So you said yesterday.'

Maddie took an extra breath. She could feel her anger rising and needed to be calmer. She had been assured at great length that they needed this woman. 'And how was your trip down?' she managed, finally. 'You're from the Midlands, is that right?' She looked to small talk to calm the room as a whole. Maybe they could start again.

'West Bromwich. I left at four this morning and drove for five hours to provide you with my advice. I do not expect to arrive to find it is already being ignored.' The woman's tone showed no signs of softening.

'Maybe we should have used someone closer.' Harry's growl carried a warning that Maddie had come to recognise. She knew he wouldn't care if a senior officer thought they needed her or not.

'Closer? If you can find anyone with my skillset closer then you go right ahead.'

'I'm not convinced we need a particular skillset just yet,' Harry said. 'Time will tell.'

The woman still had her phone in her hand. She pushed it into her pocket and fixed her attention on the inspector. 'You are aware of my CV? Of my experience in police matters?'

'No. All I'm aware of is the boy upstairs. I've been told that he needs a lot of patience and understanding before we can hope to find out what he knows. I just hope that is all part of your skillset, too.'

The woman pouted a little, as she looked Harry up and down. 'I have worked with children who have seen parents killed by the Taliban . . . who have been trained as suicide bombers at the age of seven and had the soles of their feet slashed to prevent them running from their fate . . . who have seen hangings and shootings on an almost daily basis, and some who have even pulled the trigger themselves — nine-year-old executioners. You might think there is no way back from that. But children are resilient. With the right care and attention, they can come to terms with these incidents and make sense of the world without it destroying them. My role is to assess and advise. I advise the *patient and understanding* people with just what should be done so, no, I am not blessed with a great deal of patience myself and what little I do have will run out quickly when my advice is ignored.'

'Did you read my report?' Maddie said quickly, before her boss could reply.

'Yes of course! Your description is everything I would expect from someone who has experienced some sort of trauma . . . no verbal communication at all, no eye contact and a conscious effort to nullify NVCs.'

'What does that mean? And continue to assume that I'm stupid.' Harry sounded very close to losing his patience completely.

'He doesn't want us here, Inspector. Least of all an authoritative, older man with a gruff tone.'

'NVCs?' Maddie knew exactly what they were but wanted to stall Harry's rising temper.

'Non-verbal communications. The one thing none of us can control completely. The boy upstairs is very scared. The fact he is not telling us this means we will need to read other signals to know this to be the case, and to know when he is a little less scared. It is a very delicate and lengthy process.'

'So he is not likely to start talking any time soon? And you're confident he is a witness to something?' Harry said.

Anna fixed her gaze on him. Her own NVCs were unmistakeable. She was not impressed. 'I need to see the boy to make my own assessments, but we can certainly presume from the circumstances in which he was found that he has been involved in a trauma of some sort.'

'So how long does it normally take for such a kid to be able to speak again? To tell us what they saw?'

Anna stood up straighter. 'I find it increasingly tiresome explaining such things to police officers. A child's ability to communicate is not fully developed. Indeed, it is one of the few areas of our development that never really stops. Seeing something incredibly traumatic would put a strain on you or I if we were asked to describe it. We might struggle to put into words what we experienced. It is not untypical for a child to shut down completely, to not even try. The human mind is a very protective element — protective of itself, of its own welfare. He might not even remember what happened, certainly not in any detail. Nor does he want to. You are police officers, Inspector Blaker, you are here to ask questions, to *help* him remember. You are the *enemy* here . . . don't forget that. I am confident that I can assist with this boy recovering with the right care and the right treatment, but what *you* need from him can only set him back.'

'And you say you help the police?' Harry said.

The woman licked her lips. 'No, I didn't. I help other professionals to communicate with terrified children, to help them understand what has happened, to understand that their experiences are not normal and that they don't need to be afraid of this world — that not all people mean them harm. As part of that I can sometimes assist with obtaining information required by the police. But that is not my primary concern.'

Harry fixed her in a stare. 'I can't just consider this child on his own. There's a bigger picture here. I need to consider that he was covered in someone else's blood and that at any second said someone else may pass a point where recovery is no longer possible. That is literally life and death. I don't want a kid caught up in this. I would rather they were never involved in my work. But involved he is. And I need to start making some progress with him as soon as possible.'

'And how was progress? When you defied my request to speak with him and went straight up to talk to him. How did that go? Did he speak with you?'

'He communicated. That is more than he has done with anyone else. He has a connection with DS Ives. I think we can build on that. We were starting to . . . then you came through the door and the aggression in your voice pushed him away. That's what you might call a *setback*.'

Anna's lips were back in a pout. Her eyes were fixed on Harry, who stared straight back. Maddie didn't think either was ready to back down.

'Right then, who wants tea?' Rose said. She must have sensed the same. It seemed to do the trick; it breached the impasse at least.

'I am assured two social workers are on their way from a local provision,' Anna said. 'I will utilise them. They will make contact with the boy under my supervision. You are requested not to attempt to speak with him any further. My presence here has been ratified by a superintendent who I have worked with a couple of times in the past, someone I know well enough to have been speaking with directly on the way down. Should you need me to request his opinion on who leads with this element of your investigation, I am more than happy to do so.'

Harry turned to Rose. 'Thank you, Rose, but I don't think we will stay for tea. And thanks for your help with our little friend up there. I know he appreciates it.'

Maddie caught a glance from Harry as he turned away. She followed him down the hall. He stopped at the end and nodded at the stairs.

'You need to say goodbye.'

'Sir?' Maddie was aware that their conversation was being overheard.

'You set an expectation with the lad. You said you would be the next one back up there, and even I know the importance of keeping a promise at this stage. You need to let him know that three complete strangers will be going up to see him instead. Tell him that is what *experts* have decided, so it must be right.'

Maddie suddenly fixed a glare on Harry, who stared right back. She knew better than to undermine him here, though, and she considered it was right that she said goodbye. She padded up the stairs.

'Hey, Dane!' she called out when she got to the threshold of the room. She could still see a shape under the duvet, but this time she reckoned he was lying down. 'I'm really sorry, but I have to go. Some people are going to come and talk to you who are far better at this than me. And nicer too. They're going to look after you, okay? I will come back and see you, too. I promise that. Okay?'

Again, there was only silence. She waited almost a minute before she called out again. 'See you soon kid! I just want you to be happy.'

When she made it back down the stairs, Harry was standing in the exact same spot. Rose bustled down the hall to show them out. Maddie called out her goodbyes to Anna in the kitchen. There was nothing but silence as a response, something she was starting to get used to.

* * *

Maddie only waited for the doors to shut on the car before she launched her attack.

'What the hell was that about?'

'What?'

'You know what.'

'She was being an arse. I don't like it when people look down their nose at me.'

'So you put me on the spot to make a point?'

'You set an expectation, it was right that you went and spoke with him.'

'That wasn't why you said it.'

'She needs to know that we're not idiots. That we know a bit about looking after trauma victims.'

'Then tell her direct. That's not something you normally struggle with.'

'She wasn't listening to me, Maddie.'

'Because *we* didn't listen to *her*.'

'You think she was right? She spoke to us like idiots in there. On things like this, we need to work together. And a child psychologist trauma expert, or whatever the hell she was, should know that.'

'The second she turned up and we were already upstairs she wasn't thinking like a child psychologist trauma expert. She was angry. And then you were, too, and you weren't thinking like a detective inspector. You basically just met your female counterpart in there, Harry. You would do well to remember how frustrating that was to try and work with.'

Harry had turned the key to start the car. He looked over at her now. Maddie could see his lips had formed a shape like he was about to speak. He seemed to change his mind. The rest of the journey was in silence. Maddie had no idea if that meant he was considering what she had said or if he was so furious he couldn't speak to her.

Ultimately it didn't matter. She still reckoned she was right.

CHAPTER 6

There was no rain on the second night, but swathes of water still lay at random places across the car park like slithers of shimmering glass. The café parking area didn't seem as busy. The night before, Jack had felt surrounded by lorries; today there were only a few backed up against a low fence at the rear. One of them was ticking over, the heat from its exhaust stack making a low moon quiver.

Jack lit a cigarette. He was a few minutes early and had time to try and settle his nerves a little. He had barely got to the end of his first drag when he heard the approach of a diesel engine. He turned and narrowed his eyes to a small lorry that had swung into the car park, raking its lights across him on full beam. With the lights gone, he made out that it had an open flatbed rear and an enclosed cab at the front with both front and back seats. The driver's window was close to him, close enough that he could make out an arm along the windowsill and a face leaning out.

'Get in!' It was the man from the previous night. Even in the gloom his intensity was clear.

'In there?' Jack motioned towards the truck with his cigarette. He was trying to stall for time to consider his options. Right now, getting in that truck was not his favourite.

'In the back,' was the reply. Jack took another drag and lingered on it, watching the tip of his cigarette burn brighter, his head feeling flushed and a little dizzy. 'Now!' The voice carried anger. Jack still hesitated and looked back at his own car. He longed to be back in it and driving away, having explained that this was all a misunderstanding, that he had had a lot of fun but he wasn't keen on this idea anymore. He didn't sense that to be an option. He threw his cigarette to the floor and looked into the cab. The driver was the only occupant.

He pulled on the door behind the driver. It was locked. The driver hung out of the window. 'No, in the *back*!'

'What?'

'Step up on the wheel. Get in the back.'

The man stared at him until Jack shook his head. That was one step too far. 'This is a fucking joke. You know what . . . this was a bad idea. I'm not so into this, yeah? You might be better off playing your games with someone else.'

The driver's door opened and the man stepped out to face Jack, but he didn't move any closer. His right arm was concealed behind the truck's door pillar and his stance suggested that he was holding something in his hand. He wore dark trousers and a white T-shirt that was just visible under the same long, black coat that hung open. He looked bigger tonight somehow, wider certainly. The material of his T-shirt was stretched against the contours of his chest and the hood of his coat was pulled up over his head. His left hand hung by his side, it was still bandaged, the dressing looked fresh, as did the spotting of blood that seemed to thicken round the wrist.

'Get in the back of the truck. Last chance.' The menace was unmistakeable.

Jack swore again, but this time it was mumbled under his breath. He stepped up onto the outer tyre. It was slick with moisture. He gripped the cold metal side and clambered over. The truck moved off almost immediately and Jack was thrown to his knees. He rocked forward but he got his hands out in time to stop himself face planting. His hands pushed into a soaking piece of plastic that lay along the floor. The truck jerked again, the front wheels dipping suddenly into a trench, a pothole or some such. Jack managed a clumsy sit, the seat of his trousers soaked instantly on the metal rails that made up the base of the tipper's flatbed. He grabbed the side with one hand and a fistful of the plastic with the other. The truck made it to the smoother tarmac. They turned right towards Ashford and immediately picked up speed.

The journey took ten minutes, maybe a little longer. From the café they drove along the main road for a short time before turning away from the streetlamps into country lanes leading deeper and deeper into woodland scenery. Finally the truck turned off the road completely. The high-riding suspension bucked and rolled on the uneven ground. They slowed to a stop and the engine turned off. The silence was like a blanket thrown over them but the air was cooler here. The surrounding trees were backlit by the moon and the whole scene had the appearance of landscape art created by stencils.

There was no movement from the front and Jack considered getting out. He could run. He wouldn't look back. He got up to his knees then stretched to his feet. His chest muscles ached where they had been tensed the whole way and his hands and fingers were stiff with the cold. He plunged them in his pocket to try and get them functioning again. The driver's door opened and a weak light shone down to the ground through a light mist that was picking at the sodden floor. Jack's eyes had adjusted enough to see a familiar silhouette walking down the side of the truck.

'What the hell are we doing here?' Jack said.

'Our first task is mine.'

'What the hell am I doing here, then?'

'It is also for you. Now, fall silent. We must be sure we are alone.'

'This is all good fun, okay? And the way you talk? I see you've gone all in for this stuff. Good on you. But this isn't me, okay? I think I'll be walking away — it's all got a bit weird. I get that you're into it, but—'

The noise stopped him dead. Jack's mind tried to place it: it was like a suppressed scream, then a moan. He considered it must be some sort of wildlife, but it was muffled — maybe an injured animal down a hole? It was close too. He heard a scuffling sound. The truck vibrated a little at the same time — he could feel it through his feet. He reached out to the side to steady himself. The man in front of him was still, and not close enough to be shaking the truck. Jack turned to see if someone had got out of the other side. Maybe they had been in the back seat of the cab and he hadn't seen them. He couldn't see much of anything. Movement dragged his eye. It was by his feet.

The plastic sheet was moving!

Jack sucked in a breath and took a step backwards. Something pushed out from under the sheet and moved towards him, there was another moan and he felt a grip on his ankle. He kicked out in surprise and stepped away. He felt the side of the truck bump his calves and it unsettled him. He fought to get his balance but his momentum was still backwards. His fall was silent, he tipped out and he couldn't get his hands in a position to soften his fall to the ground. He fell heavily, taking the blow through his shoulders and the back of his head. His vision flared a bright white for a split second and his head shot with pain. He was winded instantly. In his confusion he rolled his face in sopping mud as he moved onto his side, trying to decipher which way was up and trying to get into a position where he could breathe.

'What . . .?' he managed, then a coarse moan as he tried to draw air back into his lungs. Then the voice breathed into his ear.

'Your next phase has begun. You cannot walk away from something that runs after you.' Jack moaned again, it was involuntary, his rushed breath was returning. He turned his head away from the bright torchlight that shone over him and onto the side of the truck. The man carrying the torch stepped up onto the wheel and climbed into the flatbed. The suspension squeaked then there was another moan, louder than before — more panicked now. He heard the man's voice again, maddeningly calm and monotone.

'Shush now. Your time is soon.' Then he called out to Jack. 'Get to your feet! There is work to be done.'

Jack was still on the ground, his breathing still laboured. It got worse as he sat up. The torchlight was flickering above him. He narrowed his eyes, which made his head hurt more. It took a few attempts for him to stand up and he was still unsteady as the plastic sheeting was dragged over the raised side of the truck towards him. It fell to the ground, splashing him in the face with freezing water that snapped him out of his groggy state. 'What the hell are you doing?'

'Hold the light and you shall see.' He threw the torch to the ground beside Jack and its white light illuminated Jack's feet. His canvas trainers were darkened by thick, brown water. He hadn't even noticed. His legs dripped with mud that fell off in clumps. There was a piece of flint at his feet stained with what looked like blood. He ran his fingers through his hair and checked under the light. Sure enough they were spotted red. He shone the torch towards the truck.

The man was bent forward, his arms interlinked with something heavy. It looked like a struggle. He stood up a little straighter and Jack could now see a brown tangle of something was leant against the man's knees. The man timed a breath with lifting the tangle higher, high enough to drag it to the rear of the truck. The rear panel fell open. Jack moved round for a better view. The man jumped down onto the ground. Jack could see what he had been dragging: the naked torso of a heavy-set man lay right at the edge. The eyes were open and they looked to be searching desperately; his arms hung limply over the back and didn't move. He looked like a dead weight, as if only the eyes had function. He had a voice, too; his mouth lolled open wide as he groaned again, high-pitched and panicked at its start, but guttural and melancholy at its finish. The man dragged him a little more until his weight shifted and he fell to the ground. He made no attempt to protect himself with his hands. He landed on his head and neck, his body folding around him. When he was pulled straight the eyes that still searched in a panic had to blink as muddy water slid off his hair and into his eyes. His arm jerked outwards but it was as if he had no control. Jack was rooted to the spot. He watched on in horror as the heavy-set man was laid out so that his head was almost underneath the tow-bar that jutted out of the rear of the truck, his feet at the opposite end. Jack could see he had jeans on his lower half. They were filthy, caked in thick mud, some of it looked dry. He moaned again, it was quieter and finished with a choking sound.

'What . . . what's the matter with him?'

Jack lit up the man in the long, dark coat. His trousers were filthy, too, and his hood had fallen back to reveal his close-cropped, red-tinted hair. His chest was heaving from the exertion. His eyes had the same intensity, but there was something more there now . . . *excitement*. He took out his phone and pointed it downwards at the stricken man. It flashed a white light and made a shutter sound. A few seconds later and Jack heard a sound like blowing into the top of a bottle.

'He has had some tablets and has lost much of his function,' the man explained to Jack, almost sounding like a genial science teacher. 'It was necessary to finish my work. And finish I must. But first I must pause.' He walked the length of the truck and pulled the driver's door open. Jack kept him lit with the torch; he couldn't take it off him. Jack couldn't move either. He wanted to. He wanted to run away from there — to be anywhere else — but his legs were frozen to the spot. The tall man leant into the truck. When he straightened back up he held something small and shiny — a locking-wheel nut maybe? It looked to be that size and shape. Jack watched on as the man picked at the dressing on his left hand. He used his teeth to assist, it came loose and he threw it onto the seat. He held the metal object in his right hand; his left, he laid out flat, palm up on the driver's seat.

Jack took a step closer. Now it looked like a large drill bit, he had seen one before. Only the edges were rough, jagged even, as if it had been snapped roughly from its housing. The man put it on his palm, the rough metal facing downwards. The middle of his palm looked to be a raw, bloody mess, the skin looked torn rather than cut, with white and black skin all mixed up with fresh blood. He grimaced, like the act of just laying the metal on top of it was painful. It had to be. The man took a deep breath then his position changed, his whole weight centred on his right hand as he twisted the metal object into his left palm. He snorted through his nose and seemed to be biting his lip tightly. He stopped only to twist it again, his head lifted to the sky, his eyes wide and his mouth formed into a grimace. Jack had to look away when he started twisting it for the third time. When he looked back he was pushing the metal object back into his pocket. Then he pressed the dressing firmly into his palm and tied it off as tightly as he could against the back of his hand. He looked over to Jack who was still frozen to the spot, aware that his mouth was hanging open.

'It is time.' He reached further into the truck and pulled a length of rope from the back. One end was already tied off as a large loop. Jack could only watch as he moved back to the stricken man, whose eye movements had become even more frantic, his moans higher pitched. His torso was lifted, enough for the rope to be pulled behind his back, under his arms and across his chest. He was lying back down, the loop pulled tight around him. His eyes had now stopped their searching and were fixed straight up as they followed the smaller loop at the other end of the rope that was dropped slowly over the tow bar directly above him. The hooded man pulled it tight and when he straightened up, he stared right at Jack and took something from his waistband. Jack still held the torch and it meant there was no disguising the fact that his hands were shaking.

The hooded man had a knife, an ugly thing with a jagged edge. He held it out so that Jack could take hold of the handle. It wasn't a request. Jack tried to grip it firmly to try and control the shaking.

'What do I do with this?'

'When the time is right, you will cut him loose.'

'When the time is right?'

'You will know.'

'What about now? I'll cut him loose now! I mean, come on, man! What are we doing here, dragging him behind us?'

'Yes. Get in the back.'

'This is madness!'

The man had started towards the driver's door, but he switched back and made up the short distance back to Jack. He pushed himself up so close that he almost doused the torchlight completely. His eyes glinted. 'My task is this . . . his death or yours. You can cut him loose now if you wish, you will spare him, but you will take his place.' The man cocked his head and his lips curled up at the edges. 'But you won't. You will cut him loose when you are sure he has left this world. I can see that. You should know that he was given the same choice.' He turned away again.

The driver's door closed and the engine fired. Jack swept the torch to the back of the truck. The man lying on the ground was staring over at him, his chest was rising and falling, his lips fidgeting. He was starting to get more movement back and his head was rolling gently from side to side. His arms looked a little more controlled and it looked like he was trying to reach out to Jack. He was pleading. The engine revved, snapping Jack's attention away from the tethered man. He focussed on climbing into the back of the truck. He looked down at the knife, heavy in his hand, then was thrown to his knees as the truck started forward with a jerk. The shriek from the tethered man was instant, high pitched and panicked. He could hear the sound of a mass being dragged slowly, distinctive over the crunch of the tyres. Jack dared to look over, pointing his torch downwards. The man was being turned on the spot as they straightened up. He was to be pulled feet first; the bastard had laid him out the wrong way round so he could watch himself being hitched to the truck! His eyes were wide in terror. Jack switched off the torch. They moved slowly to the edge of the road and then the brake lights came on, giving the mist a blood-red hue. The truck turned onto the black ribbon of tarmac and picked up speed. The reaction was immediate. Jack turned away from the horror, but there would be no closing his ears to the tortured screams.

CHAPTER 7

Tuesday

'You just step out of the shower, DS Ives?' Maddie looked up towards the booming voice of Vince Arnold as he strode the length of the Major Crime office. It was just after 7 a.m. and the room was largely empty. She had come in early to try and put a dent in her paperwork. Vince was a distraction she could do without, but he seldom failed to make her smile. There was a young-looking officer with him who folded his scrawny arms across his front, his stance mimicking Vince in posture if not in stature. Vince was a gym bore, the sort who judged others by how much they could 'bench.' It was an aspect of him that provided limitless ammunition to poke fun at his one-size-too-small uniform T-shirts. The officer stood next to him was at the other end of the scale. He unfurled his arms to push his glasses back from where they had slipped down his nose. Maddie scanned his force number and got an instant confirmation that he was brand new.

'Not quite, Vince,' she said. 'I just about managed to fit in a run this morning, but there wasn't quite time for my normal drying and beauty regime.'

'You coulda fooled me, Sergeant!'

'I reckon I do, too. Every time I try.'

Vince turned to his crew mate. 'Me and the sarge, here . . . we have a bit of an understanding, see. We both fancy the pants off each other, but we know we need to be professional in the workplace. It's a constant battle, but we've had plenty of practice.' Vince's laughter boomed around the empty desks and dimly lit offices that made up the Major Crime floor. His skinny colleague tried to smile, but looked awkward. Vince whacked him enthusiastically on the back. He bowled forward, the blow nearly taking him off his feet, 'I'm only joking, lad! I'm wearing her down though — I swear it. She just won't admit it just yet!'

Maddie was nonplussed. The probationer next to him still looked awkward. Vince didn't have the ability to know his audience sometimes. New recruits often left training school with all sorts of rubbish in their heads about the need to challenge inappropriate colleagues and other ways to alienate themselves very early on. This was just the sort of conversation that could end up proving difficult for all of them. She decided to move it on before that happened.

'You might not have picked up on my hint, Vince, but I was up at five for a run in the cold and the dark so I could get into work early and clear my paperwork. That's quite an investment to be able to be left alone. Did you want something?'

'See what I mean!' Vince nudged the poor lad, who was still straightening his glasses from the last strike. 'I understand, Mads. I'm not here to get in the way. I was after the old man. You seen him yet?'

Maddie glanced at the time displayed on her computer screen. 'No, actually. He's normally here by now.'

'You two lovers have a barney?'

'Funny you should say that; he's not been in the best of moods. Hopefully he's having a lie-in this morning. Maybe that will sort him out.'

Vince scowled. 'Can you imagine Harry Blaker *lying in*?'

'Fair point. I'm sure he won't be long. Anything I can help with?'

'Nah, I just wanted to talk to him about something that might improve his mood is all. Daniel Wootan is wanted. Some theft overnight from the BP garage. Small fry, but it'll be enough to stir up his recall.'

'Daniel Wootan?'

'You know about Wootan right? And the boss?'

'Remind me?'

'He was driving the car . . .' Vince, the man with no volume control, suddenly stopped to check his surroundings, then bowed his head and lowered his voice. 'The car that hit him. His wife copped it. The boss damned near lost his hand. He's wanted.' Maddie's expression must have given her away. 'Shit! I thought you would know! I thought you guys were close?'

'I knew it was a car accident. I didn't know how or who. It's not the sort of thing we talk about.'

'Shit! You mean not the sort of thing Harry talks about. Don't let on, yeah? I'll pop back in and talk to him later. I thought you'd be all in the know about it. Sorry, Mads. Forget I said anything.'

'Come on, Vince! I can't forget, can I? I'll pass on your message. I won't tell him you gave me the story. Do you know what happened?'

Vince looked uncomfortable — a rare sight. 'Yeah, but . . . I mean he ain't the sort of bloke you talk about, you know. I figured Harry had told you — turns out he ain't. I probably shouldn't be the one who does.'

'But you were happy to talk about it in front of your mate, here.' Maddie flashed angry. 'Is he a close friend of Harry's too?' She backed down just as quickly and regretted the gesture towards the probationer. The young officer looked to be praying for a ground-swallow.

'You're right. I wasn't gonna talk details. Si, do you mind doing the car checks, yeah? Me and the skipper need a quick chinwag and then we'll be good to go.' He passed over a set of car keys and Si snatched them up with obvious relief at the excuse to leave. They both watched him go.

'So?' Maddie said.

'Ain't nothing much more to it, really. The boss was in his car, going round one of the industrial estates for bathroom tiles or something. Going about his business. Our scumbag is driving some old shit heap, his missus does a shoplifting at the supermarket nearby — they get like a couple of hundred quid in perfumes or whatever — and they're off. A cop car pulls out behind them and shows them the lights and he puts his foot to the floor. He was never getting away, not round there. But he's a scag, he was desperate for his hit so he gets the mist. He pushed his way through a red light, picked up some speed and the boss was crossing in the flow of traffic at the same time . . . They reckon he hit the passenger door square on . . . You get the rest.'

'Jesus . . . His wife. . .'

'At the scene. They worked on her for a while. He did himself to start with — one-handed. Shit day out, Mads. Sorry, love, I really thought you'd know.'

'Don't be. I *should* know. Especially if this guy's back out. When was this?'

'The shit did like five years. Maybe less. It was a sudden release, the sort we don't even get told about until after it happens. You'd think they'd do better with some dirty fucker who killed a copper's wife. He was released to a halfway house in Maidstone. He's on licence for another three years. He came out on Thursday and we all knew he'd come back down this way. We all said then that we'd do anything to get his licence revoked. I figured I might be able to stop him with his score in his pocket or summin', but seems like he was more determined to go back to jail than we coulda hoped!'

'So what's the job?'

'Named offender. CCTV image of him in the twenty-four-hour garage up town round the time some whisky goes missing. I haven't seen the footage to see how good it is, but just being there and being nicked should be enough for probation to stick him back in. Fucking wants to be.'

Maddie nodded. Probation had strict conditions for offenders released from prison early. Any breach would see them returned to prison for the remainder of their original sentence at least. They didn't even need to commit a new offence; just behaving badly could be enough. This sounded like it had a good chance.

'Sounds positive. What's your message for the boss? Just that he's wanted?'

'Yeah. I'm in on overtime today, nicking outstanding offenders. It's either a lovely coincidence or fate! Anyway, someone checked with a snout who must be at the house. Seems our man got home a couple of hours ago. If he's been grafting all night, I reckon he'll be in an opium-induced coma by now! Easy. Best get going though — oh and I don't intend on being gentle!'

'I'll tell him.'

'Just don't be obvious that I told you all about it, yeah? Maybe he'll tell you the same story.'

'I won't hold my breath.'

Vince grinned. 'I'll text you if I get him in. We'll probably take him into Maidstone custody, but you can break the news. Then I say we all go out for a celebratory dinner! We don't have to invite the boss, though . . . you know . . . if you don't want to.'

'Nice try, Vince. How about you get him in first.'

Vince's laugh boomed, his volume control broken again. She could still hear him when he pushed the door open at the other end of the room. It thudded off the wall before falling shut. He never did anything quietly.

It was ten more minutes before Harry Blaker arrived. Maddie hadn't done another thing of her own work. She'd considered interrogating the computer system for information on Daniel Wootan but knew that every keystroke was recorded on the system. Instead she checked the weekly briefing page that had a section for prison releases; she had every right to be browsing that. Sure enough, a Daniel Wootan peered back out at her. He wore a lopsided smile, his head lifted slightly so he could jut his chin towards the custody camera. If it was a look of defiance it was a poor one when accompanied by shrunken cheeks, pale skin and bags under his eyes, all the calling cards of an addict. He had sandy hair, short around the sides, but with tight curls bunched up on top. The headline underneath read: PRISON RELEASE — DEATH BY DANGEROUS DRIVING. LICENCE EXPIRES 2022. MANAGED BY MAIDSTONE PROBATION. CONDITION NOT TO BE IN THE FRONT SEAT OF ANY VEHICLE. Maddie was pretty certain that he wasn't allowed to steal from petrol stations either. Harry's arrival caught her out. His movement near her desk panicked her to close her screen down.

'Maddie.' His greeting contained his standard growl. His head was bent and he didn't look up.

'You're late.'

Harry slipped off his waxed jacket to hang it on the coat stand and peered over. The scarring on his cheek dimpled as he bit down, perhaps suppressing his first reaction. It was already clear that his mood hadn't improved. 'Or twenty minutes early.'

Maddie tried to soften him with a smile. 'I know. I was joking. I don't think I've ever beaten you in is all. I was getting worried about you.'

'I had some things to do before work.'

'At seven in the morning?'

He shot a look that she had come to recognise as a warning then moved towards his office. 'I'm going to make a coffee. You want one?'

'Yeah, why not.' He swept her coffee cup up and moved away. 'Vince came down to see you!' she called after him.

'Okay?' Harry didn't slow. He was almost at his door.

'Something about Daniel Wootan?' Harry stopped in the doorway. He didn't turn — not straight away. He had her cup in one hand and his other reached out for the door surround. 'I don't know the name but he said you might.'

'What was the message?' Harry was now looking over at her.

'He's wanted. They're going out to scoop him up this morning. Apparently it's enough to ruin his day. He's on licence, so Vince said. Not sure what it has to do with Major Crime, though?' Maddie held her breath.

'Okay.' Harry moved into his office. She could see him through the glass. He pushed his chair back and stood at his desk. He picked up his own mug. The kitchen area was a short walk from there, but he stood still, as if suspended for a moment, as if unsure what to do next. Maddie stood up. She sauntered into his office, making a show of looking around.

'Did you take the chairs out of here?'

Harry looked up. 'Yes. People kept sitting in them.'

She smiled, still trying to act as casual as she could. 'Ever the gracious host!'

'Was there something you needed?' Harry's irritation was clear.

'Well, that coffee you promised me for one. I was just going to offer to make it — seeing as how you appear to be lost in your thoughts!'

'Fine.' He put the cups down roughly on the desk and pushed them towards her.

Maddie didn't pick them up. She waited for him to look back over at her. 'Who's Daniel Wootan, Harry?'

'Why are you asking me?'

Maddie shrugged. 'Your reaction.'

'I didn't give you a reaction. You're asking me because you already know.'

'Already know?'

'That's why you're in here, right? Vince delivered the message; he probably came up here all excited and you asked him why. That man would tell you anything you wanted to know, so now you do.'

'Why didn't you tell me?'

'Why would I?'

'Because it makes a difference! To you, to your work, to everything! What if we were to come across him?'

'Won't happen.'

69

'It could. And this is the reason you've been in a foul mood for the last two days. And you know what? That's fine. It makes sense. This must be difficult, horrible in fact. But I want you to talk to me if you're suffering. I might be able to help.'

'I'm not suffering.'

'Yes, you are. And you should be. Last night this Wootan clown was shoplifting in Canterbury. That means he's on our doorstep. Don't tell me that isn't a consideration for you when you go about your business.'

Harry retrieved his chair and sat down. 'Well, we shouldn't need to worry about that now, should we?'

'No. Assuming Vince gets him in. I guess that's me making the coffees then, seeing as you seem to have made yourself comfortable.' Maddie scooped up the cups.

'You're right, okay? I should have talked to you about it.'

'You should. Apology accepted.'

Harry's expression softened. 'I swear you just hear what you want to hear most of the time!'

'Or I hear what you mean to say.' Maddie turned away to finish the drinks.

'I went to see her this morning — my wife, I mean.'

Maddie stopped in her tracks and turned to face him. He was looking down at his desk. All the stern edges to his face had gone. He was almost smiling.

'She's laid in our village. She's got a good spot on the edge. I've got a row of Oriental Lilies right in front of her.' Harry spoke softer now, almost as if he was talking to himself as much as to her. 'I wanted to tell her — about Wootan's release. I wanted to tell her why and also that it didn't matter. But I couldn't. I don't really know why it does matter.'

'Of course it does.'

'I wanted to tell her not to worry and that I am fine with it. I couldn't do that either.'

'You don't need to be fine with it. You need to be calm, *professional* maybe, but not fine. Sounds like this fella is determined to self-destruct anyway so he shouldn't be a problem too much longer.'

'He's a nothing. A petty crook with a miserable life.'

'There you are then. Now, can I go and make this coffee? Now I've turned the tap on I can't cope with your outpouring!'

'Get out of my office, DS Ives.'

'Yes, sir!'

* * *

'So this is weird! I just got sent away from my till to find you! At first I thought Jamie was worried about you, but surely he's just hacked off?'

Jack looked over at Alyssa. He was in the locker room. He could barely remember how he'd got in there. It was as if he'd drifted to work on autopilot and now he had snapped awake to that familiar, musty smell. He was still in his coat. He unzipped it and sat down on the wooden bench that ran along the far wall with pegs above it.

Alyssa's expression morphed into one of concern. 'You okay? You look like shit!'

'I've been an idiot,' he murmured. His voice sounded like it belonged to someone else. He was tired, so tired. After getting in late, he hadn't slept a wink. He had been terrified to even close his eyes. He had lain on his bed with his light on, the television too, trying to focus on the flickering pictures and not let the images from his evening foray take over. He had no idea what programmes had been on. He didn't move for hours.

'What have you done?' She suddenly sounded serious.

He tried to smile. He knew it had to look empty. He shook his head. 'Nothing, really. I learned a lesson is all. I've been hanging out with the wrong people. I won't be doing that again.'

'What are you talking about? What people?'

'It doesn't matter.'

'Of course it matters. Look at you!'

'It doesn't matter, Alyssa. I'm being stupid. I should get to work.'

'You should. But you should tell me what the hell is going on first. You were fine last night — full of it. And then you fucked like a train! I left you at what — ten? You wanted an early night. If this is what an early night does to you then you should hang out with me 'til later!' She chuckled but it sounded hollow, fragile.

'I went out.' Jack regretted saying it the moment it dropped from his lips. He knew it could only prompt questions and they came instantly.

'What? Where?'

'I had to meet someone.'

'A girl?' Her tone was as sharp as a pickaxe and with a subtlety to match.

'No! Fuck, Alyssa. Of course not.'

'Who then?'

Jack stood up, suddenly aware of how hot he was, how heavy his coat felt. He brushed it off. It fell to the bench and dripped onto the floor. He turned away, unable to face her. He leant against the wall with his palm flat against the painted brick. 'Some bloke. I don't even know his name. I got talking to some people. Online.'

'Online? Like what, some gay shit?'

'No, Alyssa. Not gay shit. Are you going to listen?' Jack fixed his eyes on the wall. He considered that Alyssa was not the right person to be talking to about this. She wasn't mature enough. She wouldn't understand. But he wanted to tell someone. He had to.

'Yeah, fine. So no gay shit. I was just being silly. Sorry.'

'Gaming. I was playing online. You know Fortnite?'

'Everyone knows Fortnite.'

'I used to play a lot. I had a headset and I was talking to other gamers. It was mainly banter, you know? Mugging people off when you wasted them. But I got talking to some fella and we used to team up, like me and him versus the rest. It was kinda cool. I got talking to him outside of the game on a message board. He was telling me how he was part of something, something far bigger than anyone knew and he

72

was telling me I should get involved.' Jack shook his head and shut his eyes tightly. 'This sounds so stupid saying it out loud.' He heard the bench creak behind him and turned his head a little. Alyssa had sat down, her legs crossed.

'I don't think so.'

'I'd just left school. It was before I started here. I didn't really leave with anything — didn't really know what I wanted to do. Still don't. I don't have many friends, Alyssa. I don't fit in anywhere. I suppose he got me at a weak point, he made me think there was something out there for people like me. He made me think he was *like* me.' Jack sniffed. There was so much to say, so much he couldn't say.

'Okay, so you're a sad kid with no mates and this lad wants to be your friend. I get that. Then what? You finally meet up with him and what? He touches you where you wee?' She chuckled. Jack knew she was trying to lighten things up but he couldn't muster a smile.

'I met with someone. I don't even know if it was the same person. I think it was. This thing he is part of . . . they talk about how they follow the left-hand path . . .' Jack ran out of words, talking out loud was making all this sound far more stupid than it had in his head.

'Left-hand path?'

'Yeah. Like everyone else takes the right, but this is the alternative. It's about putting yourself first, above everyone else. It's about freedom of expression, about being comfortable disliking people that are different to you and acting on that dislike. It's about taking what you want from weaker people and having what you want and not feeling bad about it. I guess I had my head turned. There's nothing out there for me. I live in a shitty little flat, I've got nothing left by the time I've paid my landlord at the end of the month — no hope of getting out of it, that's for sure. I work on a till, serving people that wouldn't piss on me if I burst into flames in front of them. I don't feel part of this place or anywhere. This group, these people who take what they want, who don't give a shit about political correctness or kissing the arse of their boss, they gave me hope.'

'Are you drunk?' Jack turned. Alyssa was leaning forward, her expression slightly humoured. She wasn't taking him seriously. No one ever took him seriously.

'They offered me a chance to join — to be a part of something. This organisation is bigger than you could know. They have members who run big business, a lot of the powerful people in companies are just that sort of person — they take what they want! And look how it's worked out for them. And it was an adventure. I had to do stuff to show my loyalty, like I had to switch off from civilisation for two weeks. I went and lived in a tent. It was right where they said it would be and with rations for the two weeks. Tinned stuff. All I had to do was make a fire and sleep out. I was supposed to read some book about Satanism, but it was fucking weird. I couldn't get into—'

'Satanism? Like the devil? What is this shit you got into?'

'I know. I know it sounds crazy, but it was an adventure. It was a dick-around, camping in the woods and a bit of fun. Then I had to do some tasks . . . shoplifting . . . then rob something off an old man . . . then make a hoax call to a school or something like that. Each task was more serious than the last. It was about causing chaos. It was about demonstrating that you wanted to live outside of the normal rules of society. I had to send pictures . . . evidence of what I had done. And it was all building towards something. Not just a better job but a better life. These people, they made me feel like I was part of something, you know?'

'Not really.'

Jack became animated with memories of bundling an old man to the ground, striking him while he was down and forcefully pushing hands into his pockets to take his wallet, and of making a call to his old school telling them there was a pipe bomb in the canteen and recording them from a distance as a panicked swarm of kids and teachers leaked out from every exit. He had done that. Just him on his own. For the first time in his life he had felt powerful — and not just because of what he could do on his own but because of what he considered he now had behind him. A whole underground organisation was intent on taking what they wanted and he was going along with them for the ride. He had almost forgotten where it had led him, he had almost forgotten the previous night. It didn't last. The sights and sounds came rushing back. His mind replayed those sickening thuds as they turned corners and the rope extended out to the sturdy trees that lined the road, of waiting until the screaming stopped then leaning down so far that he could hear the roar of the tyres on the tarmac, loud enough to feel like it was inside his head. The rope had been coarse and tough, and he had needed to saw at it for what seemed like ages. He had tried to keep his focus on that rope, to not look anywhere else, at anything else. But he couldn't help it. When it finally gave, he had lifted his eyes. He had seen the dark lump of what was left bouncing and rolling along the sodden road. It was a split second that would never leave him. He hadn't looked when they had returned a little while later, when the door had opened with the truck still ticking over and he'd sensed a flash of light, then heard that now familiar sound of blowing into a bottle-top as something was sent.

'Anyway. It's all over now. I don't know what I was thinking.'

'All over? What happened last night? Did you talk to these people?'

'Yes. I met with them but only to tell them it was the last time. I've got rid of my computer, closed it all down for good. I just need to get my head straight, get back into the real world. That devil worship shit isn't for me! It never was.'

'Devil worship, eh? Why didn't you tell me about it sooner? I might have come along with you!'

Jack shook his head. 'I wouldn't bother. Just a bunch of weirdos, really. I intend to forget about it.'

'And you can do that? Forget about it, I mean? With stuff like that, can you just leave?'

'I don't intend on asking permission. They don't know anything about me really. I won't be going along to meet with anyone again.'

'So what now? You gonna throw yourself into your work?' Alyssa laughed harder this time. It was enough to prompt a smile from Jack. He suddenly felt better, like saying it out loud had given his situation a better slant. These people didn't know him, aside from his gamer login and his first name. They didn't know where he lived. There was no way they could find him. He would stay offline, keep himself to himself and do his best to forget about what happened. It all sounded so silly out loud.

'I suppose so. Best I start by actually getting out there and doing some work though.'

'Yeah, you should. You got a shitty little flat to pay for don't forget!'

CHAPTER 8

Maddie ducked under police tape that flapped in the chilly breeze. Harry was holding it up for her, his expression as stoic as ever.

'I believe her,' Maddie said. She referred to a short conversation they'd just had with the poor woman who'd made the 999 call that had brought them all here. She'd provided a breathy account of how she'd been driving along a quiet, country road, one she had driven a million times before, and turned into a hilly section with a slow turn around to the right when she'd come across a dark bundle in the road. She'd thought it was a coat at first and she was going too fast to stop. She did her best to swerve and slow but it was too close. Both wheels on her right side went over it. The jolt told her that it was a something more than just a coat, but she hadn't counted on it being a near naked man with a length of cut rope wrapped around his torso.

The woman was still in shock. Her account was mostly given in a low monotone and Maddie had struggled to hear her. It was as if she might have thought that saying it quietly would make it untrue. The woman was well into her fifties, dressed in a tartan suit jacket with patches on the arms over thick leggings and welly boots. She looked every bit like she belonged to the area. Though her story rang true, detectives were driving her to the nearest police station where they would get a full statement. Every word would be checked and corroborated, just to be sure.

'I do too,' Harry grumbled.

'You sound disappointed!' Maddie said.

'Of course I am. I always prefer a body with the offender still on scene.'

'It makes things a lot easier, I suppose.'

The hill got steeper quickly. They rounded the corner and it was just like the woman had described: a dark bundle laid out in the middle of the road.

'The poor woman has convinced herself she killed him,' Maddie said.

Harry shrugged. 'She might have dealt the final blow. I'm not sure we'll be able to tell her otherwise. The skipper wasn't sure she was the first one to run him over either.'

Maddie slowed, letting Harry take the lead in the walk up to the bundle. 'Can't say I'm looking forward to this one!'

Maddie's first impression was surprise at just how dark the body was. Now she was closer she could see that it was a bare-chested male. He had dark coloured jeans on his lower half and no shoes, but the skin that was visible looked like it had been smeared in a paste made out of charcoal. 'He's a strange colour? The skin goes that black after a week or more, not a few hours. We're not considering he's been here that long, are we?'

Harry pulled on a pair of bright blue gloves and knelt over the body. It was on its side, the face covered by hair that was matted and slick with moisture. Harry rolled the head to the side. Shocked eyes turned to the sky. The skin around them was a washed out, almost wax-like white — more like what Maddie had been expecting. Harry ran his hands over the head, grabbing with his fingers like he was sizing up a melon for ripeness. He then moved down the body. He lingered on a length of rope then chased it to where it ended in a frayed mess near his feet. He stretched it out; it went on for another couple of metres. 'I'm not sure she needs to worry about dealing the final blow after all,' Harry said.

Maddie stood over him. She was still fixed on the face that had a strong jawbone shaping prominent cheeks. His shoulders and chest looked muscular, too, and he had thick forearms. Her eyes ran down his arms and stopped at a point where the blackness was punctured by a shocking white lump that was ringed by a dark red. Maddie recognised it as a bone. Initially she assumed it was a compound fracture, where a bone breaks so bad it punctures the skin. The truth was to be much worse. 'What makes you say that?'

Harry straightened up, peeled off his gloves, and dropped them in a bag. He pulled a new pair out of his pocket. 'This man was dragged by a vehicle of some sort. And for quite a distance.'

'Dragged?'

'Dragged. Long enough to remove most of the skin on his back and legs. You see there?' He pointed at the shocking white lump that had grabbed Maddie's attention. 'That's his elbow. The skin's come right off around it. His head's mush — it's not so much a fractured skull as a collapsed one. Being dragged behind a car at speed, you'd suffer catastrophic injuries pretty quickly.'

'Being run over wouldn't help.' Maddie pondered the muddy tyre mark across his jeans.

'Maybe not. What was the ETA for CSI?'

Maddie was still trying to take in the man lying out on the damp tarmac. Dragging made sense. Now she could see that the blackening to his skin was actually a layer of loose tarmac, mud and grime mixed up with dried blood and clumps of peeled skin. The position of the rope matched Harry's assessment, too. It was hooked under both his arms and ran along his back. He had been dragged feet first with his bare skin to the ground. Maddie couldn't imagine what that might be like.

'Maddie?'

'Oh . . . CSI . . . I spoke to Charley — it's Charley on shift. She's early turn, but she said she would still come out. She might hand it over to the late turn.' Maddie was mumbling. She'd only heard part of the question.

'And her ETA?'

Maddie looked up and met Harry's eyes. He looked expectant. She glanced at her watch. For a moment, she struggled to recall what time had been given. 'Any minute. She said half twelve. That's now.'

'You okay?' Harry said.

'Yeah. It's not a good way to go is it?'

'No.'

'And then just being left in the middle of the road for other cars to come along and run you over. Like some roadkill . . .'

'It's not nice. Murder rarely is, Maddie. Use it. Be determined to find the animal that did this.'

She needed to step away, just for a moment. She moved further back up the hill and took some gulps of air. When she turned around, she looked down at Harry. She could tell he was concerned about her. 'I'm okay!' she said. She smiled, too. It was meant to reassure him. She looked away from the body and at the scene as a whole. It was a tight country lane, just like any number of lanes they had taken to get there. It was quiet, too. She knew the road was blocked off at each end by police cars but reckoned that even if this was a normal day, they still might not see another car the whole time they were there. The road itself had a cracked surface with weeds and grass pushing up the middle, most of which was slicked down where it would brush the underside of the occasional car. She looked further up. The road was muddy in general; it would come off the high banks that were steeper on the left. There were two cleaner tracks running down the road that were the same width as a standard car. Her eyes rested on the bank. It was missing a large chunk, it looked fresh and thick clumps of it were scattered across the tarmac, as if something had hit it at speed. The mud on the road had marks on it where something might have been dragged across it. That made sense, of course, but it also made something else clear to Maddie.

'Harry!' she called. His head was down, searching through the pockets of the man's shredded jeans. He looked up. 'Come up here a second.'

He stood up and dropped his gloves in the same bag as he had before and walked towards her. 'What is it?'

'You see the chunk out of the bank there?' She pointed. Harry nodded.

'Our man's muddy, we can assume it was him that made that dent.'

'We can.'

'And look . . . that's where he spun across the road after he hit the bank.'

'Looks that way.'

'But there are no skid marks from the tyres. Let's say the vehicle towing him came round here quick enough to drag him into the bank at speed then stopped to cut him loose. He would have had to stop quick if he was leaving him there. It's wet and muddy. He would have skidded. And if you're doing that, if you're cutting him loose, this place doesn't make sense.'

'Okay. So what does that tell us, detective?' Harry rubbed his chin like he was teasing her.

'Someone cut him loose. Whatever was towing him . . . it didn't even stop.'

'Okay. The rope is frayed, but a cut rope under tension wouldn't be a clean cut. Forensics will be able to tell us more about that. So what does that mean?' Harry's face was as close to a smile as it typically got.

'You already know, don't you!'

'What are you thinking?'

'That you can't drive around a tight corner at speed with a body attached, keeping control and cutting the body loose at the same time.'

'Meaning?'

'There were two of them.'

'At least. Well done, detective. I think I agree.'

Maddie screwed up her face.

'What?' Harry prompted.

'Are you just gonna pretend that you'd already worked that out? I mean, really? You had no idea!'

Harry did now break into a smile. 'I had an inkling.'

Maddie turned to the sound of an engine that was soon cut off. Then a car door closed and CSI Charley Mace appeared wearing bright blue overshoes and a wide smile.

'Hey! You promise me this one is dead today, right?'

'I'd say so,' Maddie said.

Charley's smile dropped away as her eyes fell to the ground. 'What the hell?'

'I know. It's a bit of a mess, I'm afraid,' Harry said.

'I'm not interested in the body right now, where the hell are your overshoes?'

'I didn't . . .' Harry blushed. Maddie had never seen that before.

'No, you didn't! What if there is evidence on the ground? You think your boot marks are going to help expose that or cover it up?'

'Funny you should say that!' Maddie said. 'I've just been pointing out the significance of what is on the ground here. I was trying to make the inspector understand, Charley, but he's a little slow on the uptake.' Maddie giggled. Harry didn't. Charley was back to smiling too.

'He can be a little slow,' Charley said. 'You just need to wait for the penny to drop.' Her eyes lingered on Harry, who still looked awkward. She shrugged and held up her palms as if she was prompting him for something.

'What?' he said.

'Get the hell out of my crime scene! And you'd better not have touched him!'

Both the detectives made for their car. They would brief Charley there while she got fully suited. They had seen enough for now anyway.

CHAPTER 9

Jack leant on his own front door for support. Somehow he'd made it through the day. He'd gone back out onto the shop floor and managed to put all his focus into his work. For once it helped that his job was repetitive, he just had to run items through his tills, one after the other. No small talk, just focus on doing one item at a time. He had managed to relax a little, enough even to giggle when Alyssa had walked past with two stubby carrots held up against her head as devil horns. She had followed it up with a text message: *Just trying to think of ways to get you to worship ME now that I got competition.*

He hadn't replied. He hadn't seen her at lunch or during his afternoon break either, preferring to stay at his station and work through. He didn't want to talk to anyone, least of all Alyssa. He knew she'd have more questions about last night. Right now, he just wanted to forget, to move on.

He pushed open his front door. Even that had him exhaling with the effort. His flat was the top half of what was once a house in a tightly packed terrace that came to a sudden dead end. His front door was directly next to that of his ground floor neighbours. His was battered and wooden, resplendent in faded blue, whereas theirs was in bright white

UPVC renewed within the last couple of months. He didn't have much to do with them. At least they were quiet.

Once inside, he bent down to pick up some post. Immediately in front of him was the steep staircase, just what he needed when his whole body was sagging with exhaustion. They never normally bothered him, but then he wasn't usually denied sleep for forty-eight hours while spending much of his waking hours rigid with tension. He paused to take a breath as his tired eyes lifted to the stairs. They rested on a small indistinct object halfway up, dead centre on one of the stairs. It looked like a small bump in the steps, like a little ball maybe, but flattened. He scowled. He must have dropped something in his rush to get in last night, or during his zombie-like walk getting out that morning. He couldn't think what. There was no natural light on his stairs. The switch for the overhead light was a push button that slowly popped back out. Such was his lack of strength that he had to use his bodyweight to push it in. The light didn't help him; he was still too far away. He started up the stairs. It only took a few steps for him to realise what it was.

He froze.

He was half on one step, half on the next, his hand shot out to steady himself. It wasn't a flattened ball. It was a round and jagged piece of metal, like a locking wheel nut. Jack recognised it from the night before. The light was directly above him. It reflected a little from the layer of dried blood caught in its crude teeth.

He managed a step closer. He could see the corner of a small piece of paper trapped beneath. He held his breath. He managed to pull it out without the metal object moving. It was a note — handwritten:

6 when you wake.
6 when you work.
6 when you sleep.

Jack turned it over; it was blank on the other side. He finally had to breathe and it came out in a rush. He found himself looking around, as if there might be something else.

84

At that instant the light popped and he was plunged into near darkness. He moved up the stairs to the landing and turned left into his living area. His kitchen was to the right, his sofa and TV to the left. He turned on all the lights and took time to scan the room. Nothing was out of place or looked like it had been touched. He moved through to the only bedroom — still as he had left it: his duvet still on the floor where he had thrown it off in frustration at around 4 a.m.; his computer still showing a screen saver where he had tried playing an old video game that didn't connect to the internet — anything to occupy his mind.

He shook his head. No one else had a key to his place, not even his mother. But even if she had, Jack knew it wasn't his mother who had entered his property and put a bloodied twist of metal on his stairs. He knew exactly who it was. And he knew what it meant.

CHAPTER 10

Maddie looked round at the faces in the briefing room. They smiled mostly and a few still chuckled. The blinds were pulled so they could see the pictures of the country lane taken earlier in the day by the attending CSI. The last picture was still on the screen, a medium distance shot of the victim lying on his side, his eyes just visible from the front of a skull that she knew was damaged so badly that it was held together only by its thin layer of skin. He was laid out on a cold, damp road and she could see his blackened arms where the skin had been scraped off to leave a layer of black grit and mud. Any sane person would struggle to find anything to smile about, let alone laugh, but one quick-witted DC had brought the briefing to an end with a quip about a drag act and the room had immediately descended into chaos. Maddie had smiled too. The funniest moments were often in reaction to someone else's tragedy. Perhaps it was human nature to always look for a release. It was certainly in the nature of a police officer, possibly a way of surviving a career of turning up first to the worst that humanity had to offer.

Harry hadn't laughed — Maddie couldn't remember a time when he had — but he didn't close it down either; a recognition perhaps that such black humour had its positive element. The tension in the room was released and now the horror from that scene might not be the thing these detectives took with them before returning home to their families and having to respond to the question: *How was your day?*

Harry had wanted to brief his team with what they had so far. It wasn't much from an investigative point of view, but one thing they did now have was a name for their victim: Jarod Logan.

As part of processing the scene, Charley Mace had sent a close-up picture of the thumb that wasn't ground down to a stump to the fingerprint bureau. A result had come back within the hour. The prints were known on their system, meaning he had been arrested before, a number of times it turned out. Jarod Logan was a name that raised a few eyebrows round the room. He had been a regular to custody once upon a time, typically on the weekend when he liked a drink with a fight chaser. His arrests were always for assaults or public order offences and he was always a pain in the arse for the arresting officer. The last anyone could remember of him, he'd been working in a nightclub on Langthorne's seafront, the exotically named La Parisienne, a name it had never really managed to pull off. The club was gone now, as was the last known address of Jarod Logan. It had been within spitting distance of his place of work and both had been demolished as part of the same seafront development. All else about Logan was a blank. The intelligence around girlfriends, associates and the locations he frequented was six years old. Maddie knew that to stand any chance of finding his killer they would need to fill much of that six-year gap.

For now, Harry's fast-track actions had been centred on finding the site where Jarod's final journey started out. They had explored the possibility that there was no such site, that Jarod had been bound and then thrown from a moving vehicle, but it had been dismissed for now. Harry had pointed out that a fall like that might have done the job straight away and that wasn't what this killer wanted. Dragging someone to their death was not an easy option. It carried a lot of risk for the offender. You didn't take those risks unless you were looking to make your victim suffer — and how! Maddie could barely imagine Logan's final journey on this earth as he was being tethered to the back of the vehicle. He would surely have known what was coming. He might have been started off slowly before gradually building up speed — perhaps it was a means of extracting information? A torture element would certainly explain the wound that had since been identified under the layer of dirt on his left hand.

There were so many questions, but Maddie didn't mind that. She revelled in the early part of an investigation. It was like shaking jigsaw puzzle pieces out of their box and looking at the pile, debating where to start.

The DCs filed out. It was the end of the day shift and, while the searches were still ongoing, there wasn't too much for a room full of Major Crime detectives to do yet. The scene where the body was found had been searched and stood down. The body was in for an autopsy over the next forty-eight hours and wasn't expected to reveal many surprises — or clues. There was nothing in the way of house-to-house and only one witness: the woman who had driven over poor Jarod and then called the police. Her lengthy statement was now largely corroborated. Maddie looked back at the image of Logan on the screen while Harry shuffled papers. They were the last two in the room. An idea came to her. 'Are we doing social media work? Around Logan, I mean. We might be able to find a next of kin and fill in some of the blanks.'

Harry stopped his shuffling to look over. 'I had one of the DCs have a look this afternoon, but they couldn't find anything for him. I've tasked Rob with it, but he won't be doing anything with it now until tomorrow.'

Maddie grinned. She couldn't help it. It was like a natural reaction when someone mentioned his name.

'What?' Harry said.

'Rob. He just makes me laugh. If I was ever asked to describe an IT geek I'd just close my eyes and picture him!'

'What you do in your own spare time is down to you, Maddie.'

Maddie's grin widened. 'Did you just make a joke, DI Blaker?'

Harry's stoical expression didn't shift. 'I've been practicing my delivery. How was it?'

'Flawless.' Maddie giggled. She looked back up at the image hanging over them. 'Did you ask if Rob could have a look tonight? If anyone can find something, it would be him. It might make tomorrow a lot more productive. I think social media's our best bet, you know. Everybody has something, don't they?'

'I don't, and I bet you don't either.'

'Good point! Not in my name at least.'

'I told him we could really do with him looking before he finished today, but you know what he's like. He's got some gaming competition or some such rubbish. I struggle with civvies.'

'You mean you can't order them to get something done? I might go and ask him again.'

Harry shrugged. 'Feel free.'

The door opened and Detective Chief Inspector Julian Lowe strode in looking hassled. He looked up at the projected image. 'By Christ, he looks even worse on the big screen.'

'There are worse angles than that, boss,' Harry said.

'He's upset someone.'

'I hope so,' Harry's growl was back.

'You hope so?' DCI Lowe frowned.

'It's either that or someone did it for fun.'

'I see your point.'

'What do you need, boss?'

The DCI bit down on his lip and turned to linger on Maddie.

'Sorry, I'm just leaving,' she said.

'Thank you, Maddie. Just a personal matter with DI Blaker, here, is all. Do you mind?'

'Daniel Wootan?' Harry said. 'Maddie is well aware, boss. If there's an update on that she doesn't need to leave.'

'Well, yes. Okay then.' He cast another glance at Maddie. She was already on her way out but she stopped, unsure if she should continue or not. Lowe shrugged and she stayed.

'He's been released.' The DCI seemed to brace himself, but when he got no reaction he continued. 'He's still under investigation but it doesn't look like the job is a runner. We went to CPS. The evidence is not enough for beyond reasonable doubt.'

Harry took a moment. 'I don't know the exact details, but he was on CCTV stealing something from a garage, right?'

'Technically, no.'

'Technically?'

'Yes. And that's the bit that CPS are unhappy with. See, he was captured entering and leaving, not actually stealing.'

'In the early hours of the morning? Was anyone else in there at the material time?'

'No.'

'I see.'

'So the evidence is strong, but not strong enough for a charge. They didn't get the property back when they searched his bedsit — that would have sealed it, of course. The CPS are saying that we can't prove conclusively that he stole the item, despite being pretty sure it was stolen at that time. Not enough to charge at least.'

'You went to CPS? For a shoplifting?' Maddie was thinking the same but was keeping quiet. Police only really consulted with CPS for an instant charge decision on major cases or any type of domestic violence. Nicking a twenty quid bottle of whisky was not the sort of thing that would usually prompt that call.

'Yes, I insisted. If we could have charged him today then we could remand him back to prison and he would be back to serve the rest of his sentence — no question. His feet wouldn't have touched the ground.'

Harry shrugged. 'I appreciate the effort. So now Probation revoke his licence and he goes back anyway? He was driving a car, for one — he's not allowed in the front seat, driver or passenger. And he was stealing. Even the sniff of a dishonesty offence would normally be enough for them to put him back behind the door.'

Maddie watched Harry as his sentence finished. He was a big man, broad and strong, but looked more so when he stood with his feet apart and tensed his chest, like he was now. His body language was of someone bracing himself for a fight.

'I thought you didn't know the details?' Julian's tone carried a warning.

'I read what was on the weekly briefing. I read every one.'

'I spoke with Probation personally. They won't be taking him back to prison. There's not enough for them.'

Maddie watched Harry closely. His chest actually shrunk as he took a breath. The DCI had spoken softly, as if he was trying to appease him. Finally Harry scooped up his papers. 'I appreciate you letting me know.'

'That's it?' Lowe held his ground between Harry and the door.

'What did you want from me? Does my opinion change anything?'

'It might make you feel better,' the DCI said. 'Sorry, I didn't mean it like . . .'

'It's done. Nothing I can do.' He took another step towards Lowe, who turned to let him pass.

'What are you going to do now, Harry?' Lowe called after him.

'It's the end of my shift, boss. I'm going home.' Harry didn't turn around. He left the door swinging open.

Lowe turned to Maddie. 'Can you keep an eye on him, DS Ives?'

'No,' Maddie said.

He rubbed his face. 'No, I suppose you can't. What do you think he'll do?'

'Honestly? Nothing. I think he'll sulk for a few more days. Lord knows he's been sulking for the last few. But then he'll get on with his life. Harry knows the system and he knows the shits. This Wootan fella will come again. He'll be back in prison soon enough.'

'You might be right.'

'It wouldn't be the first time, boss.'

Lowe's looked up to the image on the screen. 'Maybe this inquiry is a good thing. Keeps you busy, gives you something to think about.'

'You're right, sir.' Maddie thought of the reams of casework littering her desk. 'Because we were basically twiddling our thumbs before this.'

'Point taken. And, talking of twiddling thumbs, did you find a solution to your blood-soaked boy problem?'

'You mean the problem of having no one to investigate it? I have a solution, sir. I just need your endorsement.'

'Go on.'

'Rhiannon Davies in CID . . . You know I have a lot of time for her. She's been acting up as a skipper in there as part of her development. I want her to run this job as the officer in the case. At least internally.'

'It's a big job, Maddie. There'll be a lot of scrutiny on it.'

'I know that. She's very capable. We were going to use CID detectives on that job anyway. This just means that there won't be any resistance. She'd still be reporting back to me and ultimately to DI Blaker. She found that boy a place to go and she already knows the job . . .'

The DCI started waving her away. 'Fine, I'm sold. It does make sense. But stay involved. I know there's a lot going on right now but I'll need regular updates on the boy. It's going to attract a lot of attention. I assume Harry is happy with your choice, too?'

'He will be, once I get round to telling him. He's a little distracted at the moment.'

'Now is not the time to be distracted. I need you all on your game.'

'Harry's always on his game. And thank you. About Rhiannon, I mean. You won't regret it. She's going to be a real asset for us and for a long time. I'm still working on bringing her over to Major Crime.' She was, too. Rhiannon had worked with Maddie on a couple of occasions on some high-profile jobs. At first, this was dictated by coincidence and circumstance, but then Maddie had increasingly sought her out. She was sharp for a twenty-year-old and Maddie was sure she had a big future. She'd resisted Maddie's efforts to get her in her team so far, explaining that she wanted a little longer in CID to learn 'bread and butter' investigations. She was right, too, but it only made Maddie want her more.

'On your head be it! Are you going home too, DS Ives? Sounds like you'll need to be fresh and ready for the morning. Once the scene stuff is done, your work will really start.'

'True. Not just yet, though, boss. I need to speak very nicely to a certain techy geek.'

'Very good. Just don't call him that.'

* * *

Maddie walked past Rob Ford's office first to make sure he was there. His shifts were set: a five o'clock finish every day and it was close to that, close enough for him to be getting to his feet and for his computer screen to be announcing that it was shutting down. He already had one arm inside his jacket.

Rob Ford was one of three Forensic Media Technicians working out of a sweaty little office on the fourth floor of Canterbury Police Station. Its windows were permanently covered, the door usually closed and with keypad access. The room itself made Maddie think of student halls. The desks were a mess of fast-food wrappers and broken laptops spewing their insides. The floor was cluttered with stacks of computer towers, some in see-through evidence bags that constricted the area around Rob's feet. Maddie couldn't work in an environment like that.

'Oh, Rob . . .' She leant in like he was an afterthought.

Rob turned to her as he zipped up his jacket.

'Yeah?'

'From the boss . . . Don't worry about those social media checks for our victim. We're gonna have a night duty DC take another look. The boss said you didn't think you'd be able to find anything anyway.'

'That's not what I said! I said I'd have a look tomorrow.'

Maddie stepped into the doorway and frowned, as if confused. 'Oh, well. Whatever. Don't worry. This DC reckons he's a bit of a whizz at this sort of thing and he's late turn. So we should have some sort of result by the morning.'

'Someone already looked. They couldn't find anything.'

'Yeah, I know. This lad though . . . he's pretty shit hot on the internet an' all that. Anyway, like I said, you're not needed. See ya!'

Maddie was quick to turn and walk back the way she'd come.

* * *

Jack's car fell silent in the car park of the Ports Café. Of course it had been the car that had given him up in the first place. Jack couldn't believe he had been so lapse as to not even consider that his car, registered to his home address, was basically a projection of his personal details. His insurance might still be registered at his mother's address unless she had changed it over, in which case there would be two direct links to him. He knew it wasn't just the police who could link his car to his address quickly and easily. That must have been it. He thumped the steering wheel and cursed himself for being so stupid. Then he cursed himself getting involved in the first place and once more for not having the balls to just call the police and tell them what had happened. They might even understand. He'd only taken part because he was intimidated — terrified more like.

But he still was. He had looked the hooded man in the eye, seen how he'd relished tying someone to the tow bar to be dragged to an unimaginably horrific death. You didn't mess with people like that.

He stepped out and shivered violently. It wasn't as cold tonight but he felt a chill race down his spine as he tried to push the key into the door lock. The car locked with a clunk. The ceiling heater seemed hotter than ever as he stepped in to the café. He pulled the hoody away from his neck at the front and made his way over to the far table, the same one he had sat at on the first night. He sat on the same chair too, facing out over the room. Only one other table was occupied. It was ten minutes to midnight; he was purposely early and the reason for this appeared promptly and walked towards him. He managed a weak smile and stiffened in his seat. It was the same waitress that he'd seen on the first night. She didn't smile back or even make eye contact. She held a coffee cup in her hand and plonked it on the table in front of him. It was a watery black with a film already forming on the top.

'Can I ask you a question?' he said.

'I'm a bit busy.' She turned to move away. Jack reached out and took hold of her arm. 'Do you know him?'

She stopped dead. Her arm was rigid and her whole body looked likewise. 'Who?' She still faced away, not turning to look at him.

'The man I met with. The man who came in here . . . you know who he is, don't you?'

'None of my business who you meet with.'

The door pushed open and Jack looked over to see the subject of his questioning enter. His hood was up on the same long, black coat. He pushed the door shut. The waitress tugged her arm away and Jack let her go. He watched her scuttle back into the kitchen, her pace noticeably quicker. He dropped his attention back to his coffee and presently heard the chair opposite being scraped out loudly. The table was nudged enough for the liquid to fidget in the chipped mug.

'We have work to do.' The voice never seemed to change in tone. Jack lifted his head. The man was staring down towards Jack's hand.

'Did you use the gift?'

'What gift?' Jack played dumb.

'You're not doing it right. It should cause you pain. It should break the skin. It will hurt at first but do it often enough and there's no pain anymore, only joy. It is your connection.' Jack remembered something about members being required to inflict injuries on themselves, to their left hands specifically, as a symbol of their loyalty. It was also a way of sending a message to other members. He'd been directed to it online — it was some devil worship crap. Whenever it got too weird he would play along, but he wouldn't really read it. Jack had no intention of showing his loyalty to a devil, real or not, and he certainly had no intention of trying to gouge out his own palm.

'Oh,' he said. He was floundering. Those intense blue eyes were now staring straight through him. 'Need practice, I guess.'

'The next task is yours,' the man said.

'Yeah, look . . . I'm really not comfortable with all this. I respect what you're doing and . . .' Jack paused to look around, slunk a little lower to the table and lowered his voice. 'I'm sure that bloke last night deserved what he had coming and that was between you two. But this isn't for me. I was after a bit of adventure. But last night was too much for me — too intense. Does that make sense?'

'Too intense?'

'Yeah. I know I was talking to you lot and you were saying there's all these opportunities out there for people like me and I was dead keen, but now I don't think I'm cut out for it. I'd just be holding you back, you know?'

'Opportunities?'

'Yeah. Whoever I was talking to online — you, I assume? I got caught up in it all. They said I could have pretty much whatever job I wanted, work anywhere I wanted and go on to earn, like, loads of money. A big salary, bonuses and all that jazz. They said I could be someone. Right now, I just work on a till. I guess I wanted options, it was an easy sell but to be honest . . .' Jack ran out of words.

The man just let him stumble to a finish, staring all the while. He let the pause became uncomfortable before he spoke. 'You have an option. You complete your task or you become the task. Tomorrow night you can reveal your decision. The task you saw last night, that was an expression of my loyalty. We must now see yours. The life you are leading is not compatible. You must understand that it has already gone.'

'Not compatible? What are you talking about?'

'Your house . . . your job . . . Alyssa Mills. None of it is compatible. You take the task or you are the task. There is no other choice.'

The man stood up suddenly and a spell was broken. Jack sucked in air after having been holding his breath, but his lips bumped together as he floundered for words. He wanted to shout at the man, ask how he knew his girlfriend's name, tell him that she had nothing to do with any of this. He wanted to say that he was walking away, that this was *his* life, but he couldn't. All he could think about was the words *expression of loyalty*. He'd heard it before, when he'd knocked that old man over after the prank call. But this was different. Everything was different now.

No words had come by the time the man had made it to the door. Jack still floundered as he watched him leave. He looked over to the counter. The woman hadn't reappeared. He gave it a minute, took a swig of the bitter coffee and then couldn't wait anymore. He walked up to the counter. 'Hello?'

There was no answer.

'I know you're back there. I just want to talk.' Still nothing. He stepped around the counter and looked over at the only other occupant. He was a muscular-looking man with short, dark hair. His T-shirt was stained with something down its front. He stared straight back and slowly got to his feet.

'You shouldn't be back there,' the man said. He moved a step closer, making it clear that he was willing to back up his point.

'Fuck it!' Jack said. He turned away from the counter and pushed back through the door to leave.

CHAPTER 11

Wednesday

Maddie looked up from her desk in response to the booming voice projected from the other side of the room. For the second day in a row it was early and she felt aggrieved that someone was seeking her out for a conversation. It was the same culprit, too. Vince strode across the office floor towards her. Today he was on his own, but the lopsided grin remained.

'Did you say something, Vince?'

'I did. I said that you need to stop doing this to me. Filling my mind with images of you in the shower in the morning. I swear you're just trying to upset me.'

'If I was trying to upset you, Vince, I'd just buy you a mirror.'

'Well I never! She has a tongue sharp enough to match her looks!'

'Did you need me for something? Or even better, maybe you came to see me because you have something of use to *me* for once?'

'No such luck, I'm afraid. Although tomorrow I'll bring you a hairdryer. Two days on the trot you've tied back a damp barnet for me. I appreciate the effort, Maddie, really I do, but there's no need. You had me at "hello!"'

'And how do I get rid of you?'

Vince smiled. Maddie couldn't help but smile, too. She had to admire his persistence. His attention was tiresome at times, but it was also a little flattering in a ham-fisted kind of way. He still sailed close to the line, but he lurched over it less and less. That, or she was just getting used to him.

'You're just going to have to sleep with me!' Vince said.

Maddie's smile dropped away. 'Too much, Vince. Too much for this time in the morning.' There he was crossing that line again.

Vince looked genuinely shocked, then hurt. 'Shit, Maddie! I was joking. I was just trying to be cute.'

'Well, I'd give that up for a start. What do you want, Vince? You should know by now that I don't have much patience at this time in the morning. You should have learned that wet hair just means I had an early start and a freezing cold run. I'm not going to be in the best of moods.'

'You went out again, hey? What is it with all the running?'

Maddie huffed. 'I signed up for the London Marathon next month. I always kind of fancied it, but with the previous job I could never have done it. I had this great idea that I will now, because I can. I wish I'd never put in for it.'

'Marathon eh? You know that's like twenty miles.'

'And the rest, yes. That's why I'm out every morning at the moment.'

'Rather you than me. Although I'd make a great running partner.'

'I bet you would. Tell me, Vince . . . you think my mood is better or worse at five a.m.?'

Vince held up his hands and started to move away. 'Fine. But it's your loss . . . you should see me in lycra!'

'What *did* you want?' she called after him.

'The old man again. They let that fella go yesterday with no plans to stick him back behind bars. I wanted to tell him that I intend to go looking for him. I'm going to stop him with something on him, whatever it takes. He's going back to prison, it's just a matter of time.'

Maddie's smile was definitely genuine this time. 'I'll let him know. He's with the DCI.'

'Okay then. Need anything done this morning? Any of the dirty work? Heard you had a nasty body yesterday. Is there an offender to bring in on the end of that?'

'Jesus, Vince! I'm good but I'm not that good! There will be.'

'Of course there will! I heard it was Jarod Logan. Is that right?'

'Yeah, someone you know?' Maddie already knew from his expression that it was.

'Someone I used to know. Reckon we all did. He used to come to Canterbury for a beer on the weekends. Bit of a lump.'

Maddie narrowed her eyes. 'Were you a bit scared of him, Vince? It's okay if you were, you know. I heard that he was a bit handy in a fight.'

Vince's booming laugh filled the office. 'You'd love that, wouldn't you! Some sign of weakness — me showing my feminine side!'

'It's okay, you can continue to hide it if you want to. I know it's important to you. I'll let you know if I need anything dirty doing, okay?' Maddie knew what she'd said immediately afterwards. She waited for Vince to seize on it but he just beamed at her.

'You do that, sergeant.' He turned to leave again.

'Nice restraint, Vince! I'm impressed!' she called after him. He stopped in the doorway as her phone started to buzz on the desk.

'I've grown, see. I'm a lot more mature now. I know you said that was on your wish-list, so that's two ticked off now.'

Maddie lifted her phone; it had Harry's name displayed on it. 'Two?' She put her phone to her ear as Vince shouted back.

'Two! Mature *and* dirty. Laters!'

Vince was gone but Maddie was still smiling and it carried in her voice. 'Morning boss.'

'I missed your call.' Harry was abrupt, enough to take the joy from her voice immediately.

'You did. You're not coming back up?'

'I've got somewhere to be this morning — unless you have something important. In which case I can do it later.'

'Rob Ford left me something on my desk from his social media trawl. He's found a link to a female who was Logan's girlfriend at some point. She still might be.'

'Rob? You asked him to have a look last night then?'

'Nope. I just told him I didn't need him to.'

'I see. Local?'

'We don't have an address for her, just a place of work. But it's a start. A hotel, too. So she might be there now. And if she isn't, they should have her home address.'

'Okay . . .' Harry sounded unsure.

'I can go on my own — it's no problem. This thing . . . is it an all-day thing?'

'No, not at all. Don't worry, I'll meet you in the front yard.'

Maddie was about to assure him that she could go on her own or take a DC, that there was no need for him to put off whatever was important enough to take him away from the first day of a murder inquiry, but he was already gone.

CHAPTER 12

Maddie slid into the passenger seat of a car that was already ticking over.

'You want me to drive?' Harry usually drove an automatic. The injury that claimed his wife's life had also left him with lifelong scarring and damage to his left arm. The job had provided an automatic; his arm ached when he drove a manual. She'd noticed that he'd stopped using it recently. They moved past his usual car towards the gate. It had a layer of frost.

'No thanks.'

'Yours not working?'

'It's fine. I fancied a change.' He prickled as if there was more to it. 'So what have we got?'

'Rob found an old Facebook profile for Logan. It was in a slightly different name, apparently — hence us not finding it immediately. Then he went through everyone who had commented, liked, or been tagged to see if he could make any links . . .'

'What?' Harry said.

'Do you have any idea what any of this means?'

'No. Do I need to?'

'Okay, no! Basically, we've tracked down someone who we think was in a relationship with our victim two years ago and might still be. And we know where she was working three months ago.'

'It's a start.'

'It might be.'

'We have a media appeal ready to go out at nine o'clock this morning,' Harry said. 'Someone out there knows where our Jarod has been and more importantly what he's been up to.'

'That should get us a response.'

'It should. The media appeal for our barefoot boy goes out later today, too. I'd expect that to get all the interest — and rightly so.'

'I guess so. A mute ten-year-old covered in blood . . . that would get more attention than most things.'

'I think so.'

'I thought someone would have called in about the boy by now. It's not a good sign that they haven't, is it?' Maddie said.

'No.'

The hotel in question, The Burlington, was a twenty-minute drive away in the town of Langthorne, which fitted in with what they knew about Logan and his previous addresses and employment. It was just a hundred metres from 'the Leas', a stretch of flat grass on top of high cliffs overlooking the English Channel. The area was well known to Maddie as it featured on her running route.

Harry pulled into one of the marked bays outside the hotel and they stepped out. Harry straightened his waxed coat and Maddie wished she'd brought a jacket of her own as a chilly breeze whipped in from the sea. She couldn't complain; it was a clear morning and there was nothing like the rain that bombarded this corner of the county over the previous nights.

The entrance was grand: a huge, dark wooden door with a curved top and darker hinges bolted to its front. It was heavy to open. In the lobby, a man stood at a desk and beamed a welcome.

'Good morning!'

'Hello. I'm just here to see Sharon Oaks.' Maddie tried her best to give an impression that this was a pre-arranged meeting and that Sharon was expecting her. The man looked confused. A young man walked past with purpose, wearing the same shirt and trouser combination as the man on reception, who called out to him.

'Yannie, these people are here to speak with Sharon. Is she in breakfast this morning?'

Now Maddie could detect an accent. Polish or Czech, she thought, but subtle, like a man who'd been in the UK for a long time. Yannie stopped mid-stride and then looked them both up and down. He was more wary than his colleague.

'Is she expecting you?'

'Of course.' Harry pulled his police badge out of his pocket and lifted it for Yannie to see. 'It's about her boyfriend. Do you know him?'

Yannie's nose lifted in a twitch. 'I know he is not allowed. Barred.'

Harry nodded. 'He doesn't handle his beer well, does he?'

Yannie shook his head. 'Or his temper. She is serving breakfast. I will bring her to you.' The man strode off.

Harry flashed Maddie a glance then set off after him. He did well to keep up. Maddie did the same. The breakfast area was down a set of wide stairs with thick carpet. It was half full and the sound was a low murmur and the chink of cutlery on bowls. In the middle, a number of guests queued at tables arranged in a horseshoe shape. A woman in a white shirt and grey apron put a fresh loaf of bread in a basket. Yannie made straight for her. Maddie held back with Harry stood next to her. She expected Yannie to say a few words then lead her away from the public area. Maybe there was a quiet room or an unoccupied suite perhaps. She crossed her arms and leant on the wall. The woman spun to Yannie's touch on her shoulder then her eyes jerked to Maddie and Harry. She looked them both over in an instant and then she started moving. She was fast; she pushed past Yannie and broke into a sprint before Maddie could even unfold her arms. By the time Maddie started after her, the woman was already a blur on the stairs.

Yannie was protesting. Maddie ignored him as she used the post of the banister to swing herself around and sprang up the wide stairs. She heard someone cry out in front, the stairs curled round to the right and as she followed it, she almost crashed into a couple coming down. They were holding hands, filling the stairs, they must have cried out a split second before; Sharon wasn't too far in front. Maddie got to the top of the stairs but couldn't see anyone. To the left was the entrance door, to the right a long corridor that led further into the hotel. The man at reception leant out with a startled expression, the sort of expression someone might have if a waitress had just sprinted past. Maddie made for the big oak exit and thundered down the steps. A car door slammed to her left and an engine fired an instant later. Maddie made for it. It was a silver beetle — an old shape. The rattling noise was distinctive: it was high-pitched in reverse then a crunching sound as the driver tried to engage first. Maddie ran to the driver's side and could see Sharon through the window. Maddie slapped on it with her palms. 'SHARON! WE JUST NEED TO TALK, IT'S IMPORTANT. YOU'RE NOT IN ANY TROUBLE!' The car pulled away, it juddered a little, the exhaust popped and nearly stalled. Maddie grabbed at the door and it came open.

'LET GO! GET OFF!' Sharon screamed as she scrabbled to shut the door. Maddie could see the keys and they were close enough. She lunged forward, grabbing them and twisting them in the same movement. 'WHAT ARE YOU DOING?' Maddie pushed back off the car and stepped back, the keys in her hand. The car was still rolling, moving towards the wall of the car park.

Maddie heard the ratcheting sound of a handbrake and the car stopped roughly. She stepped back. She held the keys up, suddenly aware that she didn't really have the right to be stopping the car and taking the keys. She was about to apologise. She had her hands lifted with her palms towards Sharon, her body language designed to diffuse the situation. Sharon lunged out of the car — straight at Maddie. Maddie stepped to the side instinctively. The weak sunlight caught on something metal as Sharon stumbled past her. She turned quickly to face Maddie. Now she could see that Sharon was holding a knife. She lunged again. Maddie stepped back, quicker this time but a little unsteady, her feet caught beneath her in her panic.

'Sharon! What are you doing? I'm just here to talk to you! Put the knife away!' Sharon was still coming and the knife flashed towards Maddie again. Maddie still hadn't sorted out her tangled feet and was still stumbling backwards. It meant Sharon was quicker than her — much quicker. The knife lunged towards Maddie. She saw the glint again, then felt its impact on her chest. It was like a punch. It pushed her backwards quicker and she toppled over a kerb, her fall softened as she sprawled onto damp grass.

'HEY!' Harry's voice was powerful enough to cut through the confusion. Sharon was looming over Maddie, but she snapped her head towards Harry, then she seemed to come to a decision. She broke back into a run. She didn't make two steps before Harry was upon her. He hit her hard and fast in a rugby tackle, taking her back down onto the grass. He wrapped her up tight in his arms and her head was thrown backwards. The knife clanged onto the tarmac of the car park. Maddie was on her back. She now pushed herself up onto her elbows. Instinctively, she put her hand up to her shirt, expecting it to come back bloody, expecting to see a large gash, already considering a firm compress.

There was nothing. No blood, at least. It was painful; her breastbone hurt like hell and her shoulder smarted with pins and needles. She looked down at the knife. It was close enough for her to pick it up. She moved to where Sharon was now on her back, Harry was still holding her down. His wide eyes turned to Maddie. Then he relaxed.

'If you're gonna stab a police officer, you need to do better than a butter knife, love,' Maddie said. She waved it in front of where Sharon stared up at her.

'Police officer?' Sharon's voice was breathy and high-pitched.

'That's right. So I guess that means you're under arrest.' Maddie pulled her shirt far enough apart to see a white dip in her rib that was already ringed with a black smudge. 'That's gonna bruise up nicely.'

'The police!' Sharon beamed a smile. 'Oh thank you, thank God! I thought you were here to kill me! He said they would come, he said they'd come and kill me!'

Maddie and Harry exchanged a glance. Harry hauled her to her feet. 'We don't have to nick you, okay. Seems like this might have been a misunderstanding — is that right?' Sharon managed a rushed nod. 'You just need to tell us about that. We need to have a chat and we'll see where we go from there. But you have to talk to us. No more making an old man run, okay?' Harry grumbled. Sharon nodded again, allowing herself to be walked back to the hotel. A man stood at the door, a man in a suit that Maddie hadn't seen before. He tutted as soon as Sharon was in earshot.

'This is it! This is last straw for you, Sharon. First comes trouble with your man and now this! Now you run around with the cutlery! You lash out and making a scene! This is no more. You must leave!' This man had an accent too, but thicker, and every word was accompanied by thrusts of his hands in every direction.

'She's had a bit of a scare,' Harry said. 'She didn't know who we were and that was our fault. She did the right thing. She thought we were a threat so she took us away from the hotel guests. You should be very proud, Mr . . .'

'Anak. Alek Anak.'

'Mr Anak, I'm Detective Inspector Blaker and this is Detective Sergeant Ives. Are you the manager here?'

'Yes. The manager, yes. I cannot have this. This is nice hotel. This is quiet hotel. Except when Sharon is around. Except when Sharon's boyfriend is around!'

Harry smothered Alek's hands in a firm grip, as if the constant gesturing was getting on his nerves. 'Listen to me . . . Sharon has done you proud, okay? She chased us out of the hotel. She thought we were a threat. And she did this with just a butter knife. And her boyfriend . . . he won't be bothering you anymore, you have my word on that, okay?'

'Okay. This is not okay, but okay. I understand you.'

'You should be grateful. Now, we just need somewhere quiet to speak with Sharon. Is there a room we can use?'

'A room? Yes, there is a function room. This is free at this time.' Alek turned from the two police officers to his employee. 'Sharon, you can use the function room to speak. But we must speak after. This cannot happen. I know what he say, but we still need to speak.'

'Okay, yeah,' Sharon managed.

'And I think Sharon here could do with a sweet tea, don't you?' said Harry. 'And we're both coffee. Leave the milk separate.'

Alek turned away, murmuring something. Harry ignored him.

Sharon looked directly at Maddie. 'Are you okay? I got you, didn't I?'

'I'll live,' Maddie said.

Sharon dipped her head again. 'It's over here.'

They walked through a set of double doors into a spacious room with light flooding in through tall windows lining the far wall. A long, bare trestle table was set up and other tables were folded and stacked against one of the side walls. It looked like they were being set up for a wedding. Maddie was still pressing her chest with her finger. It was raised and painful, but nothing more.

'So,' Maddie said, 'you wanna tell me why I just got stabbed in the chest out there?'

'I didn't know what you wanted. I panicked.'

'I've been doing this job a long time, Sharon. I've introduced myself as a copper more times that I can guess. The only time anybody ran was when they were in a lot of trouble and knew it. Is that what that was?'

'Trouble? You mean like I've done something wrong?' Her eyes were watery and fixed on Maddie.

'Have you?'

'No!'

'So you've got nothing to worry about with two police officers wanting to speak to you.'

'I didn't know you were the police . . .'

'Did your colleague not tell you who we were?'

'No. I think he was trying to be discreet, but I saw . . . I saw a big man with a scar . . .' She glanced over at Harry. 'Sorry.'

'He gets it all the time. He's a softie really.'

'He don't tackle soft.'

'Well, no. Make him run and you'll see a whole other side!'

Sharon shook her head. 'It wouldn't have mattered anyway . . . he told me not to believe anyone, not to trust anyone. Not until . . .' Her eyes dropped back to the floor. Maddie was desperate to hit her again with a question, to ask her to explain what she meant, but she'd picked up the effectiveness of silence from Harry. She waited until Sharon started up again. 'I mean, he said that someone might come for me.'

'Who did, Sharon?'

Sharon shook her head. 'What did you want anyway?'

'We need to talk to you about your boyfriend,' Harry said. 'About Jarod.'

Sharon stared at him. 'I don't have a boyfriend.'

'When did you see him last?'

'I didn't see your ID.' Sharon was still standing and now took a step backwards. Her eyes flickered to the row of windows as if she might be considering an escape route. Both officers stayed still. They let her back away a little and slowly produced their warrant cards.

'Whatever you're scared of, Sharon, we can help you,' Harry said.

'A week ago, okay? I saw him a week ago.'

'And that's who told you to be careful?' Maddie asked. Sharon rushed a nod. 'You're still friends then, at least?'

Sharon shrugged — she seemed to relax at the same time. 'Friends, lovers, exes . . . you tell me. He couldn't.'

'What happened?' Maddie prompted.

'He changed — and I mean a lot. Over the last six months or so, I suppose. He actually stopped drinking. Just like that! I never thought I'd see that.'

'Did something happen to prompt that?'

'No. I mean he got himself in trouble here when he was drunk and we had a big barney, but that wouldn't have made a difference to him. He was always upsetting someone, especially when he had a beer in his hand. I don't think he ever once considered it a problem. Jarod wasn't someone who cared about how he made other people feel . . .' Sharon looked dejected, but Maddie wanted to keep her talking.

'So that wasn't the issue. Why else would he stop drinking?'

Sharon turned to Maddie and looked her up and down. It was as if she was going over her options. 'He got mixed up with some people. Before you ask me, I don't know who they were — just some people who seemed to be promising him a better future.'

'Better?' Maddie gave another prompt.

'Better, yeah. I know Jarod better than anyone — better than he knows himself, even. He has a lairy exterior . . . people stay away from him. He doesn't have too many friends, but it's just frustration with him. He sees other people with a family, a regular job and house to sit in and he just wants that, I know he does. He's getting worse as he gets older. He's said enough times to me that he should be settled down by now and he means that in every sense. I assume that's why you're here, is it? I assume he really hurt someone this time. I guess me telling you he's just misunderstood won't help him out any. I was doing my best to keep him out of trouble, but he's even kept me at a distance for the last few months.'

Maddie looked over to Harry. She didn't feel they could delay any more. Harry must have felt the same: he took a step closer; his voice was lower than normal and with some warmth, too. 'Jarod has been found dead, Sharon. I'm very sorry.' He stopped. There was no point saying anything more, not right then. He was letting it sink in; she wouldn't hear his next words no matter what they were. It took a while. Sharon snatched her gaze to him instantly and then away again almost as quickly, then her eyes lost their focus.

'Dead?' She stepped away again, looking unsteady, as if trying to keep her balance. Maddie moved in and put an arm on the small of her back.

'It's okay. Let's get you a seat shall we.' Harry took the prompt and dragged over a chair from where they were stacked against the wall. Sharon felt for it with her hand then fell into it. The door crashed open at that moment and a young woman entered, having pushed the door with her foot. She wore the same uniform as Sharon and carried a laden tray.

'Hey Shazza . . . the boss sent me up with all this! How come you're getting the special treatment and I have to . . . Jesus! Are you okay?'

Harry took the tray. 'Thank you. She'll be fine.'

The woman kept her attention on her seated colleague. 'You know where I am if you need me, yeah?' Sharon didn't react. The woman hesitated but she did leave.

The tray had three cups, saucers and teapots. There was a bowl of sugar and a jug of milk — standard hotel stuff. Harry noted the lack of coffee but silently made up the teas. He added two sugars to Sharon's without asking how she took it. When he gave her the tea it was like she came out of a trance. She fixed him with watery eyes.

'How?' she said.

'We're still working it out. But he was found in the middle of a quiet road with a rope around him. We're not sure if he was hit by a car, or if the act of . . .' Harry hesitated while searching for the right words.

'Dragged to hell!' Sharon dipped forward in her chair to start a rocking motion. The tea she was holding rattled and shook in the saucer, the liquid slopping over the sides.

'Here, let me take that.' Maddie reached for the tea.

'Oh God! Oh God, oh God, oh God . . . he said it would happen. He said that's what they did . . .' Sharon stood up and paced towards the windows with her hands on her head.

Maddie put the tea down on the floor. She exchanged a glance with Harry then walked over to Sharon. When she put an arm around her, Sharon didn't push her off. She might not even have noticed.

'What did he say, Sharon?'

'I don't know! He was all over the place! It was all so messed up. I figured he was on something. I mean, I've known him to mess around with substances . . . a bit of coke when he was a younger — nothing recent — but he just wasn't making any sense. At first he was so excited. He was passionate about this new thing he had going on. I'd never seen him like that before. But he wouldn't tell me anything about it. He just kept saying that he was meant for better things and that I would see it for myself soon. He called it the *left-hand path*. He said he'd chosen it. What the hell does that even mean? It was like he was manic — I've seen that before . . . my brother . . . he was bipolar. His manic phases were just like that . . . everything was amazing and positive and incredible — and then it wasn't. I thought it was that . . . I was waiting for Jarod to crash back down but he pushed me away, told me that he didn't want me around anymore. But I knew that the crash would be coming. My brother . . . he used to crash hard. He never made it through the last one.'

'You think Jarod was bipolar?'

'I don't know! Something was going on. It was such a change. He was self-harming, too — I'm sure of it. I thought I knew him. But the Jarod I knew would never do that. And the excitement *did* go — all of a sudden, too. But all that was left then was fear. I'd never seen Jarod scared, but he even told me he was. I never thought I would hear him say that.'

113

'What was he scared of, Sharon? This is really important.'

Sharon shook her head like she was trying to clear her mind. 'He was involved with some group. It was all secretive and he would disappear for days, even weeks at times. He said he was performing *tasks*, that he needed to express his loyalty. Those were his words. I don't know what the tasks were. He wouldn't tell me. I did keep asking, though — that was when he said that we couldn't be together anymore. This group . . . these people had totally taken over his life — *became* his life. He disappeared again for nearly three weeks then he turned up a few days ago. That was when he told me he was scared. He had a drink with me, too. Just a tot of whisky, but it was the first time I had seen him drink in six months. He told me that I needed to keep my head down. He said he was going away but no one could know that we had been together. He scared me, too. He made me remove every trace of him from my Facebook, Instagram — everything! He'd already deleted his own and he said that if anyone came to speak to me — no matter who they said they were or what they wanted — I should run.'

'Hence your reaction today,' Maddie said.

Sharon jerked a nod. 'He just kept saying how sorry he was. Jarod never said sorry! Not to me anyway. I asked about his hand — the self-harming . . . His bandage was soaked in blood.' Her eyes were glazed now, her voice low and hushed.

'His hand? What did he say happened to it?' Maddie persisted.

'He didn't. He just said it was nothing. There was quite a bit of blood. And I could tell it was painful — he could barely use it for anything.'

Maddie and Harry exchanged glances again. Maddie picked back up with the questioning. 'What was the dragging thing you said? About being dragged to hell?'

'When he was drinking, the last time I saw him . . .' Sharon was suddenly overcome and Maddie could see the emotion sweeping through her. It was as if she had suddenly made sense of their message. The tears came thickly and they bundled down her cheek, leaving tracks to the corners of her mouth. She got herself together eventually, enough to speak again. 'The last time I will ever see him! He said that he was too far in, that the tasks were different now and that if he didn't do them they would punish him.'

'Punish him how?'

'Drag him to hell. That was what he said! Do you think this is what they meant? Did they drag him on that road? That was what you were going to say wasn't it?'

Maddie nodded. 'Yes, we think someone did.'

'Jesus!' Sharon sobbed again. Maddie wrapped her up in a full hug this time. She felt Sharon grip her back then she tried words. Just mumbles into Maddie's shoulder at first, mixed up with sniffs and snorts. 'He came back to warn me. He had a new task. He said it was me! He said everybody who wants to join gets the same task — a final expression of loyalty. *Cutting ties* he called it.' She pushed Maddie slightly away to make eye contact. 'I was so scared. He was looking at me like . . . like he was considering it. I knew what he meant, when he said his task was me. He meant hurting me — or worse. He said he had to take photos of what he'd done and send it off as proof. I don't know where to, but he took his phone out. I could see the screen was on the camera. He looked at me — the way he looked at me! All that I have seen him do . . . I know what he's capable of, but I never once thought he would hurt me. But he was battling with himself, right in front of me and I couldn't move. I just waited to see what was going to happen. Then he just ran. I didn't see him again. I swear that's what happened! I swear it!'

Maddie wrapped Sharon back up and looked over her shoulder at Harry. He was rubbing his hand over his closely cropped head, backwards and forwards. Maddie had seen him do it before when he was deep in thought. She wondered if he was thinking the same as her: that filling in the gaps of Jarod's life might not be as simple as they had hoped.

* * *

Jack was back sucking on a cigarette when Alyssa appeared. He was on his break, looking out over the bleak, grey loading bay at the back of his workplace with one hand gripping a metal bar that flaked both yellow and black paint. He swung his legs absently, his heels knocking against the concrete step.

'Groundhog day!' Alyssa said.

Jack snorted his agreement but didn't turn around. He heard her lighter sparking. He took another drag on his own smoke. He was already over his time.

'Am I coming round yours tonight, then?' Alyssa said. 'I was kinda hoping we could have the same sort of night as we did on Monday. You know . . . before you went all weird!'

'I didn't go weird.'

'I was joking! Shit, I was just trying to lighten it up a little. Forget about it. You didn't reply to me is all. As long as you're okay.'

Jack stood up and slapped the dust from the seat of his trousers. 'Sure, you can come round. But I do need to have an early night — and for real this time. No more weird people out of hours, I promise!' He put on his best smile, which seemed to appease Alyssa. She burst into a wider grin and he felt her tap him on the backside as he walked past.

'Maybe I get to stay over this time, too? I make a mean breakfast.'

Jack slowed his walk. They had talked about it but he had never been keen. He wasn't sure they were *there* yet. But he liked the idea of keeping her close for now, just until he knew what sort of danger she might be in, if any. Part of him also quite liked the thought of coming back to someone at the house too, especially as he had no idea what his task was to be tonight. There would be the problem of sneaking out, but there were ways to make that easier. 'We'll see,' Jack said, 'as long as you promise to behave.'

'Definitely not!'

CHAPTER 13

'How is it?' Harry gestured towards Maddie's torso. She'd been lost in her thoughts over a steaming kettle in the kitchenette off the Major Crime floor.

'Oh! It's fine, really. I was just thinking that I'm glad she was rearranging the cutlery and not putting the bread knife out!'

'Yes, it could have been a lot worse. You're sure you don't want to be doing anything about it?'

'No. I don't think arresting her for assault-police achieves much, not all the while she's talking to us.'

'Well, I agree with you, but then I wasn't the one jabbed in the chest with a butter knife. I hear she's giving a very detailed account. Everything she knows.'

'There might be something of use in there then.'

Harry nodded. 'One thing she mentioned . . . the *left-hand path* . . . I had a look at what's available on the internet. It is a thing.'

'A thing?'

'Yes. Part of the occult. Not strictly devil worship. More a way of life.'

'And I assume not a calm and peace-loving way of life? Maybe more of a dragging people behind cars way of life?'

'You guessed it. And on that, I've put in a call to the national analyst team to see if this execution method is particularly prominent. They couldn't tell me anything over the phone. They needed it via an official police email account. I'm expecting a reply today at some point.'

'You think it might be the chosen method for this group's members?'

'From what I can see about this left-hand path nonsense, they're big on symbolism. Jarod told Sharon about being *dragged to hell*. I can only assume his death was symbolic of that.'

'Sharon was definitely thinking the same.' The kettle clicked off. Maddie spun a clean cup from the bench and gestured at Harry.

'Yes please.'

'Black coffee . . . strong.' She lifted a heaped teaspoon. 'So I assume my theory is the same as yours at this point? We have a man who got mixed up in some occult group and to prove his loyalty he was given the task of what? Hurting his girlfriend? Then he couldn't go through with it. He reported that back and they took it all rather personal.'

'Cutting ties,' Harry said. 'As far as theories go, it's as good as any.'

'It's the only one we have! Sharon also said something about Jarod having his phone out. Something about how he needed to take a photo. I guess that was intended as proof of what he had done. There'll be a trail.'

'There will. We didn't find a phone with Jarod's body, but Sharon gave us the number she has. I've put in an urgent request with the phone company, but I don't think that will get us much further. Again, they wouldn't say much over the phone, but they did say that it didn't show any activity at all for months.'

'Switched off?'

'Must be. Certainly it's not connecting to any masts. Nothing.'

'So he wasn't using that phone.'

'Sharon said she saw him with a phone. She knew he had an iPhone and she assumed it was the same one. I think he just got another one.'

'Or he was given one.'

'Quite.'

'He won't be sending those pictures as text messages either, will he? There are a lot of messaging apps out there now with end-to-end encryption. Even your common or garden drug dealer knows to use one of those to run their business on.'

Harry lifted his coffee to take his first sip. He pulled his lips back from the bitterness, 'I agree.'

'We're not getting much further here. Anything from the searches?'

'Not yet. So far they've identified almost thirty sites in the three square miles of countryside I asked for. And I was being conservative with that. They've put the VRD's in first. They'll be quickest, but the weather's closing in. If we don't get anything by sundown today it's not going to be a line of enquiry.'

Maddie exhaled. They were running out of options. VRD's — Victim Recovery Dogs — could detect a spot of blood on a piece of open ground the size of a football pitch, but the conditions had to be right. She thought back to the injury to their victim's hand. She'd hoped for some spilt blood if he was stationary, but his girlfriend had described a dressing. It wasn't looking positive. She stiffened suddenly. 'The injury to his hand . . . which one was it?'

Harry looked at her over his mug. 'The girlfriend said the left, but the preliminary report from our CSI states he had injuries to both his hands.'

'He had injuries everywhere, Harry!'

'He did. One of the wounds was deemed to be older than the other, I remember that.'

'The left. The one that Sharon talked about being bandaged.'

'What's your point?'

'Just that the symbolism might be significant, surely?'

Harry looked like he was considering this for a second. 'The left hand for the left-hand path. Branding or scarring would make sense, not sure about an open wound, though?'

Maddie shrugged. 'Maybe the wound in the left hand had to be fresh. So the devil would know. When he was *dragged to hell* I mean!' She shook her head. 'I may be clutching at straws there?'

'Hey, I thought I'd find you in here!'

Maddie jumped. She'd been lost in her thoughts of devil worship and open wounds when Rhiannon had walked in.

'Kettle's just boiled,' Maddie said.

Rhiannon waved her away. 'No, thanks. I just wanted to let you know that the media appeal has gone out.'

Maddie didn't reply immediately.

'For our boy with the blood?' Rhiannon clarified.

'I guessed that. Sorry, I thought there was more. That's good. Surely we'll get a lead or two from that.'

'I'm quietly confident. Someone knows who he is and what happened. They have to.'

'And I don't doubt we have the right person in charge to find the answers!'

'Technically you're still in charge.'

'That's what I meant!' The two women chuckled together. Rhiannon had been tense but seemed to relax a little.

'Is it a full release?' asked Maddie.

'It's on all the social media and the media team are contacting the nationals.'

'I think it'll gather momentum. I can't see how this isn't a huge public interest story.'

'We've set up an information line. I'll let you know if anything comes from that.'

'Yes, please do.' As well as overseeing the investigation, Maddie was also intending to offer her services to speak with the boy again later on. She felt invested in him. She wanted to know his story and to be part of making it better. 'How are you getting on with our child psychologist?'

Rhiannon smirked. 'Famously.'

'Sounds like you are having the same experience we did,' Harry said.

'I think my experience might be down to your *groundwork*. No offence, sir, but she doesn't seem to like you much.'

'People like that don't like anybody.' Harry's growl was immediate.

Maddie chuckled. 'Harry Blaker just said that!'

Rhiannon's phone was ringing. She apologised and swept out of the room. Maddie watched her go.

'She's going to be a fine SIO one day,' Maddie said.

'She would have had a good mentor.'

'That much is true! What have we got on this afternoon? I've got case review chasing me for a file upgrade on a not guilty plea. I know it's only a matter of time before Jarod Logan takes over my life. If I can sit at my desk for an hour I reckon I could clear the decks.'

'Go for it. I plan on going to see CPS anyway.'

'Face to face?' Maddie couldn't hide her surprise. The Crown Prosecution Service was based at the courts these days and far less accessible. Gone were the days of knocking at an office in your own police station where a CPS representative would be sat, ready to assure you that your evidence was nowhere near ready for prosecution. Now their nearest base was at Canterbury Crown Court and the personnel there would only talk to you about cases at that court on that day. To have a face-to-face about a case that wasn't live, you needed to go up to their office at Maidstone. Maddie had never been there herself; she had always been pointed towards secure email and phone lines. CPS had always made it clear that they didn't hold meetings with the likes of her.

'Face-to-face. I'm old fashioned. It still has some advantages.'

'And they didn't fob you off?'

'I didn't give them the opportunity.'

'Which case?'

'Trevelyan.'

'The husband and wife rape case? How's that one going?' Maddie could guess the answer. Rape cases when both parties were in an intimate relationship were far more common than people realised, but were also notoriously difficult to get across the line. There was no other type of offence where the evidence was so flawed from the outset. Maddie had a real dislike for domestic violence offenders; they could make her angry in places she hadn't known she could feel. The Trevelyan case was nasty, and the last she heard the husband looked set to walk.

'It's not going. I need to look someone in the eyes to get it kick-started.'

'Well, good luck with that!' Maddie chuckled a little, but she meant it.

Harry checked his watch and consequently downed the last of his coffee. He squeezed back past her to put his cup next to the sink. 'I shouldn't be long. Though I might need more than luck.'

* * *

Harry felt bad about lying to Maddie. He knew that wasn't how you operated in a partnership; you couldn't, not when you both wanted the same thing. But this was to protect her as much as anything else. He shouldn't be here. He knew that.

It was just over an hour since he had left his office in Canterbury to head to Maidstone. He was in the right town to see CPS but that had never been his intention. Instead, he now had a tight grip on the handle of a very different type of entrance door, one he had been watching from the other side of the road for a while. It looked dirtier up close, its wooden surface scuffed, pitted and generally worn. It had been busy with people coming and going, but not for the previous ten minutes. This was as good a time as any.

Still he hesitated. The handle was cold enough to make his hand ache. Finally he pushed it open. Maidstone's

Probation Office opened up immediately into a waiting room. The chairs were empty but added to the same worn impression overall. He walked through the reception area and his leg was brushed by stuffing that burst out from one of the chair backs. The reception was really just a small glass window cut into a brick wall. Harry had been to a few Probation Offices in his time and the look and atmosphere was always the same. A lad stood behind the window with his shirt sufficiently open to show off a rack of beads resting against a bony chest. His hair was floppy, his face littered with the onset of stubble.

The lad looked him up and down. 'Hey, can I help you?'

Harry lifted his warrant card. 'I'm Detective Inspector Harry Blaker. I'm dealing with an offender who attends Probation here. I spoke to his Probation Officer a few times on the phone but I've come down to speak with him in person . . .'

'Okay, who's your offender?'

Harry hesitated. This was the moment when he needed to overstep the mark, when his tale became a lie and with no plausible denial. 'Wootan, Daniel Wootan,' he said firmly.

'Yeah, I know him. He was in here not long ago.'

'Great, I was speaking with his officer . . .' Harry tutted and he shook his head. 'His name escapes me? I have it written down somewhere . . .' He made a show of starting to rummage his jacket pockets.

'Rob Aitkins, right?'

'Rob! I feel bad. I've been speaking to him a lot! Is he here? He did say he would be.' Another lie. Harry had discovered that Wootan had been summoned to Probation for a meeting after his arrest and subsequent release. Harry had timed his visit for an hour after. Late enough for Wootan to be well clear; soon enough for his officer to be still typing up his notes.

'Yeah. I'll let him know you're here.' The boy turned to move away from the serving window.

'Actually . . .' Harry called out. The lad stopped in his tracks. 'I'll go through and speak to him in there. Some of

123

the people that come through that door might not like me very much. I've had a bad experience or two in these places!'

The boy eyed him. He smiled, but it took a few seconds to appear. 'I bet. I'll buzz you through.'

The door was to the side of the office. It led to a corridor, which Harry walked down until he reached a gap in the wall opening to a bigger room at the back of the building. There were three L-shaped desks and a round meeting table with an array of chairs pushed against it, a box of overflowing paperwork on its surface. Two of the desks were occupied. At the one closest to him was a larger man who leant back in his chair to look up at Harry. He wore a white short-sleeved shirt and the material was tight around his upper arms. His elbow was dug into his belly to hold up the thing he was chewing on while crumbs cascaded down his front. The only description Harry had of Wootan's Probation Officer was a mention of him on an intelligence report where Wootan had become abusive in his presence and referred to him as a 'fat shit'. This was his man.

'Afternoon, Rob,' Harry said.

The man cocked his head to one side and his chewing became a lot more pronounced. 'Have we met?'

'Some time ago,' Harry lied.

'Once met, never forgotten, eh Rob?' The slimmer, older man at the other desk laughed too hard and too loud. Harry screwed up his face while Aitkins pulled his shirt taut to help the crumbs to the floor.

'You're managing Daniel Wootan, right?' Harry said.

'That is my dubious pleasure, yeah.' Aitkins still peered down his body, completing a final sweep. His chin wobbled with the movement.

'We got him in recently for theft,' Harry said. 'I was expecting him to be back inside by now, serving out the rest of his time. What happened?'

'I don't think you said who you were.' Aitkins looked past Harry to where he'd come in. 'Or how you got back here?'

'Detective Inspector Harry Blaker.'

'Ah! So that makes a bit more sense! Look, I get it, okay? I get this all the time . . . senior police officers calling me up or whatever about some petty shit we've got on our books and who's been out of jail for like a week and they've already seen their crime stats go through the roof. I know Daniel's a shit. I know he's back on the steal again. But I have to do this right. I've got my own pressures and we don't work for the police.'

'I would prefer it if you didn't swear in my presence. And I won't in yours — a respect thing.' Harry noticed the skin on Aitkins's neck and face flush. His face bunched up into a sneer.

'I tell you what . . . I promise I won't swear *at* you, how's that? But this is my office, this is where I work and sometimes I swear. Like I said, whether you're a police inspector or a wooden top makes no odds to me. Daniel Wootan is for me to manage and how I do that is not up for conversation. Not with you.' Aitkins got to his feet. He was even taller than he was wide. It was rare for Harry to lift his head to make eye contact with anyone but he didn't step back. Aitkins threw his wrapper into a bin.

'Shoplifting isn't enough to breach his licence conditions?' Harry persisted.

'Well, it might have been, but he wasn't charged with shoplifting as far as I know. Your lot never *proved* it.' The *proved* was accompanied by a morsel of food that narrowly missed Harry.

'He was seen on CCTV going in and out of that shop at a time when there was no one else in there. When he leaves, the alarm goes off and a bottle of whisky is missing. He made off when he heard the alarm. And that's not enough?' Harry's tone was still flat.

Aitkins shrugged. 'I agree. You people need to pull your fingers out of your arses!'

'I don't mean for a charge. Your threshold is much lower. That's enough for you to send him back to prison — no question. Theft is a dishonesty offence, it's all you need.'

'What I need is to get on with it. What I don't need are police officers telling me what I should be doing and how. Happens all the time and it isn't as simple as that. There's this whole bigger picture out there, where the prisons are full to the rafters and there's just about room for only the most horrible. So, a nicked bottle of whisky? Let's just say he might not be a priority to push back into the mix.'

'Daniel Wootan went to prison because he killed someone.' Harry shuffled on the spot. He pushed his hands behind his back and dug nails into his palm until it hurt. For the first time he was aware of emotion leaking out in his words and he didn't want his big fists hanging loose.

Aitkins huffed. 'Killed someone! Come on! He was out on the rob and he crashed his car. Yeah someone died but that ain't a murder now, is it? That's a petty thief who can't drive for shit!' Aitkins chuckled and it shook his whole belly. Harry fixed him in a glare and stepped in a little closer, close enough to make him uncomfortable.

Aitkins leaned back, his expression only somewhat contrite. 'The swearing thing, yeah? It's habit is all—'

'He's dangerous. Part of his conditions include a ban on driving. This shoplifting took place at a garage and was committed by the occupant of a car. The *only* occupant. So he's driving, too.'

Aitkins started moving some papers around on his desk. 'Look, it's done, okay? He stays out so the rapists, the paedos and the murderers get to stay in. It's the way of the world these days.'

'He won't stop driving — you know that. He was high when he crashed the last time and he's back on the gear. What if he kills someone else?'

Aitkins grimaced. He stopped what he was doing to lean forward. He had started to look rattled, now he seemed angry. His face and neck flushed brighter. 'Well, I promise I'll recall him then. How's that?'

Harry's nails dug so far into his own hand that he almost yelped. He broke away first, though — he knew he had to. It was time to leave. He walked back along the corridor and out into the waiting area. He was back to his car when he finally pulled his fingers apart. The last few paces he made were slower and more deliberate. He shoved out at his car, both his hands slapped against the driver's window and the car shook on the spot. He stopped to look around. He was parked on a busy road with traffic passing in both directions. No one seemed to be taking any notice of him, but they might. He could already have caused himself problems; he didn't need to be making them worse. He turned his hands so they were palm up. He could see the deep marks pressed into his flesh and pulsing white. They were still painful when he turned the key to start the engine.

CHAPTER 14

'What have you got, then?' Maddie was at her desk and had started to make some headway with her case file when Rhiannon's name had flashed up on her desk phone. She had been largely ignoring calls, but her hand had shot out to pick it up. She hadn't heard anything since the media appeal had gone out. Maybe there was an update.

'Can you come over?' Maddie thought that Rhiannon's voice was tinged with excitement.

'Now?'

'If you can. There's something I want to show you.'

CID was in a separate building from the main police station at Canterbury. The building was known as 'the range' as it had once been exactly that: a big, open-plan building used for firearms training. Firearms had moved away, leaving the facilities team scratching their heads, trying to work out how to make a long, slim building with barely any windows and soundproofed walls into a comfortable, functional and not-at-all-oppressive building for detectives to work in. They had largely failed on all counts. Rhiannon's desk was down the far end on the top floor, close to the DCI's office. It had been Maddie's first desk when she had moved down from Manchester and it always made her smile to see it. Not because of happy memories, but because she was happy she didn't have to sit there anymore. Rhiannon and another DC lent over the desk.

'We've had a good response,' Rhiannon said. She straightened up and shook her hair with her fingers. She looked a little tired and blinked like someone who'd broken away from a computer monitor after a long stint.

'I thought you might. Anything that stands out?'

'Mainly offers to foster the boy. So . . . no — until this came in.' Rhiannon brought up her email screen. She clicked on an attachment which took a second to open. It was a bright white screen with writing in a font that made it instantly recognisable as a CAD. This is how a call from the public was recorded. It showed the initial typed notes of the call-taker. Maddie skimmed over it. The top part usually gave the caller details: name, address, and the phone number they were calling from. This one was blanked out. The *name* box was the only one with an entry: *anon*.

'What's the summary?' Maddie said. CAD's were not laid out very well. There were lots of lines of jargon before you got to the meat of the call.

'It was in the pile for a follow-up. It started off like someone who was a bit of a crackpot. This sort of thing always attracts their interest.'

Maddie made a listening 'Umm' while fighting the urge to just tell Rhiannon to get to the point.

'But this bit here . . . was anything put out about the boy's dad?'

Maddie leant back and followed Rhiannon's slender finger to a line of text: CALLER STATES THAT THE BOY IS KNOWN TO HIM. THAT HE WAS THERE WHEN HIS DAD WAS HRT. WILL NT SAY WHO BOY IS OVER PHONE, OR DAD. SAYS DAD WAS HURT BAD. HE MAY NOT BE OK. WILL ONLY SPEAK TO THE SIO. VRY INSISTENT.'

'No!' Maddie said. She bit down on her lip. 'I mean I could double-check nothing went out on anything official, but—'

'It didn't. I checked those already.'

'Okay, what about the press?'

'We've not made mention of anyone else, the release as a whole was pretty bland. A young boy with staining on his clothing that suggests he was present when an assault took place. That was about it.'

'So this caller might actually know something?'

'He might. Or it's a lucky guess?'

'He?'

'The description gives the voice as adult, male. That's all we have, though.'

'Have you had the caller details run?' Maddie said. Anonymous calls to the police were rarely actually anonymous. The details could be retrieved if they put the right justification on the right form.

'A phone box on Stone Street. The Canterbury end.'

Maddie stepped back. 'So it's the right sort of area. Seems too specific for a crank just getting lucky. But he'll only speak to the SIO. How does he want to do that?'

'There's a time and an address.' Rhiannon's finger ran down the screen until she found it.

'The Ports Café,' Maddie read. 'I know it. It's just off the A20. It's not exactly the most police-friendly place. We'll need to try and blend in.'

'We?' Rhiannon said.

'Sure. I'm still the Senior Investigating Officer as far as DCI Lowe is concerned. I told him as much! We can't have you going on your own.'

'Okay . . . I just thought you and DI Blaker would go out?'

'The whole idea of you running this is for your development, Rhiannon. You're just as capable. Besides, Harry's busy talking to our CPS overlords this afternoon. And, like you said, this may well be just some crackpot who got lucky with one of our buzzwords. Have you seen this bit?' Maddie was back to scanning the CAD. 'The more I read it, the more I think it *is* a crackpot.'

'What do you mean?'

'This bit here? The bit about *how* he wants to meet?' Maddie pointed at a line of text.

'Oh yeah, I was hoping you wouldn't see that!' Rhiannon chuckled. 'I think we still have to go.'

Maddie read from the screen, *'When the SIO enters, he or she will need to order a black coffee and the pancakes.* What does he think this is, some spy film?'

'It would appear so. It still could be something, though.'

'We definitely need to go and bottom out his comments. I'm just not as interested as I was. At least he should be easy to spot.'

'Easy?'

'Yeah, he'll be the one sat in the corner holding a newspaper up with eye-holes cut in it!'

Both of them laughed, then Maddie was suddenly thoughtful.

'What?' Rhiannon prompted.

'That dad comment . . . Harry had oversight of everything that went out. It's worth a check with him. He'd know if it was released anywhere.' She lifted her phone. It was already ringing.

'Maddie . . .' Harry's voice was loud against background noise. Maddie could tell he was on handsfree and in a moving car.

'Harry, quick question . . . We've got a lead in relation to our blood-soaked boy. He wants to meet to give us information. I just wanted to run something past—'

'Meet? Who does?'

'The informant.'

'Which is who?'

'We don't know. It's anonymous.'

'You meeting him at the nick, then?'

'No. He's given instructions to meet at a café. I can't exactly get back to him and confirm either way.'

'A café? All sounds a bit odd. When?'

Maddie glanced her watch. 'Not long, actually. We need to get going.'

'What café? I can head there and meet you.'

'No need, Harry. Rhiannon's leading this. I'm heading out with her. She's very capable.'

'I get that. But I don't like someone setting a time and place to meet you. Not when we don't have a clue why.'

'We'll handle it. I didn't call for you to attend, I just wanted to know if you were aware of any release of information about the boy's dad — that we suspect the blood to be from him?'

There was slight pause. 'No. We actively avoided giving any details, didn't we?'

'That's what I thought. I was just checking. I know you have oversight of everything that goes out.'

'To my knowledge that was never mentioned.'

'Okay then, thanks.'

'Make sure you take a cover car, someone to have your back. And get a CAD created so the control room knows you're there. Are you both in kit?'

Maddie rolled her eyes at Rhiannon. 'It's all under control. Don't worry. I'll let you know how it goes.' The call ended.

'Has he got a problem with us going out?' Rhiannon said.

'Not with us going out, just with us being competent! I think it's a man thing. They see us as something they need to protect. I should be glad, really.'

'You should.'

Maddie smiled. 'But I'm not! Let's get this done. We don't want to be late for our crackpot, now, do we?'

* * *

The Ports Café wasn't far from the M20. It was somewhere Maddie knew by reputation rather than it being somewhere she'd ever been to, a reputation that told her the word *café* was a little misleading. It might have started its life as a humble café but it was now more of a lorry park with round-the-clock services for the drivers. The building had been extended a number of times in response to an ever-increasing footfall. The car park had been extended, too, and seemed to wrap around the main building like a horseshoe thrown over it. 'You bring me to the nicest places!' she said to Rhiannon.

As they turned across the road and onto the hard standing, the going got bumpy. Rhiannon was in the driver's seat and she slowed right down to a crawl to negotiate the ruts and bumps in the stony surface. They pulled up on the left side of the building. The car park here had a few parked cars and a neat row of motorbikes close to the door. The windows had a layer of condensation that prevented Maddie seeing anything more than blurred shapes inside. It was just before 2 p.m., and she considered that any lunch rush should be just about over. She'd passed this place at night before and often seen the car park end-to-end with lorries.

Maddie walked in first. She narrowed her eyes to a ceiling heater that seemed to be angled to beat her in the face with a blast as she entered. There was a clump of empty tables in the middle; people seemed to prefer to sit around the edges. From a quick survey of the punters, she reckoned there were a couple of families, a few tradesmen, and a lot of bikers still dressed in half-leathers. They occupied the full length of a wall where a number of tables had been pulled together. Their group was in high spirits and laughter broke out. A man in the centre of them all was hanging his head, seemingly the butt of the joke.

Maddie walked through to the counter with Rhiannon just behind her. A young woman appeared from the door directly behind, where kitchen smells and sounds leaked out before it swung shut again. The woman looked to be in her early thirties and their presence at the counter seemed to make her jump. She gathered herself together and pulled a notebook from her apron.

'What can I get you?'

'Black coffee and pancakes for me, please, and she'll have a cup of tea,' Maddie said.

The woman hovered over her pad. She seemed to change her mind about something and slid it back into her apron. 'Anything else?' she said.

'Just those, thanks.' Maddie peered to her right. There was a big chalkboard with a mess of handwritten menu items. 'I don't see pancakes on there? Is that going to be okay?'

'We took them off, but I can still do them.' She gave a smile but it looked strained, nervous almost. 'I'll bring it all over.'

Maddie and Rhiannon picked a table against the far window and Rhiannon flicked idly through a local paper. Maddie was back to sizing up the other occupants. Their order came out quickly. The woman appeared by her side, catching her out.

'That was quick! You must have had some left over!' Maddie said.

'We should bring them back, I say. But who am I?' The woman shrugged then forced a laugh. 'Enjoy your meal.' She moved away.

'Do you like pancakes?' Maddie asked.

Rhiannon reached out for the plate. 'I didn't get my lunch yet. I love the syrup. I'd better not eat them all, though, otherwise how will our secret agent know that we did as he requested!'

'Just be sure you don't! I don't think he's here yet.' Maddie was still looking beyond Rhiannon. She had already disregarded the biker group and the families didn't fit the profile either. There were two tables of obvious tradesmen and there was no sign of them having any interest in anyone beyond the edges of their tables. Maddie was expecting someone on their own, someone standing out without meaning too. No one did so far. She glanced out at the car park: no movement there either. She checked her watch: ten past two. From the very specific instructions and the apparent excitement behind them she hadn't expected their informant to be late. 'How long do you think we should give it?' Maddie said.

'Well, I'm nearly done with these,' Rhiannon said with her mouth full.

'Fine. He has until I finish the coffee and then we're gone.'

'You're going to drink that?' Rhiannon asked.

Maddie answered by lifting the cup to her mouth. She hadn't tried black coffee before; it was Harry's tipple. It couldn't be too bad surely? She took the smallest of sips. It was so bitter she almost spat it straight back into the cup.

Rhiannon laughed as she pulled a face. 'I'll take that as a *no*, then!'

As Maddie dabbed at her mouth, she was suddenly aware that the woman who'd served them was staring over. She looked away as Maddie made eye contact. Maddie stood up and pulled her coat on. 'We're wasting our time here, I reckon. He wouldn't be late. He must have had a change of heart.' She reached into her inside pocket. The waitress was serving someone. Maddie walked over and waited patiently behind them until they were well clear. Then she held out her card.

'What's this?' the woman said.

'I came here to meet someone — on his instruction. Seems I've been stood up. I don't like being stood up. If you're aware of someone coming in later that might have been here to meet me, would you mind passing on my details?'

The woman took the card and turned it over where Maddie had written her colleague's details. 'It gets busy. I don't take much notice of people.'

Maddie smiled. 'I'm sure you don't. You never know, though. Someone might stand out. Maybe someone turns up looking late and hassled then asks you if someone ordered your pancakes. If that happens, hand over my card, would you. Is that okay?'

'Sure,' the woman replied, but she didn't look it. She hung her head a little and there was no eye contact now. She did push the card into a pocket on the front of her apron.

'Thank you. And the pancakes were lovely. I agree . . . you should put them back on the menu.'

'I'll bear that in mind.'

* * *

Harry had intended on just driving past this place. Probation was the other side of the town, a long way from where he had ended up. He was going to call the control room and find out where Maddie and Rhiannon were going, then hang in the area until they were clear. But at the roundabout for the motorway, he'd reached a decision. He was still angry, of course he was, but when he pulled at the wheel to deviate off at the first exit at the roundabout rather than the fourth, he realised that he was less in control of it than he'd have liked. He'd ignored the protestations of the drivers he'd cut up with his sudden change in direction and their horns did nothing to snap him out of his haze.

He was just going to drive past. And now he was parked up.

Daniel Wootan was at a property known to police and probation as a 'halfway house'. There were a number of them around the county. They were a place for some offenders to go when they were released from prison. Some people on their release didn't have anywhere to go and councils wouldn't take housing applications from anyone who was still in prison. The halfway house was designed to be temporary, a place to spend a few months until their housing and other benefits kicked in around them. It was seen as a favourable alternative to forcing newly released criminals straight back into the world of crime. The reality was that it often took much longer, so that the system was clogged with convicts who did indeed find themselves homeless and with no access to finances. Wootan had been more fortunate. He'd been housed in a bedsit on the second floor. Door number seven. Harry couldn't explain why he had deviated to drive past. Maybe he wanted to be sure it was still the rundown and dreary building he remembered from a few years before when he'd visited a man who was a likely witness to a murder in prison. In his career, he'd probably visited just about all of the halfway houses in the county for one reason or another.

He knew he should be staying well away, that he could only cause himself issues. But he was just going to drive past — no harm in that. Then there had been a gap among the parked cars. The road was always busy, always choked with traffic in both directions. Parking was typically impossible. But there'd been a gap. And he'd taken it as if he was on autopilot.

He stared over at the frontage of the building. Before being divvied up into bedsits, it would have been one very large and probably very grand house. It had a front door in the middle that was flanked by two bay windows on the ground floor that repeated directly above. There were windows in the slant of the roof, too. Harry's previous visit had been to one of those rooms. It was a cramped, dingy place with a single bed pushed under the sharp angle of the pitch. The windows were tiny. That day had been in the middle of the summer; it was sweltering and the whole building had been thick with the stench of perspiration. It was cooler on this day but he'd wager that the smell would be no better. The lower ground windows were part-covered by patchy conifers. Once, they might have been in a neat row with trimmed edges; now, the hedge on the right side of the front path was unkempt with a brown patch in its middle while the left side was largely cut to stumps. At least it allowed a clear sight through to the long, thick grass of the front garden, which was dominated by two wheelie bins that had their orange lids pushed upwards by overflowing sacks of refuse. He looked up to the second floor. The bay windows on this level both had curtains pulled across. On the right side the curtain wasn't wide enough and it left a thick, black shadow in its middle. Harry couldn't be sure on which side of the building number seven would be nor whether Wootan was even there right now.

Then Harry noticed the front door being opened and a man stepped out in a grey tracksuit with the hood up and a black body-warmer over the top. The door closed behind him slowly as if it was on a slow spring and he was bent forward, his face covered by both hands as he lit a cigarette. He straightened and blew a cloud upwards. Harry could see his face now. It wasn't him. It wasn't Wootan.

It took a large expulsion of air for Harry to be aware that he had been holding his breath in the first place. His pulse was racing and his left hand was gripped tightly around the steering wheel, but his right rested on the door handle and he was leaning forward. He slumped back in his seat as he exhaled and moved his hand away from the door.

'And what exactly were you going to do?' he said to himself and shook his head. He still watched the smoking man, who eventually turned back to the door and pushed it open. He hadn't used a key, just the handle. It wasn't locked. Harry shook his head again. He had no business noting that. He had no business being there at all.

The car was still ticking over. He was never intending on staying, after all; he was just driving past. He gave one more glance at the second floor of the building before checking his mirror and pulling back out into the stream of traffic.

CHAPTER 15

As Harry strode through the Major Crime floor towards his office, his thoughts were elsewhere, but he was wrenched from them by the sound of a familiar voice. DCI Julian Lowe was in conversation with one of his DC's. He broke away immediately on seeing Harry.

'Ah, just the man!'

'Boss.' Harry continued through to his office and Lowe followed him in. He pulled his jacket off and was hanging it up as Lowe pushed his door shut.

'A closed-door session, boss?' Harry said.

'A short one.' Lowe glanced around for a spare seat and, seeing there were none, looked uncomfortable standing. Harry sat and looked expectant.

'I got an update from your team out there on Jarod Logan. Seems he has been an international man of mystery for the last few years at least. Detectives from your team have spent a lot of time with the girlfriend and, if she's to be believed, she didn't know too much about him either.'

'Not his recent activity, no.'

'And you believe her?' Lowe's hands moved to his hips, they pushed out his suit jacket.

'I don't see what reason she has to lie. I think she's scared witless of whatever it was that got to Logan. If she knew enough to help us take the fear away, I think she would tell us in a heartbeat.'

'*What*ever?'

'Well, *who*ever. But it seems he might have been part of something — a group, rather than just an individual. I just took a call from Charley Mace as a matter of fact. I have search teams out in the area where he was found. I figured he started his journey somewhere. They've had a positive hit on some blood.'

'Positive that it's Logan's?'

'No. Positive that it's blood. CSI are running it as we speak. It might be nothing but, whatever, we'll get to the bottom of it.'

'I know you will,' Lowe said. He looked even more awkward now. Harry decided to let him off the hook.

'You didn't close my door for that, boss. What is it?'

'Daniel Wootan again, I'm afraid.'

'Okay . . .'

'Were you aware of his arrest earlier today?'

'I was aware he was wanted, something about a theft. That was all.'

'Vince Arnold went out first thing this morning to knock on his door. The arrest was . . . not without problems.'

'Problems?'

'The long and the short of it, Harry, is that a complaint has come in via his solicitor regarding the nature of the arrest and his treatment. Apparently our Vince was a little heavy handed. Wootan is claiming some bruising and being refused a drink of water among other basic human rights yada, yada. It's rubbish and will go away very quickly. The arrest was lawful. I'll speak with Vince as to when and how he put hands on just to draw a line under it.'

'And this has something to do with me, does it?' Despite an internal battle, Harry didn't think he was showing any reaction.

'Not directly. The problem we have is that any further attempts to single out Wootan will likely lead to further complaints, cause more work for everyone, and we might get to the point where one of the complaints is upheld. I've heard through the grapevine that officers are actively looking to target him for stop and search in an effort to get him back in prison. I'm sure you understand what I am trying to say?'

Harry's breathing had become deeper, he'd been taking big gulps to try and quench a growing anger. He took his deepest breath yet before his reply. 'Single him out? He's a known drug user, sometime dealer, and a prolific thief. Time was, singling out criminals like that for stop-searches was good police work.'

'Times have changed, Harry.'

'We don't target criminals anymore?'

'We play the game and we play it right.'

'This isn't a GAME!' Harry's feet were planted and he was standing upright before he had time to suppress it. His chest heaved. There'd been nothing he could do to conceal his emotions. 'Not to me,' he said, trying to gather himself back up. He picked up his cup and stayed standing, a sign that he was done.

'You're right. Poor turn of phrase. I just want to do this right. I want him back behind bars just as much as you do, but if we don't do this right — if we play into his hands — then we face a situation where he rubs our faces in this whole nasty affair. We cannot be seen to be putting any more focus on him than we do other known criminals.'

'This has nothing to do with me. If you need to speak with Vince then go ahead. I have no intention of *singling him out* as you put it, I've got too many years behind me to go looking for people like Daniel Wootan.'

'I know that. I never assumed that you would be. But this does have something to do with you. As part of his complaint, Wootan's solicitor brought up your name. The claim is that he is being targeted on your direction, because of who you are and what you do.'

'Well, he isn't,' Harry shrugged.

'I know that. But I thought you would want to know. We need to be sensible. We need to give this piece of work enough rope for him to hang himself with. And he will. We may just need to be a little more patient. Can you imagine how this would feel if he manages to get compensation as part of his complaint?'

'Compensation?'

'Yes. Of course he's asking for that. They all do. Look, it will be dealt with and he will be told to wind his neck in. I just wanted you to be aware.'

'And now I am.'

Julian hesitated like he had something else to say. If he did, he kept it to himself for now. Harry watched him leave. When he was out of sight he sat back down. Maddie Ives might have been waiting for him to finish; her appearance at the door was instant.

'You okay?'

'Always.'

'No one's okay always. How did it go with CPS?'

Harry lifted his eyes to meet with hers. 'Same old. It wasn't as productive as I'd hoped. There may be some more positive news around Logan's investigation however. Charley Mace has confirmed a blood find. No idea whose or why. I've had CSI do what they need to do. There's nothing else there apparently. I think I might take a drive out and take a look myself.'

'Do you need to? If there's nothing else there? If forensics have done their bit, we can just add it to our map showing key locations and wait for the photographs.'

'She's emailing them over. I know Charley, she'll get the full scene in, too.'

'So I'm missing something?'

Harry took his time to answer. 'I like to get a feel. And I could do with getting some air.'

Maddie did that thing where she cocked her head to one side and narrowed her eyes a little. 'You see, I told you no one could be okay all the time.'

'I will be. Once I've got some air. You coming or not?'

'Sure. I'll drive.'

* * *

The 'walk' to the car had been almost a jog for Maddie to keep up with Harry. She looked over at him in the passenger seat as he faced out of the window. 'Bad day, Harry?' she chanced. Harry wanted to get away from the station, she could understand that, but he'd asked her to come along, in his own way. He wouldn't do that unless he wanted to talk.

'Standard,' he said.

'Bad week, I reckon,' she said. They joined the endless stream of traffic passing the front of Canterbury Police Station. They were turning away from the city centre at least, away from the traffic chaos.

'I wouldn't say that. In this job, bad has to be very bad.'

'It does.' The car fell silent. Once, Maddie might have either felt awkward or tried again to get Harry to say what was on his mind. She knew him a little better now; he would talk when he was ready. She turned the radio on low. A few moments later, Harry flinched like he'd been jabbed with something.

'You okay?'

'Oh, yeah. My watch . . . it vibrates. Catches me out a bit.'

Maddie looked down at his wrist and recognised a type of smartwatch. 'Very posh. I looked at getting one of those for my running. Didn't think it would be your sort of thing, though?'

'Why not?'

'Well, it's complic—' Maddie stopped herself. She grinned too but aimed it out of the window and away from her passenger. 'It's fandangled. I know you don't like fandangled.'

'You mean you know I can't work fandangled!'

'That's exactly what I meant.'

'It was my birthday present. Today's the first day I've tried it.' Maddie didn't push him for any more detail; she could sense it coming. 'From both my daughters.'

'That's nice.' Maddie knew he had children, but not how many or what gender they were — until now.

'I'm not sold on it. Apparently I'm not so good at replying to messages on my phone. I guess they thought that an electric shock every time you get one is the best way to prompt a response.'

'Does it work?'

'It does, actually. I still think I'll go back to the old one, though.' Harry was fiddling with his phone and looked to be typing something out. Maddie waited until he put it away.

'Have you talked to them? About Daniel Wootan?'

'Yes. Well, one of them. They both know.'

'One of them?' Maddie pushed her luck.

'The youngest. The other is away at university. It doesn't make it easy.'

'I'm sure it doesn't.' Maddie let the silence return again. She thought there might be more to come. She was right.

'They were devastated. Even Faye was upset and she's the laid-back one of the two. Melissa, the younger one . . . she's struggled — with the whole thing. I talked to her, but I still wouldn't say I know what she's thinking.'

'Probably the same as what you are,' Maddie said.

'I doubt it.' There was another pause. 'I didn't go to see CPS today. I went to see Wootan's Probation Officer. It was a mistake. I know I should be staying the hell away.'

Maddie snatched a look at him. He was still looking away. 'Okay . . . Did you get to see him?'

'Yes.'

'And?'

'He assumed I was there because I was upset about our crime figures.'

'He didn't know about your history? With Wootan, I mean.'

'No.'

144

'So, no harm done then?'

'Not yet, no.'

'What did he say?'

'Well, he doesn't care. Not about Wootan and what he might do now he's released. And he certainly doesn't care about what he did to go to prison in the first place.'

'That must have been hard to hear.'

'It was. I just need to remember that no one else *does* care. They can't. I've made a career of telling junior colleagues not to absorb too much from what they see and from the victims they speak to. You can't suck up everyone else's agony. In the end it'll take you over. He's right not to care. It's just another name on his books.'

'Is that what this is for you? Agony?' They weren't far from the location now. The scenery was just trees and the dapple effect of a weak sun on the muddied road ahead. Maddie slowed up, giving Harry time to talk. Arrival at their destination would have cut him off, and she decided he needed to talk it out.

'It's hard. And you can't take anything for it — nothing deadens it. Then we get the news that he's . . . I can't look my own daughters in the eye and tell them why it is happening . . . why that man is a free man . . . why he hasn't answered for what he did and how he might be getting compensation from the police.'

'Compensation?'

Harry waved her away. 'Forget that — that bit's not happening. I think our friend Vince was a little heavy handed with the arrest. It hasn't helped.'

'You know that was his way of trying to do just that, though? Of helping? You should have seen how happy he was to be the one out there knocking on Wootan's door!'

'I do. I *do* know that. He's a good man — just in the most idiotic way.'

'That might be the best description of Vince I've ever heard.' She laughed a little, Harry didn't. He changed the subject.

'How was your meeting at the café? I assume you went out with Rhiannon?'

'I did. Uneventful. He didn't show.'

'He didn't? Anything since?'

'No. I've asked the FCR to make me aware of any other calls from that number.'

'So a timewaster?'

'I guess so.'

'That's very frustrating. The public are quick to moan that there aren't enough police officers on the streets, but they don't realise that a call like that can take a lot of resources to manage.'

'I know. I guess they don't think about it like that,' Maddie said. They were nearly at the location but now Maddie was satisfied. This wasn't the time to tell Harry that she hadn't tied up quite as many resources as he thought. She'd reckoned it to be a timewaster from the start.

They rounded a bend and the road straightened. She could see a marked car parked up in front of them and over to one side. The door to this car pushed open as they approached and a sergeant with a black jacket tightly zipped up under his chin stepped out and walked towards them. He was at her door before the car had even come to a full stop. He wore a baseball cap that had a little mud-splatter on the word *Police*. Maddie pushed open her door.

'Hey, I understand you want to see the find?' He eyed them both. He looked like he was doing his best not to ask why.

'That's right,' Harry said. 'Thanks for waiting.'

'No problem. We've completed the search and CSI have done their bit. The scene's stood down — not that it needed much managing. I haven't seen a single car in the three hours I've been here.'

Maddie peered around at the scenery. The road was a slither of cracked tarmac that was out of place in the thick woodland. Overall it looked like nature had been left to its own designs and was slowly taking back its territory. The road was flanked by muddy gullies that leaked standing water onto its surface while long grass and weeds poked out from its middle. They stood on packed-down mud mingled with stones and rocks that appeared to be the start of a vehicle track into the woods. There was a closed gate around two car lengths in with a green sign announcing that the land was maintained by the Forestry Commission. Maddie's eyes flicked around, looking for any cameras. Some fly-tipping hotspots had them, but it didn't seem they were so lucky.

They stopped close to the gate and the sergeant pointed to a small puddle of mud at his feet. 'Not much to see, I'm afraid, but this was where the dog signalled. There was a rock that had some staining to it. The CSI was able to confirm it as blood and it's been seized. She took a sample of the puddle water too. She seemed to think she had enough.'

'Great, thanks.' Maddie suddenly felt aware of herself. The sergeant was looking from her to Harry and she knew he was waiting for them to reveal the reason they'd driven twenty minutes out to look into a puddle. They didn't have one. Harry had needed to leave; he had wanted to talk and needed an excuse. This was it.

'Any tracks?' Maddie was clutching at straws. She made a show of looking around.

'More of an indent. CSI took some pictures. It's too wet to take a mould apparently and there wasn't enough tread detail. She didn't think she'd get anything.'

'Okay. Right then, I think I've seen enough. Thanks again for your time.' They shook hands. Maddie could see the sergeant was still looking over at them when she got back into the car. She was glad of the phone ringing to drag her attention as she drove away.

'Rhiannon, you okay?' Maddie answered.

'Yes, can you speak?'

'Sure. You're on speaker. I'm out with Harry following up a lead on Jarod Logan. We're just coming away.'

'A lead?' Rhiannon sounded enthused. 'What have you got?'

Maddie exchanged a glance with Harry. 'Well, a muddy puddle really. But it might turn out to be something.'

There was a pause at the other end. 'Okay . . . well, we might have something on the Alex Thompson case, too.'

'Alex Thompson?'

'That is the name of our boy covered in blood!' Rhiannon nearly sung the revelation.

'How did we get to that?'

'We did what you asked. We put out a good picture of the boy to Social Services in just about every county to see if anyone recognised him. We got a hit in Reading. A social worker over there reckons her colleague worked with the boy and his family a while ago. She's given us some information over the phone but I've sent two DC's to speak with her this afternoon. We should know more very soon.'

'Her colleague?'

'Yes. And I know what you're going to say but we can't speak with her. I put my foot in it a bit actually — she passed away.'

'Who did?'

'Sorry! The social worker who dealt with Alex and the family over a period of time died. Last year sometime. But the woman we're speaking to did a dual visit when they first started working with the family. Apparently, they always try and go out as a pair for the first meeting.'

'One visit?' Harry butted in.

'Well . . . er, yes.' Harry's gruff interjection seemed to have thrown their young colleague. 'I mean they worked with the family for a little while, I think — certainly with the boy.'

'But your actual informant . . . she only made one visit, is that right?'

'Er, yes. She went out on the first one. But she's pretty certain.'

'One visit over a year ago to a boy of that age? It might not be this Alex Thompson at all.'

'Noted, sir. I'm sending a couple to go and see her anyway. We'll get all the detail when we see her. There should be other ways we can confirm it.' Maddie could hear the excitement ebbing out of Rhiannon's voice.

'Send one. You don't need two on that enquiry. You need people back here,' Harry said.

'Oh, okay then, understood. I guess we could do with keeping the manpower back here. I was just thinking it's quite a way. It might be an overnighter and there might be another enquiry or two to come off it . . . But, yes, I'll whittle it down.'

'We're heading back in now,' Maddie cut back in. 'I'll catch up with you when I'm back and we can see what we have. What are your plans now?'

'Er . . . Well I was thinking I would go up and speak to the boy . . . tell him what I think I know and see what reaction I get. I don't see any harm in it and right now it might be the quickest way of moving us forward.'

Maddie was quick to answer before Harry could. 'Okay, good idea. Let me know if you want me to come with you. I know he still hasn't reacted to anyone else.'

'He hasn't, but he might now. I know you're tucked up with Jarod Logan. I'll go and see what happens. It might be that I ask you to go back and speak to him if he still won't engage with me.'

'I think it makes sense for you to try first, for sure. Good luck!' It was easy to read between the lines with Rhiannon. She had been given an investigation and she wanted to deal with it herself and she didn't want help unless it was desperately needed. Maddie was pretty certain she would have done exactly the same.

'Thanks.' Some of the enthusiasm seemed to be back in her voice. Maddie cut the call. She glanced towards Harry. He appeared to be oblivious, his attention out of the window. She swallowed her first reaction, took a few moments and a couple of deep breaths with it.

'You didn't have to bring her down so hard, you know. She's a young detective excited about a lead. We shouldn't ever beat that out of someone.'

'Beat? Having a lead is one thing, seeing it is another.'

'And managing someone with one is another thing altogether. She's bright. She has a hell of a future.'

'So you keep saying. She's naïve.'

'She's young! We all were once, even if some of us can't remember it.'

'That's just another way of saying the same thing. And we all had to learn from those that weren't quite so *young*. She may have nothing.'

'And she may have everything.'

Harry fell silent. Maddie hadn't finished making her point but she knew that continuing now would get her nowhere.

'And I'm not sure we need to go and see the boy with a possible name just yet. If we're wrong, we might just lose any of the confidence that boy has in us keeping him safe. It's a big risk.' Harry picked it back up.

'Rhiannon's made a decision. I think it's a good one.'

'You should go with her to see that boy at the very least.'

'You heard me offer. She's going on her own. One thing I know about that boy is that he doesn't like crowds. That *young* thing she has going for her just might be in her favour. She's closer to that boy's age than any of us — by a long way.'

'If the name is right, she's making good progress.'

'I never doubted she would!' Maddie snapped and immediately wished that she hadn't. It had been as close as Harry ever got to a climb-down. She needn't have worried.

'That was good advice you gave her, about checking with Social Services.' Harry's face was creased into something she had come to recognise as a smile. Maddie couldn't help but smile herself.

'I knew you couldn't let that go! Fine, Social Services was a good suggestion of yours and you've proved your point about how I should call you for your opinion. You happy?'

'Well, I am now.'

CHAPTER 16

Rhiannon knew she was going to have to get out of the car at some point. She didn't know why she was hesitating. She didn't need to. She'd already broken the ice by calling ahead and talking to Rose on the phone. Rose had cried, of course she had, but that conversation had meant a lot to Rhiannon too. She didn't like how she had left it with Rose all those years before.

The house hadn't changed a bit. Rhiannon had lived there for a very short time — a couple of weeks, maybe. But it had been the most significant couple of weeks of her life. She still believed it had changed her course entirely. When she entered that place, with its mismatched furniture, pinging radiators and creaking floors, she had been a terrified sixteen-year-old who'd just lost the last family member she had. She had never felt more alone, and Rose had been able to change that almost immediately. She was wonderful, warm and genuine, while also seeming to know just how much space to give her. There'd been other occupants with her there, too, another kid who had needed an emergency foster placement just like her and a permanently fostered girl. Rhiannon had caused problems. She hadn't meant to and the numerous times she had looked back at her time there she still wasn't sure if she could have done anything different.

When she had left that house she was a different person. Still alone, but more aware of who she was, of what she could be — of what she wanted to be. She started researching police recruitment almost immediately and she would apply the moment she turned eighteen. Now she was going to step back into that house as a police investigator — not yet an accredited detective, but she would be soon. Among a number of lessons she'd learnt in her short time in that house, the most significant perhaps was that she could do anything she set her mind to.

She knocked on the door firmly. She was suddenly happy that she had assured Maddie that she didn't need anyone to come out with her. This was something she wanted to do on her own and the fact it was her first time leading an investigation as serious as this was only part of the reason. The sun was low and felt warmer than it had for a while. It was beating straight at the door, giving the effect of a flash when it pulled open. Then the same light illuminated the face of the woman who had taken her in at a time when she was at her lowest, at her most vulnerable. Rose's hand snatched to her mouth, her face creased, her sobs were big, like everything about her. She stepped forward suddenly and swept Rhiannon up in a big hug. When she stepped back her hand was still over her mouth.

'Look at you! Look at you! Rhiannon . . . you're a woman! And what a woman!'

'Hey, Rose. You look great.'

'A detective! I always said you were sharp. I've never known a girl like it. I said that when you were here and after you left . . .'

'I'm sorry, Rose. I know I caused you problems. I never got the chance to speak with you after, but I never wanted that.'

Rose stepped forward again, the hug was bigger still, stronger too, and it pushed the air out of Rhiannon while trapping her arms by her sides and pushing her notebook against her chest.

'Don't you apologise! I had no idea what was going on. The police, they came and spoke to me. They told me what happened, what happened to you — to you and to Sam . . . I don't think she was as strong as you, Rhiannon. She's doing okay now, but it took her some time.'

'That's good. I was going to look her up but it wasn't . . . it never seemed like the right time.' Sam was the other girl in emergency foster care at the time. Rhiannon could still remember her cheery innocence and how it had been snatched away in her time in the house.

'You should. I think she would appreciate that.'

For the first time, Rhiannon felt awkward. Rose had stepped back again and was looking her up and down while biting down on her lip. She looked to be beaming with pride.

'How's your latest guest doing?' Rhiannon said. It seemed to snap Rose out of her daze.

'Oh, he's doing okay.' She lowered her voice and her eyes flickered momentarily to the ceiling. 'He's going to need time. Some of your lot don't seem to recognise that. But come in! Let me put a pot on. We can talk better in the kitchen.'

Rhiannon pushed the heavy front door shut and followed her through. The kitchen was just as she remembered it: the big table that dominated everything was chipped and stained in equal measure; the old range oven against the wall; the same oversized teapot with its tea-stained spout and the scorched-metal kettle on the hob with a bright blue flame bending around its base.

'I assume he still hasn't said anything?'

'Not a word. He'll do things that he's asked, so I know he understands me, and if he's hungry he'll come down and point at a cupboard or some bread or something. But he doesn't speak at all. I'm sure I've heard him crying in there, though. I went up there the first few times, I wanted to see if there was anything I could do. I've lost count of how many children I've had through here and just about every one of them has shut me out to start with. I understand it — I'm a stranger. But I make it my business not to be a stranger for long and not one of those kids has kept their barriers up for as long as he has. Sometimes I do get the impression he wants to talk to me and I really don't think he wants to be sat up in that room all day. It's like something is stopping him.'

'Is that all he does?'

'I've got one of those computer consoles. He uses that. I hear him on it a bit, but most of the time there's nothing but silence. I've suggested taking him out — the cinema, the park, swimming — anything he wants. I just wanted to get him out of these four walls, but he won't go anywhere. It means I can't go anywhere either of course, but I'm not complaining. The woman your lot sent in here — the child shrink lady — she said the last thing he needed was any pressure to do something he didn't want to do, so he won't be getting that from me.'

'Is that all she said?'

Rose shook her head. 'There was a lot more. She did up a big report. It was for Social Services but she gave me a copy, she said it might help. Just as well she did, no one else is talking to me. This report was all wordy, but she dumbed it down a little for me. Basically, all I need to understand is not to put any pressure on him. She thinks the same as me . . . that he'll start talking when he's ready.'

'I see.'

'So if you're here expecting a chat with him, I'm sorry to disappoint you.'

'I wasn't expecting anything to be honest. I just wanted to talk to him about what we're doing. I want to keep him up to date at least. He doesn't have to respond. He can just listen.'

'I agree.' Rose beamed again. 'I'm so proud of you, Rhiannon.' She clapped her hands as she turned to finish the tea.

Rhiannon carried hers up the stairs. She stopped at the top. The window at the top of the landing was covered by a pulled blind, but a little light still leaked in from the sides. There were no other sources of light. All of the doors were closed bar one; that at the end hung open. This led into the very same room she had occupied just a few years earlier. Rhiannon stepped towards it but was careful to stop a few metres short. She was close enough to see in. The layout was the same as she remembered: the bed on the right with a small bedside unit next to it that almost touched the other wall. It was a box room, really. Rhiannon remembered a wardrobe on the right side, too, but that would be concealed by the open door.

'Hey!' she called out. She got the silence she expected. She leant against the wall on the left side of the landing so she had the best angle to see in. The curtains were pulled across the window, but she could see the bed. She could see the lump in it too. She reckoned it was about boy-sized. Maddie had told her he'd hidden under his covers when they had been here before. It seemed to be his place when he was scared. Rhiannon knew what that was like, to be scared and alone in that room, on that bed. She suddenly filled with emotion that turned quickly into a new determination to help this boy, to find out what had brought him here and to help him past it.

'My name's Rhiannon,' she said. She watched and listened. There was neither movement nor sound. 'I'm a police officer now, but I was a scared little girl once. In that room where you are.' She paused again. Still there was no reaction. Her eyes had adjusted a little. The bedsheets looked to her to be a light grey. She thought she could see them rising and falling — just gently, but enough to confirm that someone was in there at least.

'I lost someone I cared about. The last person I had in this world, really. The police, they brought me here and Rose looked after me. Just like with you. Is that what happened? Did you lose someone you care about?'

Rhiannon slid her back down the wall until she was sitting down. She pulled her legs up so her chin could rest on her knees.

'I didn't like it here at first. I remember it was so hard. I had a nice life with my family and then suddenly I was here. I didn't know anyone. I didn't know Rose and I just wanted my old life back. That was all I wanted, but that wasn't possible — that life was gone. The only time it started getting better for me was when I came to understand that. You take all the time you need here. I just came here because I wanted you to know that I am doing all I can to find out what happened to you so I can help you get your life back. Or whatever life you want. Does that sound okay?'

Rhiannon got no response. She took the opportunity to look around. She considered getting up and walking away now, maybe she had put enough pressure on the young lad's shoulders. But she remembered when she was here, when everyone around her was keeping her in the dark while they tried to sort out her life. She had been older than the boy in there, but she was still more capable than they gave her credit for. She didn't want to make the same mistake.

'I think I know who you are, Alex.' She fell silent again, straining her ears for the slightest reaction or movement. There was nothing, and she continued. 'I know you lost your mother a couple of years ago and your life can't have been the same since.' All of her attention now was on the rising and falling of the duvet. She waited a few more seconds and this time it did move. Something pushed upwards. The boy had sat up. When he stopped moving, she waited a little longer to see what he would do. He stayed still.

'You're Alex Thompson. You have an older brother and sister — a lot older, right? And a dad. But someone was hurt and you might have seen it. As much as I want to help you, I would love to help that person, too, Alex. If you think I can, if there's something I can do, you need to let me know — any way you can.'

The figure under the cover made no more movement. Rhiannon was disappointed, of course she was, but not surprised. Knowing this boy's identity for sure would change everything for her and her investigation, but it changed very little for this boy. Whatever he had seen, whatever he had been through, nothing was going to change that. It didn't matter who knew his name or even if someone like her thought they knew a bit more about his past. No one would ever know everything about him — about what he had been through and about how he was feeling now. That was another lesson this house had taught her. No matter what support you had around you, what promises people made, there were going to be times when you had to face up to things on your own.

'I'm going to leave now, Alex, okay? But Rose downstairs, she can contact me anytime. So, if you need anything from me, or if you just want to talk, it's never a problem. One thing you should know . . . you're safe here, okay? You can trust me on that.'

She got back to her feet and stepped close enough to be able to lean on the door support. The upright figure was still unmoving. She left it long enough to know that she wasn't going to get a reaction.

'And you're not alone,' she said into the room. She moved away. She had said enough for now. She wanted to tell him just enough that he would have a lot of questions. She hoped it would prompt him to ask them. Time would tell.

* * *

Jack's watch lit up when he pushed the key into the lock of his own front door. He didn't turn it straight away. His other hand rested on its surface and lingered on the sensation of the peeling paint, the raised bobbles under his fingertips. His mind was a blur; he couldn't make sense of it all: what he could do next, how he could get out of this whole situation. He could think of nothing. He was desperate.

He took one last look at the street. The rain was lighter tonight and mingled with a mist that distorted the mustard-coloured street lighting. It was as quiet as he would expect for the early hours; the only sound was the dripping of moisture from guttering and the trickle of water into the drains. He could wait no longer.

When he closed his front door the hallway was pitch black. He didn't push the light switch in. He had left Alyssa in bed and the last thing he wanted to do was disturb her now. He was silent as he moved up the stairs. Every step felt laboured. He couldn't remember the last time his whole body didn't feel drained of energy. He reached the top. The street lighting seeped through his front window sufficiently for him to move around the furniture and to the closed door of his bedroom. He stopped to listen for sounds from within, any sign that she was still awake. He'd half-expected her to be up with the television on, waiting to ask him where the hell he'd been. He still felt bad for plying her with wine and then sneaking out, but there was no other way. He wouldn't have had the answers to her questions. Now there was only silence.

Slowly, he dipped the handle and pushed open the bedroom door. As the hinges creaked, he froze on the threshold. A gap in the curtains provided enough light for him to see her outline in the duvet. She was on her side, facing away. He could hear her breathing, long and deep. She was still asleep. He became aware of pain in his bottom lip where he was biting it so hard. He had to move forward. He walked up his side of the bed, still fixed on her outline. His foot collided with something heavy and hard and there was a loud thump as the computer tower on the floor went over. He held his breath and froze again with one knee on the bed, leaning towards her. She stirred. Her next breath was longer, her arms pushed out in a stretch, but he still didn't think she was awake.

'What are you doing?' Her voice was croaky and soft, but to Jack it broke through the darkness like a scream. He pushed back off the bed.

'Sorry, just going to the toilet.'

Alyssa raised herself up onto her elbow. One hand swept her hair from her eyes, the other moved under her pillow. When it came back out, a bright light shone on him — the torch function on her phone. 'You're fully dressed, Jack, and you're wet! What the fuck?' Jack tried to think fast but he'd never been any good at it. 'If you're gonna run out on me, you should remember that this is *your* place!' She rubbed her eyes, keeping the light on him. When he raised his hand to block it a little, she turned it off and sat up. 'Did you go out?'

'Yeah. I had to.'

'Your devil mates?'

'You need to go.' Jack's voice was a low monotone. He was trying almost too hard to hide any emotion.

'What? Now?' She sounded instantly angry.

'I'm really sorry . . . rough night.'

She lifted her hand to her head. 'I've had quite a bit to drink. I just need to sleep it off. You can put me on the sofa if you need your bed on your own—'

'It's not that!' He took a moment to calm himself down. 'It's not like that . . . I just need you to leave. I'm sorry — I know it's odd. I've got the cash for a cab.'

Her movements now were quick and agitated. She stood up out of the bed and moved to the switch on the wall. The light was sudden and it hurt his eyes. Alyssa was naked. She stared straight at him.

'Do you mind? At least leave while I get dressed. You don't get to see this anymore.' There was nothing he could say. He moved out into the living room and stood at the window overlooking the street. The rain seemed heavier, though the mist still swirled and picked at the street lamp. There were thuds and bangs from his room. He could hardly blame her for being upset. After a short time it went quiet. Then he heard her voice from the other side of the room.

'I'll just leave then!'

Jack didn't turn around at first, he didn't want to see her. 'Okay. There's a taxi waiting. I'm so sorry.' He dipped his head.

'You're not even going to look at me? Why are you treating me like this, Jack? I thought this was what you wanted.'

'It was.' He turned around but took a few moments before lifting his eyes.

159

'*Was?*' she snorted. She strode the length of the flat and disappeared out of sight to the top of the stairs. He followed slowly, almost as if his legs were moving against his will. He leaned on the doorframe and resisted turning the corner to where he'd be able to see down the stairs. He could hear her though, stomping her way to the bottom. Then he heard her scream.

There was a scuffle and the scream was quickly stifled, as if something was pushed into her mouth. There were more scuffling noises, a thud and a suppressed shout. He could only hear heavy breathing now. That was all that was left. Now he did move to look down the stairs, just as the light was clicked on. Alyssa was laid over the bottom three steps, her head over to one side, her eyes shut, her chest heaving, the man stood over her. He lifted his eyes as Jack appeared and pushed his hood back up from where it had fallen down. He was the source of the heavy breathing and his face was flushed enough to match the colour of his hair.

Jack started down the steps. He descended the first few but felt suddenly weak, overcome. He sat down heavily and looked down at Alyssa, failing to stifle a sob. He wanted to cover his eyes or to look away, but he couldn't; it was as if he was being forced to watch. 'I'm so sorry!' he spluttered. 'I didn't have a choice.'

The man's voice was deep and strong. 'We all have a choice — the same choice. Them or you. You were very clear. Now we need to finish this.'

The light clicked back off. The man pulled the front door open and leaned out. He paused for a moment before stepping out into the mustard hue of the night. Jack knew he would be back for Alyssa — for him as well. It took every ounce of his energy to stand. His feet felt like they were moved down the steps. His eyes were heavy, too, as he wiped at the tears he hoped wouldn't be seen in the darkness.

* * *

Harry sat up in bed with his heart racing and a shrill squeal in his ears. He lashed out with a shout at the sinister bright light that pulsed in the darkness. It was his phone . . . it was ringing . . . he was alone in his bedroom. He was safe.

The phone stopped and the darkness was complete. He swung his legs around and took a few moments. He could feel his heart racing in his chest, the rhythm so strong and fast that he could hear it thumping in his ears. His breath was short. He sat up straighter to let more air in and tried to calm himself. He was used to waking up startled in the night and had been coping better. It had been a while since he'd woken and been unable to function straight away, and the nocturnal panic attacks had not been this bad since soon after the accident. He reached for his alarm clock and felt for the button on the top. A row of numbers appeared on the screen: 01:17. He suddenly remembered what had woken him up and the implied urgency at this hour was obvious.

In his haste to reach for the phone, he knocked it from the bedside table. He stood up and clicked on the main light, squinting until he found it on the floor. The screen showed: *Josh Adams — missed call*. Then it beeped with a message announcing voicemail. He had to focus on his movements so he didn't drop the phone again. The rhythm in his ears was back stronger. He pressed to listen.

'Mr Blaker, sorry to bother you. I'm on my way to hospital with Mel. She's had another one of her episodes . . . Look, I'll give you a call when I know a bit more. She's okay, that's the thing. She didn't want me to call, but I couldn't not . . . sorry.'

Josh was Mel's on-off boyfriend. Harry had never approved but he had come to realise that he never would. No one was ever going to be good enough. At least Josh seemed to genuinely care about his daughter and he was worried about her tonight; that much was obvious in his voice. Harry pulled open his wardrobe, trying to work his phone at the same time to call Josh back. It went straight to voicemail. He hadn't said to what hospital they were going but it would likely be the William Harvey at Ashford, assuming she was at home. He'd keep trying to call on the way.

It took twenty minutes. A section of the motorway had a reduced speed limit for roadworks. He had ignored them, and the bright yellow speed cameras towering above them. He dumped his car on yellow hatchings and strode into Accident and Emergency, knowing it to be the only area that was manned twenty-four-seven.

'Can I help?'

Harry lifted his warrant card, thinking it might skip some of the formalities. 'Melissa Blaker. I think she was just brought in here by ambulance.'

'Okay.' The woman behind the desk looked expectant.

'I need to see her.'

'I'm sure you do. I can't just let you through. What are the circumstances? I'm supposed to assist the medical staff with preventing police officers hindering any treat—'

'I'm her father.' He lifted his warrant again, pointing at the bit with his name and face on it. '*Blaker*, see? I'm not here on official business. I just need to see my daughter.'

The woman fixed him with an exasperated look. 'That makes more sense.' She fidgeted on her computer. 'Yeah, she came in half an hour ago. She's in an obs room. I'll have someone come through for you if you'd like to take a seat.'

Harry pushed away from the desk and turned to the waiting area. He had attracted some attention. Most of the seated patrons were looking over. A lot of them turned away instantly, their attention dropping back to their phones. He considered he had been loud and forgotten his surroundings. He didn't care. He couldn't sit down. Instead, he leaned against a wall close to the hatch through which he had just spoken. He got some further looks of exasperation from the woman behind the counter but he didn't care about that either. It was just a few minutes before a young lad in dark blue scrubs stopped next to him, his plimsolls squelching on the rubber floor. Harry read *Stephen* on his name badge.

'Mr Blaker? Would you like to follow me?'

Melissa was sitting up in a hospital bed wearing a white vest, her right arm supported by a couple of pillows and bandaged from wrist to elbow. The bandage was tinged with scarlet that was turning brown as it dried. Josh stood up when Harry entered.

'Jesus, Melissa,' Harry uttered.

'I'll get you that tea,' Josh said. 'Can I get you anything, Mr Blaker?' Harry didn't reply; his attention still fixed on his daughter. He heard the curtain swish back where Josh left. *Stephen* in the scrubs said he would give them a few minutes and then pop back.

'I didn't want you told.' Melissa hadn't looked up yet. She seemed to be staring at her bandage.

'What happened?' Harry concentrated on keeping his voice low. It still came out as a growl like it always did.

Melissa took her time to answer, then sniffed. 'I'm sorry, Dad.'

'Don't be sorry.' His reply was instant, well practiced. They'd been through this more than once before, this exact exchange. He imagined the rest of the conversation would be a familiar one too. Harry was trying to keep the message to his daughter consistent. He wanted her to keep speaking to him and knew that wouldn't happen if he sounded like he was allocating blame. He wasn't. He was learning all the time what depression was. He knew this wasn't her fault. He also knew that he should be delighted all the while she was saying she was sorry. It showed an awareness of the impact on other people. When depression took a proper hold it could take away that concern for upsetting others, and that could be the last barrier to finishing the task.

'I didn't want to. I didn't want to have to come here again,' she said.

'I know that. No one wants to feel like this. I'm only here to help.'

She flickered a faint smile. 'Thank you, Dad.'

'What happened?'

'Cutting.' She was so quiet Harry almost missed it.

'Okay.' Harry fell silent. He wanted Melissa to feel that she didn't need to give more detail, but that it was okay to do so. He suppressed all the questions he had.

'I've been struggling. I was getting there, you know. But it was on the news yesterday. Did you see it?'

'See what?'

'That man . . . the man who killed mum. It made the news and someone shared it on social media. I know you said it would happen. My mate shared it and she just asked if I was okay. I might not have seen it if they hadn't tagged me.'

'I didn't see it.' He hadn't, either. He wasn't on social media and he rarely bothered with the news anymore.

'They named you. Mum, too . . .' Melissa took a moment and sniffed again. She was able to lift her eyes now; they looked heavy, puffed and red. 'I think it just caught me at a weak moment.'

'Okay. And how do you feel now?'

'Stupid!' She choked a laugh and shook her head. 'I'm so sorry.'

'Like I said, you don't need to be saying that. Is it bad?'

She looked back at her arm. The fingers on the hand flinched. 'I had a couple of goes. It was just superficial at first, just seeing if I could. But then I had a good go. At the wrist. Josh . . .' She broke down. Harry waited her out. He wanted to hear the rest; he couldn't rush her. 'If Josh hadn't been there . . . I don't know. I don't know what would have happened. I got it really deep. The second time I thought it was going to go. The scary thing . . . I was trying by then! I just want to stop feeling like this . . .' She broke down again and Harry moved in for a hug. He took hold of her tightly, felt her shudder against his shoulder as she sobbed. He swallowed hard to control his own emotion, but it wasn't sadness he was desperate to control, it was anger — rage even. He could feel it. It started as a knot in his stomach and it tensed his limbs as it spread out. He held his breath, his hug on his daughter got tighter. He let her go when he heard the curtain go again.

'Hey. Your tea.' Josh was back. He put a steaming cup down on the table beside Melissa. Harry stepped right back. 'I'm sorry I called you. I didn't know what to do, really. I was waiting for the ambulance and just putting a lot of pressure on her cut, you know. It seemed like the right thing. I saw you called back. I couldn't answer.'

'It's fine.' Harry couldn't say more; the rage was threatening to take him over.

'Melissa didn't want me to call. She said you spoke recently and she told you me and her . . . we weren't . . . together, you know. We didn't want you to find out like this. I should have been more up front . . . I could have spoken to you or something . . .'

Harry had to step away. He'd barely been listening. He couldn't speak. He pushed open the curtain and stepped through it. He walked a short distance away. There was movement all around him, he balled his hands into fists and rested them both on the wall so they took his weight. He stayed like that just long enough for his head to clear then he walked back to his daughter. Josh turned to him as he pushed back the curtain. He was clearly tense, too, rigid and leaning away. Harry made right for him. Josh flinched, brought his arms up to his midriff as if ready to defend himself. Harry jutted out his hand. Josh eyed it for a second then took it up. The handshake was firm.

'You did good, kid,' Harry said. 'Thank you.'

Josh nodded.

'He looks after me, Dad!' Melissa suddenly chuckled through tears.

Stephen walked back in. He had picked up a folder and he appeared to read from the front page.

'Melissa Blaker . . . Are you okay for me to speak in front of your dad and boyfriend here?' He looked cheerily at Harry and Josh in turn.

'Yes, of course.'

'Okay. Well, we have three deep lacerations to your right arm there, one of which is particularly deep and has gone through the hypodermis layer, which is where you start getting to the really important stuff. We are going to require stitches, I'm afraid — I'm not going to be able to glue something that severe. I do have a couple of additional concerns, namely infection treatment and mental health. This is a wound you inflicted on yourself, is that correct?'

'Yes.' Melissa was back to staring at her bandaging.

'I'd like to get you assessed by our mental health team here. I have spoken to the Crisis Team and they have confirmed that you are known to them. They'll will come and see you in the morning. I have found you a bed and once we get you stitched up we'll keep you in for an assessment. I know you have been on medication previously for depression and anxiety. I'd like to get that reviewed, just so we can get you back on the level.' Stephen smiled. 'Does that sound okay?' Harry thought his manner overall was like he was booking someone into a hotel suite, as if he had just told them the number to call for room service.

'Okay,' Melissa replied.

Stephen looked at Harry and Josh again. 'Now, I might be able to swing it for one of you to stick around. I can't promise a bed — a seat next to Melissa maybe. But only one. The other can sit in the waiting room, of course, but it's not a comfortable option when we might be talking about a twelve-hour wait or more for this all to play out.'

Melissa was staring straight at Harry. 'Go home, Dad. Get some sleep. You will have work in the morning. Josh, you can go too. I'm fine now.'

'I'd rather stay. For you,' Josh said.

Melissa beamed at him.

Harry wanted to stay but could see his daughter had made her choice. 'Fine. But I want to know the moment you get out of here.'

'No problem.' Both Melissa and Josh spoke at the same time, then laughed at each other.

'One of you at least.' Harry managed a tired attempt at a smile himself. He sent Josh back out for a black coffee. He would stay a little while longer at least. He found himself staring at her bandaged wound. He couldn't help it.

166

'How are you getting on with the watch?' He was caught out. His eyes shot to his own wrist and the cheap and battered steel watch his wife had purchased for him when he had first started his police career.

'Oh, I just grabbed the first one I saw. I was in a bit of a rush to get out of bed.'

'You've tried it, then?'

'Of course.'

'And?'

'It's good at keeping me aware, like you said.'

'But you hate it? I don't think I've ever seen you bother to pretend you like something when you really don't. I mean, you're terrible at it, but it still feels like progress.'

'That's not . . .' Harry petered out. 'I'll give it another go, okay? Maybe it's something I can get used to.'

Melissa chuckled. 'It was Faye's idea. I told her it was a bad one.'

'I never said it was a bad one. I just need to give it some more time, to get used to it.'

'Don't worry, I'll tell Faye you love it. And I'll be far more convincing than you.'

'I'm sure you will,' Harry conceded. 'You mother said the same: I never have been much good at pretending.'

'That's the best thing about you, Dad. Don't ever change!'

Harry smirked. He was supposed to be here building his daughter back up. Once again the roles had switched and the shift had been seamless.

'You're just like your mother. That means you can't ever change either.'

Melissa suddenly seemed overwhelmed and sobbed again. Josh chose this moment to reappear with Harry's coffee.

'You okay? What happened?'

Melissa gave a sob that was mixed up with laughter.

'My Dad! That's what happened.'

* * *

When Harry made it back home it was nearly 5 a.m. and there didn't seem like any point in going back to bed. He sat in his armchair instead, considering that he might be able to doze despite feeling wide awake. He clicked through the channels for a short time then, with a sudden realisation, he paced back into his bedroom. When he returned to his chair, he clutched a state-of-the-art smartwatch in one hand and the instruction manual in the other. This seemed like a far more effective way to doze off. Sure enough it was a couple of hours later when he woke from his nap. He still had the open booklet in his hand and the television was showing a young woman stood in front of a map of the UK. She instantly beamed a good morning and told him that, overall, it was going to be a beautiful day. Harry clicked the television off and walked stiffly towards the shower.

'We'll see,' he said to the silence of his home.

CHAPTER 17

Thursday

Maddie's stride felt stronger that morning, stronger than it had the day before at least. She'd slept better for a start, but the wind was gone, too. Her morning route took her from the promenade just across from her flat in Sandgate and then left at a building used as a Rowing Club to head in the general direction of Langthorne. Most days there was a coastal breeze at the very least, but on this occasion there was nothing at all. It wasn't far before the promenade widened and there was some hard standing on her left that met with a road. It provided vehicular access to the seafront and to the rear of a number of million-pound houses dug higher up into the cliff edge above. There were about ten of them in total and all had paths chasing up their steep gardens from the pebble beach.

Maddie's eyes, though, were invariably pulled right to the sparkling, heaving sea. She loved the shoreline especially. On this day the water had a gentle rhythmic movement over the glittering pebbles, like it was a huge living thing, breathing in and out. The day before, with a stronger wind, it had been a constant churning. Both were beautiful in their own right. She had planned on this being her last run of the week but the run this morning felt almost effortless and, with the sun making a better effort to warm her face, it was a genuine pleasure. She closed her eyes to it for just a second. Her phone rang.

'Goddammit!' She remembered a time when she didn't need to take her phone out with her. But she had been convinced that training for a marathon required a fitness-planning app to track her heart rate and steps among other things. Her first instinct was to ignore the call but it was still before 6 a.m.: it had to be important.

By the time she'd peeled off her gloves and wrested the phone from its holder, the caller had rung off. She saw that the missed a call was from Rhiannon. She called her straight back.

'Did I wake you?' Rhiannon said instantly.

'You did. I was having a lovely dream. It was all about having another hour of sleep before I even needed to think about getting up.'

Rhiannon didn't answer immediately. 'You're lying, aren't you!'

'Yes, but you're lucky!'

'I figured you're always up. Is today a run day?'

'It's always a run day too. Maybe one day you'll come back out with me rather than just saying you will.'

'Is that healthy? Training every day?'

'Nice dodge.'

'I will come back out with you. I'm building up to it. But again, is it healthy to be out every day?'

'I don't know, Rhiannon, but it's bad enough having a smartphone telling me when I need to run and when I don't — I don't need you getting involved too! I'm worried that if I stop, I won't get going again. This marathon thing was a stupid idea.'

'I did tell you that.'

'You did. Is that why you phoned me? To remind me it's a stupid idea while I'm stood on the promenade getting cold?'

'I thought I could hear the seagulls! I couldn't sleep, Maddie.'

'So what, you thought you would call me and make sure I couldn't either?'

'I wanted to see if you fancied a breakfast meeting before work. I wanted to run a few things past you about my investigation. Usual place?'

Maddie looked at her watch. She still had plenty of time. 'Opening?' she said, knowing that it opened for 7 a.m.

'Perfect.'

'One condition.'

'What?'

'You come out with me. Tomorrow! You'll love it — the sunrise over the sea, the sun in your face, the endorphins.'

'This hasn't quite gone to plan. I can get up for a cooked breakfast, but a run . . .'

'Your choice.'

'Fine! You win.'

'I always will, Rhiannon. You'd do well to remember that.'

'See you there for my cooked breakfast! I'll be the one smiling with a menu. Then I'll see you tomorrow for a run . . . when I won't be.'

Maddie chuckled. She could tell from Rhiannon's voice that she was beaming too.

* * *

The smell was a mixture of everything: muffins, bacon, avocado and coffee and it struck Maddie all at once. She was always hungry after a run but that smell amplified it to the point where she knew she was going to have to be careful not to undo all of her morning's work. Rhiannon was already sitting down with a steaming mug in front of her. She waved as Maddie entered. Maddie ordered her drink and made her way over.

'Been a while.'

'A while?' Rhiannon eyed her like she was expecting more teasing.

'Since we've done this.' Maddie gestured at the quiet interior of the café. It was early and the staff were still setting up. Maddie had just passed a man battling with the sandwich board outside.

'Oh I see! I thought you were still going on about how I haven't been out for a run in a little bit.'

'A little bit?'

Rhiannon shrugged. 'A big bit, then!'

'It's fine, it doesn't matter at all, really.'

'Good.'

'Because you're coming out with me tomorrow!'

'At six a.m.?'

'Thereabouts. That's a little late to be honest.'

'Jesus, Maddie.'

'A deal's a deal. We're here doing your thing and I'll help where I can and then tomorrow you have to come and do my thing. You'll love it when you're out.'

'There is literally nothing I *love* before seven a.m. I've ordered us both the usual anyway. It was going to be my treat but you can forget that now!'

'Fair enough! You obviously want something. So how can I help?'

Rhiannon suddenly looked a lot more serious. 'I just wanted to talk about the developments from yesterday. I didn't want to come and talk to you in the office about it . . .'

'In case Harry was there?'

Rhiannon looked a little awkward. 'That might have been a consideration. He just didn't seem impressed with what I was doing. I wanted to check with you, to see if maybe I'm making mistakes,' she said.

'Not at all. He used to make me feel like that all the time too, he's very good at saying exactly what he means but in a way that makes people think he might mean something different.'

'He wasn't upset with me, then?'

'No. And why would he be? Harry's job is to question everything we do — all of us — to make sure we're doing the right things. He has no ability to soften that.'

'Okay. He was probably right about not needing to send two detectives and about the ID — it's not really an ID yet. I guess I just got excited—'

'And you should be. Police work is a lot about what-ifs. You could send two detectives and have it turn out to be a waste of their time, or you could send five detectives and it turns into a major lead where you haven't got enough manpower. Harry has the experience to know that you keep your resources central and allocate them when you *know* what you have, but experience is the one thing you can do nothing about. It comes with working cases, with leading investigations like this, with doing what you're doing. And you're doing great.'

'Thanks. I mean it. I don't think I've done anything yet without second guessing it.'

'Me neither. That is something that may never change! So what do we know?'

'Well, I sent Mick Pearson to pick up the enquiry. I reckon he falls into the *experienced* category too.'

'I should say.' Mick had been on Maddie's team for a short time when she was a CID sergeant. He was the sort of detective that had you wishing for six more to complete your team. He was a seasoned detective who knew the job inside out. You could give him a job at the start of shift and then just sit back and wait for a good resolution by the end. Detectives like that were few and far between.

'He was able to talk to the social worker who got in touch with us. He met her at her home address quite late last night. I put him up in a hotel but he sent a written report. It was nearly midnight when it came through. I'm just after some advice really about where we go next.'

'Okay, so what do we know?'

'Well, yesterday I gave you a possible name of *Alex Thompson*. That was from a single picture that we sent out to Social Services across the country. Mick took another few pictures with him and the social worker's more convinced now — says she's ninety-nine percent. I know what the boss might say, but I'm working on the assumption that it's Alex Thompson. For now at least.'

Maddie grinned, delighted that her confidence hadn't been knocked too badly. 'So what do we know about Alex Thompson?'

'Not too much, there are still a lot of gaps. We have a very slanted view based on the experiences of social workers. The woman who went out worked for something called *Early Help*. They get kids referred to them who need assistance at school. In this case, Alex was referred because his performance took a sudden dip and the suggestion was that this was due to circumstances at home. They work with the family and the child to try and get them back on track. The social worker was working with Alex a couple of years before and met some of the other members of the Thompson-Garner family. The story we have is that Alex lived with his mum and dad. Alex has two much older siblings, a brother and a sister. The older siblings have a different dad and resent the stepdad for whatever reason. This seems to have caused a lot of trouble in the home. I think it was untenable. I think one or both of the siblings left the home and when this happened there was an improvement in Alex's performance, to the point where they closed his case.'

'So nothing since?'

'She was involved again around a year after that and this is when our informant met Alex — around eighteen months ago. The school contacted Social Services to say that the mother had passed away and they were worried about how it might affect him. Social Services ran a few sessions but he was deemed to be okay and again his case was closed. The informant only went to the first session. There is some anecdotal evidence that there was a dispute over the inheritance. I think the siblings' dislike for the stepdad reared its head again. The theory is that either the mother wrote her new partner into the will, or didn't include their natural father. Certainly something caused an issue.'

'And what about the boy's speech? I assume she was able to talk with him at least?'

'I asked the same thing. She seemed genuinely shocked to hear that we hadn't heard a word from him. She said he's an intelligent kid and had strong opinions that he seemed to enjoy sharing. She didn't always agree with him, but she always knew she would have a good conversation about it at least. She described him as *old beyond his years*.'

'Okay. And this father-stepfather figure, do we know who he is?'

'No. Social Services were not heavily involved; they only visited the family home once and that was after the mother died. Other sessions were done on the school grounds. Social Services seem to work very different from us . . . where we would get the details of everyone there, they don't seem to. She's sure her friend would have got those details, but there's not much hope of getting them now. I do have the details of the siblings. There's nothing on the local police systems to help either. I was hoping we'd been there for a domestic or something. Social Services provided the home address and I passed that on to Thames Valley Police, who cover that area. They sent a patrol around and there are new people living there who said they've been there eighteen months or more. They weren't sure who was there before.'

'So we don't know where they are?'

'Not a clue. The house was rented. I spoke to the agent and they said they barely heard from the previous tenants — then they just upped and left.'

'Did they have a record of all the occupants?'

'I asked. It was all in the mother's name. They know she lived there with a partner but it wasn't a joint tenancy.'

Maddie sat back to let the information sink in. 'So they could be in Kent too? The rest of Alex's family, I mean?'

'That has to be the most likely scenario. And not too far from where we found Alex, right?'

'Alex. We're just calling him that now, are we?' Maddie chuckled. Rhiannon did too.

'Now you're starting to sound like DI Blaker.'

'Experience, see? That's what I was talking about! Are you still thinking of going to see Alex? A lot could be learned by his reaction I suppose.'

'I did that already.'

'You did?'

'Yesterday. Not long after I spoke to you. I got a reaction, too, nothing that means I can say for sure I was right, but I know I am.'

'A reaction?'

'Well he hid under the covers like you said he would, but he went from lying down to sitting up. I know that doesn't sound much. At the time though, it felt like all I needed.'

The same man Maddie had seen wrestling with the sandwich board out the front of the café now put two plates in front of them. Maddie had to lean back, she was grinning the whole time. Rhiannon waited for the man to leave, then spoke immediately.

'What?'

'You're right then. You learn to trust your instincts when you've been doing this job a while. You have good instincts.'

'I hope you're right. Just to prove the boss wrong for one!' Rhiannon grinned then seemed to suppress it instantly. 'Sorry, I don't mean that disrespectfully . . .'

Maddie waved her away. 'You wouldn't be proving him wrong, he doesn't think this is the wrong line of enquiry, he was just concerned that you were following it and disregarding any others. We still need to keep an open mind. But I think you're aware of that.' Maddie started on her breakfast. She used the time to think. 'So, is Alex Thompson not a reported misper?'

Rhiannon shook her head. 'He left school a little while back. After his mum died, his older sister, Michelle Garner, became his primary carer. A few months later she withdrew him from school and said he was going to be home educated. As far as the school are concerned, he isn't missing, he left.'

'How old is he?'

'Ten. Nearly eleven. Bang on what we thought.'

'So a ten-year-old can just leave school?'

'Not entirely. Different areas run it different. In Reading, it seems, you can opt to home-school your child but a specific school still has to assign you work and they have to meet a minimum standard. A teacher is supposed to do a home-visit every three months too, but the school are being a little coy about that. I only phoned them. I should have got Mick to go in there and speak face-to-face. They've asked for official data protection forms, but I think they're stalling.'

'You don't think they've been doing their visits?'

'I don't.'

'So a child can go missing without ever being reported?'

'If he's living with his primary carer and being schooled at home, he's not technically missing from anywhere. All his work is sent to him online. He was doing it, too, judging by what little information I did get from the school.'

'So he gets sent work online. I assume he returns it the same way? There's no sending anything out to an address or taking it out by hand?'

'No, aside from these three-monthly visits, it's all online.'

'So you could be *attending* a school in Reading and living in Canterbury.'

'It is quite feasible.'

Maddie sat back and huffed.

Rhiannon nodded. 'I know, it feels like one step forward and two steps back.'

'It's not quite as bad as that. It gives us lines of enquiry.'

'It does. Mick has sent over the details of all the family members. We'll be running all the checks we can on police systems. We'll get Thames Valley to do the same. I'll go back to the school, the renting agents again maybe. The Department of Work and Pensions may have an idea what area they are in at least.'

'Assuming they're claiming benefits,' Maddie said.

'Yes, of course. I was going to try and find out who dealt with the will, too. Which solicitor, I mean. I might be able to get a steer on what happened — maybe even a contact number.'

'From a solicitor? You might . . .'

'I know, it's a longshot.'

'But one you have to take. You're right to give it a go. So what did you need to speak with me for? You seem to have everything under control?'

Rhiannon sat back and looked thoughtful. 'I suppose I just wanted to run it all past you. See if there was anything I was missing.'

'Not that I can think of. But it's always better to get as many opinions as you can when it comes to complex investigations.' Maddie lingered on Rhiannon long enough for her to take her hint.

'You mean DI Blaker?'

'Yes. And I tell you why. If nothing else, when you sit down and tell him what you've told me, he'll see just how much you've done and just how much you have considered. He'll be impressed. He has to be.'

'I'm not sure it's possible to impress him at all, is it?'

'I know what you mean, but trust me, it happens. And then he shows it when you least expect it! In all seriousness, though, use him. Use his experience. He may well have another angle neither of us have considered.'

'Of course. Sounds good to me.'

'Excellent. Let's get this finished up and then head in. I suggest you take half an hour to get a briefing prepared and we can speak with him pretty much as he gets in. Harry's always at his best first thing in the morning.'

'Is he?' Rhiannon said.

'Of course not!' Maddie laughed hard. Rhiannon did too. Maddie noticed the DC was pushing the food round her plate more than eating it.

'You not hungry?'

'I was. You get a lot here.'

'You do. I suggest you eat it, though. You need to keep your strength up if you want to come running with me in the morning.'

'I don't want to come running in the morning!'

'All the more reason to keep your strength up. Sounds like you might need enough to run *and* moan about it.'

* * *

'Morning, Harry. How did you sleep?'

'Why would you ask that?' Harry's reply was immediate and defensive.

'Because it looks like you haven't.' He was at his desk. Maddie had spoken while putting a black coffee down for him. He swept it up and gestured a thank you with it, then brought it to his lips. 'And that'll be hot,' she added.

'It's fine and you're right . . . I didn't sleep so well. I need this today.'

'You want me to put another shot in it?'

'No. A refill, maybe. Too strong and it makes my heart race.'

'And there it is! I'll just go and tick that one off.' She turned to leave.

'What? Tick what off?' he called after her, sounding irritated.

'On my *List of Things I Know About Harry Blaker*. It took me a year to get the first two things, but now there are three! And never did I think I would answer the question *what makes Harry Blaker's heart race?*'

'Very good,' Harry grumbled. 'You're just what I need, aren't you?'

'Don't you want to know what the first two things were?'

Harry stood and picked up his notebook. 'No, I think it's fair to assume I should know them both already. Aren't we meeting Rhiannon now?'

'We are.' She turned sharply towards the door and her grin dropped away quickly as she almost ran into Charley Mace on her way in. 'Shit!' Maddie called out in surprise, then she scowled. She was still turned away from Harry and she spoke to Charley. 'Do you think he heard me?'

Charley nodded. 'I think he might have, yes.'

Maddie turned back into the room. 'Sorry, boss, but this no swearing thing is killing me. The things we see . . . the people we deal with . . . sometimes there's only a very few words left to describe them.'

'I don't care. *A strong dislike of profanity.* There's another one for your silly list.'

She shook her head. 'That's one of the two things I already had.'

'Charley, did you want to speak with me?' Harry said.

'Well, both of you, I suppose. Good timing. Do you have a minute?'

'We were just on our way to a briefing,' Harry said, 'but you can have a minute. If you need longer, we can come and see you straight after?'

'The blood from your country puddle . . . I had it couriered yesterday so it got to the lab. I put you down as authorising the cost. Anyway, they ran an urgent comparison against the database . . .'

Maddie couldn't resist. 'And it's Jarod Logan's blood!'

'No. It's Jack Knight's blood.'

'Jack . . . Who the hell is that?' Maddie said.

Looking pleased with herself, Charley put a folder down on the desk. 'This is why I'm in forensics. Black and white, see? I work with confirmed results and definites. And it's definitely Jack Knight. Who that is, why that is, and how it got there is down to the detectives. He's known to us following an arrest two years ago for some minor offence. Lucky for us it was serious enough to get his DNA on the database. You let me know if you need anything more, okay?' Maddie and Harry exchanged glances, then both pairs of eyes fell to the folder on the desk.

'We need to put this briefing back,' Harry said.

Maddie was already on her way out the door, 'I'll let Rhiannon know.'

The meeting room was just across the floor. Rhiannon was already there with a couple of her detectives. She was shuffling paper and had fired up the monitor on the wall. Maddie felt bad; this was all her idea in the first place. But she knew Rhiannon would understand. And she'd make it up to her.

'Rhiannon, I'm so sorry. We're going to need to put this back. Something's come up. I'll explain later.'

Rhiannon nodded dumbly. She may even have looked a little relieved. Maddie didn't stick around. This development was important, perhaps critical. By the time she got back into Harry's office he was staring into his screen and he already had an update.

'Jack Knight is just a kid. He was arrested for criminal damage a couple of years ago — graffiti. We have a home address, looks like he lives with mum. That's about all we know.' Harry half rose to his feet, leant on his desk and scribbled something in his notebook.

'Let's go.' Maddie felt her pockets for her keys and led the way.

* * *

Maddie drove slowly along a row of twee cottages in the village of Littlebourne, on the outskirts of Canterbury, then came to a stop outside the third dwelling from the end. It had a red door that was brighter in the sunlight and it stood out from the whitewashed walls. Harry knocked on the door with two hammer blows. There was movement at the window first. She couldn't see any detail, the light was wrong for her to be able to see through the glass. She lifted her warrant card and smiled, hoping it would reassure the occupant that they shouldn't be judged on her colleague's apparent attack on their front door. It seemed to work. The door was pulled open a few moments later.

'Can I help you?' A middle-aged woman opened the door, although not much. It was just enough for Maddie to see that her dark hair looked to be damp as it clumped over her shoulders. She wasn't wearing make-up either and it looked like she was wearing a robe. Harry held up his own police ID. Her eyes flickered over it and then beyond him to Maddie.

'Are you Mrs Knight?' Harry said.

'That's right. Is there something wrong?' She stiffened and the hand that was gripping the door slid a little higher as she stood straighter.

'Is Jack here?' he said.

'Jack? No. I mean . . . he doesn't live here. Has he done something wrong?'

'We're not sure what he's done,' Harry said. 'When was the last time you spoke to him?' His permanent growl rarely gave away his emotions or the motives behind his questions. Maddie was very aware that the woman in front of them was starting to panic. Maddie stepped a little closer. 'Do you mind if we pop in for a minute? Maybe we should explain why we're here. I'm sure it's nothing to worry about, but we do need to speak with him.'

Mrs Knight didn't move straight away. Her hand was still gripped round the door but she let go and pushed it further open before disappearing into the shadow behind. Harry stepped in next and Maddie followed. The front door opened directly into a living room and Mrs Knight had backed into a small, two-seater sofa. There was another one on the wall where they had come in and a small television on the opposite wall beside an open fireplace. There wasn't much room for anything else.

'I'm DS Maddie Ives and this is Inspector Harry Blaker. We work out of Major Crime at Canterbury. When was the last time you spoke with Jack?'

'A few days ago, I suppose. We speak a couple of times a week, I was seeing if he was coming out for Sunday dinner.'

'Is that a regular thing?'

'It seems to have become regular, yes. He was here for the last few. He misses it if he has to work, but he doesn't do too many Sundays now.'

'Where does he work?'

'What is this about? Can you at least tell me if he's in some sort of trouble?'

'It's a bit of a strange one, the sort of thing that Jack could probably explain away in a minute or two if he were here. We are working a crime scene and there is something in the area that is linked to your son. We just need to ask him if he was in the area at the material time. He might be a witness — a really important one.'

'Oh, I see. Well I haven't spoken to him for a few days, but if he saw something bad he'd call me, I'm sure of it.'

'I'm sure of it too. The thing is, sometimes people can see something and not even realise how important it is. We get it all the time. If you could let us know where he's living, we can go and ask him a question. That's all we need.'

'Yes . . . I have it here somewhere. He's in a flat in Langthorne. Not a bad little place — the only one he could afford on his wages. He works at the big supermarket in the town. Just on the till, but it's a start at least.' Mrs Knight pulled her phone from her gown pocket and fiddled with it as she spoke. 'I've got friends with kids the same age. I don't think any of them are working. It's not much but at least he's working, you know?'

'I agree. That's half the battle, getting your foot on the rung. Can I take his phone number too?'

'Yes, of course. Did you want me to give him a ring?'

'No.' Harry cut in with his usual decorum. Maddie glared at him and Mrs Knight spun to his gruff voice. 'If he's at work we might get him into trouble,' he said. 'We need to head over to Langthorne anyway. We can pop in on him on the way past.'

'Well, okay then. 38b Marshall Street is his home address. That's in Langhorne, like I said. His is the top flat, the right-side door. You'll know what I mean when you see it. He works most days though.'

'That's great, thank you.'

'And when you speak with him, could you ask him to give me a call? There's little point me calling him anyway — he never picks up to me. I've lost count of the amount of voice messages that have gone unanswered. You're welcome to try calling him yourself of course.' Mrs Knight turned her phone screen towards Maddie displaying Jack's number. Maddie noted it down and nodded.

'That'll be useful if he's not at work. Thank you. I assume you may not be the right person to ask about his associates then? Any mates? A girlfriend maybe?'

Mrs Knight chuckled as she shook her head. 'Well, normally I wouldn't have the faintest clue, but I did get someone up here a day or so ago. He said he was a friend, but I didn't recognise him. I used to know a few of his school mates — they'd turn up with Jack after school and I'd be expected to feed them! I never minded — good kids generally. Jack is, too. A good kid, I mean. He's never been in any real trouble. He had a little run in with the police, but it was a minor thing — boys being boys, as they say. I think he got a fine and a ticking off.'

'What did his friend want when he came up here?'

'I don't know really. He struck me as an odd fella. Quite a bit older than Jack. I got the impression he was a bit of a chancer rather than a friend. Like he wanted something from Jack. I'm not sure how he knew to come here. I mean he was nice enough but sometimes you just get something behind a smile, you know what I mean?'

'I think I do, Mrs Knight. What did he look like?'

'Tall. Older, like I said — more than thirty. White, clean-shaven, a woolly hat pulled right down — it was almost covering his eyes! Black coat. It wasn't a very cold day . . . he didn't look like he was dressed for the weather. That's all I can tell you, I'm afraid. I only talked to him through the crack in the door.'

'Did you give him Jack's address?'

'No. He didn't ask for it either. He just said that when I see Jack, I should tell him that his friend from the café was asking after him. He said Jack would know what that meant. Like I said, he was an odd fella.'

'And no girlfriend that you know of for Jack?'

'Not that I know of. Sometimes he hints that he's seeing someone, but I guess the mother is usually the last to know. Jack has always been a bit . . . shy? He can be awkward around girls. A lot of lads are, I suppose, all those hormones flying around and no idea how to quieten them down long enough to just say hello! He could do with meeting someone nice, someone who understands him. He's a nice lad. He'll be a good husband to someone one day.'

Maddie nodded. 'I'm sure you're right. Thanks again for your time.'

Langthorne was around twenty-five minutes from the address in Littlebourne. The car park at the superstore took half the time again to negotiate and Harry's pace through the front door suggested to Maddie that he was running low on patience. Jamie Dunn, the shift supervisor, was not about to appease him any. He was pointed out by a hassled-looking woman at the cigarette kiosk and, despite Harry calling him directly, he continued his walk towards the rear of the store. Harry strode after him and Maddie followed. The man's head was turned slightly to one side, there was no doubt he had heard the call. Harry didn't call him again. Instead he followed him silently towards a set of blue double doors with a thick plastic lip running horizontally across its middle. Jamie pushed one open, keeping it in his hand as he turned.

'Can I help you?'

'You could have helped me all the way back there.' Harry stepped in a little too close to emphasise his point.

'Sorry? I didn't realise you wished to speak with me. We're very busy as you can see. Any staff member can help you.'

'I need to speak to the shift supervisor.'

'Okay then.' Jamie sighed and he looked expectant.

'I'm looking for Jack Knight. I need to speak with him, please. I shouldn't need to keep him for long.'

Jamie now looked Harry up and down, then his eyes shifted to do likewise with Maddie. 'Who are you? Are you the police?'

Harry took out his warrant card. 'Yes.'

'I should have known. I see enough of you people. Is Jack in trouble?'

'No, not that we know of. I just need to speak with him for a minute or two. Is he here?'

'No. He didn't come in this morning, nor did his bloody girlfriend. That's why we're so busy, I was two tills down before we even started.'

'Is he unwell?'

Jamie shrugged. 'You tell me. I get the impression he doesn't want the job, put it that way. I'm very close to making that wish come true.'

'So he didn't call in?'

'Hasn't yet.'

'Is that normal for him?'

'He doesn't miss many days. He can be a few minutes late and his work ethic is not of someone pulling up trees for me, but I'd come to think I could at least rely on him to turn in. More fool me.'

'And his girlfriend . . . she works here too?'

'She does.'

'What's her name?'

Jamie hesitated. 'What's this about again?'

'It's just a check on his welfare.'

'What makes you think you need to check on that?'

'Well, he hasn't turned up for work for one thing.'

Jamie seemed to recognise that he wasn't getting much more out of Harry. 'Alyssa. She's Alyssa Mills.'

'And do you have contact details for her?'

Jamie took hold of the door. 'I do. They're in the office. I'll warn you though . . . I've tried them both this morning and all I'm getting are two phones that are switched off.'

Alyssa's home address was walking distance from her place of work and in a row of sturdy, brick-built Victorian townhouses looking out over the central bus depot. The traffic noise was a constant din and the pavements busy with passing people.

Maddie waited for Harry to finish on the phone. He'd put a call into Mitch Evans in the Major Crime office. He was their civilian investigator and the one person you could always rely on to be at his desk. Harry had asked for the picture of Jack Knight to be sent to his email so he could access it on his mobile phone. Alyssa Mills was not known. He asked for a social media trawl to commence on her, that way they would have photos of both and know who they were looking for.

When he finally lowered his phone, Maddie pushed open a gate that squeaked as if in complaint. The communal entrance was up a few steps. The noise of a passing diesel engine seemed to be even louder now they were elevated above it. There were three doorbells in a row. The top and bottom bell had neatly typed surnames. The middle one was handwritten in blue ink that seemed to have run in the rain. It looked close enough to Mills for Maddie to hold it in. She counted to five as she did so. She wanted any occupants to be sure that they needed to answer. No one did. This time Maddie counted to ten before letting go. It seemed to have the desired effect.

'What THE FUCK!' It was a man's voice, angry, slurred, and from directly above. Maddie turned to Harry, who was already stepping back from under the cover of the vaulted overhang.

'Could you buzz us in, please,' he said. 'And there's no need for the profanity now, is there?'

Maddie heard a thump. She guessed it was the sound of a window being slammed shut. 'Maybe you could pick him up on his language when we're *through* the door?' she said.

'I like to set expectations.'

Maddie's expectations were met in the next couple of minutes when no one appeared at the front door. 'I'm not sure he's coming down to let us in after all,' she said. She leaned back on the bell, this time she had no intention of letting it go. Harry stepped back again, his face angled up towards where the voice had come from. Maddie had nearly counted to sixty when the communal door was suddenly wrenched inwards.

The man on the doorstep was out of breath. His chest rose and fell, moving an off-white vest as it did so. He was also in a pair of tracksuit bottoms but his feet were bare. He had short, greasy curls on the top of his head that looked to be thinning out. His cheeks were flushed a bright red and the same colour also featured in the whites of both his eyes.

'I don't want anything! Nothing of what you're selling. Now FUCK OFF!' He leaned forward, his vest pulled apart where his arms were stretched to grip the door surround. Harry lifted his badge.

'Swear in my company again and the only thing I'll offer you is a night in the cells. On me.' Harry stepped forward and into a stand-off. The man blocking the door grinned. It was sudden and looked almost manic. Maddie could smell the sickly sweet scent of consumed alcohol, even from her position further back. She couldn't tell if he was breathing it out or it was emitting from his pores. She decided it was likely both. He looked to be struggling to focus. Maddie considered that his stance might not be so much an attempt to block the door as to keep himself upright. He pushed off it and stepped backwards. His turn away was clumsy. He stumbled on the bottom step of the stairs that were almost directly behind him and started making his way up. He was laughing, too. It sounded forced — certainly there was nothing to be laughing at. She stepped in behind Harry and they followed the man up.

When they got to the landing, the front door of a flat hung open. Maddie walked into a long hall. The room at the end of this was the living room and she entered to find the man was already lying on a sofa. He was on his side, his back to her and his attention on a television by the window. There was little else in the way of furniture or belongings in the room. The light was lower up here. The bay window would overlook the street, but it had a curtain pulled roughly across. Maddie walked over to it and pulled it open. The resulting daylight wasn't strong by any means, but it was enough for the man to squint and complain.

'What the hell did you do that for? Close the curtains down would you?'

He gestured towards her like he was blinded. His attention remained on the television anyway. A game show was playing, the room filled with the sound of audience laughter and a jingle that seemed even louder.

'Are you Alyssa Mills's dad?' Maddie said. She was aware that Harry was moving around in the flat. She had seen him in her peripheral vision a couple of times as he crossed the hallway. She got no reply. The TV remote was on the bare, wooden floor near where his hand trailed from the sofa. She picked it up and clicked the TV off completely. He looked at her instantly. 'Alyssa Mills,' she said again.

'Alyssa! My princess!' the man chuckled. He sat up slowly, his hand lifted to his head. He was still squinting.

'So you're Mr Mills?'

'You, my love . . . you can call me Kevin. I like it when people call me Kevin. No formalities here, the world's got too many formalities.'

'Kevin. Is Alyssa here?'

'Alyssa. She's a free spirit that one. She comes and goes as she pleases.' Harry appeared at the back of the room and shook his head.

'When did you see her last?'

'She comes and goes does that one.'

'Last night . . . Was she here last night?'

'Nope.'

'Does she normally stay here at night?'

'Not when she can help it. Not anymore.' He started to search the area around the sofa for something then tutted. 'I think I might be out of supplies. Can you believe it? Alyssa's

189

a good girl. I'll get her to bring me some supplies back from work. She works at the shop, see? Handy!'

'So when did you see her last?'

The man shrugged again. He tapped his pockets then pulled out a carton of cigarettes. He took three attempts to light one. 'All blends into one, love. We don't get on so well. Alyssa's a little ashamed of her old man, see?' He expelled smoke in a chuckle. 'Can't blame her for that.' The man's attention moved to where Harry walked round the front of the sofa. His smile fell away. 'Look out! Here's the big man!'

'You haven't once asked if she's okay . . . why we're here.' Harry's bassy tone seemed to fill the space.

Kevin seemed to consider this for a moment. Then he shrugged. 'You would tell me if there was anything up, right? A strong girl that one.'

'She's had to be, I'd guess,' Harry said.

'Do you have any pictures of her?' Maddie asked. 'Of Alyssa. So we know what she looks like?'

The man shrugged again. 'An angel!' he beamed. 'Looks just like a fallen angel, that one.'

'So no pictures?' Maddie said.

The man tapped gently on his temple. 'All up here, love. All the time.'

Harry had already moved to the door. 'Come on, we're wasting our time here.'

The next waste of time was waiting for them at the end of a ten-minute drive to Marshall Street at the top end of the town. They knew Jack Knight's flat was accessed by the right-hand door of two that were directly next to each other. Jack's door had lighter colour bricks around it and Maddie assumed it was the more recent addition as part of adapting the terraced house into two flats. The door itself, however, looked to have seen far more years. The blue paint on its surface was peeling away in chunks. It was gone completely around the handle, leaving just an off-white patch where the peeling had been hastened along by daily contact. There was no answer to ringing the bell or to their knocking on the door. It was the same story when Maddie tried the smarter looking, white UPVC door next to it. Bending to peer through Jack's letterbox revealed nothing more than the first few steps that would lead up to the flat above. They tried a few more doors either side and, despite a couple being answered, their questions about Jack and his whereabouts drew a complete blank.

They did at least manage to get an update on one of their outstanding lines of enquiry — PNC showed a green Vauxhall Astra car registered to him at this address. It was parked outside. Its appearance was every bit as battered and dejected as the registration date of eighteen years earlier might suggest. It was locked. There was nothing on show through the windows of any relevance. Harry marked the tyres and took a picture of its position so they would know if it had moved. He also called through to Mitch to request ANPR movements for the last month to be sent to him, and for it to be added to a live database so he would know of any activations.

The expressions of the two detectives were every bit as dejected as the ageing hatchback by the time they sat back in the car to return to the station.

'We could really do without wasting a whole morning at this point in an investigation,' Maddie moaned.

Harry looked thoughtful. He seemed to be fixed on Jack's car as she drove away.

'Nothing's ever wasted,' he said.

CHAPTER 18

It was almost midday by the time Maddie arrived back at Canterbury. Harry had been silent for most of the journey back. This wasn't unusual for him, a fairly regular occurrence in fact, but recently it had felt different. Maddie decided that there was more he needed to talk about.

'You okay, Harry?'

Harry reacted as if he had been snapped out of a trance. 'Sure! I was just thinking . . . about where we go next.'

'And?'

'And I don't know. I want to go through the ABE interview from Jarod Logan's girlfriend, see if anything more came out of it that we might be able to use.'

'Makes sense.' Harry had insisted that Sharon Oaks's statement was taken using a video interview as a method. Known as an 'ABE', *Achieving Best Evidence*, it was common practice in Major Crime inquiries as it often did just that. A written statement could be very dry and it often had a slant to it provided by whichever police officer was taking the account. This might be an unconscious slant, but it was there all the same. Harry liked to try and engage or watch them in a natural conversation. He liked them to forget themselves,

192

to forget where they were and to whom they were talking. Maddie couldn't argue with the benefits.

'Then, I think we should put the two kids out as high-risk mispers.'

'Both?' Maddie was a little surprised. Nominating someone as a high-risk misper meant creating a list of standard, fast-track actions that would immediately be tasked to their uniform Response colleagues. These would include searching the home address, speaking to next of kin, monitoring social media, and visiting known associates and places frequented — much of what Harry and Maddie had already done. But once someone was a high-risk misper, these checks were repeated as often as possible and at different times of the day. It was labour intensive and their uniform colleagues wouldn't thank them for making the decision lightly. There were other time-consuming components, too, such as checks with the missing person's bank and mobile phone company to see what was being accessed and where; these would be carried out by detectives in Major Crime. Some of these were very intrusive, breaching a number of human rights, and needed top-end authorisation. Maddie considered that they might just about be able to justify the nomination for Jack, she was far less sure about his possible girlfriend.

'Yes, both. Why not?'

'From what I understand we have a patch of blood out in the rural that is a ninety-nine percent match to Jack. It's not a lot of blood either, not enough to suggest he's in serious trouble, and now we can't find him. Alyssa is just his girlfriend.'

'Who we can't find either.'

'Who we can't *account* for. She doesn't know we're looking for her. We can't say that she's missing. No one else has flagged her up as such.'

'We've met her father. I imagine the only time he notices her missing is when his drink runs out.'

'I agree. But we would still normally need that ratification, someone to report someone missing is where we'd usually start, wouldn't we?'

'It can be. But we can declare someone high risk. The patch of blood was close to where we found a murder victim don't forget.'

'Half a mile. And there are no known links between the two.'

'That's exactly why we need to find him. And her. I'm comfortable with the justification. There's too much we don't know. Why would a young lad living in the middle of a town travel up to the rural, bleed, and then travel back. And then he leaves his car outside his flat — assuming he was using that car in the first place — but doesn't turn up for work? And his girlfriend doesn't either and doesn't check in with her boss, which is described as *out of character*. There are questions here, Maddie, questions that I need answered and we're not getting any closer.'

'Okay then. So we go in and figure out what we do have. We review the interview and we identify the gaps we still need to fill.'

'Gaps to fill?' Harry grumbled. 'This whole investigation is just one big *gap*.'

* * *

The night edged in, despite Jack wishing it away with all he had. He knew he had to return to his flat, if only briefly. And if it wasn't to his flat, it would have to be somewhere — he was starting to attract attention. Jack was sitting in a McDonald's in the town of Langthorne. He had moved to a corner booth with a view over the entrance and the food counter as soon as he had seen it become available. The restaurant wasn't too far from where he worked and he didn't want to be spotted. He'd purchased a meal when he'd first come in, then a coffee that he had nursed for as long as he could. He'd seen the shift change and made small talk with a couple of employees. It was starting to become awkward.

When he stepped out of the artificial glare of the restaurant the evening seemed instantly darker. It was cooler too. He zipped his jacket right up and dug his chin into the material, leaving just his nose and his darting eyes visible. It was still enough to be recognised.

'Jack!' He snapped his head to the voice as if it was the sound of a car skidding towards him. He had to gasp a mouthful of air to be able to reply at all.

'Hey, Rich.' Jack recognised a man who worked with him. He was out back in the stores. They had started around the same time but Rich's move behind the scenes was a fast one; it seemed he was a little too rough round the edges to be customer-facing.

'*Hey, Rich?* That all you got, nobhead? Where the fuck have you been? Called in Tom Dick, I heard.' Rich's eyes lifted to the lit-up yellow arches looming over them both. 'Your quack prescribe a Happy Meal did he?' Rich's laugh was powerful and irritating at the same time. Jack had to wait for him to finish before he could be heard.

'Something like that. I'm feeling a bit better. I didn't have anything in. I've been told I need to eat.'

Rich lifted his hands. 'You don't need to be swinging the lead with me, mucker. I don't give a shit. That Jamie lad, though . . . you wanna watch that one. I reckon the man's got a broom shoved right up there somewhere! He's a career rat . . . someone like that'll have your legs if it helps them up the ladder.'

'Yeah, I know what you mean,' Jack said, despite only really getting the gist. 'I'd better get back to my bed anyway.'

'You in tomorrow then?'

'I plan on it.'

'What about that little dolly bird of yours?' Rich winked. 'She was off today, too. I heard you two were seeing each other. Maybe you didn't fancy work, maybe you fancied spending a whole day *seeing* each other!' Rich lifted his hands again and stepped back with it. 'None of my business, though. Now, I gotta get a Big Mac inside me . . . ooh er!' That all-consuming laughter again.

Jack smiled politely until it petered out. 'See you tomorrow then!' Rich said something in reply and there was more laughter with it, but Jack was already walking away. He didn't look back. His stomach was suddenly so knotted with tension that he was terrified he might be sick on the pavement right there. At least it would have backed up his story.

His flat was twenty-five minutes on foot from the centre of town. It took nearly forty. Jack took the long way at a dawdle. The town was in the midst of rush hour, as much as Langthorne ever experienced a rush hour, and the roads were jammed with what seemed like a steady procession out of the town. Jack found himself glancing over at the drivers. They were sat with their cars idling, waiting to edge forwards. He could see their radio screens and the condensation on their windows. It seemed suddenly to him that everyone else was safe, warm and content. He yearned for that — a normal life, even the life that was his just a few days earlier. His mind soon wandered, filled up with images of his last few days, things he had never wanted to see, things he knew he would be seeing over and over for as long as he lived.

In contrast to the white noise and movement of the busy town, the dead-end road he lived on was quiet. Again he found himself hesitating at his own front door. As he pushed the key into the lock he closed his eyes, as if Alyssa might still be at the bottom of the stairs and he might have to look into her eyes again, eyes that had been full of confusion while those lips he had kissed a thousand times had pleaded with him to let her go. He'd wanted to. He'd told her that. He'd whispered it into her ear when he'd had the chance. But it was her or it was him, and he'd made his choice.

The door swung a little too hard, enough to thud off the wall. He forced his eyes open in a moment of self-loathing. He shouldn't be protecting himself from what he had done. He should be made to face it, to re-live it. His exhaustion as he climbed the stairs was worse than ever. He was in the flat for just a few minutes — just as long as was needed to retrieve his car key from the pocket of his jeans on the bedroom floor. He stopped for a brief moment on the way out. He considered if there was something else he might need. He couldn't remember the conversation about tonight, other than the meeting time being a few hours later. He was dreading that. Midnight was bad enough, but tonight he had instructions for 4 a.m. There was little chance of him sleeping beforehand — not there, at least, not in that flat. He needed to get far away.

He couldn't remember if he had been told to bring anything. He didn't think so. He remembered being in a bit of a daze. The man had told him that this latest *task* might take longer, he remembered that much. He peered around the interior of his flat without really knowing what he was looking for. He was on autopilot when he moved to the cupboard under the sink. He had some latex gloves in there as part of an oven cleaning kit. He stuffed them in his pocket. He didn't know why, but he had a feeling that he might need them.

* * *

It was the flash of light that woke him every time.

Harry lay on his side, a roar coursing from his mouth, his eyes suddenly thrust open. He fell silent and tried to make sense of the blood-red digits etched in the darkness that showed 3:28 a.m. He pushed himself into a sitting position while his heart beat like a hammer against his ribcage. He checked his phone, considering that it was what had woken him the night before. There was nothing on the screen. Tonight's reason for waking was all too familiar.

His eyes took a while to adjust before he could make out the edges of his bedroom furniture. An ironed shirt hung on the outside of the wardrobe for his day at work, its lighter

197

colour meant it came into focus a little quicker than the rest. He fixed on it. His heart was slowing, the adrenalin flowing out of his system. He knew he was over the worst. The dream at least always ended the same, even if the build-up to it could be very different. The flash of light that always woke him was a memory of the last moment of the crash that had claimed his wife. It was the moment the car had struck and a bright white flash had filled his vision where they were hit so hard the car had tipped towards the bright sun in the sky. It was the moment that had replayed over and over since. The changing build-up to that point was cruel, meaning that he could never know when it was coming. He could be dreaming about anything, about anyone, and then that same ending — the block of white light with a scuffed movement next to him, a suspended scream in his ears and the feeling of a tugging on his arm, as if the afterlife itself had reached for him and then settled only for his wife. He never used to dream at all; how he wished for that state again.

In the one counselling session he had been forced to attend, he had been told that his condition was likely to be a form of PTSD, that the moment had come from nowhere and had left him traumatised, that his mind was now set up to accept that everything could change in a moment and from nowhere, and how it might make him struggle to relax and switch off to life's dangers — even when he was lying in his own bed it seemed. Harry had scoffed at him. Everything had its own label these days. He was having nightmares and he was grieving for his wife. Calling it a 'disorder' made it sound like there was something wrong with him for reacting like that. And there was nothing wrong with him.

His throat felt dry. He pushed the covers off and his feet found the carpet. He rubbed at his face and stood up. He padded through the open door and into the hallway. A low moon was distorted through the frosted window in the bathroom as he passed it. It seemed to soften every edge as he passed through the dining room and into the kitchen, where the window was bigger and the light was brightest.

The moon held in the top right corner of the kitchen window like a stamp on an envelope.

As he held a glass under the tap, a bright lamp flickered on in his back garden. His eyes flicked to it then to what had set it off. A fox lifted its nose from the ground. It was on their path, close to the pond that Robin had made him dig out. It would be after the frogs, maybe, or even his fish. He slapped the window. The fox turned to him. It didn't run. It didn't even look as if it felt vaguely threatened and soon put its nose back to the grass. The garden light clicked off and then came instantly back on again. Its light fell over the bench that was his wife's favourite place to sit.

There was a happier vision of his wife that he was sometimes able to recall. It was late spring a few years earlier and the garden had been an assault of colours and scents and she was sitting on that bench. She looked so at ease and peaceful. He handed her a drink and she smiled up at him and just announced from nowhere that here and with him was her favourite place in the whole world. He could still remember her smile: big and bright. She'd never looked happier. But that was not the recurring vision that punctured his nights and invaded his days, and it was no longer the image that came to mind the second anyone said her name. Instead, it was that flash of light, that suspended scream. It was as if the crash had taken her so suddenly from his world, it had also scrubbed her very memory at the same time.

Harry's heart was racing and his adrenalin flowing again. He still held the glass tumbler and took a step back from the sink. The fox was still out there, moving again slowly but enough to drag his eye. He slapped the window again but it still didn't move away. He put down his glass of water and balled his hand into a fist, winding himself up into a frenzy. The window shook with the force and he was shouting, too, his booming voice adding to the strength of the blows. The window flexed as if it might go in. He took a step back and his right hand swept up the glass of water. He brought it down in the sink and it smashed instantly. In the darkness he could hear splintered pieces bounce off the window behind, skid along the work surface and scatter across the floor.

The sound broke through his rage. He was left leaning forward, his breathing heavy from the exertion. He shook his head. Maybe this was what they had meant about him not being able to relax? He needed something to change; he needed closure. He couldn't go on like this. *They* couldn't go on like this. His mind filled with the image of his youngest daughter propped up in that hospital bed, blood seeping through the bandage around her self-inflicted wound. Except it wasn't self-inflicted. None of this was.

His mind now rushed with a blur of options but only one had any clarity to it. He pushed back off the unit and went quickly to his bedroom, turning on the lights as he went. There was no chance of him going back to sleep now and anyway, that was the furthest thing from his mind.

* * *

The traffic lights changed and Jack stared right into the lurid green light. The whole unit fidgeted in the strong wind. The harsh light flooded the interior of his car and when he closed his eyes to it, he could still see a blob of green. The car horn behind him snapped his eyes back open. He selected first gear and turned right to join the Ashford Road. The Ports Café was a few hundred metres further. This time it was a left turn onto the rutted surface. He had come the long way and he was late. He had considered not turning up. He could have just kept on driving and seen where he ended up, but he knew he had to show. Anytime he considered making a run, he just had to remind himself of the text message his mum had sent him, letting him know that his *friend from the café* had turned up at her house. She said there was no message; he just wanted him to know. Of course he did.

When Jack pushed through the door and scoured the interior of the café, his *friend* was nowhere to be seen. There was a clock on the wall, the hands fashioned out of rusty knives and forks that showed he was ten minutes late. The café was empty, hardly surprising for just gone four in the morning. He walked to the counter and the same waitress appeared from the kitchen area almost immediately. Despite the time of day, she looked wide awake — on edge even. She ripped a piece of paper from the top of a pad, leant over it and stayed looking down, her pencil readied for the order. Jack considered talking to her again, asking her what the hell was going on, but everything about her, the tension in her body language, her quick short breaths, the speed with which her eyes had met with his and then dropped to the floor, told him that the last thing she wanted was a conversation with him.

'A white coffee, please. As strong as you can make it, though. I haven't exactly been sleeping well.'

The woman pushed off the counter, her pencil dropping onto the empty pad as she did. She went straight to the coffee machine.

'I'll bring it over,' she said. Her voice sounded hoarse.

Jack walked to his usual seat. The door opened as he sat down and the man stood in the doorway to stare. Jack stared right back. He was beyond being intimidated anymore; he was tired — exhausted really. His confused mind couldn't remember the last time he had slept properly. From leaving his house earlier that evening he had driven to a spot he knew on the North Downs that overlooked Langthorne. He'd made his car as warm as he could and put his chair right back. But sleep hadn't come. He was beginning to think he might never sleep again.

The man in the entrance half turned, his bandaged hand hooked around the door. Jack knew that he was meant to get up and follow him out, that the man had no intention of staying.

'I've got a coffee coming. I'm drinking it,' Jack said. He crossed his arms to emphasise his point.

'You're late!' snapped the man.

'You're later,' said Jack.

The man's lips curled into a sneer and he paced across the floor and pulled out the chair opposite. He sat down heavily and leant right forward. He had his dressed hand balled into a fist that he caressed with the other. Jack ignored his stare as his coffee arrived — plus a black coffee for the man. The waitress put down the drinks silently and then she was gone.

'Friend of yours?' Jack jabbed his thumb towards the kitchen area where the waitress had stepped out of sight. The man opposite glared back. Jack was considering if he'd ever seen him blink before. He had a sudden urge to throw his hands out, to try and make him flinch, to get some sort of reaction at least — anything to get a sign of something human.

'Tonight's expression of loyalty is yours,' the man growled. 'We are so close to everything that we desire.'

'And what is that?'

'Access.' The man licked his lips and his nostrils flared with excitement.

'Access to what?'

'You have stepped a long way to know nothing about the path you have trodden. You should have kept your eyes open.'

'Honestly, I love the way you talk. It's very cute and I bet it gets all the girls. But you should know that I'm exhausted. I haven't slept for days. I've seen things I never wanted to see and after last night . . . what we did . . . I'm a little bit fucked up right now, okay? So you'll forgive me for not quite having a clue where the hell I am headed. What the fuck does *access* mean?' Jack could feel himself getting angrier. The man repositioned his hands and snatched his dressing off. As it was folded back it flashed an angry red. He rolled the dressing up and stuffed it in his pocket. The palm of his left hand faced towards Jack, propped on the table at the elbow. A thick blob of blood leaked from the middle of the torn skin. It looked like a piece of shredded meat. Jack couldn't help but watch the blood roll down his wrist and out of sight. His brave front went with it. The man pulled a clean dressing from another pocket. He ripped it out of the packet and applied it while he spoke.

'Access means everything. This world is controlled by those with access. You want to succeed in this world, you want to be someone, you have to earn your access — you have to prove you are loyal. We are close. This is our final task.' The man finished dressing the wound on his hand. He reached into a pocket and flicked a small rectangle of white card onto the table. Jack hesitated, but he did pick it up. He spun it over. The other side was busy with typed font. He read the words through the middle.

'Who the hell is Maddie Ives?' he said. The man didn't answer, just stared right back, his eyes still unblinking, his growing excitement obvious. Jack looked back to the card and scanned the other words on there too, below the name was a rank and contact details and in the top corner was a crest he recognised.

'A police officer? You have got to be kidding me!'

The man's expression was suddenly more serious, his cheeks rippled where it looked like he was biting down hard. 'I don't kid. The final task is to be a statement. A statement that cannot be argued, that cannot be questioned, that cannot be bettered.'

'Are you crazy?'

'Crazy? I am on the brink of greatness. *We* are! Do you wish to remain on the side of the ordinary, pushing other people's items through your scanner at the supermarket?'

'I m-mean . . . H-how even?' Jack searched across the table as if it might provide some answers. 'How are you going to get access to somebody like that *and* hope to get away with it?'

'I made contact. She came to me but we did not meet. She does not know who I am. But I was patient. I followed her movements thereafter. She has a routine. We have an opportunity. But it is soon. We must move.'

'I can't! We can't do this! What are we doing?'

'This is your chance to be something. People like you, like me, we cannot succeed any other way. This is how we become someone.'

Jack took a moment to check the café was still empty. 'Greatness is doing in a copper, is it? My life before really wasn't so bad after all. I would really quite like it back.'

The man leaned forward further this time, forcing Jack backwards.

'There is no *back*. There is only forwards or the path falls from under you.'

Jack shook his head. He could feel his chest tightening. He was going to have to go through with this. The man was still talking in riddles but he was clear enough: there was no longer an option.

'This is it? Nothing more after this?'

'Our final reckoning!' The man stood up and stared down at Jack's coffee. It was still untouched. Jack stood up too. Suddenly he didn't feel like he needed anything to make him feel more awake. He snatched a desperate glance towards the counter. There was no sign of the waitress.

CHAPTER 19

Friday

When Jack came to his senses, the first thing he was aware of was the breaking dawn. The sun was low and piercing and he had to turn away from it instantly. His exhaustion must finally have got the better of him for him to have dozed off.

After leaving the café, he'd been taken up to the front passenger seat of the truck. Conversation had been stilted at best then dwindled to nothing. He had tried to get some sort of clue of what was expected of him, of what they were doing. He gave up quickly. They had stopped at a clifftop location in his home town of Langthorne and occupied a space among a few other parked vehicles. There had been a child's play park on their left side and beyond that was an elevated view of the sea. When the truck fell silent he had tried again with his questions, but he still got nothing. Then, with just an hour of darkness left, they had moved again. It had been a short drive to the other side of the town and down a steep, unmade hill to where they stopped again. This was where Jack was now squinting at the rising sun. They were at sea level and almost on the promenade itself.

The sea dominated as he peered out at it over the empty driver's seat at the sunrise. On another day he might have appreciated the view, but that morning it was the last thing on his mind.

He reached for the door handle, suddenly aware of how hot and uncomfortable he was. He stepped down from the truck to stretch and look for his missing driver. There was no sign of him. A chilly breeze swept in off the sea and he pushed his hands into his pockets. He felt the business card that had been tossed at him in the café, the one with *Maddie Ives* written across its front. He'd spent much of the last couple of hours with the card in his hand and must have read the details on it a hundred times or more, each time pondering a different idea as to how he might get out of this mess. At first, he was going to wait for an opportunity to text a warning to the number. Then he decided he would just make a run for it when they pulled up somewhere, and when he got far enough away he'd call this DS Maddie Ives direct — or even just 999. He reckoned if he gave them the whole story they would have to help him. They would have to keep him safe at least — him and his mother.

But he hadn't. He hadn't done anything. He'd asked a few questions, trying to find out what he could, and when that had failed, he'd just sat there waiting, not really knowing what for. He became resigned to letting this play out; there was nothing else he could do. Maybe it was this resignation that had relaxed him enough to finally get some sleep.

Now he had daylight, he took the opportunity to have a look around. The 'road' they had driven down was more a coarse ribbon of crushed stones and grit that moved into and across the expanse of rough standing where they were now parked. Underfoot was a firm layer of worn pebbles with determined sprigs of wild grass jutting out among assorted lumps of driftwood. The grassy area and the beach itself were separated by a strip of promenade, which looked out of place with its smooth, flat surface and sharp edges.

The thud of something against the metal bed of the truck made him jump and he jerked his head to the source.

The man appeared, standing at the back end of the truck and staring at Jack. He was holding a length of rope in his hands and it was pulled taut across his chest. He had fashioned a large loop at one end. Jack grasped its grim function straight off and the horrific images of a few nights earlier swam to the surface of his memory. All of the questions he had reeled off in the preceding hours were now answered in the form of a length of rope and the excited stare of the man holding it.

'Your hand.' The man beckoned to him. 'You have your tool?'

'Tool?' Jack knew exactly what he meant.

'We go to work. Six times when you work. You must break the skin.'

'Now?' The device was loose in Jack's coat pocket. He could feel its weight whenever he moved.

'Now.'

The truck's front passenger door was still open. Jack leaned in and fished the metal lump from his pocket. The teeth were still stained despite Jack having scrubbed it. He laid his left hand flat on the seat, palm up. With his right he laid the metal against his skin, teeth downward. He clenched his jaw and twisted it. The pain was immediate, though he didn't break the skin; he wasn't applying enough weight. The man must have moved closer; Jack was suddenly aware of his voice in his ear. He pushed in, his hand fell over the metal and he grabbed it firmly to twist it again. He put as much weight through it as he could and Jack screamed in agony.

His palm ran with blood. The skin around it was white and puckered.

'Four more!' The man said. He stepped back to let Jack continue. Just resting the metal on his hand was painful now. He knew the remaining twists were going to be agony. He started to feel sorry for himself, his head shaking slowly, wondering what he had done to deserve this. Then he remembered. He remembered what he had done, whom he had hurt, and what he was about to do. He realised that this pain was exactly what he deserved, every second of it. When he twisted the tool again, he pressed with all of his weight. His teeth gritted as he silently cursed his very existence.

* * *

Maddie Ives finished tying off the laces on her jogging shoes. She stood up straight to walk away from her apartment and down to the street. She used the walk as part of her warm up, her strides longer and more deliberate than normal. When she got to the High Street she hooked the heels of her feet on a low wall, one after the other, and leant in for a long stretch. Her legs still felt a little stiff from her previous run, when she had pushed herself a little longer and a little faster than she had intended. Today she would take it easier, certainly for the first few miles until she loosened up. She had considered not coming out this morning but Rhiannon's grudging confirmation that she would accompany her had been the incentive she needed.

'Hey!' Maddie stood up as Rhiannon approached.

'Hey yourself!' Maddie replied. Rhiannon started using the same wall to stretch out on.

'Well, this was a stupid idea.'

'You think? You should have said if you didn't fancy it. I'd have stayed in bed.'

'You mean I don't have to be here at all?'

'No, you do! But I could certainly have taken a day off. This will be six in a row.'

'I only came out because you made me feel guilty.'

'Then I did you a favour! Sooner we get going, the sooner we get back.'

They walked towards the alleyway that cut through a row of buildings. They had only a teasing glimpse of the sea at first, but its shuffling blue mass opened up in full when they made it to the end. Maddie loved how it constantly changed its appearance to match with its mood. Today there was some cloud cover, but it was thin and with gaps. The sun broke through regularly to change the colour of the water, and added a little sparkle as it did. It was calm, too.

The promenade looked to be empty of people for at least as far as she could see. It was a big reason why Maddie dragged herself out of bed so early and why she always took the same route along the beach. At that time of the morning she could almost guarantee not meeting another soul.

They reached the promenade and broke into a loose jog. Maddie's legs still felt tight, but she knew they would loosen up quickly. She lifted her eyes to a turn in the promenade up ahead. Here the path took a hard left to curve around a part of the coast where the sea had pushed in as if overstepping its territory. The path never came back out as far. Instead it cut through an area of hardstanding then continued into a coastal park with trees and wild grass on either side. Maddie shifted her gaze from the path ahead to where the sun was dipping its toes at the horizon. Maddie felt her lips curl into a smile as she felt the warmth on her face.

* * *

Harry was hurried and untidy in pulling the car over. The engine was still running. He could still hear his pulse beating in his ears, still powered by anger. He hesitated to turn the engine off. He didn't expect to attract any attention. A running car in the middle of Maidstone shouldn't sound out of place, even at dawn with the sun still struggling to shift the shadows.

He had to stoop a little in his seat to see the second-floor rooms of the large property. Wootan's room was on this level somewhere. The curtain positions, the lopsided hedge, the battered-looking wheelie bins — all was identical to the day before. Maybe one wheelie bin was a little more central than it had been; its right side seemed to obstruct the path to the front door. There was no movement anywhere, nor was there likely to be at this time of the morning. Maybe that was the reason he'd made his snap decision. He was awake, he was angry, and there was no one around to see him. He knew he shouldn't be here, but his restraint was all but gone.

He turned off the ignition and lingered on the keys in his palm. Stepping out of the car would be another threshold crossed. He knew that he would cross it; there was little point in delaying. He opened the door. The sky was layered in grey clouds that looked to be losing a battle with the sun. He was penned in by tall buildings, and the air was unmoving.

He sidestepped to get a better view of the door. The bins had definitely moved. He remembered how they had been overflowing; now the lids hung down and there was nothing visible over the top. The rubbish from the outside of the building had been taken away to leave just the scum that was inside.

He started his walk towards the door.

* * *

Jack stared dumbly at the vicious-looking knife that lay across the palm of his right hand. His left hung by his side, a dressing tied tightly across it.

'You know how to hold one of those?' the man said.

Jack stayed looking down. He did, of course he did. He just couldn't bring himself to wrap his fingers round that handle, to hold it like he meant it. Once he did that, he was one step closer to using it. 'Sure.'

'Give it here!' The man snatched it back. Jack watched it go. 'You just take hold of her — it needs to be firm. I will use the blade. I will push this in her face, as close as I can. I will cut her, break her skin to break her spirit. She needs to know we are serious; she needs to know she can't put up a fight and win.'

'Take hold of her?' Jack knew his voice was lacking any strength. He could do nothing about that. The man eyed him closely. He had been staring at the knife and it seemed to have increased his excitement. He'd moved it closer to his face to study it and licked his lips. Now his expression had changed to

210

disgust. He was looking at Jack. 'Take hold of her firmly and move her towards me. I will push this into her face and she will know. Then it is easy. If she picks up that you do not mean what you say, that you are weak, she will fight or she will run. You should know again that the task today is either the two of us with Maddie Ives or it is me on my own with Jack Knight.'

Jack flinched at his own surname. He knew he had never shared it with the man. Given the previous revelations, he shouldn't have been surprised, but it still caught him out.

'Can you do that?' the man persisted.

Jack nodded in resignation.

'She will run past. You will need to take her as she passes. With the element of surprise you will need to silence her first. But I say again . . . you must be firm. She must know that you are not someone she can fight.'

'Okay,' Jack croaked.

The man reached into the back of the truck and pulled out the rope end over end, making large loops. When it was all out, he hung it diagonally across his body like a sash. He seemed to have a sudden realisation. He moved past Jack to pull open the tailgate of the truck and rummage in a metal box Jack had seen bolted to the floor. When he turned back he was holding another knife, smaller but looking no less vicious. The glint was back in his eye and he licked his lips again.

'When you grab her, push this into her throat! Draw some of her blood. Show her!' His excitement was peaking. 'You will get no problems from her.' He held it out. Jack reached for it. It felt lighter than the previous one. He still didn't hold it right but the man didn't seem to care anymore. Jack heard the clunking of the locking system on the truck and then the man was already walking away. He made the promenade before he even looked back. He didn't say anything. He didn't beckon to hurry him along or tell him to catch up. He didn't have to. He knew Jack would follow. He took a firmer grip on the knife and did just that.

* * *

Maddie was starting to feel stronger. She always seemed to struggle for the first mile or so and it was always when she got to the area of hard standing at the foot of her dream house that she started to feel like she was getting her second wind. The house was off to her left and elevated high over the promenade. The back garden was cut into zig-zag lines that led to a wooden beach hut two-thirds of the way down. It had a balcony with seating and a steel barbeque. Every time she passed it, she fantasised that she was out on the wooden deck on a summer's day with a glass of wine in hand, waiting for the barbeque bricks to turn grey.

'That place is mine one day!' she said. Rhiannon was still alongside her. She seemed to have got comfortable in her stride a little quicker. Her breathing was already more measured, her strides seemed more natural and with the exception of the reddening to her cheeks she didn't look like she was exerting herself too much. Such was the joy of being young. You could miss two weeks of training and then turn up to pick up where you had left off. Rhiannon cast a glance over to where Maddie had gestured.

'As long as I can come round for dinner!'

'Anytime.'

Maddie looked ahead. Her favourite part of the run was when she entered the coastal park that she could see half a mile away in front of them. They passed an open-backed truck on their left side. It was beaten up enough to ruin the ambience. Maddie turned away, to where the sea still lapped gently at the shore. She considered that the ugly truck might have ejected a kayaker, but couldn't see anyone enjoying the water. A dog-walker maybe — and who could blame them? The morning was getting more beautiful with every minute that passed.

The coastal path approached. It was made up of thin slivers of grey concrete cut through trimmed lawns, with maintained flower beds and freshly planted trees among the native rocks, driftwood, and beach pebbles. And all was to be experienced with that constant sound of the sea sighing gently in the background. She quickened her pace to make for it, now feeling as strong as she ever had.

'This a race now?' Rhiannon exhaled.

Maddie had almost forgotten she was with her; she had got used to running on her own perhaps. 'Sorry! I feel good this morning.' Gazing forward intently, she thought she had seen movement — someone crossing the path a few metres in from where they would enter the shade of the trees. She reckoned it would be her dog-walker from the parked truck. It didn't matter. She could chirp a pleasant greeting while keeping up their pace. The few times she had walked this route rather than run she had found herself engaged in small-talk when all she wanted was to be left alone. That was the beauty of running; you could avoid all that.

* * *

Jack stared down at the knife that hung from his gloved hand. With his heightened awareness he jumped at the movement of a leafy bush shivering in the light breeze. They had walked a short distance, maybe half a mile, to where the path continued through wooded parkland. It looked man-made. The trees were lined up in formation, their roots dug into areas marked out with low fencing and scattered with shredded bark. On the opposite side of the path, his mentor stepped into the trees and was instantly out of sight. There was a steep bank behind a row of bushes on that side and he had said that the elevated view would allow him to see anyone approaching from far along the path. Jack was supposed to take up his own hiding place but the man was already back, bursting out from cover.

'It's both of them!' He struggled to contain his excitement. 'Two!'

'Two?' Jack's eyes fell back briefly to the knife in his hand. When he looked up, the man had stepped closer to him, too close for comfort.

'This is perfect. Maddie Ives will know we mean business when we strike down her friend in front of her!'

'S-strike d-down?'

'Maddie Ives is the older woman. Take her as we discussed — a firm grip. But rather than pushing her towards me, hold her so she can see.'

'So she can see?'

The man took out the large knife and moved it from one hand to the other.

'When she sees what we are capable of, she will not fight, she will not argue. She will be ours. Take hold of her and turn her towards me so she can see. The younger one is mine — be sure to show her! Now, find your place!'

The man turned away and was quickly invisible again. There was the sound of movement as he must have climbed higher but it soon stopped, leaving just the gentle hissing of the sea behind him.

Jack turned towards it. He was standing at the edge of the path. The trees were younger on his side, the trunks nowhere near thick enough to shield him from view, but there was a thick bush planted where the wooden fence made a corner. It would be thick enough to hide him from the view of a casual runner, he was sure of it. He managed to get himself moving and ducked stiffly behind it. He shifted his weight onto one bent knee and leaned a little to peek out. He could see twenty metres or so down the path. He still couldn't see anyone, but now there were rhythmic footfalls — two sets. They were getting closer. A loose stone was kicked and skipped across the concrete towards him. He took another deep breath. He glanced for a moment at the knife gripped tightly in his right hand. He could feel his heart beating hard as he tried to console himself, his head shaking from side to side, his lips mouthing over and over, 'I'm sorry, I'm so sorry, I don't have a choice, I don't have a choice!'

The footfalls were louder. He closed his lips tight and held his breath.

* * *

As Harry strode across the silent road, his feet kicked something loose. He heard it skip and roll across the path by his feet. He didn't look down to see what it was. His attention was in front of him, on whatever might halt his progress, like the wheelie bin pulled roughly across his path. It had two plastic half-lids that, when shut, met in the middle. Now they hung open so the stench of rotting detritus washed over him like a wave. It did nothing to stop his advance.

He stopped at the front door. It was as he had already assessed: wooden construction, inward opening. The handle hung limp and at an angle as if it was broken — ineffective at least. Sure enough he was able to push it open with his gloved hands. He paused. He could feel the pulse in his temple and his chest at the same time. The door gave him access to a sparse porch with just a crumpled mat on the floor, covered in dried mud and leading to a more solid-looking door with a handle that hung like it should. He stepped forward onto the mat, which crunched under his feet, and his mind flickered with doubt for the first time that morning. This door would surely be locked. He couldn't knock for access. He wasn't intending for people to see him.

He considered that he didn't know exactly what he was there for. His right hand rested on the door handle, his left was flat against the surface of the door, and he had positioned his feet further back so he was leaning against it, ready to push. But what then? He hadn't thought this through at all. Harry dipped his head. This was so unlike him. He was running on pure emotion — something he never did. Harry's strength was his ability to be rational, no matter what was going on. His colleagues had called him cold in the past, cold and unfeeling. This was a massive mistake. His grip loosened on the door handle until his hand slipped off completely. His left still pushed against the door. His eyes lifted to it. His sleeve had fallen down a little, enough to expose the sliver of a scar before his leather gloves covered the rest. The scar on the top of his wrist where the surgeons had needed to push a pin to meet with a metal rod that ran up his forearm. The scarring was worse on the other side: a jagged line, an angry and raised flash of red. Harry didn't need a physical reminder of that day, of that incident, of the moment his life changed forever. But he had got it. Fate had chosen to brand it on his skin — or at least Daniel Wootan had. Some of his scar was further concealed under a sleek-looking smartwatch, a present from his daughters so he would answer them when they needed him. Not that he felt like he could help. He had never felt so useless, so utterly lost. They wanted their mother back. They *needed* their mother back. Melissa was still adding to her physical scars. In time they might heal, but the psychological scars could only ever fade — but not while Wootan wasn't getting what was coming to him, what he deserved for what he did. The justice system had let Harry and his girls down. He knew why he was here: to put it right, to start the healing process.

His pulse had quickened, the beat so strong in his head that it felt as if his brain might burst out of the sides. He took a step back then shifted his weight forward, his right foot lifting at the same time to meet with the door halfway up. The kick was solid. Harry was a big man and every part of him was behind it. The door crashed in and bounced off a wall on the other side. Harry was already stepping through. He was lost again, back to running on pure emotion, no longer caring about any noise he was making. Once his foot found the bottom step in the dimly lit hallway, he swept up the stairs two at a time, his attention on the door numbers he passed, counting them up. Numbers one, two and three had been on the right side of the corridor on the ground floor; the first-floor landing had numbers four, five and six. The landing turned back on itself to another flight of stairs. Harry's pace didn't slow.

The seven was missing on this door but the process of elimination had done its work. He didn't stop at Wootan's door. He didn't try the handle either. He simply used his momentum and raised his foot. The door folded in. It clattered and thudded against the wall. Harry pushed through it. The light was low, just a triangular patch of light directly opposite where something was pulled roughly across the window. A man stood close enough to the window to be revealed by the poor light. Harry froze as he turned towards him. The man froze too. He was bent forward and there was something at his feet. Harry didn't look at it, staying focussed on the man. It wasn't Daniel Wootan — Harry was sure of that. He was too short.

'He was just like this! When I got here!' The man's eyes were wide and unblinking. Harry took in the rest of the room: at the man's feet was a mattress and someone was laid on it, the head almost at the man's feet. The face was turned away, and Harry could just make out a clump of dark hair. 'I think he's dead!' the man said.

Harry found a light switch on the wall next to him. A single bulb cast a dirty orange glow. The figure on the mattress was still and the man standing over him had something in his hand.

'What's that?' Harry forced the words through a throat that felt tight.

The man looked down at the item in his hands. When he lifted his head to Harry again, his eyes were just as wide. 'His wallet, okay? I was just looking. I wasn't gonna take nothing, I swear! He's dead, man — OD'd. The needle's down there. There's some brown left, too. I just woke up and he was like this!'

The room was a bedsit. The bed, a low table and a sofa with a messy blanket on it comprised the only furniture. The table was cluttered. Several spoons were laid out, the stubby, distinctive types given out as part of needle exchange kits by drug charities. At least one of them was scorched black. There were paper filters next to a packet of baby-wipes, one of which was pulled out and looked to have a spot of blood on it. A ripped open sachet of citric acid lay on the floor.

Harry moved forward to see the face of the figure on the floor. It was Wootan. His eyes were open, unmoving and glazed, but there was a quiver from the lips. He knelt down and slipped off the glove from his right hand. He pushed two fingers into Wootan's neck. There was nothing. He pushed more firmly — a pulse! It was slow and very weak, barely registering. He wasn't dead, but without intervention he would be very soon. Harry stood back up.

'You're police, right?' the man said.

Harry's gaze was downwards, his jaw locked so tight with tension that he couldn't answer. He was fighting the urge to lash out with his foot, but the word *police* seemed to cut through his haze. He seized on it. The man looked at him intently. He was still frozen, his stance unnatural, knees twisted and feet turned to fit between the mattress and the wall.

'Look, I ain't taking it!' The man looked less shocked now, his expression more uncertain as he gestured with the wallet.

'No.' Harry managed finally. 'I'm not police.'

The man looked him up and down and seemed to relax. He moved the wallet back closer to his body and flicked through the compartments, his tongue running over his lips. Harry had pulled on a tatty hooded top, jeans and old boots along with his beaten old waxed jacket in his hurry to leave the house. He might not have looked like a police officer but criminals had an uncanny knack of seeing past their attire.

'There ain't nothing here to have, yeah? Nothing in his wallet and nothing here. I've looked. Wootsy never did have nothing. But I got dibs on the brown, yeah? I was first in.' The man's eyes fell hungrily to the cluttered table. Harry stepped back. He was back looking at the figure on the mattress, his eyes dragged to movement of the lips. He was still fighting for his last breath.

'You take what you want,' Harry said.

'You see that!' The man must have noticed movement from Wootan. 'He ain't gone! You know that CPR stuff? Compressions, right? You got a phone? We should call an ambulance!'

Harry stepped towards the man. He was much shorter than Harry. He tried to step back but his heel was wedged against the wall. He arched his neck to meet Harry in the eyes.

'He's gone,' Harry growled. 'He's beyond help.' He fixed the man in a stare. He nodded, it was hurried, and his lips broke into an uneasy smile.

'I get you . . . Fuck him! He ain't no friend of mine, yeah? This was just some place to crash and he was taking a big rent. All he did was mug me off.' The man chuckled. 'And at least I know you ain't no copper now, right?'

Harry stepped away. He snatched a baby-wipe that was reaching out of the packet and rubbed Wootan's neck where his fingers had searched for a pulse. He pushed the wipe into his pocket and slipped his leather glove back on. The man by the window now had his hands on his hips.

'Ain't no one else gonna be checking on him. You think I should call it in? I got a mate who's got a phone. Wootsy ain't got no family or friends no more. He pissed 'em all off! He could lay here for days, mate. I could call it in anonymous like.' The man shrugged.

Harry moved to the door and cast a last glance around the dingy room. 'Let him rot,' he growled.

'You too then!' The words followed Harry out of the door. There was laughter too, it sounded almost manic.

Harry made it out of the house and left the door swinging behind him. He pulled out his phone, fumbled over it then pressed it to his ear. He was still hearing a dialling tone as he clambered into his car, then it cut to voicemail. He cursed, cut it off and tried again with the same result. He checked his new watch: 06:32. He'd been sure Maddie would be up. Usually she was out for a run at this time. He dialled again. This time he spoke when the voicemail finally cut in.

'Hey, Maddie . . . It's me.' At that moment Harry regretted calling, it washed over him in a wave. He glanced back at the halfway house and hesitated. But he had to say something. 'Look . . . I made a mistake. This morning. Just now. I just needed to talk. I know I made a mistake. I'm not after anything. I just wanted to talk about it.' He exhaled and hesitated. 'I guess this was what I was talking about, when I said about how we call each other for opinions — to run something past them. Maybe I should take my own advice. It doesn't matter, okay? I'll see you at work. It's six thirty. I'll make my way in now, I think. If you get in early maybe . . . Maybe we can get a coffee. Okay . . .' He fizzled out, hung up and cursed again. The phone went back into his pocket and he started the car.

He had been a fool.

CHAPTER 20

Harry's face scrunched up as the car's display read *Maddie IVES calling*. He was back in Maidstone's one-way system, heading out.

'Hey, Maddie.'

'Harry, you okay?' She sounded out of breath.

'Yeah. Sorry. I shouldn't have bothered you.'

'Yes, you should. Like you said, that's what we do. You sounded upset?'

'I'm fine.'

'Okay, then. You still want that coffee, though? Maybe you can tell me just how okay you are?'

Harry rubbed his head. His very first reaction had been to call Maddie. He didn't even know why. Whatever his reason, it was fading now. Perhaps it was better he didn't talk about it. Not straight away. Not until he'd considered what he should say. 'It doesn't matter. It was nothing, really. Moment of weakness.' He waited for Maddie to answer. She took her time.

'There's this Harry Blaker I know. He's the sort of bloke where there's no such thing as a moment of weakness. I've turned back now. You've already ruined my run. I finally get Rhiannon out and I had to leave her to finish on her own! I have a training programme and we had a breakfast planned after. It's all ruined, Harry. You did that. The least you can do is buy me a coffee.'

'When you put it like that . . .'

'Usual place. I need a shower, so I'm an hour away.'

Harry glanced at the clock in the car. He'd probably need half that. It suited him. He could have some time on his own first. 'An hour it is.'

* * *

Harry headed straight into work. When he moved through the Major Crime floor at Canterbury Police Station he was accompanied by the sound of clunking overhead as the sensors to the strip lights activated. The blinds were drawn; the night duty DC was based out of Margate, so the office would have been left empty since 11 p.m. The sensors were slower than he was and his office was still half dark when he sunk heavily into his seat. When the light did erupt above his head he had to narrow his eyes. He ran his hand over his face and pulled his cheeks down, trying to massage some life into them. His eyelids felt heavy and his monitor was reflective enough for him to see that they looked puffy, too. He was exhausted. He'd only managed a few hours sleep and, since waking, had been through just about every emotion. Now he just felt empty. And foolish. The feeling was amplified by the silence of his office and he was surrounded by reminders of what he was, of the career choice he had made. He considered what he had risked, what he might have *done*. He shook his head.

Wootan was dead. Harry was sure of this. If he'd done what he could to save him he would almost certainly still be dead — but he hadn't. He had walked away, and he was damned sure Wootan's pickpocket had done the same. A few hours earlier and Harry might have considered this to be all that he wanted, but now he wasn't so sure. The image of Wootan laid out on that mattress stuck in his mind while the conversation with the man stood over him played over and over. Daniel Wootan was the epitome of a miserable existence. His life was nothing and allowing it to ebb away meant nothing. It might even have been his preference. By contrast, Harry stood to lose everything. He shook his head again and thought about what he should do next. He was pretty certain there was no CCTV in that block; he had looked for it on the way in. There was nothing council-owned; he knew that at least. If Harry still had a mortgage, he would confidently have bet that on the man stood over Wootan, the only witness, snatching the heroin that had just taken his mate's life and getting as much distance between him and that bedsit as he could. Harry's mind flashed with the possibility that it was a bad batch, that it might take the man's life, too, and then any possible lead back to him would be gone. He shook his head again — just for thinking it.

He *would* talk to Maddie. He needed to talk to someone. Someone he could trust. He knew she was sensible. She made good decisions and she would be able to do so without all the emotion and the anger that he was struggling to control. Maybe he would take up that offer of the counselling, too. Maybe this PTSD was a thing — certainly he hadn't behaved rationally. He looked over to the wardrobe in the corner of his office. He had some smarter trousers in there and a few shirts, a shaving kit and some shower stuff, too. There was a shower a few floors up. He felt like he needed it, as if a layer of filth and death was still clinging to him. It might make him feel better — more awake, at least — and Maddie would be here by the time he was done. He took a few more minutes just to sit, to try and calm his mind. When he walked out and towards the lift, the lights had to clunk on again.

* * *

'Good run?' Harry dropped into a seat opposite where Maddie was playing with a sugar sachet. He pushed her drink towards her and she sat back. She was eyeing him the whole time.

'No. The best bit about a run is not the start, when you're cold and maybe a little stiff, or the end when you're knackered and just want to go home. It's the middle bit. I was just about getting there when you called.'

'I didn't ask you to turn back.'

'Rhiannon was delighted! She thought it meant she could turn back too. I had to be quite insistent. She needs the training.'

'What did you tell her?' Harry suddenly stiffened a little.

'That the night duty DC had a query. That it was probably nothing but I said I would come in and take a look before they went off-duty. Nothing about you calling, don't worry!' Maddie smiled and her head cocked to one side. He knew she would be picking up on his tension. He would be exuding it and she was good at reading people.

'I'm not worried.'

'I'm playing with you, Harry, of course I am. Did you have a bad night?'

'A bad night?'

'Sleep. I assumed that was the issue?'

'Oh, well . . . yes. But that wasn't why I called. It was just a reaction. I think I just needed to speak to someone, you know. I wouldn't have called — I know you're into your running . . .'

'A reaction? To something that happened at six thirty in the morning?'

'Yes. I went out. Early. I don't know what time.' Harry was aware Maddie was staring at him. He was also aware that he'd started as if there was more to come. He was struggling to say it.

'You realise you called me and said you wanted to talk about something? You're not making it easy, Harry!'

'I went to his house. To Daniel Wootan's house. I don't know why, but I did. I couldn't sleep. I haven't been sleeping well for a while and I just made a decision. So I drove there.'

'You drove there?'

'That's right.'

'And what did he say, Daniel Wootan, when he saw you?'

'He didn't see me.'

'So you didn't talk to him?'

'No!'

'You say that like it's ridiculous, like *of course* you didn't speak to him. But you drove up there. What did you drive up there for?'

'I don't know, okay? I don't know why I drove up there. I didn't have a reason. I didn't go up there to speak to him.'

'Because you know how stupid that would be? Driving to his house in the early hours of the morning and knocking on his door? That would be pretty stupid, wouldn't it?'

'Yes, Maddie, I do know that.'

Maddie huffed. Harry could feel his face burning up. He tried to hide it by lifting his coffee cup. He lingered on taking a swig.

'Look, Harry, if this is something you need me to cover you for then you're going to have to tell me every—'

'It isn't. You don't need to cover for me. He didn't see me. I didn't talk to him. But I drove up there. I just wanted to tell someone. It's not like me — that's not what I do.'

'And you wanted someone to tell you that it's okay? That it's understandable and maybe someone else would have done exactly the same thing?'

'I don't need patronising, no. I know I've been an idiot. I'm not trying to justify it.'

'It's okay, Harry. You drove to the house of the man who was responsible for your wife's death and you sat outside. It's understandable. Someone else might have done exactly the same thing. Someone else might not have shown the same restraint, though. Someone else might not have come away and phoned their mate to tell them they'd been stupid. Someone else might have made everything a lot worse. Forget about this morning, it doesn't matter. But it is out of character. It isn't like you. Maybe this has hit you harder than you realise?'

'No. I know exactly how hard it's hit me. And my girls.'

'Your daughters? Are they struggling too?'

'Mel . . . She cuts herself.' And there it was. Harry had never said those words out loud before, certainly never to another soul and never so curtly. He had used *self-harmed* before to health professionals and counsellors. But that sounded different — like it wasn't such an issue. But *cutting* yourself . . . that was serious. That's someone with serious problems and that wasn't his Melissa. Except it was.

Maddie's expression didn't change. She wasn't surprised or horrified. She didn't baulk at him or immediately ask if she shouldn't be admitted to a mental hospital. He was wringing his hands. He felt where he had dug his nails in earlier. Maddie reached out and placed her hands on top of his. He felt her warmth. 'That must be really difficult. You're a miserable old bastard, Harry, but I know you have a big heart for those girls. It must be near to bursting.'

He bit down hard, the sudden wave of emotion catching him out. 'I'm here to protect them. That's all I have to do now. That's all that's left. To keep them safe. But how can you protect someone from themselves?'

'Go to the source. I assume Melissa has struggled with Wootan's release?'

'She has.'

'Is that why she cuts?'

Harry shook his head. 'This time maybe. She struggled with depression for a little while, too, before even . . . The harm stuff got quite bad when she was at school. It's all linked together. Robin was so good. She handled it in a way that I never could. I just couldn't get my head around it. She was a teenage girl with her whole life ahead of her. She should have been having the time of her life, not lying in bed all day. I know better now . . . but I was harsh on her. That just makes it worse. I know now.'

'You didn't understand.'

'I didn't try. I didn't have to.'

'Because you had Robin?'

'She was so many things. Most of them I didn't even realise. A big one was softening me for the kids — she was like my translator. She knew that I was frustrated with Mel because I wanted the best for her, because all I wanted — still want — is for her to be happy and I couldn't understand why she wasn't.'

'And now?'

'Now?'

'Now you understand?'

'She's ill. It's not her fault. But we got her on the level, between us all, and it was so hard. Then Wootan gets out and the media run with it.'

'And she takes a dip again.'

'She didn't tell me. Her boyfriend phoned me out of the blue. She was in hospital. She had a good go at it, went for the wrist.'

'She okay now?'

'I left her with Josh. He's a good kid.'

'Jesus! What does a bloke have to do to be good enough for Harry Blaker's daughter?'

'I never said he was good enough!' Harry managed a smile. He took another swig of his coffee and used it as an opportunity to peer round the café. It was quiet on the whole.

'You said you weren't sleeping.'

'Not well. I get off okay . . .'

'Nightmares?' Maddie probed.

'Sometimes. Sometimes I just wake up. I couldn't tell you why, but once I do there's no going back to sleep.'

'Have you spoken to anyone?'

'About my sleep? I tried some tablets the pharmacist recommended.'

'Counselling?'

'No!' It came out strong — maybe too strong.

Maddie sat back a little but she was smiling. 'How did I know you were going to say that?'

'It's not a pride thing.'

'Yes it is. That's exactly what it is. Grieving is a weakness, right?'

227

'That's not what I think.'

'Well, it shouldn't be. Grieving would be enough on its own, Harry. Plenty of people need help when they lose someone so close. But you were right there when it happened. I can't imagine what you saw that day, what you went through. Did you ever talk to someone about any of it?'

'The police.'

'The attending officers? Then the investigating officers you mean?'

'Yes.'

'What about Welfare? The job have a good setup. I've used them. It's what they are for.'

Harry had an instant reaction. He swallowed it. He sat back and considered it. He had never considered it before. 'I don't know. I don't like it being linked to the job.'

'Private, then. Or go and see your GP and get referred through.'

'Maybe you're right.'

'Maybe?' Maddie grinned.

'Maybe. You get nothing more than that.'

'That'll have to do then. Do you need to be here today? You could go see Melissa, see how she's getting on.'

'We're busy. I can't be taking time away.'

'Of course you can. There's nothing I can't handle. Just take a few hours to go see how she is. It'll make you feel better to know. Give me a call when you're done and I'll fill you in on whatever you missed.'

'I don't like missing anything.'

'Which is half your problem, Harry. You need to start looking after yourself. We have a dead body to investigate. He's not getting any deader. Take the morning.'

'And a blood-soaked boy. I still need to get up to speed on that.'

'No you don't! Our Rhiannon is doing a fine job. She has an update that even you will be impressed with! I'll catch up with her shortly. I owe her a coffee for ditching her this morning anyway! I'll make sure her update is part of your debrief so you won't miss a thing. Now, go and see your daughter.'

He finished the last of his coffee. He hadn't considered seeing Mel today, not during his working hours at least, but it didn't seem such a bad idea. The last he knew was a text message from Josh telling him they were heading home. He could check in at least. Be it work or home life, Harry couldn't stand not knowing.

'You sure you can cope?' Harry struggled to keep a straight face.

'For a man who doesn't like swearing, you have an uncanny ability to make me want to.'

CHAPTER 21

Once they left the coffee shop, Maddie stopped to lean against the rail outside. Harry turned a tight left to make for his car. She watched him pull up the collar on his waxed jacket then dig his hands into his pockets so that it pulled tight over his broad shoulders. He didn't look back. They had said their goodbyes and he was not one to linger.

But today he had been different. There was a vulnerable side to him that Maddie hadn't seen before. It made her happy. She felt a little bad about that, but he needed to open up to someone and she was delighted that he had chosen her. He disappeared out of sight and she turned her smirk down to check her phone. She'd sent Rhiannon a couple of text messages. The first was just after getting out of the shower: a short note asking how her run was and joking that she suspected Rhiannon had waited for her to get out of sight before immediately turning back. The second message was sent a few minutes earlier, when she was wrapping up with Harry: She let her know she was in the coffee shop near the police station if she wanted to walk round. Rhiannon was normally quick to respond, but there was no reply to either as yet. Maddie re-read her earlier message to make sure there was nothing in there to which she could have taken offence.

There wasn't and, besides, she didn't think she could offend Rhiannon if she tried. She was still keen to meet with her. Maddie was aware she had cancelled on her the previous day, but Major Crime was like that: you had to react to whatever was coming in. Rhiannon would understand, but Maddie still wanted to make it up to her. With Harry out for at least the morning, she could give her all the time she needed.

She pressed to dial her number. It rang out. The coffee shop was a lot busier than when she had first entered but she looked up as the door swung open for someone leaving and the queue looked to have almost gone. She pushed off the railing and stepped back in. It was just a few minutes before the start of her shift time. She would take Rhiannon a coffee back anyway and maybe grab another one herself.

The walk back was less than ten minutes, time enough for the heat to warm her hands a little too much and she was glad to be able to put the drinks down. She had gone straight to Rhiannon's desk in the range building. Rhiannon was stepping up to lead a team of DC's on day shift that week and they were filing steadily in. Rhiannon's desk had the look of a workplace that had been tidied the night before and not disturbed since. She pulled open the top drawer. Her day book was there. No on-duty detective would be out without it.

'Hey, anyone seen or heard from Rhiannon this morning?' she called out. There were shaking heads and shrugs. She checked her phone again. Still no reply. The DCI's door was shut firmly but there was murmuring behind it. She knocked twice and pushed it open.

'Sorry, one second,' the DCI said into his desk phone. 'Maddie? I'm on a call right now.'

'Sorry, sir, I know the door was shut. I just can't get hold of Rhiannon this morning. Has she called in sick?'

'Who? Rhiannon. Well, no, but she wouldn't call me direct. The sick line goes through to the FCR. I normally get a notification . . .' He huffed and thumped his keyboard to wake it up. He apologised again into the phone, which Maddie

231

knew was for her benefit, not for whoever was on the other end. His eyes searched his screen. 'No. Nothing on here.'

'Sorry to bother you.'

The DCI started talking again almost immediately. Maddie left the door open on purpose. She was a good few paces away when she heard it slam behind her. She was still smiling when she made it back to the stairs.

'Hey, you've called Rhiannon. Sorry I can't answer the call right now. I probably saw your name and ignored it. But leave me a message anyway — let's see if I call you back!' Rhiannon's cheeky voicemail message had always made Maddie smile. It didn't today.

'Rhiannon, it's me. I can't get hold of you this morning and you're supposed to be at work. If you're skiving that's just fine, but can you let me know? Call me back okay? It was only a short run! I'll head out your way anyway so that if you're really not well I can at least fill up your hottie bottie or something. And I can check, too. That you're unwell, I mean. I'll bring a thermometer. I can't promise to warm up the tip, and it isn't one for your mouth.' Maddie ended the call with a nervous laugh. She was back out to her car by now. She slid into the driver's seat and waited a few seconds to make sure her phone paired. Then she rolled up to the gate before turning in the general direction of Rhiannon's home.

* * *

Maddie had quickly fallen in love with Sandgate and she was reminded why when her vision was filled with the sparkling blue vista of the English Channel. She had found a place to park almost where her and Rhiannon had started their run earlier that morning. Parking in Sandgate could be a nightmare. It was genuinely her only grumble, but the road leading to this point was well hidden and part of a one-way system, so there were often spaces. The low wall separating the promenade from the beach was just visible through her nearside windows as she silenced the car. Stepping out was an assault on the senses. The warmth of the sunshine brought with it a sense of the changing season while the light breeze accompaniment bore a blend of every British seaside smell at once. A bold seagull cawed at her as it unfurled and folded its wings then continued to eye her with clear distrust as she moved away, keeping the sea to her left to head towards Rhiannon's flat.

The building was an impressive, whitewashed block. Maddie counted up to the third balcony on the left side, knowing it to be Rhiannon's. With the angle of her approach, she couldn't check the sliding doors at the back for any signs of life. The communal door was on the side, accessed through a gate that seemed to push back. There was a block of buttons on the wall. She pushed the one marked as *Appt 4* and rattled the door in its housing. There was a brief flicker of a light behind the button, nothing more. She pushed the button marked *Trades* while still tugging at the door as her impatience got the better of her. It was heavy, too, and she had to adjust her feet to get it open wide enough. Once inside, she walked up two flights. Every scuff of her foot seemed to echo off the clean walls that were broken up with an occasional block of colour on a canvas. They all had handwritten notices stating: *For Sale. All enquiries to Appt 6.*

Rhiannon's door was a crisp white. Maddie knocked straight away then stepped back to peer around the corridor. There were two more front doors on this corridor, one she had walked past that had the number six on it and one off at an angle behind her that showed as number five. Maddie knocked again. She knelt down to push open the letterbox. Her view was restricted by tight bristles. She did her best to part them but she could only see snatches of the interior behind. Maddie knew Rhiannon's flat well. In the summer she was a regular. They would take advantage of her balcony and stare out over the sea, toasting whatever career decisions had got them to this time and place. She knew the flat opened up almost immediately as you stepped through the door, but through the letterbox it was hopeless.

She thumped again, this time hard enough to sting her knuckles.

'Rhiannon! RHIANNON!' She leant against the door, desperate to hear a scuffle, to hear Rhiannon's voice that might be slightly annoyed and full of the cold that had come on sudden enough to catch her out. There was nothing. Then there was a sound. Maddie held her breath. It came from her left and she jerked her head towards it.

'Can I help you?' A middle-aged woman stood in the doorway of the neighbouring flat, the one Maddie had seen to be number six. She sounded annoyed. Her eyes flickered to take in all of Maddie.

'The artist, right? I love the pictures.'

The woman visibly warmed in an instant. 'I try!'

'My friend lives here. Do you know her?'

'Your friend? Do you hammer the door like that for all your *friends*?' She seemed to tense back up a little.

Maddie stepped closer. 'I'm worried about her. She didn't turn up for work today and that's not like her. When did you see her last?'

'Work? I don't even know what she does. Where do you work?'

''The council. We're both on the planning side. We've worked together for years and I don't think she's ever missed a day!'

'No. I hear her go out every day. I assumed she was shift worker from when she goes out and gets back. Not my business though.'

'And this morning?'

'This morning was early. She woke me up. Nothing you can do — these halls echo, I suppose. I heard her door go. It was before six.'

'So you generally hear her when she leaves?'

'I do.'

'And when she comes back?'

'I guess so. It's not like I'm listening out for her — she's a grown woman and none of my busin—'

234

'I'm not suggesting you do! And even if you were, it's good to have someone listening out for you. I wish I had that in my place.'

'Is she in some sort of trouble?'

'No. At least I certainly hope not!' Maddie tried a chuckle; she knew it would sound forced. 'What time did she come back?'

'I didn't hear her come back. I assumed she went out to work. She does do that sometimes. She'll have an early start.'

'You're sure? Did you go back to sleep?'

'I don't sleep very well, lightly at the best of times, but once I get woken up that tends to be me. This morning I started breakfast shortly after I heard her leave. I had the news on low but I can still hear what goes on. I can tell you, she never came back.'

'Thanks for your help. Could I leave my number with you?' Maddie was already scrabbling for a piece of scrap paper in her bag. She pulled out a post-it pad and leant on the wall to write her number. 'It's just for when she comes back, if you could let me know.'

'Can she not let you know herself? I don't really like the idea of reporting on someone. Especially when, with all respect, I have no idea who you are.'

Maddie nodded. She plunged back into her bag for her warrant card. She and Rhiannon had talked before about neighbours and keeping their day job a secret from them. She didn't want to be the one to break that, but this was an exception.

'I'm Detective Sergeant Ives.' She held out her card for the woman to see. 'I'm not prying. I'm just worried about her.'

'Is she in trouble with the police?'

'Not at all. It's a missing person investigation and we're pretty sure it's nothing. I think our Rhiannon has just gone out for the day and left her phone switched off, but I like to be sure. So if she comes back, could you either give me a call or maybe give Rhiannon a nudge to call me?' She handed the piece of paper over. 'I can give you a card if you like? They're more professional.' Maddie held one out. The woman beamed at it.

'Detective Sergeant, eh? I always wanted to be a detective! I'm just not sure I'm the right sort.'

Maddie smirked. 'Well, you do have to be comfortable getting your nose into other people's business. It's not for everyone. Do you mind if I take a contact number for you, too?' Maddie took out her book and copied down the woman's details. She put her number directly into her phone.

'Thanks for your help.'

The woman waited at her door and Maddie stared at her to prompt her to close it. Once she did, Maddie dialled Rhiannon again. She was certain there would be no answer. Surely the missed calls and messages would have prompted a response by now, but she could feel herself starting to panic. She'd had a tense knot in her stomach from the moment she had walked away from the police station that morning and it was only getting tighter. Rhiannon's recorded message clicked in. She was chirpy, her voice light and humoured. Maddie longed to hear it for real. She hesitated at the top of the stairs. She peered back over at Rhiannon's front door. She couldn't think where to go next, what to do. The only place there might be any answers was behind that front door. When someone was reported missing, the first thing you did was search their home address. Maddie knew she hadn't called it in yet, so Rhiannon wasn't officially missing, but there was no plausible explanation for her lack of contact.

She strode back towards Rhiannon's door with purpose. She didn't slow her momentum and brought her boot up to meet with the white wood. It flexed against the blow but remained sealed. She stepped back to launch herself forward again. The door flexed again, but this time there was a splintering sound that accompanied it. She was aware of the front door opening to her left, the same woman appeared. Maddie ignored the questions. The door took another two blows before it flung inwards and bounced off an interior wall. The sound echoed around the hall. Maddie stepped in. She was still aware of the woman's voice, she turned to it and saw that she was on the threshold.

'You need to stay out. This is a crime scene now.' The woman's eyes widened. She could barely contain her delight. She was actually rubbing her hands.

Maddie turned back to the room. The living room was neat. The kitchen was off to the left and open plan with the units running along the wall. She could see a plate stood up to drain next to the sink and a few items of cutlery too. Last night's dinner. No sign of a breakfast bowl. No signs of any disturbance either. The bedroom was off to the right and she could see the open door from where she was standing. She walked to it. The bed was against the far wall, the curtains tugged open. Rhiannon had always boasted that the first thing she did when she woke in the morning was to pull open those curtains to the view. The bed was messy, the duvet pulled back from one corner and left folded like someone had got out in a hurry. A dressing gown was thrown onto the bed. It was lying beside a pair of neatly folded trousers and a white shirt, Rhiannon's usual choice of work clothes. They were the only things not stowed away in the fitted wardrobes. Maddie moved to the en-suite bathroom. The shower unit was glass and enclosed, she tugged the door open to find it bone dry. Maddie knew that Rhiannon had gone out for their run. Now she also knew that she hadn't made it back.

Maddie stumbled over her phone, nearly dropping it as she tugged it out of her trouser pocket. Her hand shook as she pressed to dial a number. She walked back out into the living room area. The phone picked up on the second ring.

'Harry . . .' She was breathy until she composed herself. 'Harry, it's Rhiannon. She's missing. It's not right. It's not right at all.'

'Where are you?' The gruff reply was instant.

'Stood in her flat. Sandgate.'

'I'll be right there.'

'Your daughter . . .' Maddie couldn't manage any more. It was as if the panic that had been building slowly was now choking off her words.

'She's fine. It's job done here. I'll be with you in fifteen.'

Maddie ended the call. Her eyes fell to Rhiannon's shoe rack, a hole where her designer running shoes would normally sit.

'Where the hell did you go?' Maddie breathed.

CHAPTER 22

Harry's finger hovered over the button to make the call, but he pulled back quickly. He hadn't been exactly sure where Rhiannon lived, but the sight of Maddie pacing down a short side road leading directly to the sea answered his question. She was hovering by the entrance door to a white building with a phone held to her ear. She looked up to the sound of his approaching car and seemed to end her call abruptly. She stood at his door as he opened it.

'I've made some calls. I checked again with the FCR and the boss. She hasn't called in. She's gone, Harry. And not in her car — that's still parked round the corner and it's stone cold. I don't think she ever came back from her run. I kicked in the door to her flat, her running shoes are gone, her clothes for work are laid out . . . That's about all I know! Where do we start?' Maddie was close to panic. Harry hadn't seen her like this before.

'Okay, start from the beginning and slower. What do we have?'

Maddie seemed to take a breath. 'She didn't turn up for work — that's never happened. I tried calling and her phone just rang out, so I came out here. I spoke to a neighbour. She went out early, the right time to be meeting me. We went for a run. She was fine. We ran along the promenade until you called and I turned back. We would have been halfway then, so she would have had another five-k to do.'

'Do you know her route?'

'Yes. It's the same one I do. Through the coastal park and up the zig-zag steps, then along the Leas and back down the hill.'

'Did you see anyone else?'

'Anyone else? This morning? No. No one. We need to walk that route; we should do that now.' Maddie set off, Harry held his ground and called out after his colleague.

'Is the flat secure?'

Maddie stopped. Her head was shaking fast. 'I pulled the door back to. It will push open though. The lock popped, there's a little damage but it pushes closed.'

'We need to stay with it. Who else have you spoken to?' Harry stepped back to take in his surroundings as he listened for the answer. The seafront consisted mainly of tall buildings that contained flats and maisonettes, all designed to take advantage of the sea view. He could see some of the High Street from where he stood. This was made up of tightly packed houses and then a row of shops with flats overhead.

'What if she's laid out somewhere? What if she had a turn on the run and she collapsed? We should walk it. I could run it even . . .' She stopped. Harry had his hands out, she had paced back a little closer.

'It's a nice day,' Harry said. 'The promenade here is always busy. If she was lying on a path she would have been found. When you spoke to the FCR, did you ask if there might be any linked calls from the area?'

'Yes, I asked that. There's only one call for the whole area and that's an RTC on the way to Hythe.'

'Okay, so we can be pretty sure she's not there. But something relevant might be. Go back upstairs and stay with the flat. We'll get a search team out. Is she reported as a misper?'

'Yes. I spoke to the DCl. We shouldn't be lacking resources.'

'No. The whole world will want to turn out to this. You live here right?'

'Just round the corner.'

'What's open at six a.m.?'

Maddie was shaking her head, it looked like an unconscious thing that she didn't even realise she was doing. Her speech was fast and breathy. 'Nothing. The coffee shop a bit further down the road sometimes sets up early. They open at seven. We go there, too. They'll know her.'

'Okay. Anywhere else?'

'Not that I know of.'

Harry peered across the road. 'Go back up to the flat and stand with it. I'll free you up as soon as we get more officers here. I'll start knocking doors in the meantime. The shops opposite seem a good place to start.'

'Okay.'

'You okay?' Harry said.

'No, not really, Harry. I don't like this at all. This is nothing like her.'

'I agree. We'll get to the bottom of it. It's a missing person search and she hasn't been gone long. We're good at these, Maddie. Remember that. We just need to go through what we do.'

'Okay. Thanks, Harry.'

Harry watched her step back through the door. He hoped he had been effective at hiding his true concerns. His smartwatch said 11:00 hours. The optimum time to start a search that might lead to a successful conclusion was long gone. They were already chasing shadows. He took advantage of a lull in the traffic to cross the High Street, taking in his surroundings as he walked away from the sea. When he made the pavement on the other side he turned to see if he still had a view of the communal entrance to Rhiannon's building. He did, but only just. Very few buildings would have a view of Rhiannon's front door and it was highly unlikely that she had returned here anyway. But Harry was using the walk to clear his head more than anything. He needed to try and work out their next move and he needed to be away from Maddie's panic to do that. No one had called in reporting finding Rhiannon on her run-route. That was good and bad. Good that she hadn't been found lying injured or worse, bad because it meant that wherever Rhiannon was, Harry was now certain it was a long way from here.

CHAPTER 23

Harry's pace was a fast walk. The path was flat and a light grey in colour that flared a bright white when the sun emerged. He reckoned they were halfway around the curve he had seen from their starting position. On their left were expensive-looking homes dug into the hills, on their right was the sea, but it was further away here. The pebbled beach was a long stretch that dipped away sharp enough to conceal the shoreline. Maddie was close behind; the first arriving patrol to arrive had been directed to relieve her at the flat. There were a lot more resources on their way but Harry wanted to walk the route as soon as possible. There was nothing of significance from the people living or working near to Rhiannon's flat. He hadn't expected anything. Now his attention was downward. It was a cursory search at best, too fast to be truly effective. He would get the search team to do it again, his check was for anything obvious; anything from a smattering of blood or a clump of hair to personal items dropped or torn off. But this was a good area. Harry was pretty sure that if anything obvious was on the path, they would have had a call about it. He had almost convinced himself that this search was entirely pointless.

'We're two miles in, Harry,' Maddie said. 'The path splits when you get into the wooded area. One way goes through the park, the other goes round the outside and carries on as the prom. We always run through the park. We stay on that path to the end, then the route doubles back to go up Remembrance Hill to the Leas and we then come back down some steps. We run this bit of the path twice.'

Harry was pulled from his darkening thoughts at just the right time. He needed something to focus on. 'Remembrance Hill is quite a way from here. Can you get on the air? Any patrols arriving . . . have one start from that end and meet us in the middle. Another patrol can start on the Leas.'

'No problem.' Maddie immediately lifted her phone and her voice drifted over him as they came to where the cover of trees started and the paths split. He slowed to take it in. The path that pushed into the park was wider than it had looked from a distance. The edges had flat soil beds and a low wooden fence on both sides. The left side remained soil, but it rose quickly and was punctured by wild ferns, grasses, and mature tree trunks that got thicker as they moved up the slope. On the right, the trees were more juvenile, the grass longer and denser, and the ground looked to be covered by bits of chopped bark. Most of it was flat, almost pristine, but there was a patch that looked disturbed, where some errant bits of bark had been pushed out onto the path, like a foot had been dragged through it. A squirrel fidgeted at the base of a tree. It didn't seem to take much notice of them and it didn't seem to be disturbing the ground either.

Maddie had stopped, too. She was still talking on her phone. Harry lifted his head. The path curved left around the steep cliffs that seemed to protrude more and more into the park as they went. He took a few steps forward, looking left and right as he moved. He stopped ten metres in and turned to look back out over the path they had just walked. It was still a bright white and it curved away into the distance. If he took another few paces he would have been around the bend and the path would be hidden, as would anyone approaching. He looked over to where the ground sloped upwards to eventually meet steep cliffs a third of the way up. The ground here was scuffed, too, but it was more like a trail that moved up behind a boulder. He moved closer, careful to stay on the path. A footprint was clear. It was smudged, as if someone had pushed off from there rather than walked over it. He looked back at the path. From here the view was excellent and it would only get better if you could get elevated.

His eyes moved directly opposite to where the disturbed bark was lying on the path as if it had been kicked out. Beyond that, he could see spindly trees and a thick bush to their right. He moved across the path, his eyes fixed on the bits of bark, then he looked up to the trees. He stepped into the hedgerow. Now he was closer, he could see something: it looked like a brown stone stuck to the other side of the tree and at eye level. He moved closer. Just another step was enough to reveal more: it wasn't a stone — it was a knife handle! He stepped around to see where the blade was stabbed firmly into the trunk. The knife flexed a little, Harry must have disturbed the trunk as he passed. He swore loudly.

'You alright in there?' Maddie called out. Harry could see her through the thin trees.

'You gave your details, when you went to the café, right?' Harry growled back.

'My details?'

'When you went out to meet the informant who called in from the phone box — the one who mentioned the boy's dad — you gave out your card, right?'

'Yes. To the waitress.'

'And Rhiannon's details?'

'I wrote them on the back.'

'I know you did.'

Harry heard the snapping of twigs and the sound of branches flexing against Maddie's clothing as she pushed her way through to him.

'What has that got to do with anything?'

Harry stepped back. He was still staring at the flexing knife. Maddie saw it too. She would have seen it pressed an inch into the slim trunk, hard enough to expose the green of the tree's insides. She would have seen the point dissecting the name *Maddie Ives* on the front of one of her business cards and if she dipped her head slightly, she would be able to read her own handwriting on the back, where Rhiannon's name and contact number were scribbled. And under that where she had written *pancakes and coffee* in writing that was distinctively different.

'What? H-how is this p-possible?'

'What did you do? When he didn't turn up? When you left the café? Were you careful like I told you to be?'

'Careful?'

'You took a cover car. They were behind you when you left. Did you get a gap — deviate at all to see if anyone followed? You know better than anyone what I mean.' Harry did nothing to hide the anger in his voice. 'I told you to be careful, to treat it like a hostile meeting. Did you do that?'

Maddie shook her head. 'It was just a line of enquiry, a standard—'

'Standard! It was an appointment where somebody else was directing your movements entirely. It can happen. But we take precautions because we don't know what we're walking into! You know better.'

'I do . . . I didn't . . .'

'What did you do? When you left?'

'We drove back to Canterbury. To the police station.' Maddie's voice was a monotone, her eyes down to the floor, her face a mask of shock.

'Direct?'

'I . . . yes. Direct.'

Harry shook his head and pushed his way back out onto the path. He pulled his phone roughly from his pocket. Maddie followed him out.

'But . . . here? It makes no sense . . .'

'*Still?*' Harry spat. 'This still doesn't make any sense to you? I assume you didn't take any notice of any cars that might have been following, or of anyone out of the ordinary?'

'We were talking . . . about the case . . . with the boy . . .'

'And when your shift ended what did you do then?'

'What do you mean? I just went home.'

'You drove directly home? Were you parked in the police station car park? Did you go from there?'

'I was . . . I always do . . .' Maddie was still breathy, her voice even weaker now, murmuring to herself. 'But . . . how . . . I mean, what has this got to do with Rhiannon?'

'Really, Maddie? Your arranged meeting didn't show. So you drive straight back with no cover car watching your back, chatting about who-knows-what. Then you leave in your personal car from the station car park and you drive straight home, still not paying attention, I assume. You go for a run every day, right?'

'I have been.'

Harry shook his head, his anger building. 'And the same time, same route, you said. All your training, Maddie . . . You've forgotten who you are. You've forgotten *what* you are! Rhiannon is gone. She's gone because of you!'

Maddie's eyes were wide and unblinking, now they rested back on Harry.

'But if someone followed me, why take Rhiannon?' Her eyes flicked back to the tree, where the blade still stuck out from puncturing her name. She sucked in a breath, her hand went to her mouth and she stepped back out onto the path. She turned left and walked with purpose the way they had come. Harry watched as she emerged from the cover of the trees to be drenched in the sunlight. She stumbled a little and her body drooped to the point where she was bent double, her hands rested on her knees. He knew this was her moment to realise what he had already. She turned back to him. He had stayed still, his phone still in his hand, and she had to shout for him to hear. He could hear the strain in her voice.

'I got to here, Harry! You called me and I turned back, but I was right here!' Harry didn't reply, but he did start to walk towards her. Her attention fell back to the floor as if she was searching for something. As he got closer, he could see that her eyes were glazed over. She was lost in thought, close to being consumed by panic. She lifted her head as he got close to her.

'It was supposed to be me, wasn't it?'

'Yes,' Harry said. His anger was seeping away a little. Maddie was suffering; he could see that. She had been careless and she was now realising just what that meant, but he had been taking out his own frustration on her. He should have been here. He should have been focussed on the investigation, on watching his colleague's back. But he wasn't. He was sitting outside a halfway house, useless and bitter.

'Whoever this is . . . why did they want me?' Maddie said.

Harry put his hand out to rest it on her shoulder. He leaned in, forcing her to make eye contact with him.

'We find that out. We find Rhiannon. Simple as that. I need you focussed, Maddie. I was harsh. This isn't your fault.'

'Focussed? You were right . . . I've forgotten who I am. I've been careless.' She stiffened. 'We need to find her, Harry. I need to put this right. I messed up!'

Harry nodded. '*We* need to put this right.' He detected a quiver in her lips. He *had* been too harsh. He needed to build her back up.

'And we will.'

CHAPTER 24

'Coffee?' Harry said then turned away from his colleague before she had a chance to reply. He pushed open the door to Loaf Café on Sandgate's High Street. A young woman smiled from behind a counter to his left. 'Black coffee, strong,' he said. He turned to where Maddie stood in the doorway. She still held the door open and stared at him.

'You want to get a coffee? *Now?*'

They had walked the path back to Sandgate's seafront just as soon as a search team had turned up to do a more thorough search. Harry had asked for hands and knees and raking up the bark. They would fan out from where the knife was still pushed through Maddie's card. It would be painstaking and slow at a time when they needed to be anything but. Harry had also seen the CSI van flash past. Their focus would be on the knife, initially, he couldn't see too many other forensic opportunities there, but they would also survey the wider area. A fingerprint hit was the best they could possibly hope for; it could give them a swift result. DNA could provide something in twenty-four hours but even that might be too long. Harry wasn't hopeful. Even the dumbest burglars these days were aware enough to put a pair of gloves on.

He considered that they needed to stop and think. They couldn't rely on the scene to give them the answers quick enough. Maddie was the key, and right now she wasn't functioning. Harry knew this was partly his fault; he had reacted badly. He was struggling to fix it. She had taken herself away to sit on the low wall of the promenade while they had waited for the search team. She looked to be staring out to sea, no doubt using Harry's words to beat herself up.

'We need to step back for a moment and talk it out,' he said.

'What? We need to be out there finding her, Harry!'

'Go and sit down.' Harry's anger flooded back all at once, it was all he could do to conceal it in a hiss. He turned back to the young woman who was still peering at him over the counter. He felt Maddie bang into his arm as she pushed past him.

'And a white coffee.'

The woman nodded. Harry sucked in a breath to calm himself then walked over to the table Maddie had occupied. She was sitting with her back to him, her phone to her ear.

'Who are you calling?'

'Vince. I missed his call. He's heard what's going on. He wants to come in early for his nightshift to help. I figured he could come in and crew up with me. He can—'

'Hang up the fucking phone, Maddie,' Harry snarled.

Maddie's mouth flapped open. He leant forward, his eyes fixed on her, refusing to let her off the hook. He heard a tinny version of Vince's voice from the phone's speaker. '*Hello? Mads? Hello?*' She lowered the phone and ended the call without breaking away from Harry's stare. Her face and neck were suddenly flushed. The phone started vibrating almost immediately. Maddie let it ring out on the table. The silence between them remained for another few moments.

'We need to stop and we need to think. Someone pre-planned the abduction of a police officer. They were waiting for you while holding a large hunting knife. Why?'

'I don't know!'

'Your previous life . . . your undercover work in Manchester . . . any suggestion that has followed you down?'

'Nothing I am aware of.'

'The media releases for the boy covered in blood, or Jarod Logan for that matter . . . did your name get mentioned at any point?'

'No. Why would it?'

'Okay, then. Let's run with the assumption that the person making that call from Stone Street set up that meeting. Let's further assume that same person followed you out and is responsible for taking Rhiannon. That being the case, we have three options as I see it. First, that person was targeting the officer on the case because he has some link to that boy and is upset that there's an investigation at all. Second, they have nothing to do with the boy but they have become aware of you running it and they saw an opportunity to isolate you. Third, their intention was to isolate a police officer, *any* police officer, and this gave them an opportunity.'

'I don't think it can be about me. If we're saying I was followed home from work then they know where I live and there would be other opportunities. Taking Rhiannon makes it *less* likely of getting another chance at me. And my card at the scene . . . that wouldn't make sense either? If you're after me, don't tip me off.' Maddie was starting to think again.

'The card as a whole doesn't make sense,' Harry said, 'unless it's someone you upset in Manchester and they are trying to mess with you maybe? Make you suffer?'

Maddie shook her head emphatically. 'The people I was in amongst up there are vicious criminals, of course they are, but they're business people, too. They would deal with a problem like me quickly and quietly. I would suffer, I know that, but it wouldn't be like this. I would just disappear — no one else involved. No clues stuck to a tree either.'

'Okay. So we're left either with someone linked to the boy or an opportunist targeting police and after anyone they can isolate.'

'I'm not sure which one is more likely,' Maddie said.

'It doesn't matter anyway. We need to cover off both. But the business card . . . that's our biggest lead.'

'It's our only lead, really.'

'Which means we know where to go next, doesn't it.'

'It does?' Maddie suddenly looked excited.

'It does. And you need to make some calls on the way. Your old boss up in Manchester for one. We just need to be sure there's nothing on their radar about you. We don't rule anything out completely. Then we need to call someone on Rhiannon's team. We need that update we kept putting off. We need to know everything Rhiannon found out and everything she did to get it. *Everything*. Get what you can over the phone but we'll need to run through any material Rhiannon has in her day book — anything on her desk, too . . . any scraps of paper . . . her personal locker — everything.'

'Okay.'

Harry stood up over his full coffee. Maddie did the same. They both made for the door with new purpose.

* * *

Harry knew the Ports Café. He had stopped there on a pursuit driving course previously. It wasn't somewhere he had ever wanted to return to. He thought it an ugly building overall. It looked like it had started its life as a small, detached bungalow, but was now extended on just about every side, growing to match the increase in passing trade. Distinctive green tiles formed a sloping roof that looked to be reaching out and gathering in the newer built areas that jutted out of its base. The whole of the extended front and its two sides were largely glass and the sun was aimed straight at it. The patrons sat to the front had pulled cheap-looking blinds to try and abate its strength. It seemed that spring had arrived all at once.

The café was in the throes of its lunchtime rush. Harry took a moment on the threshold. He immediately matched a couple of middle-aged men sat on their own at separate tables to one of the numerous lorries stacked in silent formation on the area of hard standing they had just crossed. It was just as easy to match the numerous tables of tradesmen to the transit vans and the family taking their elderly parents out for lunch to the polished, seven-seater MPV that was nose-in and close to the entrance door. No one looked out of place. Harry walked to the empty counter. He was aware of Maddie close behind him. The door to what Harry assumed to be the kitchen was just beyond it. He considered just pushing through and announcing himself but decided he would wait — for a minute at least.

The door opened in half that time. A man walked out backwards. He turned to reveal two laden plates. He didn't acknowledge the two detectives or break his step to sweep past them and out onto the café floor. When he returned, he took a pad out from his apron pocket and put it down on the counter. His pen was readied.

'What can I get you?' He cleared his throat as he finished his sentence. His voice sounded strained — a sign of tension, perhaps? There was an accent, too. Harry thought it might have been Italian.

'Maybe I should get you a wet-wipe?' Harry said. The man looked up at last. He looked puzzled at first then his face broke into a nervous smile. He lifted hands that were blackened at the fingers. It looked like dried grease, the sort that gathered on an engine bay.

'I have scrubbed and scrubbed. They are clean, believe this or not.'

'And your jeans?' Harry said. The man's black apron was by far the cleanest part of him. It looked brand new, still with straight lines running down the material like it had just unfolded from a packet. In contrast, his blue jeans seemed to have the same black dust over most of both legs, with the knees taking the brunt.

'These are probably a lost cause, no!' He still wore a grin but it dropped away pretty quickly. Probably when he realised Harry did not.

'You don't strike me as the waiter type.'

'You got me there!' the man replied. 'I help out sometimes in here when it gets busy. But I can help when the trucks need a bit of attention, too. This is my main job.'

'This is busy is it?' Harry made a show of looking round. They were still the only people at the counter. None of the tables appeared to have anyone still waiting for service. The man shrugged.

'The woman who works here . . . I assume she's just out there in the kitchen?' Harry said.

'Woman?'

'The waitress. My colleague, here, met her last time she came in.'

'Her apron was a little more worn in,' Maddie said.

The man glanced at her very briefly. 'I can take your order. There are gloves — new ones. I'll put them on to bring your food. I was just in a rush.'

'A rush?' Harry had no doubt of that. The man looked like he had been dragged from a truck repair and pushed into the kitchen while an apron was hurriedly lifted over his head. Maybe around the time the two officers had entered.

'I hear the pancakes are good.' Maddie said.

The man had readied his pen again. He was leaning over it, using it as something on which to focus. Harry waited for him to look up. It took a count of two.

'They took those off the menu. Shame. They were my favourite, too!' The man seemed to force a chuckle.

'That is a shame,' Harry said. He fell silent. The man was back to staring down at his pen.

'So . . . anything else?'

'You know who I work for, right?'

The man looked nervous. 'You ask a lot of questions, you see a lot of things, so I think you must be police.' He snorted to show that he found that amusing. Harry didn't.

'Are you known to the police? Do you have a record?'

The man's eyes flickered from Harry to Maddie and back. His tongue flickered out to wet his lips. He leant on the counter, his arms locked out and tensed.

'Are you here for food or are you here for me? I am just worker here!'

'I get that. The waitress who was here . . . it's very important that I speak with her.'

'The waitress?' Now he pouted like he was unsure.

'She works here,' Maddie said. 'I met her.' She stepped forward, too, increasing the pressure on the man.

'Sure, I know who you mean. She is not here.'

'She's not?' Harry said. He had been leaning forward on the counter. Now he pushed off and stepped back. He turned to a shuffling noise. Someone else had joined the queue behind them. The waiter looked delighted, as if it might let him off the hook. Harry had no intention of doing that.

'I will be with you in just one minute, thank you,' the man said. He fixed back on Harry and shrugged.

'She is not. I am cover. So if I cannot get you anything I will need to serve these nice people here.'

'You have her name and phone number though, of course you do. I'll take that for now.'

The man shrugged again. 'I do not. I do not speak with her away from here. There is no need.'

'Her name?'

'I don't know. We don't really work together. She is not the talkative type, you know.'

'Excuse me, are you in the queue?' Harry heard a voice behind him. Maddie answered it firmly:

'Yes.'

'I need to help these people. This is business here. We cannot be upsetting customers!'

'My colleague here gave her card over.' Harry paused, but not for a verbal confirmation — he knew he wasn't going to get that. 'Do you still have it?'

'Not to me she did not.' He stepped further back, his hands lifted. He glanced back to Maddie, who stayed quiet.

'But you know about it?'

'I know nothing about this!'

'Of course you don't. There's a manager, right? An owner?'

'Not here.'

'No one else is here?'

'No one else. This is why I am here! I just fix some lorries. I use the site. It is an agreement. Sometimes I help out if they are really in need.'

'Who pays you?'

'This is not for pay!' he laughed as if the notion was ridiculous.

'You work for free? Out of the goodness of your heart?'

'The drivers . . . they have petty cash — a budget to keep their lorries on the road for minor repairs. I speak with them. I help them with the work. Maybe with the parts. They do not know England. I can source what they need.'

'I bet you can.'

'I can. They pay me for this; it is how I earn my money. The people here . . . they let me use the site. They do not let anyone else. It is a good deal. Sometimes I help in here to keep them happy. I need to keep them happy!'

'The card . . . where is it?' Harry flicked back to his original question, trying to catch him off guard.

'I do not know! Maybe she throw it away?'

'What makes you say that?'

'Because you want me to say something! I do not know.'

Harry moved back to leaning on the counter, this time his fists took his weight, he pushed himself so far forward he could feel pain in his knuckles. 'She might be dead,' he growled. It was out of the blue, out of context to someone who had no idea what he was talking about, but the man opposite him froze, all his movements stopped, his lopsided smile dropped away, as if Harry's words had frozen time itself. It was just for a moment, but long enough.

'Sorry?'

'Maddie, here, she came here before with a young girl. She's twenty years old. She's missing.' Harry used another silence. The man stepped back again, avoiding eye contact.

'I need to find her. Her disappearance has something to do with *here*, with your pancakes. If you don't help me and something happens . . .'

'I do not know about this! I cannot help. I would help if I could. I do not want people hurt!'

'I think you *can* help. I think you know more.' The silence was longer this time but still it didn't prompt a response. 'I saw the cameras on the way in. What do they store to?' Harry moved on again.

'Store to?'

'We're going to need to review the footage. Some store to a hard drive, some to a cloud. I just need to know before I make arrangements for someone to come out and download what we need.'

'The CCTV does not work. I have never known it to.'

Harry scowled. 'This place is twenty-four-seven, right?'

'Yes.'

'People work here alone?'

'Sometimes. At quiet times I know there is one person here.'

'So you need security. You need CCTV.'

'There are cameras. Maybe they do the trick. Maybe she tells people they are working if there's any trouble, but this is not that sort of place. At night there are tired truckers until the early hours and then nothing really.'

'She?'

'The waitress. She does the nights. Sometimes she is here in the day, too. I do not know her pattern. She seems to be here a lot.'

'Anyone else?'

'Else?'

'She can't be the only person covering this place?'

'No. There are other girls. Young girls, they come in at the weekend. And there is an older lady who I think has worked here for a long time who does the mornings.'

'But today, is it just you?'

'Right now!'

'And your name? I assume you know that?'

His expression hardened a little. 'This is good for me. I do not find job easy here in England. I find it harder if I speak too much to the police.'

Harry stepped back. The people who had joined the queue were gone. He took a moment to look around the café, his attention moved to the outside, to where a lorry was turning slowly onto the hard standing.

'What is it that you source for these lorry drivers? Because I've been a detective for a long time. I've heard of a few different scams that seem to do the rounds. We know it goes on. A lorry driver with a small budget for repairs? That's not something that is too difficult to take advantage of if you know what you are doing. You just need a driver who can be sold an opportunity and a man who can print a receipt for work completed. Am I right?'

'About what? What is this you are saying?'

'And you said you can source what they need. Is that just parts for lorries? A man on the road may have other needs. Do you get yourself involved in that too?'

'You know nothing! You are making this up on spot! This is how I earn a living. I am honest man, making honest living and this is not easy. I work hard.'

Harry slapped his hands back down on the counter, loud enough to attract attention. 'So do I. I can assure you of that. I work tirelessly, and when I get hold of something, even just a scrap of something, I don't let it go until I've dug out every stinking detail. Do you understand? You do not want me crawling all over this place, over your receipts, your tax records, sitting with the Department of Work and Pensions who have an office next to mine at the station . . .' Harry let his words sink in for a moment. 'I assume you are claiming benefits?'

The man shrugged. 'This is not a job. This is a service to help. Sometimes they pay me for my trouble, but this is not a job!'

Harry's face twisted into a wide grin. He could feel the pulse in his temple and the counter pressing against his waist.

'You are a man stood in a café, in an apron, serving me a black coffee, extra strong. Maddie here will have a white coffee. We'll be sat over there. And seeing as you're not getting paid for your trouble, I wanna see you doing it for the love.' He turned away to sit down and Maddie followed him.

'Sit on the same side,' he muttered. She did as she was told. They both sat facing the counter at the closest table. Some people stood up from a table nearby, the same people who had been stood behind a few minutes earlier. They walked back to place their order. The man took it, but his attention remained with the two detectives in the form of hurried glances. Harry watched his every move. He was far from fluid in his actions; he didn't seem to know where much was. It was a couple of minutes before he brought their coffees over.

'Extra strong. The Italian way!' He tried a chuckle. Harry fixed him with a stoic stare and he hurried away.

They sat in silence. Harry had nothing to say and Maddie must have got the message. He sipped at his coffee. It was stronger than his usual even, at least three shots. The man fidgeted behind the counter for a while before taking a final glance in their direction, then disappeared through the door to the kitchen. Harry resisted standing up and following him in. He narrowed his eyes as he took another sip of his coffee. The door pushed open again a few minutes later. The same man reappeared and fidgeted some more behind the counter. Harry still stared.

When he finished his coffee he stood suddenly, his chair scraped loudly. Maddie stood too. He walked back to the counter.

'You enjoy the coffee?' the man said.

Harry pulled his card from his pocket and slapped it down on the counter between them.

'*My* card. I expect a call from your nameless waitress. If I don't get it, I will be back — and by then I will be in a bad mood. Do you understand?'

'I will pass on your message,' he said, but the grin was gone.

Harry was aware of Maddie's voice calling after him the moment they made it out of the café.

'We're leaving?' Maddie said the moment they were outside.

He didn't answer her until they were back in the car with the doors shut and the engine started. 'We are.'

'That waitress was there. It was written all over his face.'

'It was.'

'And we're leaving? She was avoiding us. Why would she do that? She knows something — something that can help. We've got nothing else, Harry. We can't walk away now!'

'We have to. We were getting nowhere and we don't have time to waste. We need to keep the pressure on. I don't know how just yet.' He pulled the car forward. The ground was bumpy and one of the front wheels clunked into a deep pothole.

'The CAD — the call that came in to arrange your visit here . . . it came from a phone box?'

'It did.'

'Close to here?'

'Not far. A couple of miles along the road — towards Lympne.'

Harry turned right out of the car park and onto the A20. They were silent again. Maddie's frustration was obvious, palpable even — close to boiling over. It was better that they didn't speak. The road was fast and straight so the village of Lympne was only a five-minute journey. The long, straight road also meant that he could see the red outline of a phone box from some distance away. He slowed, taking his surroundings in as he approached. The phone box stood on a junction. Both sides of the road at this point were fields. He could see some houses in the distance. All the places he had passed so far had been large and with a good amount of ground around them. When he reached the junction he could see some smaller houses, closer together and further up the road that turned off the main A20 and shrunk down to a single-track very quickly. He could see a sign labelling it as

Thorn Lane. The phone box stood out against the greenery. He couldn't recall the last time he had seen a traditional style phone box like this; the shiny red colour and the rounded roof were both present and correct, as were the slatted windows on all four sides. He could see the handset was hanging down as he stood out onto the road.

A car sped past and he turned to it. There was a 40mph speed limit here, it dropped from 60mph just long enough to take in this tiny cluster of houses and the junction and then it was back to the national limit. Harry didn't reckon that most people would slow at all. The road was just about wide enough to warrant the national speed limit, but the banks holding back the fields were a few feet high and butted up against the road. He moved away from the phone box, stepping past Maddie, who had got out of the car but hadn't moved any further. Her arms were folded. He walked to the other side of the road and peered left and right.

'What's the matter?' Maddie asked.

'If you wanted to use the phone you would have to drive here. Unless you lived in one of these houses.'

'Okay.'

'You wouldn't park in Thorn Lane. It's too narrow. So you'd park on the main road.'

'You would.'

'It's a quick road. You'd want to park somewhere you could get your vehicle out of the way.' Harry started back the way they had come and walked a hundred metres or so. Maddie called out something but he didn't hear what she said. Another car whooshed past — it had to have been doing more than sixty. He stopped where a car could pull in. It was an area where the steep banks levelled out enough and vehicles had pulled up. He could tell they had from the long grass that was flattened in a thick line — a tyre track. It looked to Harry like it had been driven over a few times at least. But a car parking here would still stick out in the road a little. Maybe it was enough to give them an opportunity.

261

'You think this was where he parked?' Maddie said. 'The man who made the call?'

Harry was squatting down and didn't answer straight away. He pushed the wild grass to one side to see the mud bank underneath. There was no chance of a tyre print; the grass flattened down to form a layer that would prevent an imprint in the mud. He stood back up.

'I do.'

'So we do some house-to-house. We knock all the doors in a mile radius and we ask if anything was parked up. We have the exact time he made the call on the CAD.'

'I agree. But I need to make a call. I need to get someone to speak to the media. They might be our best chance.'

'I heard the DCI was already planning on doing that. The press have got wind of a missing police officer somehow. They're going to use the interest around it to see if anyone's seen her.'

Harry stiffened. A car swept past in a roar of white noise. He waited for it to pass. 'Soon?'

'That was the impression I got. Why waste time?'

'What are they saying?'

'What you would expect. That Rhiannon was snatched from Sandgate seafront and appeals for any information.'

Harry ran his hand over his head. 'That might be a mistake.'

'A mistake?'

'A missed opportunity at least.'

'You're not making any sense.'

'We need to keep the pressure up. Putting an appeal out like that makes us sound clueless . . .' Harry fumbled over his phone.

'We're not clueless then?'

He put the phone to his ear. 'We might not be as clueless as they would like.'

'Surely we shouldn't reveal too much, either? Not if you're talking about a hunch. Doesn't that put Rhiannon at risk?'

'It's more than a hunch!' Harry snapped. Then he murmured as the phone rang out to voicemail. He hung up and dialled again immediately. This time it was answered on the second ring.

'Harry, I'm in the middle of something if this isn't urgent.' Julian Lowe's voice was a hissed whisper.

'Are you speaking to the press?'

'Not right now. But soon. I'm with the SLT discussing it now. They want me to do the speaking — we're just working out who will be sitting next to me. Is this urgent?'

'What are you telling them?'

'What? What do you think? That we have a missing officer! We have a picture of Rhiannon to put out and we want to know if anyone saw or heard anything that can help us find whoever took her.'

'Find whoever took her? What about actually finding Rhiannon? Before she comes to serious harm.'

'Well obviously! That's what I . . .' The DCI huffed. 'Look, Harry, you and I both know the odds when someone's been missing as long as she has—'

'She's not dead. And I can give you an alternative that still uses the media and might be more effective.'

'How do you know she's not dead?'

'Because he would have killed her there, if that was the intention. It was early in the morning. A wooded area. Nobody about. If the motive was sexual or a violent assault, we'd have found her body on that path or close to it. The tide wasn't right to dump a body, either. She would have just washed up on the beach a little further up.'

'Jesus, Harry,' the DCI exhaled.

'And the card left at the scene . . . It's a message. To us. I think we still have some time.'

'And you have a media release that solves all our problems?'

Another car sped past. Harry had to wait for the noise to pass.

'Dashcams. I want all people with dashcams that used the A20 within a two-hour time period to make themselves known.'

'Dashcams?'

'A lot of people have them now. Someone made a call from a phone box on the A20. They arranged to speak with our officers at a nearby café. I think it's linked to Rhiannon's disappearance. I think this call was to lure police officers — I just don't know why. I'm at that phone box now. It's pretty remote. They would have needed a vehicle. I'll send you exactly what I need you to say.' Harry stopped talking. Two more cars whooshed past in the silence that followed, a silence that had started with a clearer sigh from the other end of the phone. 'Please boss, you have to trust me on this one. Someone took her. They did it before six o'clock in the morning and from a remote location that they had the chance to choose carefully. And they knew they were planning on taking a police detective — they would be extra careful. There's no way they would have taken her anywhere where they could be seen by members of the public. We have an opportunity to put a bit of pressure on them here. I visited the café today. We need to keep up the pressure on that place and this is the only way to do that.'

'Do we have any definite link to this café? I haven't heard one yet.'

'No. Or I would be signing up a search warrant. But someone there knows something. With enough pressure we might get to know what. People under pressure make mistakes.'

'And sometimes they kill victims, too, Harry.'

'Sometimes they do.'

'That isn't what you mean by a mistake is it?'

'Of course it isn't. I need them to know that I'm not going to go away, that there are other ways of getting answers and they are better off helping me now.'

'I don't know, Harry. The SLT had already signed off on the release. It goes out in forty minutes. You want me to tell them to put the emphasis on a stretch of road that is — what, ten miles from where Rhiannon was last seen to put pressure on someone at a nearby café that *might* be linked?'

'We have house-to-house going on down in Sandgate. That covers any sightings of her or of any offenders. You don't need to put that out as an appeal. It's doubling up.'

'I thought the call from the phone box was just some crackpot after police attention?'

'I don't think it was.'

'You *don't think?* You want me to brief this out, to change our whole appeal on the back of something you *don't think?*'

'I'll call the Chief direct if you need me to.'

'I wouldn't do that. If I go with this, I may need to make it more palatable.'

'I'll send what I need you to say in a script. You'll just need to read it out. Please. You have to trust me on this one.'

Another sigh — deeper this time. 'I can't make any promises, Harry. I'd go as far as to say it's not likely. If I'm struggling to see your viewpoint on this, I can't see the SLT being convinced easily. Get me your script in the next ten minutes, or sooner. I'll need time to consider it.'

The call ended. Maddie was standing close.

'What did he say?'

'Bring up the details of the call that was made from here. I need another look.'

CHAPTER 25

Forty minutes later, just before 14:00 hours, Harry was back at the police station. Maddie was with him among a gaggle of detectives. Most of Major Crime and CID were back in and the nervous energy was tangible. They were all desperate to be tasked, desperate to help, just desperate to do anything.

The immediate response actions and subsequent searches were coming to an end and the house-to-house in key areas was just about done. Uniform colleagues were still knocking on doors but they had branched out. Just about every door in Sandgate would be knocked on by the end of the day, notwithstanding a long list to try again where they had found no one at home. Harry knew it was frivolous; when Rhiannon Davies had disappeared, the world had largely been asleep. But they had to do all they could.

This media appeal was their last hope. Harry was sure of it. But the subject matter was key and Harry had no idea if his pleas with the DCI had fallen on deaf ears and the agreed script had remained unchanged. He still had an unshakeable feeling that the call that had prompted Maddie and Rhiannon to visit that café was linked to the disappearance, a feeling that had only deepened since he had attended the place himself and talked with a man who had looked decidedly out of place in an apron. He was so convinced in the involvement of that café that he had even found himself calling the superintendent to discuss surveillance authorities. But he was unprepared and had made a fool of himself. That wasn't something he did often. He had wanted something set up on the Ports Café, on the staff going to and from. The superintendent had listened to the request, readied a pen, and then asked for the justification. Harry had applied for surveillance authority before; he knew how it worked. It was one of the most intrusive policing tactics available. The justification required was colossal and you had to demonstrate how you had considered future court processes and legal challenges from the highest courtrooms in existence. Surveillance was a breach of a person's human rights, no less. And yet Harry had nothing more than a feeling. He tried to put that into words, into something tangible, but he had failed. He was unprepared and desperate, and he couldn't help but sound like it. The superintendent was someone he had known a long time, he felt like there was a mutual respect, but it wasn't enough — not nearly enough. The subject was quickly moved to how he was doing since his 'time off'. It was humiliating. Harry knew what he meant; he knew that he was being questioned for even making the call in the first place. The superintendent had finished the call by asking how this might play out if the situation was reversed. *'Would you give me authority, Harry? With what you have presented and knowing that it's in your name as the authorising officer?'* It was the worst end possible: Harry effectively calling a superintendent to refuse his own permission.

Now he watched an oversized TV screen clinging to the wall of one of the Major Crime briefing rooms, knowing that it really did represent their last chance. It was the same room where he and Maddie had stood just a few days earlier while Jarod Logan's gruesome end was projected onto the wall. The projector screen was rolled up now and put neatly to one side — just like that whole investigation. Harry tried to put that out of his mind. He would always prioritise the living over the dead and he had to believe that Rhiannon was still alive.

The television was tuned into the BBC News channel. The screen was busy, there were two talking heads split into two smaller screens and a blood-red banner running along the bottom: *Breaking news — Lennockshire Police update on possible kidnap incident.* The newsreader looked stern as she sat behind a desk. The talking head in the box next to them was suddenly replaced by the image of a longer desk with three empty seats. There was a cluster of microphones in front of each and the occasional flash as a member of the gathered paparazzi got their eye in. A graphic appeared showing that someone was turning the volume up.

Harry rubbed his top lip and his finger came away damp. The box with the empty desks suddenly expanded to fill the screen and the flashes became constant. DCI Julian Lowe emerged. Harry's hands were fists that he squeezed tighter and his chest felt almost too tight to breathe. He knew this was it. If they came out with their original, dry appeal asking for witnesses on a deserted seafront at 6 a.m., the pressure was off the people who had taken Rhiannon and it was all over. They would never find her — not alive. Harry had never been more convinced of anything. He'd sent off his script like the DCI had asked, he'd tried to type out a reasoned justification too, but had deleted it all and replaced it with simply, *trust me.* It was just fifteen minutes since he had ended a call with a superintendent when an appeal to *trust him* had been not nearly enough. This had to be different.

'Ladies and gentlemen, thank you for coming.' A woman was seated in the centre. Harry didn't recognise her but she went on to introduce herself as the Head of Media Operations for the force. She introduced the man to her right as the Deputy Chief Constable and then to her left DCI Julian Lowe as the Senior Investigating Officer for the case. The Deputy Chief then took his turn to give a stern and generic, pre-prepared statement, in which he appealed for the help of the general public and thanked them for their assistance to this point

so far. He handed over to DCI Julian Lowe to provide the specific requirements. The camera had been taking in all three officers but now moved to focus on the DCI. He thanked both persons who had spoken already, shuffled a paper and pushed his glasses back up his nose. When he finally looked up to the room, he was immediately flashed a hundred times.

Thank you for being here today. You, as the gathered press, are our mouthpiece to the people of the UK in our time of need. The reports are correct . . . Lennockshire Police have a missing police officer. But she is more than just a member of the police family . . . she is a member of her own family. She is also a friend and decent member of the community who spends her days trying to make Lennockshire safer for all of us. We are asking for that work to be repaid.' Harry ran his tongue between his lips as DCI Lowe paused. So far, nothing he had said was part of his script, but he hadn't got to the appeal yet. This was it.

'The circumstances of her disappearance mean that we cannot rule out foul play.' The DCI looked up again and his glasses reflected another glut of flashes. Harry tensed his jaw. He felt a run of sweat on his temple; he was burning up in there.

'Unfortunately, for operational reasons I cannot reveal these circumstances or any more details just yet. What we are asking for is very simple and any members of the public who live in, or have travelled through the county of Lennockshire may be able to assist us — specifically, anyone who has a functioning dashcam who has travelled the A20, Ashford Road between Ashford and Langthorne — any part of it. We would like for you to get in touch. It might just be that your dashcam's memory is storing a vital piece of information, the sort of information that can assist us with finding this young woman. The number is on the bottom of the screen. This goes directly to the incident room, but you can also call us on 101, come into any of our stations or make contact with us in any way you know how. Please . . . get in touch and do it as soon as possible. Thank you.'

The room erupted into a cacophony of voices as the camera pulled back out.

Harry exhaled and looked around the room. They had used his script — some of it at least — but the key message was delivered. There were puzzled expressions among his own staff; it wasn't what they'd been expecting. He'd not had the chance to brief them. He would have to now. He would speak to the force control room, too. He wanted to be sure they were ready to field the calls.

On the screen, the Head of Media had her hands up, to refuse questions at this time. Harry knew why. It was simple: they had more questions than answers themselves and they had taken a risk. Harry had a sudden sense that he had to be right. This was all on him now.

CHAPTER 26

When Harry looked up this time he was just about out of detectives. The response to the media appeal had prompted a lot of work. Experience told him that most of the enquiries would be a waste of precious time. The FCR were sending everything they were getting through to him, even stuff that was very obviously irrelevant. Harry had ensured his script was deliberately vague. He wanted to be the one ruling out what wasn't relevant rather than members of the public doing it for him. Only the public liked to help — or at least they liked to feel that they were helping — so he was getting everything from sightings of cars 'never seen in our road before,' to 'suspicious noises last night' — whatever that meant.

The response to the request for dashcam footage had been far larger than he had expected, too. Their use was far beyond what he had hoped, with some insurance companies now insisting on their use. Harry had wanted to pick up his keys and respond to every lead himself, but he had to be restrained. His most important job now was pulling in all the information coming in from his team and prioritising what they followed up on first.

Right now he needed to step away from his screen and his phone for just a moment. He didn't think he'd done that for two hours solid. He stood and stretched, aware that his eyes were heavy and dry. He made for the coffee pot. It was darker outside. The cloud cover had thickened as the day had gone on and now threatened rain. The kettle was cold to touch as he clicked it on.

'Hey, you needed one too.'

Harry turned to Maddie. She was smiling but it was fixed, as if she had suckered in a breath and held it since pushing through the door to Major Crime.

'Yeah. How are you getting on?' While everyone else was out chasing shadows and dead-ends, Harry had asked Maddie to find out all she could about Rhiannon's investigation into their blood-soaked boy. It was still a relevant line of enquiry — that someone linked to that boy was targeting the police officers working the case. That didn't make sense to Harry, given the circumstances of Rhiannon's disappearance, but he couldn't ignore it as a possibility. He had also needed to give Maddie something to do, something that allowed them to work apart for a while.

'Good. Rhiannon was all over it, it would seem. She was pretty certain he is Alex Thompson from Reading. She had done a lot of work with Social Services and got a lot of information around him and his family. Seems they were well known to the Social. All except the stepdad — or the dad in the case of Alex. She was struggling to get any information on him. Not even a name yet.'

'Anything standing out?'

'It seems they're a family who have their issues but they certainly don't like interference. They seem to have done their best to resist it. Alex's mother engaged with Social Services to an extent but the older siblings definitely didn't — the brother in particular . . . Mark Garner. He has his issues. A few run-ins with the police, too. Rhiannon did a lot of sound things . . . She's put the blood up for comparison against Garner. He was nicked for some public order stuff and criminal damage at the family home.'

'Any confirmation?'

'Not yet. She fast-tracked her request and it was couriered. I've put in a call to the lab, I was worried there might be results sat on her email. They haven't sent them yet. It might not be today, which means it'll be Monday. I've made sure they know to copy me in to any emails, just in case . . . in case Rhiannon can't pick up hers.'

'Can they work quicker?'

'It's four thirty on a Friday afternoon. I got a lab assistant. I asked to speak to someone higher and I was told no one was available. You know how these places work.'

'They're at home already?'

'Or in the pub more likely.' Maddie stood straighter than looked natural, her shocked smile still in place.

'You okay?'

'Not really, Harry. I just keep thinking about how lapsed I was. It's like I got comfortable down here. You were right, I didn't even think—'

'I was frustrated, not at you. It wasn't fair for me to say that.'

'What if they've hurt her? What if—'

'Then *they* hurt her. Not you. You can't be beating yourself up about this. Not now. We need you sharp. A sharp Maddie Ives is quite something.'

Her shoulders dropped a little, some tension released, perhaps.

'Thanks.'

'Dream team!' Harry turned to the sound of a booming voice. Vince's raucous greeting was accompanied by the door crashing off the wall as he strode through. 'I thought I'd come in early. Solve this shit for you. Only took me an hour! You can thank me later, Mads.' Shaun Wilson appeared from behind Vince's bulk. Harry knew him as one of the CID detectives normally based in Thanet. He wore a creased shirt and an unruly beard. On another day Harry would have sent him home until he could come back looking presentable. Today he needed every pair of hands he could get.

'What are you talking about?' Harry said.

Vince inclined a thumb at Shaun. 'Your shiny-arsed detective mate here got a bit excited — unearthed what you might be looking for. I turned out on blues to go get him. He's got something you need to see.' Shaun held up a USB stick.

'What's on it?' asked Harry.

'Footage from a work's van,' Shaun said. 'Shows a truck pulled over, right where you said and at the right time. Some fella's getting out as he goes past. The van has to swerve!' Shaun was breathy, his words tumbling out on top of each other. 'I couldn't make out the registration, but I only watched in on the little camera screen. I thought you might manage to see it better in here. It just plugs in. We seized the camera too.'

Maddie had already got to a desk and thumped a keyboard to wake it up. She booted up her media programme and snatched the USB from Shaun. A circle did somersaults in the middle of the monitor to announce it was loading. It seemed to take forever. Harry broke the tense silence.

'You're nights, Vince, right?'

'I was boss. I heard about Rhiannon so I came in. Little Maddie I call her! She's a scrapper, too, you can tell the sort. Wherever she is, she'll be giving them shit 'til we turn up and bring her home.' He grinned. It was aimed at Maddie. She smiled back, tired-looking but still more genuine than Harry had seen her all day.

'There's no overtime code, Vince. There—'

'Overtime?' Vince turned on him and pulled his lips back in a snarl. All his warmth dropped away in an instant.

Harry lifted his hands. 'You didn't let me deliver my punchline, Vince. I know you'd work for free. I know why you're here. It's all been a bit tense is all, I figured a joke might help.'

Vince looked more at ease and shook his head. 'Honestly, boss, I have two days off, I come back and Maddie's lost her shadow and Harry Blaker's making jokes! What the hell happened here?'

Harry smiled. Vince was the sort of bloke you wanted around you in a crisis.

The computer screen changed to a bright blue with the force crest in the middle — the standard media player. Maddie's fingers blurred over the keys to get past a password request. When she plugged in the USB, the screen changed again. A few more clicks and a small window showed movement that was visible through a windscreen of a view ahead. It filled the screen. The van passed a parked car. Harry couldn't read the registration number; the camera was too central. He was disappointed. This didn't look like getting them the result they needed. He leaned in a little closer. 'This isn't the A20,' he said.

'Not yet.' Shaun lifted a handwritten note. 'Less than a minute. You can fast-forward it but it runs away with itself.'

Sure enough the camera showed a junction approaching. The van slowed but didn't stop completely. It turned right, giving a sweeping view of the road it was now joining. Harry recognised the A20 now. The general direction was towards Langthorne — and the phone box. The van picked up speed. Harry tried to pick out what was in the distance.

'Can we slow it down?'

'No. It only pauses, but it's tricky to time it right.'

The van was still accelerating. The scenery was becoming more and more of a blur. A parked car flashed past on the left side, Harry made out the last two digits of the registration this time. He could see a junction in the distance and a red smear on the nearside bank: their phone box. They were approaching it quickly, too quickly. The junction flashed past, the red box did too. Harry could see something a few hundred metres further up. It was a dark, square object, a truck or a small lorry he reckoned. The camera was still moving too quickly and the scenery was mainly a blur. It moved out, already starting to overtake, there was nothing coming the other way. It was too fast. Harry leaned in. He was already certain they would have no chance of reading a registration at this speed.

Suddenly the dark shape changed: the driver's door pushed open. The van reacted; it slowed quickly and lurched further out to the right. A figure stepped out of the door. He was in a long, dark coat with the hood up. The van must have been close to hitting him but he didn't seem to react. Harry's attention had been on the figure; he hadn't checked the registration plate. The van's speed was slower now, much slower.

'Anyone get the reg?' Harry snapped. Maddie didn't reply, no one did. A few more clicks and the footage moved backwards to where the truck was just a solid shape. She started it again and clicked to pause it. She muttered under her breath as it rolled too far again. It took a few goes but finally the footage was stopped at the optimum time. The registration number was a block of yellow, the letters and numbers within it looked to be running together. To the right of this, a figure was halfway out of the door, his front leg planted, his back leg trailing into the truck. The footage was blurred, his face nothing more than a block of dark grey with a hood rounding off the top.

'I think it starts GN,' Maddie said. She stepped back and ran her hand roughly through her hair, her voice close to breaking. 'It's not good enough is it? To get an ID? Jesus, Harry, are we staring right at whoever took her?'

Harry's eye flicked to the digital display on the footage. It showed 11:15:20s. This was less than a minute before the phone box was used to make a call to the police control room, the call that summoned Maddie and Rhiannon to a café, to a meeting that never took place. Harry knew that it had served its purpose, however. The man on their screen, with his hood up on a clear day, with his lack of awareness to the speeding van, was exerting signs of someone distracted maybe, someone who was there to do something that was important to him — something that was consuming him entirely. There wasn't much that could make you focus like that. An abduction of a police officer might just do it.

'We need to know who that man is.'

'There's systems out there,' Vince said. 'I've heard of them used — stuff that can make pictures and videos clearer. They use it on CCTV, right?' Vince was gruff, as if his throat had dried up.

Harry stepped away. The rest of the office suddenly seemed darker as he moved from the brightness of the screen. He was still turned away when he spoke, talking to himself almost.

'There are. I've used them a few times, but it's a Met resource. It took a week. I had an urgent request once that still took three days.'

'Then call them,' Vince said. 'Tell them what's at stake here! This isn't an ordinary case, this is one of us, Harry.'

'I know what it is!' Harry snapped back.

'The GMP might have one.' Maddie was digging in her pocket for her phone. 'There's a programme that can clear up footage. Our covert teams used it when their footage wasn't great.' She already had the phone to her ear and it must have been answered on the first ring.

'Sir, I need your help!' she barked.

Harry paced further away to rest on a table next to the window. The clouds outside seemed darker still. There was a strip of whiter cloud and some sunlight getting through, but it was some way in the distance. It gave the sense that the darker clouds were gathering over the station. His attention stayed fixed on the sky while Maddie spoke down the phone. She explained hurriedly and it was obvious that she was doing all the talking. It sounded positive but she was frustrated too, as if any offer of help wouldn't be quick enough. There was no such thing as quick enough, not in a case like this. He waited for her to finish then turned back into the room. Maddie was staring over at him; all the tension was back in her face.

'It's not a GMP function. They use the NCA. That was Ian Jackson, my old superintendent. He has a senior contact over there. I need to send the file to him and he will see what he can do. He's going to try and get someone to look at it now. He carries a lot of weight in the police but the NCA don't have to lift a finger for him. He made no promises.' Maddie was running her fingers frantically through her hair. 'The file's huge, too. I'll need to send it as a zip file . . .'

Harry had no idea what a *zip file* was. He was aware that Maddie had stopped talking and was staring silently over at him. Vince and Shaun were doing the same.

'I can do it, though,' Maddie said. 'Then what?'

Harry turned back to the gathering clouds. 'Then we wait.'

CHAPTER 27

When she awoke, she gasped for air. Her first instinct was to move, to lash out, to try and make sense of where she was. But she *couldn't* move! Not anything it seemed. She let out panicked squeaks and expulsions of air. She scrunched her eyes shut. They were working at least. Her head moved too, she could move it from side to side and her eyes could scour her surroundings, not that there was much to see. She was lying down, she was sure of that. Something lay over her. It rested against her face and sucked against her lips to make breathing difficult. She had to keep her face to one side. It was cold and the plastic had a strong odour. She tried to lift her arms but nothing happened. She rolled her head to try and see them but she couldn't see much under the cover. She focussed on her breathing, trying not to let her panic get the better of her.

'So, I can't see anything much, can I?' She always talked to herself when she was nervous. It helped. Sometimes she could talk herself into a solution.

'So, what else is there? What can I hear that tells me where I am?' Her voice was high-pitched. In another context it might be mistaken for an excited voice, but it was the tension; it was squeezing her throat so that speaking was a strain. She had to force her swallows too.

'Well, there's wind in some trees I reckon.' The swallowing seemed to unleash a metallic taste in her mouth. She tried to cough it away and it boomed loud in her head.

'Something squeaking, I can definitely hear that.' The sound seemed to be behind her, and was like a child's swing moving in a breeze.

'So what else do I know? I can feel the cold.' It was through the back of her head especially. 'And something stiff against my neck.' It was tight and coarse. Like a thick rope.

'That's about it. Hang on, I can see . . . a light . . .' She took a moment while her eyes became a little more accustomed. The thing lying over her was a little clearer. It was some sort of plastic sheet. It was dark blue mostly, but there was a bright blue spot just above her head. She had to strain her eyes to see it. It was a light source, bright and localised, like the end of a torch held close to her.

'Is there someone there?' she called out. Her voice was still high-pitched. She was trying to sound calm, almost jovial, but her voice broke at the end.

Suddenly there was movement. The tarpaulin ripped back and she had to slam her eyes shut. The white light was suddenly overpowering and hot, too; it was a low sun. She twisted her head away from it. What she thought was a squeaking swing changed to a deeper sound. Now it sounded like a big spring. She felt her whole body dip, then a swaying movement as if she was lying on a water bed. She could also hear the movement of feet to both sides of her, and each footfall sounded like it struck something metal. Suddenly the sun's heat was doused and she dared open her eyes. She still needed to squint, but could focus enough to see that she was laid out on the floor of a lorry, the sides of which were barely knee-height. Above them she could see leafy trees and white clouds. There were noises close by. Someone was moving. The movement seemed to be timed with the re-emergence of the bright sun. She twisted her head to try and look up but it was too strong and she had to scrunch her eyes tightly again. Then there was a sound like the clicking of a camera shutter.

There was a tutting and then a grunt — a man's grunt she thought. The shutter clicked again, then came another grunt, but higher pitched this time: someone trying to contain a squeal of excitement.

The intensity in the light was gone again and she opened her eyes. The dark figure of a man loomed above her, a block of black with a vivid outline of sunlight. He was bent over and he was holding something small in a bandaged hand; all his attention was on it. Then she heard a sound like a single low note blown from some kind of flute.

'Before!' the man exclaimed, then gave another excited squeal. He moved aside, the bright sun blinded her again and she rolled her head away. Presently, she felt herself bobbing gently again and the squeaking noise returned. The plastic sheet fell back over her face and she was grabbed and rolled onto one side. Now she could see the loop of rope tight across her chest and under her arms. When she was rolled back, the plastic was tighter, tight enough to be firmer against her nose and lips. Her breaths became panicked again. She couldn't speak out loud to calm herself, not now. Her throat was all but closed up and the plastic sheet felt like it was pushing into her mouth with every breath.

CHAPTER 28

Maddie cast a look over her shoulder as she hurried away from the police station, almost breaking into a jog. She'd been assailed by what was almost a full-blown panic attack, though she was pretty certain no one had noticed. Harry had been on his phone when she'd realised that she had to get out. She'd experienced such attacks before. Early on in her undercover career they were almost a common occurrence and they typically accompanied *first times*: the first time she walked into a room of career criminals and was required to blend in; the first time she spoke to the head of an organised crime group, the sort of person who would kill her in an instant if he knew what she was; the first time she was accused of being a grass.

Each time, Maddie had remembered her training. She'd been taught grounding techniques, ways of occupying the mind with simple tasks to divert the panic from taking it over completely. She had been using those simple disciplines to keep a lid on things, but then Vince had asked her what time they were out running that morning. Maddie had checked the clock as part of her answer that she had last seen her at around 6 a.m. Then it struck her: *Rhiannon had been missing around twelve hours*. And she'd tried to think of how many cases where a young woman had been abducted and been missing for twelve hours or more and had been found alive. She couldn't think of any. Not one. The anxiety that had been rising like floodwater finally burst its banks and she had almost collapsed there and then. She just about managed to excuse herself before making for the exit. She needed some air.

Friday evening always seemed to be the busiest rush hour. A thick blur of traffic crawled past the front of the nick, although every daylight hour seemed like rush hour in this town. She turned right out of the building and kept walking until she was concealed behind a high wall. Only then did she feel safe enough to root around her bag for her cigarettes.

It was ridiculous — she knew that. She was a grown woman. She could smoke if she wanted to and it was very rare. The packet she kept in her bag was mainly for other people; a cigarette introduced at the right time when talking to a victim or a witness could make all the difference. Three months before, she had bought a packet of twenty and she still had a few left. She only ever wanted a smoke herself when her stress levels were at their highest and there was no other way to get them down.

She'd had to get away from that room, just for a few minutes. The atmosphere was stifling, the tension tangible. Police investigations were always feast or famine — major ones at any rate. Whenever something big happened there was a rush of activity, a million things to do, information coming in from everywhere and a need to work out a response. Then there was the lull. Often it was welcome, it was a time to reflect on everything you had, to start again, to get a sense of direction and to prioritise. But when it was something like this, something as important as the life or death of a colleague, there was no sitting down and calmly prioritising, no stepping back from the investigation to see where you were; there was only the nagging anxiety that you should be doing something, you should be *out there* doing something. She just didn't know what. Maddie was too terrified to even think straight. She was terrified that Rhiannon was already dead. She was terrified that they might not ever find whoever took her. And she was terrified that it was all her fault.

She sucked hard on her cigarette. Too hard, the rush of coarse chemicals forced a cough and then her head swam. The cough bent her forward and she thumped her own chest with the back of her fist, cursing between each one.

'Well, that sort of language don't suit you!' Vince stepped around the wall and Maddie looked up at him. Her eyes streamed where she had been choking and she started coughing again.

'You smoke, Maddie Ives?'

'Not very well it would seem.'

'I had no idea.'

'Only when I'm very stressed. I know its counterproductive before you start the lect—'

Vince held up his hands. 'We all need a release. This job will get you to that point often enough. You have to find your way.'

Maddie's gaze lingered on him long enough to prompt a reaction.

'What?'

'I was waiting for the punchline, Vince.'

He leant against the wall, hands behind his back, one foot lifted to rest on the rough stone. 'I ain't got a punchline today, Mads, I get the impression you ain't looking for one neither. Your mate . . . she's gonna be alright.'

'I hope so.' Maddie took another drag, making sure she was slower this time. 'She's missing, that's bad enough, but I can't shake off that it's my fault.'

'Your fault? Who told you that?'

'Harry.'

'Harry said that?'

'He did. It was just a reaction, I don't even think he meant to say it, but he was right. I got sloppy. I've got comfortable down here. Just because I'm not under the noses of dangerous people every day, doesn't mean I'm not under the noses of dangerous people every day.'

Vince frowned, plainly confused.

'It doesn't matter, Vince. I underestimated this town . . . this county. It won't happen again. Not that that helps Rhiannon.'

'You'll find her. I know you will.'

'Right now I'm leant on a wall smoking a cigarette. It's not like I'm hot on the trail, is it? I keep thinking that that she won't last the night, too. If she's still alive now, she won't see another day.' She felt the panic rising again; the knot of anxiety was back, increasing with every word.

'We just have to find her before tomorrow, then,' Vince's matter-of-fact tone made her flash angry. She turned away from him, gave herself a moment to calm back down. She knew he was trying to help. She was aware of a vibrating in her pocket and she lifted the phone out to read *Ian Jackson* on her phone.

'My super,' she explained to Vince. 'Boss . . . tell me you have news.'

'Good and bad.' He sounded flat.

Maddie had been holding her breath and she let it out in a sigh, her body slumping forward with it. This was it, their last chance and already she could feel it slipping away. 'Go on.'

'Are you with Harry?'

'No. I just stepped out for a moment.'

'Okay. Well, sorry for the delay. Not everyone can do this, it seems. The NCA had to make a few calls to get the right person back in. But they've cleaned up your image. The registration is GN18 EKO.'

'Hang on!' Maddie dumped her bag on the floor to start a desperate search for a pen.

'Don't worry, I've sent it over as part of a summary on your email. It will be with you already.' Maddie made eye contact with Vince as she moved towards the building, her pace just below a jog, the cigarette already discarded on the floor.

Ian Jackson was still talking. 'I took the liberty of getting our intel team to have a look at it. PNC shows previous keeper details only and there's no insurance.'

Maddie swore under her breath. She hesitated with the door pushed open and Vince bumped into the back of her. 'So I guess that's the bad news,' she said. She could feel her chest tightening. This was a good lead, it might be their only one, and already there was a chance it was going cold. 'When did it change hands?'

'Only two months ago. So you'll have a line of enquiry there.' They would. There was a spark of hope, enough to get Maddie moving again. Change of vehicle ownership involving private purchase was a common hindrance for the police. When one member of the public purchased a car from another, the emphasis was on the new owner to register that ownership with the DVLA. There was little incentive for someone with criminal intent to register as the owner.

'Okay, we'll get right onto it,' Maddie said.

'We obviously can't check your local system. Maybe that'll have something on there about the ownership. And the previous keeper lives in a place called Sturry? We put it into our mapping system — a ten-minute drive from your police station, right?'

Maddie thumped through the last door that took her into Major Crime and the noise had caused Harry to stand up from his desk. Maddie made eye contact with him but she still spoke into her phone as he walked out onto the floor. 'I'll get my email up and see what's on there. Finger's crossed and thanks for your help.'

'Maddie . . .'

She was just about to end the call and she held off. 'Boss?'

'Best of luck with finding your colleague. If it were me, if I was lost, I would hope it was you coming for me.'

Maddie bit down hard. She turned away from Harry and took a moment. 'Thanks,' she managed. The call ended.

'Previous keeper details only on that reg. They cleaned it up. I've got a summary on my email. It's Sturry. Only changed hands two months ago. I'll get it up on my phone on the way — we need to go. Vince can flash us there.'

'Too right!' Vince said.

Harry was already pulling on his jacket.

CHAPTER 29

Sturry was on the other side of the city and the address was further off still as they found themselves in what was more like the Thannington area. It was one of Canterbury's more deprived suburbs and the hope of knocking on the door of someone keen to assist police with their urgent enquiries dwindled as they pushed into an area of social housing. The target address came up on the right, one in a row of detached bungalows that seemed separate from the more modern-looking council stock on the opposite side. The house was set back off the road. Vince pulled straight onto the drive. The traffic was heavy and there was nowhere to pull it over.

Maddie was out of the car first. The light was fading quickly now, to the point where it took a moment for her eyes to adjust when the car's interior light turned off. The drive was two strips of clumsy concrete cutting through a block of unruly grass. The front lawn to their right was also overgrown but for patches where the growth had been stunted by what looked like abandoned cars parked untidily over it. There were four vehicles visible in total: three on the lawn and one on the drive in front of them. It looked to be the only one in use.

The front door was on the left side of the building. An engine block sat in its own oil stain just beyond it, one end looked to be resting against a filthy garage door that flaked white paint from the edges. Maddie thumped the door before her two colleagues got to her. With the sun just about gone, it was down to the cloud cover to hold onto the warmth. It felt close, sticky almost. A wall light clicked on, she wasn't sure if it had been turned on from inside the property or if it was a security light that was just slow to detect her movement. The door pulled open.

'Yeah?' A man in his late thirties pulled the door open a crack. His watery eyes flicked to her feet and crawled slowly back up her body. The end of his tongue appeared and wet his lips. He opened the door a little further to reveal ill-fitting tracksuit bottoms and a once-white T-shirt. As a whole, his appearance matched his garage door: greasy, flaky, and worn out. Maddie had her warrant card out and the man's eyes moved from it to where Harry and Vince stepped in behind her. He pushed the door back to its original position, just a slit, just enough for a conversation.

'We need your help, that's all,' Maddie said hurriedly.

'I don't help the police.' The man's nostrils flared, he was still looking out over the top of her.

'A lorry you own . . . it's being used regularly in crime. I think you might have sold it but I need to be sure of that. Otherwise you're going to get a lot more visits from the police and you might end up getting yourself arrested.' It was a half-truth.

'I don't own no lorry!' he spluttered.

'Did you sell one?'

'I sold a lot of stuff.'

'A lot of lorries?'

'No actually, I don't do many of them. It came up and it was a good earner.'

'Tell me about it.'

'This takes three of you, does it?' He looked back over the top of her.

She considered how it might look: a simple vehicle enquiry carried out by a DS, a DI and a uniform cop built like Vince. 'No, actually. I don't think it does. Gentlemen, I'll have a quick chat with our friend here. I'll meet you back at the car, okay?' Harry frowned at her and neither of the men moved. 'I'll just be a minute.' They both held their ground for another few seconds then looked at each other and turned slowly away.

'We'll be at the car, then,' Vince said.

'Yeah, you can move that off my drive too if you like. I don't want to be getting no reputation round here. People don't appreciate people what talk to you lot.'

'I suggest you hurry up then, mate,' Vince snapped back. 'The car stays.' The man sniffed and Maddie smiled at him.

'It's cold. Do you mind if I step in for just a moment? I guess the paperwork is in there anyway, isn't it?'

'I don't do paperwork. Not really. You see, I'm a sold-as-seen kind of bloke. Someone buys something from me, it's down to them to let you lot know or whatever.'

'It is. So you're in the motor trade?'

'I spin a few cars, that's all. I get doer-uppers generally. You can make a bit if you know a bit.'

'But not many lorries?'

'No. Mate of mine runs a crew of groundworkers and he changed his wheels. They offered him scrap value, really — there were a few issues. I took it on and it sold — just like that. But I ain't giving you his name. He's known to you lot. He wouldn't like it.'

'Who? Your groundworker mate?'

'Yeah, bit of a scally in his time. Straight as now, but still trying to keep his-self to his-self — you know the sort.'

Maddie nodded. She knew them only too well. 'I don't care about him. Who bought it off you?'

'I didn't get no name.'

'You wrote him a receipt though? You took his address for the forms?'

'I told you, I don't do that. I never owned the lorry. I was spinning it for my mate. He might have filled it all out like — none of my business.'

Maddie tried another smile. She played with her hair, too. It was a way of concealing her rising panic, her desperation. She was getting nowhere here. She'd seen it enough times, the lorry would have been declared off-road then sold on, with the man stood in front of her acting as the middle man. No one took anyone's details at any time. Even if this man wanted to help, Maddie was starting to realise that he couldn't.

'What did he look like?' Maddie's voice was noticeably different, coarser, where her throat had suddenly dried up. She could feel her heart beating faster in her chest. She didn't know where they went next, if this line went nowhere. There was nothing else.

'It wasn't really him; the bird did the talking.'

Maddie ran her hand over her mouth and suddenly stood straighter. 'Bird? You mean a woman?'

The man chuckled. 'Sure, whatever! Bird, woman, bint. I didn't get her name either, though. Some fella called me up about it to start with. It was odd really . . . he didn't really care much about it — just that it was a runner and that it had a tow bar.'

'A tow bar?'

'Yeah. They're pretty rare, I reckon. You get the pikeys . . . they want a tow bar for their caravans an' boxes an' that. But most people don't care. My mate had some plant on a trailer so he fitted a bar. I guess this fella was doing the same.'

'So it had a tow bar?'

'Yeah.'

'But a woman turned up with the cash?'

'She did. The bloke was here, too — at least I guess it was the same fella on the phone. He didn't say a dicky. I got the impression he was trying to scare me maybe. He just sort of stared me out. From a distance, though. He weren't brave enough to get up in my face or nothin'. And then they paid the full asking — straight off.'

'What did they look like?'

'I ain't writing none of this down, yeah? This ain't on no record?'

'No record.' She tried to act casual despite her stomach turning.

'I dunno, a man and a woman! She had, like, brown hair. Down. A nice set of tits. What do you want from me?'

'Slim build?'

'Yeah. Nice like! You know what I mean?'

'And him?'

'I didn't take much notice. Like I said, he stayed away really. Me an' the woman talked out on the drive and he hung round near the road. Dark coat, hood up — which was weird. It weren't cold or nothing.'

'Hood up?'

'Yeah. Oh and I think he'd hurt himself. He had a bandage on his hand.'

'Which hand?' Maddie couldn't hide her desperation now.

The man looked puzzled then turned his body a little as if working it out. 'Woulda been his left hand I reckon. Oh an' she called him her brother I think.'

'Brother?'

'Yeah, she pointed and said about how her brother was well happy. They didn't strike me as no couple from the off to be fair.'

'You remember the registration of that lorry?'

'Not all. It was a fourteen plate. And the last three was E.K.O. I remember that 'cause my mate called it Echo.'

'I need your name,' Maddie snapped. She needed to leave — and she knew exactly where they needed to go. But she'd need absolute confirmation.

'I told you, I ain't writing none of this down.'

'And I told you I need to make sure no one comes looking for you if this lorry does something criminal. Right now, you're the only person linked. Give me your name and I'll put an intelligence report in that says I've spoken to you, that you sold the lorry and you should be left alone.' She handed him a piece of scrap paper. Write it on there, I need to make a quick call then I'll leave you alone.'

The man hesitated, but took the pen and paper that she thrust at him. Maddie pushed a contact on her phone.

Mitch Evans picked up on the first ring. 'Mads?'

'Mitch, there's a shared folder under CID. Rhiannon made it. It's called Op Hythe.'

'Okay.'

'There's a jpeg file in there. Headshot of a male. Rhiannon got it from the DVLA. It's his driving licence picture.'

'Okay.'

'I need you to send it to my phone right now.'

'Okay!'

Maddie hung up. The man was holding the piece of paper out for her.

'Gerry,' she read. 'Gerry Holt.'

'That's me. I've put my phone number on there, too — y' know, should you need it.' He actually winked. Maddie smiled back, she hoped it looked like she meant it.

'Date of birth? And is this your home address?'

He gave his details quickly and she scribbled his answers under where he had written his name. Her phone vibrated in her other hand. She had to suck in a breath to work it — her hands were shaking. She opened up the attachment. It was a stern-looking male. His expression looked like it was about to break out into a snarl. She turned it for Holt to look at.

'That's 'im. Same look he gave me, too. Maybe I shouldn't take it personal like.' Holt laughed heartily. Maddie didn't. She felt suddenly overwhelmed. She held it together and pushed the phone back into her pocket.

'Thanks for your help.'

He shrugged. 'Don't reckon I've been much.'

'If that makes you feel better!' She called back. She ran the length of the drive. Harry and Vince were both stood by the car.

'We need to go!' She pulled the door open and slid in. The two men were in the car by the time she buckled up, their doors slamming in unison.

'What have you got?' Harry said.

'Rhiannon was investigating our blood-soaked boy, Alex Thompson. We know he had siblings — an older brother and sister. They bought that lorry. Rhiannon had got his driving licence photo from the DVLA. His sister doesn't have a driving licence. Neither of them have passports . . .'

'Wait . . . who bought the lorry?'

'Alex Thompson's brother and sister — Mark and Michelle Garner.'

'Okay . . .'

'And from the description, I reckon I've met Michelle. She was the waitress at the Ports Café, Harry. *I* gave *her* my business card!'

Vince turned the engine on. The car revved hard and jerked to the end of the drive. The lights were already spinning and the siren announced their departure as the streaming traffic jerked to a halt to let them out.

CHAPTER 30

Maddie tutted. She had put her phone down for it to ring again immediately. She had been speaking with the FCR, updating the inspector based there as best she could. He had dedicated a radio channel for what was now an operation and he was best placed to direct the required resources to the Ports Café. Maddie and Harry had managed a brief conversation with each other and formed the same intention. They were going to get to the café as soon as possible and they would start making arrests — anyone who was there and looked to be an employee or was in the least bit obstructive. Once they had someone under arrest, they had search powers and they would tear that place apart. Rhiannon had to be there. Maddie couldn't allow herself to think any differently.

Vince was still forcing his way through the dense traffic. The car burst out onto a roundabout and a van approaching from the right only just stopped in time. Maddie was sitting in the back and just a few feet from the near-collision. She managed to cling onto her phone to answer it.

'Maddie Ives.' She peered between the front headrests and through the windscreen. It was starting to spot with large drops of rain. Vince now pulled out into a bus lane to make progress.

'You're too late.'

A taxi pulled across their front. Vince swerved, swore loudly, and braked hard. Even Harry's hand reached up for the grab handle.

'What?' Maddie pushed the phone harder against her ear. The voice was soft and low, a woman's voice. She didn't recognise it.

'You're too late. He's gone. He's taken her.'

'Who — who *is* this?'

'By now I reckon you know who I am.' The voice was suddenly more familiar: the woman who had spoken to her in the café, Alex Thompson's sister.

'Michelle Garner?' Maddie said. The name had been in Rhiannon's notes and Maddie must have read it ten times with no way of knowing that *Michelle* might hold the key all along.

'There's no point coming here. He's not here. You're too late. But you can still catch up with him.' Maddie's eyes met with Harry's; he had spun in his seat with a questioning look. He must have picked up on her sudden change of tone. She moved the phone away and wrapped her hand around the mouthpiece.

'Vince, kill the sirens!' she said.

'What?'

'Do it, now!' Maddie hissed back. Vince mashed the steering wheel with his palm. Two strikes killed the noise. The console still flashed with the lights. He jerked sharp right and Maddie had to jam her feet under the front seats to ground herself. She pressed the button on her phone to activate the speaker, levelled the phone out and leaned forward. Harry stared at it silently.

'How would you know if we were coming?'

'You found who sold us the lorry. You're on your way here. I knew you were getting close — I was trying to get him back before you worked it out. But I've lost him. I can't control him anymore. You have to stop him now. Stop him before—'

'Before what? What are you talking about? Who?'

'You know that, too, I reckon.'

'Your brother?'

'Mark. But it's been a long time since I've called him that.' Mark Garner; another name she had read a number of times in her colleague's notes.

'Where is he, Michelle?'

There was a pause and then the sound of quiet sobbing. The voice came back a little stronger. 'You have to know . . . I was only doing this to protect my family . . . to try and keep us all together. That's all my mum wanted. She told me I had to keep us together. I didn't know what else to do.'

'Where is he?'

'He's just turned off. He was on the main road. He'll be in Monks Horton soon. He'll find a place that's right. He's used there before, and then . . .'

'And then what, Michelle? What are you telling me?'

'I never wanted anyone else hurt. I know she's not part of this — she's not part of them. I did what I could to stall him. I can't do any more. You have to do the rest. I'm so sorry.' The phone went silent. Maddie stared at the screen.

'What is going on, Maddie?' Harry said.

'I don't know. No number. I can't call her back. But that was her — that was our waitress.'

'So the second we left that fella, he called her direct and told her the police had been sniffing around?'

'He must have.'

'We need him in.'

'I agree, but we need to find the brother first. He has Rhiannon. She said she couldn't stall him anymore, Harry! He's going to hurt her!'

'Vince, do you know that location?'

Vince pointed a stubby finger at the car's touchscreen. 'I brought up the A20 on the mapping system. This is our road from what she said. It comes right off the A20 and it's a left through the middle of Monks Horton. It looks like a tiny village. Can we trust her, though, boss? I mean . . . if she knows we're on our way she could just be stalling us? How would she know exactly where he was if she wasn't with him?'

'I agree. We need to get to the café. That place holds the key — it always has. I'll get whatever patrols we have there, too. But we'll have to try for an invisible perimeter on the place. We're expected now — we don't know what the threat is. It'll need a full tactical assessment for patrols to pitch up. I'll call the firearms commander. They can make the first approach.'

'I think she's telling the truth!' said Maddie. 'We have to go where she said!' She was aware she sounded desperate. 'A firearms entry will take time, Harry. A *lot* of time. They'll want to know the ins and outs of every detail and then it'll be a negotiator leading. We don't have the time for that! *Rhiannon* doesn't have the time for that.'

'No, Maddie. Maybe we *should* consider every detail. Maybe we *should* take our time. When I start sending officers in there, Rhiannon isn't the only person I might be putting in harm's way.'

Vince was rubbing his fingers over the screen, moving the map around. 'We could come in this way, boss. That almost makes Monks Horton on the way. We could go just to see if anything was moving. We wouldn't lose much time at all.'

Maddie leaned forward to where Vince was pointing at a junction that looked to be a sharp turn off the A20. It was a short road, quickly joining up with another that looked to run parallel to the A20. It would allow them to still be heading in the general direction of the café while putting them in the area that Michelle Garner had told them about.

Harry was silent. Maddie waited for him to dig in. He relented. 'Okay then. Map says the deviation makes a couple of minutes difference. We're seven minutes from that junction.'

'Seven minutes!' Maddie blurted. Suddenly that felt like an age. She could feel her panic returning all at once. She had to get a hold of it; she couldn't have Harry thinking she was panicked or he would be even less likely to listen to her. She remembered a grounding technique she had been taught that could give her back control. She reached out to grab the back of the seats and closed her eyes. She focussed on the touch of the fabric, on something she could feel. The siren started back up again to provide something she could hear, and she opened her eyes for something she could see. It was Harry. He was staring back at her and there was no doubting his own fear.

* * *

Jack tried to concentrate on his grip, on ignoring the searing pain through his wounded palm. The lorry was moving, the exhaust bumping against the steel frame with every shift in gear, the suspension wallowing over the surface and the lowered tailgate shaking and thumping with every undulation. The man's driving was more erratic than ever tonight. The safer option would be to drop to his knees or to sit down on the steel flatbed. But he didn't want to. He didn't want to be any closer to the plastic sheeting at his feet. He knew what was under it and what he was expected to do.

He looked away. The woods were closing in; the road was at its narrowest yet and they were climbing up a steep hill. At least with the slower pace he could look forward over the top of the cab without his eyes being stung by raindrops. Now the rain was just a rhythm on the thick trees and the steel roof. His fingers hurt, too. He had wrapped them round the mesh of the cage that jutted backwards from the cab. He was just a few inches from the back of the driver, close enough to hear him when he barked his instructions through the window. They were near to where he had brought him before. From what he remembered, it wouldn't be long after they topped the hill. The tight drop on the other side was where he was called into action the previous time. He scrunched his eyes tightly shut. He was so tired, physically and mentally. Mostly he was wearied by the same internal battles, the same indecision. He was tired of knowing what he should do and not having the bravery to go through with it. Instead he was still doing what he was told, and that meant being backed into the cold, soaking corner of a dark country lane, waiting for inevitable instructions. The truck slowed enough for him to check his waistband. He still had the jagged knife he had been given when he had admitted to losing the last one. He hadn't lost it; he'd left it sticking through a hurried message — a last and desperate attempt to end this madness. Then he had scuffed up the path to draw attention, but even if they had seen that and then found his scrawled note it might not mean anything to anyone. But maybe it would to Maddie Ives . . . whoever that was.

The vehicle lurched forward and the brake lights drenched the sodden woods blood red. When the darkness returned, another light caught his eye. It flashed past a distant junction and before he had time to snatch his head to it, it was gone. The blanket of darkness returned instantly, as if the night was keen to fool him that it had even happened at all. But he knew what he had seen, he had seen a flickering light in the distance and it gave him the merest spark of hope. Because he was certain it had been blue.

* * *

'I saw a light!' Maddie had undone her seatbelt and was leaning forward, her arms out and across both headrests. She pushed herself further forward now between the two seats. She moved her right hand to point at the mapping system on the car's display.

'There was a road back there! I saw brake lights!' The car slowed, but it was a natural slow; Vince had eased off the pedal but he wasn't braking. He wasn't taking her word for it; he was looking over at Harry. 'I'm telling you! I saw a set of red lights. It looked like they were on something big. It could be it! Spin it around!'

'Boss?' Vince queried. It was maddening. Maddie pushed herself back to sit straight. She thumped into the rear seat in shock and fury. She couldn't believe she was being ignored, that Vince was looking for confirmation from Harry. Suddenly this didn't feel like rank either. This was personal. She didn't know what was stronger now, her rage or her desperation.

'Turn the *fucking* car round, Vince! We need to go after it!' Maddie was beyond any grounding technique to calm her down. Anger was the hardest form of panic to control.

'We don't know what's going on here, Maddie.' Harry's retort was instant and it was strong. The car was still slowing but its direction was still towards the café and away from the lights she had seen. It seemed they were rolling to a complete stop. The urgent flashes of blue visible through the windows amounted to perverse mockery. She felt like she might implode with the frustration.

'Please, Harry. I don't think Michelle was lying. I think he's out here with Rhiannon. And even if it's half-truths or she's luring us somewhere else, there are three of us here and a whole lot more going on to the café. We can handle it.'

'We can't just go blundering into the countryside because we've been told to. We need to be more measured.'

'You mean like I did? Like I went *blundering* into the café?'

'People make mistakes, Maddie. That's not an issue. It becomes an issue if we don't learn from them.'

'That stings, Harry.' She had been leaning forward again but she pushed herself back. The car had practically stopped. 'So we should just sit here then, should we? Is that what you're saying?' her voice was laden with menace. She felt for the phone in her pocket. Her radio was in her bag, too. She'd put it on silent when Vince had turned up the volume on the car set. She made a snap decision. She would get out here. The radio was full of excited chatter from officers making their way to the area. It wouldn't take much to call up and have one pick her up. Then she'd go after her lights. She pushed the door open and swung her legs out, her radio gripped tightly in her spare hand. The car jolted suddenly to a complete stop.

'Maddie! What the hell are you doing?' Harry's voice barely contained his rage.

'I'll get a lift. You carry on to the café.'

'Don't be ridiculous!'

She stepped away from the car and immediately she felt the chill of raindrops. Harry's window slid down.

'Get back in the car, Maddie. There are updates from others. They're at the café. They know to hold back — it's a huge perimeter. I can't spare anyone coming out here to look for you in the dark. We take five minutes to chase your lights. But you remember this was your decision.'

Maddie held firm. She considered her options and lifted her eyes to the dark horizon. All around her the leaves of the trees beat the rhythm of the rain. She got back in the car. Vince's eyes fill the rear-view mirror. She could just make out where the cheeks beneath were creased, where he was smiling broadly at her. Now it wasn't just the flicker of the lights that felt urgent.

CHAPTER 31

'Straight on here!' Maddie called out as she looked up from her phone.

'Did you see more lights?' Vince called back.

'Yes. Straight on.'

'What lights?' Harry said. 'I didn't see anything! We need to take this next right — back to the A20. We're wasting our time out here. Even if you did see a lorry, it could be anywhere. The café is our best shot.'

'Go straight on here — there's a right just a little further up. I've got my mapping open on my phone. Just prove me wrong and take the next right.'

'Boss?' Vince said again. Maddie wanted to vent at him, to tell him to trust her, to get a backbone of his own. She bit her tongue; it would achieve nothing.

'Straight on,' Harry said. 'But we take the next right.'

Maddie was back to leaning forward. Vince had killed the blue lights when they had turned off the main road. They would be seen for miles around in this darkness. It was difficult enough to find anything out here, let alone someone who could see you coming. There were only the headlamps of the car to pick anything out. So far, it was just slick, muddy banks and branches hanging down over the road dripping thick globules of water. The rain was heavier still, the windscreen wipers now working on full. Ahead, Maddie could see more road rising over a steep hill.

'Harry, I know where we are! Jarod Logan . . . we found him here. Not far from here.'

'We did.' Harry's voice was lower. He didn't turn to look back at her. She could feel the panic rising again. She knew what that meant. She reckoned he did, too. 'Vince, pick up the speed will you,' he said.

She felt the car surge. She was focussed forward now, hardly daring to breathe. They swept up the hill, Harry pushed a dash-mounted button to update control with their location. His voice had a slight shake — he was tense. When they reached the crest of the hill, they must all have seen the red lights at the same time. They were bright, fifty metres in front, and there was no doubt they were attached to the back of a lorry. And they were stationary. Vince jerked the patrol car to a stop and Maddie felt herself pushed forward. Nobody said anything and time seemed to almost stop. Then there was movement: Vince reaching for the panel that activated the lights.

'No, Vince!' Harry snapped.

It was too late: the vivid blue strobes sliced up the darkness. The reaction was almost immediate. The red lights on the vehicle in front flickered, then bright, white lights reached out from the front. The light illuminating the rear number plate came on, too. Maddie could see it clearly.

'E.K.O.!' she shouted. 'That's it!' She heard the roar of a powerful diesel engine and the lights over E.K.O. shuddered as it surged forward. Vince revved the patrol car hard. It was quicker and the gap between them closed.

'There's someone in the back!' Vince shouted. His lights flooded the rear of the truck where Maddie could see someone squatting down. They were in dark clothing with an arm raised to repel the bright lights of the patrol car on full beam. The figure stumbled and reached out to grab the side of the lorry, almost toppling out. The arm dropped to get hold of the side. Maddie saw a man's face under a hood. Wide eyes peered out. He looked young — and terrified. He made it to the back of the truck and his hands dropped below the truck's tailgate. Maddie couldn't see what he was doing.

The tailgate dropped away. Even from the back of the car, Maddie heard the loud bang as it came down. Now the beams of the patrol car flooded the whole of the rear. The man in the back was kneeling next to what looked like bunched-up plastic. Maddie felt the air leave her lungs with such force that she felt she might never be able to breathe again. The soles of bare feet faced towards her from beneath the plastic. A rope trailed from under them that dipped down beside the number plate and looked to be tied off around the tow bar.

'DROP BACK!' Harry bellowed. The car slowed a little and the truck pulled away.

'WHAT ARE YOU DOING?' Maddie shouted. Her voice was a dry rasp, her chest so tight she was fighting for breath. She got no answer. The figure in the back of the truck was still battling to stay upright on his knees. He moved close to the plastic and reached under it with both his arms. He heaved, every movement looking like an unnatural jerk as it was caught in the blue strobes. The plastic turned and he fell onto his side as the truck lurched into a corner.

'DO SOMETHING!' Maddie screamed. Vince was back to keeping pace, the car's lights still flooding the rear.

Harry reached out and jabbed the panel and the blues stopped. 'DROP BACK!' he shouted again. The car slowed a little more.

'Harry! We need to get up to it! We need to stop it!'

Harry spun in his seat, his wide eyes fixed on her. 'We can't!' His head shook, his eyes glazed then ripped away from her as he faced back front. 'You need to look away, Maddie. You don't need to see this.' His voice was softer, drifting over her. Her hand pushed over her mouth. She couldn't look away. The figure was still on his knees and he heaved again. The roll of plastic was on the edge of the flatbed. The man lifted his head. His whole face was flared white by the headlights and he was still for an instant. Then his head dropped and his arms pushed out.

The plastic rolled then dropped. Maddie heard the thud as it hit the road, even over Vince's shout. She screamed as the rope tightened almost instantly and the clump of tarpaulin twitched and skipped after the van. The patrol car slowed more. The truck pushed into the distance, the darkness starting to consume it.

'Stay with it, Vince.' Harry's voice was strained and trembling with shock. 'Maddie, tell me you're looking away.' His face was still forward.

Maddie couldn't respond. She had nothing. The truck took a bend and the dark clump of plastic flicked out behind. It collided with a steep bank, spun and jerked back out into the middle of the road. The patrol car made up ground on the bend and now they were close enough to see the figure in the back. He had moved to lie on his front, his arm reaching down with a sawing movement.

'VINCE, STOP!' Maddie screamed. She didn't need to. The car was already skidding. Vince must have seen it at the same time she had and stood on the brake pedal. Maddie was pinned to the back of the front seats by her forward momentum. When she was able to look ahead again, she saw the rope give. The clump of plastic still moved forward but its motion was different now, a roll rather than a slide. It collided with the bank for one last time and rebounded into the middle of the road, where it came finally to rest. The lorry that had shed it moved off into the distance. Maddie pushed her car door open and her feet were on the ground while they were still moving. It made her stumble. The road was narrow here and dropped away sharply at the sides. Her left foot slid down a greasy bank into standing water. She pushed past where Harry's door was opening. A fallen branch banged against her shins as she lunged forward to where the bundle of plastic was still in the middle of the road. The bright lights of the car picked out a slim leg sticking out from the plastic

306

bundle. It looked shockingly pale. There was no movement and no sound. She'd been praying for screams or cries — any signs of life at all —

but as she fell to her knees, she heard only the sound of the patrol car's idling engine and the falling rain.

CHAPTER 32

Harry pushed his door open hard but it came straight back as Maddie flashed past. It must have collided with her shoulder. She didn't seem to notice. By the time he got out of the car she had already sunk to her knees and was tearing at the rolled plastic. Vince moved across him and made his way over to help her. Harry took a moment. Beyond the frantic movement of his colleagues in the middle of the muddy road, he could see the lorry. It had come to a stop in the distance; the headlamps of their patrol car reached out far enough to brush the back of it, enough to see the unmoving silhouette of a tall, stocky man with his hood up standing in the centre of the truck's flatbed. It was too dark and too far for details, but it was a different outline to the man who had been struggling to stay upright in the back. Harry squinted at what looked to be movement in the man's upper body. Suddenly a small, white light was pointed directly at him. It disappeared for an instant and then returned as a flash. *A photograph?* Harry took a step forward. His capacity to stay calm, to take a moment to assess the situation, was quickly diminishing as rage flooded his veins. The gall of someone to do what he had just done and then stop to take a photograph! As he stepped beyond his colleagues, he could hear Maddie's high-pitched tones and

Vince's low rumble. He wasn't sure if they were talking to him and he didn't look back. Instead, he quickened his pace, his attention still on the man in the truck.

The small white light reappeared. This time the subsequent flash was angled down, towards the ground at the rear of the truck. Harry could make out something there, but little more than a shadow. He moved faster. The silhouette moved to the right and clambered down to the ground. He was moving towards the driver's door. Now he was closer, Harry could see it hanging open and could hear the engine ticking over. He broke into a sprint. He still had fifteen metres to make up. The truck's engine revved hard and there was the sound of churning gravel as the wheels dug in for grip. They found it and the truck lurched forward. There was the scrape of steel on steel when the gear was changed. He slowed to a jog. The truck was gone and the darkness closed in.

He turned back to where Vince or Maddie must have moved to block the headlights from reaching him. He took out his phone and activated the torch function. It wasn't a great light but it would pick out anything obvious. He ran it over the ground as he moved towards where the truck had stopped. A few more steps and his light found a surface to reflect back from. It was a pair of eyes, wide and morose.

Harry dropped to his knees close to a young man's face. He lifted his torch to run the light down his body. His feet were at the opposite end. He had bare knees and his trousers looked to be pulled down to just below them. Harry didn't think he had been dragged, the rest of him looked too well preserved. He leant forward so his cheek was just an inch or two from the young man's pursed lips to feel for his breath. There was nothing. The young man wore a big coat and his legs were pulled up so that it covered his thighs. Harry moved alongside him. The light was still poor.

'Hello!' Harry said instinctively. He shook the man from the shoulders — muscle memory perhaps, the response to a collapsed person he had been taught a hundred times in his career. He grabbed the wrist closest to him to feel for a pulse. The hand attached to it was wrapped in a tight bandage. There was nothing. He moved to the neck, which he knew to be a more reliable point. He pushed two fingers in hard, hard enough to detect even a slightest beat. Still nothing. He needed to start working on him. The man was lying on his side and Harry pushed him onto his back. He scrabbled over the zip on his jacket and tugged it down. He pulled the jacket open to expose the chest so he could try to massage the heart and keep the blood flowing around his body until someone came to help. He stopped dead in his tracks. For that to work, there would need to be some blood left in the first place. He was pretty sure there wasn't.

The puddle under the man's side was deep and still spreading, mainly around the hip area. The inside of his jacket was soaked with it and it was also on the man's chest and the underside of his chin. The gash causing the blood loss was clear and it explained why both thighs were exposed. His underwear was pulled down from the waistband and something incredibly sharp had sliced through it. It had sliced through the skin underneath too, deep enough to sever the femoral artery that fed blood to the legs. Harry had seen it happen before: a road traffic accident where a motorcyclist had collided with an Armco. The attending paramedic had told Harry that someone would bleed out completely in under two minutes from such an arterial wound. The biker had never stood a chance. This man hadn't either.

Harry rocked back on his haunches. All he could see was blood now. It was all over the road, stretching back the way Harry had come, but it seemed to be in clumps rather than from the spurt you would expect from an arterial bleed. Harry guessed that the young man's coat had caught the worst of it and that he was on his feet when he had been cut.

'HARRY!' He turned to the voice. It was Maddie and she was shrieking. He cast one more glance down at those morose eyes and made his way back towards the car. There was nothing he could do for him now. He broke into a jog. Maddie was still kneeling down. She stood up as Harry approached. Vince was doing chest compressions.

'How is she?' Harry asked, despite already knowing the answer.

'It's not her! It's not Rhiannon! It's a girl. The girl we saw. But it's not Rhiannon! We have to go. I've called it in. Patrols are on the way. We have to go after that truck!'

'The girl we saw? What girl?'

'The *missing* girl! We got pictures sent from her online stuff — Alyssa!'

'Alyssa? Of course!' He pictured those morose eyes now concealed by the darkness. 'Jack Knight!'

'We need to go after that truck!' Maddie screamed.

Harry shook his head. 'How? We can't get past her. And there's another body up there — Jack Knight, the boyfriend. He's bled out. He's dead.'

Maddie seemed to hesitate for a second. She shook her head gently like she was clearing her thoughts. 'We can drag her out of the way — him too and get after him! We know what he'll do. We *have* to stop him!'

'NO!' Harry gripped her by the arms. They were side on to the headlights of the patrol car and the light was so bright that he struggled to make out her expression. She jerked her hands back and Harry let her go. He had stained her sleeves with blood.

'We have to try!'

'We get someone here first *then* we go. He could be anywhere by now and we can't move her, you know that. We need to think. We need to be careful.'

'There's no time! We need to be doing something.' Maddie suddenly snatched away to the sound of a distant siren. It was getting closer and the lights soon broke the treeline. Maddie moved towards it.

'You okay, Vince?' Harry said. The moment Vince looked up Harry could see he was weary.

'She's right, boss. We need to get after him.'

Harry turned back to the slamming of car doors then the sound of running footsteps. Two officers came into view in front of the headlights. Another car announced its arrival with a burst of noise and lights behind the row of cars. Harry addressed the first two officers.

'Take over with the compressions. I need you and the other patrol to do what you can to guide the ambulance in. I can't spare any more patrols. There's another body further up the road. I'll sort a road closure the other end. There's nothing you can do for him. Work on *her*. Okay?'

Two sets of wide eyes nodded back. One of them snatched the radio that hung from her chest and announced that she had arrived on scene. She checked on the status of the ambulance and was told that no ambulance had been requested. Harry shrugged.

'There's been a lot going on. Get it here.' He got more nods. The other officer was already knelt beside Vince. The handover was seamless.

'Are we going after him?' Vince spoke the instant he was freed from his work on the ground. Harry could detect an edge to his words despite his breathlessness. This was a question Vince had already answered for himself.

'Yes,' Harry said. Two more uniform officers paced up to him.

'What do you need?' the leading officer said, but his attention soon shifted to the bundle on the ground.

'Do what you can to help. And we need to swap car keys.'

'Mine are in the ignition,' Vince said. The officer handed a set of keys to Vince with no further questions.

'Since we can't get out, we're taking the car at the back!' Vince shouted to Maddie. She stood by the back door of the car in which they'd arrived. Her head dipped out of view and then she reappeared with her radio. She ran quickly to the rearmost marked police car and Harry and Vince joined her. Vince had to reverse for a good distance to a point where it was wide enough to turn around. As the car whined back up the road, Harry reached up to turn on the interior lamp and its harsh white light exposed the amount of blood on him. It coated his hands, ran up his arms, and was splattered on his chest and lap.

'You okay, boss?' Vince said.

'Yeah, it's not mine. Are we all okay?' There was a pause before anyone answered.

'We're okay,' Vince said, 'but we need to find this piece of shit.'

'I know where he is.' Maddie's voice rasped from the background. 'I've been getting messages from his sister. She must have a way of tracking him — his truck at least.'

'Tracking?' Harry turned to her.

'Yes.' She lifted heavy eyes. They were fixed open, part-glazed. She looked close to breaking, as close as Harry had ever seen her.

'She must have been tracking us, too. That's how she knew which way we needed to turn. When I said to go straight on it was because she told me. I got a message. I didn't tell you. I didn't explain in case you wouldn't follow. I'm sorry, Harry, I'm still blundering on. I got caught out — it must be me she's tracking. I've been lapse. And we didn't get her back, did we? Rhiannon, I mean.' Harry could hear the desperation. He wanted to tell her not to worry, that people made mistakes, that everything was going to be okay. He couldn't. The images from those two kids laid out on the road were still fresh in his mind and he didn't believe it himself.

'No. But she wasn't the one lying out on that road. We still have a chance. Where is he?'

'At the back of the café. A few miles out. The truck has stopped but there's access on foot that way apparently. From mapping it looks like there are fields between it. No roads.'

'And she's tracking the truck, not him?'

'So she says.'

'He's heading back to the café. On foot. That would make sense. He knows everyone will be out looking for his vehicle.'

'He can't know we're close or that we know who he is, then? Maybe his sister is telling the truth?'

'A good liar will always stick as close to the truth as they can.' Harry ran his hand over his head. 'But, like you said, we don't have anything else. Take us back to the café, Vince. I'll call up and get whoever's left to be in the area.'

'You don't want to go in en masse?' Vince asked.

'No. Right now he might not be expecting us. Drop the car short, somewhere out of sight, and we'll walk in.'

Vince revved hard to pull away pinning Harry to his seat. 'We might be walking in, Harry, but this piece of shit ain't walking out. I'll tell you that now.'

'I might need you to hold back, Vince. Your uniform might spook him. I need to know what's going on before I start announcing us as police.'

'You're joking right! I ain't missing out on all the fun!'

'And there's my other reason, Vince. Just get us there. You'll be the first person I call when we need to take action.'

'You mean when the fun starts?'

Harry sniffed. He reached up to turn off the interior light and got a good look at the red staining up his arm.

'This isn't what I would call fun.'

CHAPTER 33

Harry and Maddie moved briskly across the broken surface of the café car park. Vince had parked the car up just a few metres short, just before the end of a thick hedgerow. He would be seconds away if he was called. Harry and Maddie both had radios in their coat pockets and also had their standard kit: an extendable baton, a pair of handcuffs and an irritant spray. It suddenly didn't seem much as they strode into the unknown.

The café was eerily quiet. Harry slowed up to take it fully in. He could see inside now. The lighting didn't look right; only the middle of the room was lit as if the rest of the lights had been turned off. It wasn't how he would expect it to look if it were open. He approached the door. Sure enough a *Closed* sign hung against the glass.

'This place is twenty-four-seven, right?'

'Yes,' Maddie said.

Harry peered through. He could make out the figure of a woman sitting at a table facing the door. She was in the only area that was lit. Her eyes were down and she was playing with her hands. Harry pulled at the door. It was locked but the sound made the woman jump as if she was suddenly plugged into the mains. She gathered herself together, stood up, and straightened her apron. She walked slowly towards them but struggled with the door, it took her a little while to open it. Harry tried his best to stay calm, to stay patient. He could tell that Maddie was doing the same.

Finally, the door unlocked and the woman made her way back to sit at the same table. Harry moved after her. He pulled out a chair and sat opposite her. He could sense Maddie stood off his right shoulder. The woman was back to looking at her hands where they rested in the middle of the table.

'I . . . I don't lock it often . . . Sorry!' She lifted her eyes and flickered a smile.

'You need to talk,' Harry said. The empty café had a strange atmosphere but his growling tone seemed to fill it instantly.

'I know that. I don't quite know where to start.'

'Where's Rhiannon?' Maddie cut in. Harry shot a hard look at her. This woman had the upper hand. Harry didn't like that and he sure as hell didn't want to be reinforcing it. They needed to be measured.

'She's here, on this site, but you need to understand. You need to know everything before you can help her.'

'Is she okay?' Maddie asked.

'She's okay. She's not far from here but you need to understand if you want to get close. Even then I can't promise anything. He's getting more and more unpredictable.'

'What do we need to understand?' Harry said.

'That I still have some control.'

'Control? What do you mean?'

The woman sighed. 'There's so much . . . I don't know—'

'The beginning. The short version. But make me understand.' The woman looked terrified. Harry thought that was genuine at least. 'Let's start with who you are . . . Michelle Garner . . . is that right?'

The woman nodded. 'We've never been a *normal* family — whatever the hell that means!' She tried a chuckle but it sounded cracked and brittle. She took a short while to get her thoughts in order. 'But we've always been a family. You know . . . together thick and thin. They tried to split us up more than once when my mum was alive. It didn't work. She knew that when she died they would try again. And they did. I couldn't let that happen. I told her I wouldn't let that happen. It was the last thing I said—'

'What did you do?' Harry's tone was a little warmer. Just enough he hoped to encourage her.

'My brother . . . he has issues — his mental health. He always has. If he were born now it might not be such an issue, but he's thirty-four. When he was a kid, no one understood him. They put him on a million different types of medication. Every doctor had a different idea, a different diagnosis. Schizophrenia was the most popular, but nothing they did seemed to help him. Anxiety, acute paranoia . . . we've heard them all. Now they say he has a Personality Disorder.'

'And what does that mean?'

'Well, it means there is nothing anyone can do for a start. Mark sees the world differently. And his place in it? He sees that different too.'

'And how is that?'

She finally lifted her eyes to meet with Harry's. 'He wants the same as you and I, deep down. I understand him. I've always been the only one who could. He has things that are important to him, just like we all do. He has needs and frustrations, just like we all do. And he wants to be liked — loved even — and part of something . . . Just like we all do. Once I understood that, I understood him. Imagine if *you* saw the world different to every one of the seven billion plus others you shared it with.'

'He's a murderer.' Harry lifted his arms and laid them on the table. He had zipped his waxed jacket up to hide the clump of blood on his chest but now he pulled up the sleeves to show the bright red staining on his white shirt. Michelle's eyes fell to it and she bit down on a bottom lip that still quivered while Harry continued. 'This is the blood of a young man lying out on the road, sliced down to the bone so he would bleed out. He's dead. Your brother killed him — his girlfriend, too. That cannot happen to my colleague and I suggest we are running out of time.'

The woman's hand rose to cover her mouth and she sobbed a little behind it. 'I never wanted him to hurt those kids. They were just teenagers messing around. I knew Mark wouldn't like that. I knew the boy was in danger from the off.'

Harry pushed his jacket sleeves back down. He needed her to be able to focus.

'What *did* you want, Michelle?'

'To keep my family together. Mark was always the problem. He caused issues at home; he was a threat to my little brother when he was born. No one knew how Mark would cope with that. He was okay, but only because I was pulling his strings, *telling* him it was all okay. Alex is our half-brother. He has a different dad. Mark doesn't understand things like that. He doesn't cope well.'

'So what did you do?'

'I made him see Alex for what he is. *Half* our brother is still our brother. I played on the fact that our mother loved him so much. It was easy enough. But his dad, our stepdad . . . I could never get Mark to even acknowledge him.'

'Alex turned up in the middle of my city covered in someone else's blood. His dad's blood. Your brother killed him, didn't he?'

Michelle nodded. 'He just got out of control.'

'Tell me about that?'

'Someone got hold of Mark — or some group at least. He used to spend all his time online, playing games or watching videos. A lot of it was disturbing stuff. He could never hold down a job, he's never made a friend in his life. He wouldn't even know how to talk to a girl! But he wanted all these things, just like we all do. He just wanted to fit in, but he was never going to be able to do that. Someone got hold of him.

They told him they were part of some organisation, like an underground organisation with members all over the world. Like the Masons, you know, but a lot darker. They asked him to join. Sold him the benefits and he fell for it hook, line and sinker. He's always been the type to fixate and this became it — became his everything, his obsession.'

'Organisation?'

'They have a name — something about the *left-hand path*. It's linked to devil worship but they don't actually believe in the devil. It's complicated, but basically you have to prove you can live like the devil would. The thinking is that if the devil *was* a real thing, if he were alive today, he would be in charge because he would take what he wanted and he wouldn't be held back by the sort of things that we would. Like being part of a society with rules that looks after the weak. Does that make sense? It all sounds so ridiculous out loud!' She snorted a little and gave a strained smile.

'Carry on.' Harry was stern. This was all sounding familiar after what he had read of the Jarod Logan investigation, but he wanted her to explain what she knew.

'I really don't know how to explain it. My brother has been walking around with his left hand bleeding for nearly six months. Every day he digs at his palm with some piece of metal. It's all part of the commitment apparently. It's idiotic. But it was more than just some symbolic self-harm. These people were getting him to do things. *Expressions of loyalty* they called them. At first it was silly things like shoplifting or running up behind someone and slapping them. He had to get evidence of what he was doing on his mobile phone and he would send it off. It was done over something like a messenger app that was all encrypted. Some of the stuff he was sending and the people he was talking to . . . I could see they were going to get him into a lot of trouble. His *tasks* were . . . escalating, the things they were telling him to do getting nastier. He punched some pensioner to the ground then kicked him. He looked like such a frail old man. This was just in the High Street and in the middle of the day.

He was going to get himself arrested and that was where our troubles had come from before. When mum died, Social Services had already been back in touch. They were already saying that I wouldn't be able to cope when I said I would be Alex's primary carer. We were on a six-month trial period. Mark was living with us and he was out punching pensioners to the floor! It wasn't going to end well. Either Alex was going to get taken away or Mark was going to prison. Either way I wasn't keeping my promise to mum.'

'You seem to know a lot about what your brother was up to. Fine details, too. Did he confide in you about all this?'

'No. I cloned his phone a while ago, before all this started even. I know what you're going to think about that. I know you won't understand. You can't. I was trying to keep him out of trouble. To do that I had to know who he was talking to, what he was looking at. It was so simple to do . . . I could see everything he was seeing on my own handset. I saw this thing escalate so quickly! So I stepped in. It wasn't hard at all. His contact wasn't using a real name and there were no personal details. Anyway, I had seen everything that was said between them. I just approached him using another fictional name and I said there had been a security breach, that the phones had been compromised and they both needed to change their names. I told Mark he should ignore anyone else. This group used odd language — distinctive. It was easy to talk like they did. Whoever had been in touch with him lost interest almost instantly — so quickly that it just confirmed to me what I suspected from the start . . . that this organisation didn't even exist. It was just one person — maybe just some kid winding my brother up for fun for all I knew! I was the only one left communicating with Mark and he really believed I was this organisation.'

'So if this negative influence stopped, how did we get here?'

'I lost control. I planned on phasing it out, moving him onto something else if I could . . .' Her eyes flicked between him and Maddie as if she was choosing her next words very carefully. 'Then I saw an opportunity. There was this one social worker . . . she had it in for us from the start. As soon as my mum died, she came for Alex. She wanted to put him into care. Mark was waiting for a task, so I thought I would give him one more. He was just supposed to rough her up, scare her a bit . . .' Michelle was suddenly racked with sobs. Harry sat back. The outburst was sudden. 'He drowned her!'

Harry didn't say anything; he wanted her to continue. He did his best to remain impassive.

'He made it look like she did it herself. I saw the photos. These people — or this person . . . when they had Mark do one of his *tasks*, he had to send proof. He would send a *before* and an *after*. I think he just walked her into a lake. He'd made her write out a note. He sent a picture of that, too. I don't know how he did that. How do you make someone do something like that? I wouldn't even know where to start.'

'What did you do then?' Harry said.

'I was panicking, as you can imagine. The whole idea was to get him *out* of trouble and now he was responsible for someone's death! My mum hadn't been gone long — there was so much to sort out. I just didn't know where my head was. I still had access to her bank accounts. She had savings. I took everything I could and I told the letting company that we were leaving. I just took the money and I moved us all away. I don't know . . . maybe I thought I could run away from everything. I bought into the café down here. It was just an opportunity that seemed to be the right distance away. The only thing Mark had ever done for work was selling a few loads of firewood. He used to know a lorry driver who delivered cut wood in bulk and he would chuck Mark some to sell. That driver came through the café here and he told me they were looking for an investor. It seemed to make sense. I put mum's savings into buying a share of the café. It gave me a job and a place to live upstairs. I bought Mark a lorry so he could carry on with the wood business but he quickly lost interest.'

'Because he wanted to carry on with expressing his loyalty to what he thought was some underground organisation?'

'It was all he cared about. Whoever had first got hold of him had filled his head with what he could achieve if he was part of this group — or rather how he would never achieve anything if he wasn't. And he was convinced that he'd get accepted sooner if he escalated quickly — he was desperate to prove himself. They'd told him there was extra kudos for recruiting others so he started trying to pick up contacts through online gaming or just on social media.'

'How many did he recruit?'

Michelle's head dropped a little. 'Two.'

'Any more? Only you don't look too sure?'

'Two, only two. I just didn't want to be telling the police all this. All I've been trying to do for the last eighteen months is trying to keep a lid on him. And here I am . . .'

'What two?'

'What two? You mean who? I didn't get names — I didn't want to know.'

'So how do you know there were only two?'

'Because of his phone. He found them the same way someone found him, through video games. But then he would contact them on his phone via a messenger app. He was now the one setting *them* tasks and they were sending their own pictures as evidence. But he would meet up with them quite early on, before the tasks got too bad and once they had proven themselves with some minor stuff. He's never trusted anyone. He would meet them here. It was tearing me up. I saw these people come in here to meet him for the first time and they had no idea. But I did! I knew exactly what was waiting for them, what was expected of them.'

'And now they're both dead.'

Michelle nodded. 'I saw the older one on the news. They said the name on there and were asking for information about him. I had to turn it off. I saw the pictures of when . . . Of *after*.'

'One of the worst scenes I have attended. Why? If he was recruiting these people, why kill them?'

'Because they refused. Because they weren't as sucked in as Mark, weren't as committed. That would upset him more than you can imagine. They both got to a point where they realised this was serious, that this wasn't right, that the end wasn't the means even if it was all true. Mark didn't take that well. He took it personal, like it was a slant on him, on his judgement.'

'So why didn't you cut it off? Tell him it was all made up, that these violent acts were not for anything! There were things you could have done!'

'I would have done. But Alex . . . I didn't know how Mark would take it. But I was certain he would be humiliated — crushed! Then he'd become enraged and unpredictable — more of a threat to me and Alex.'

'So what was your plan?'

'To wind it down. I was trying . . . I just couldn't.'

'And your stepdad?'

He found us. I moved away without his knowledge but he came looking for Alex, but also the money. He was probably entitled to *some*. But I'd already spent it, and if he got hold of Alex then that was the family splitting up and I'd promised mum . . . So I used Mark . . .'

'You tasked him to kill him? As part of him showing his loyalty?'

'It was just supposed to be a beating — nothing more. I know the sort of man he is — was! He would have backed right off if Mark had reared up at him, especially if he knew my mum wasn't around to intervene. He was a gentle man, no fighter. But Mark read the task his own way. I think he was starting to get frustrated. He wanted to make a point. He thought that he could speed up his entry into this secret organisation *and* he suddenly talked about trying to secure Alex's membership too. I didn't see that coming. He'd never really cared about Alex, but now he said he was committed to "setting him up for life". That's what he said he was doing.'

Michelle stopped. It seemed to Harry that she was preparing for the next instalment of her story, breathing deeply, but even as she began her voice broke with emotion.

'He strung my stepdad up, a rope under the shoulders. I've never seen anything like it. I didn't know it was going on until I got the picture — the *before*. I could tell where he was and I tried to get there in time. He was held up under his arms by a rope and he cut him — the top of his leg. There was so much blood! He did it here. Out the back. By the time I made it there he was already gone and Alex was just stood looking up at his dad. He wasn't crying. He wasn't doing anything! He was covered in the blood. I'll have that image for as long as I live!' She was sobbing uncontrollably now. She pulled a phone from her pocket and fidgeted with it. A few seconds later, she spun the screen around. The image on the phone was sharp. It was their boy dripping in fresh blood, his eyes bulging wide, his right hand gripped tightly around the handle of a knife.

'This was the *after* picture. He's holding the knife but Mark mocked that up — I know that. The way he was positioned, Alex couldn't even have reached. Mark figured a young boy like that, doing something so horrific, would be instantly accepted into this fantasy group of his and be sorted for life. Like I said, I didn't see that coming.'

'No wonder he won't talk if that's what he saw!' Maddie's voice was hushed, not directed to anyone, But the woman seized on it.

'He won't talk because I told him not to! I panicked. Mark was out of control. I knew I had to get Alex away from here. I waited until Mark went to sleep. He doesn't sleep at night, not like normal people, and he's often up all night. He doesn't sleep much, truth be told. He dozed off at like six a.m. I waited. Then I got Alex up. He was still wearing the same clothes, still covered in his dad's blood, I did try to clean him but he wouldn't let me. Then I had an idea to get him safe. I drove him into the nearest town, I was in such a rush I didn't even put his shoes on! I pushed him out near the shops. I told him he would be safe. I thought that the blood might actually help, that looking like that he'd get straight into emergency care and he wouldn't need to say a single word. I knew you lot would be all around him and he would be safe. I told him not to talk. I made him promise. I said the police would come and he should let them look after him but not to talk to them — not a word. Not until I could figure all this out and he could come home . . .' She sniffed. 'I told him I'd come back for him then. I never did.'

'So Mark doesn't know you handed him over?'

'He did. He must have followed me. He never told me but I got a photo. It was of Alex. He was sitting down, pushed against a shop window. He looked so scared!' She lifted her eyes to Maddie. 'You were talking to him. He called it *before*! It made my blood run cold. I didn't know what *after* meant for sure in that instance, but I knew that he intended for someone in that picture to die. I thought it was going to be Alex.'

'But he meant me.' Maddie's voice was a low monotone. 'And now it's Rhiannon! You need to tell us where they are. He's sent you a picture, hasn't he? A *before*?' Maddie was more animated now and leaned in closer.

'Yes.' The woman gestured at the phone.

Maddie snatched it up. After a few seconds, she dropped it clumsily back on the table as if it was burning hot.

'Harry!' Maddie breathed.

There was a full-screen image of Rhiannon. It looked like the photo had been taken square on to her but from lower down. She was hanging up with thick rope running under her shoulders, her arms pulled over it and behind her back where they looked to be restrained. She looked so vulnerable with the ropes dug deep into her armpits. She was still in her running gear.

'You said we have an opportunity?' Harry said. He was fighting with himself to stay calm. He wanted to stand up, to stomp around the site, to call in everyone he could. But he remembered Jack Knight. He remembered it was two minutes for someone to be beyond help. He needed to be able to get close.

'My mum was wrong, you know, about keeping the family together at all costs. I saw how she worked at it. In the last twenty years of her life it was all she was doing, trying to pretend like we were a normal family. But she was wrong. We can't be anything all the while Mark's around. Maybe prison is the right answer.'

'I think you're right. Where is he, Michelle? This needs to end.'

Michelle shook her head. Her eyes dropped back to the table. 'There are two caravans together, static ones. They were on the site when we got here. He uses those. He lives in one of them most of the time now. The other one is where he . . . It's where that photo was taken of your friend. It's out the back and just walk north. He'll be in there.'

'Is that a guess or do you know that for certain?'

'I told him to wait there. As part of his task, I mean. I don't know for sure.'

'You're tracking him, though, right?'

'His truck.'

'And us? How were you tracking us?'

Her eyes lifted to Maddie. They rested on her coat pocket. She dug around, her hand came out and she opened her palm to a receipt, a black square of plastic and a key.

'That's a tracking tile. It works with an app on that phone. When you were in here, I dropped it in your pocket. You can register as many tiles as you want. I just needed to know when you were close . . . I was just trying to keep him out of trouble.' Maddie's jaw hung open.

Harry turned back to Michelle.

'Quite the controlling type, aren't you?'

'I've had to be. You don't understand what it's like living with someone like Mark. He's always been violent. It's like he's got no idea what it's like for someone to be on the receiving end. He doesn't care. It was only a matter of time before he hurt someone close to him.'

'How long do we have?'

Michelle shook her head. 'I told him to wait. I told him he would get further instructions. He was going to drag her behind his lorry tonight but I convinced him to save the police officer as his final expression of loyalty. I said that the final one should be the most impressive and that it needs to be seen first-hand. I was trying to think fast. But that's what I meant by an opportunity.'

'So Mark is expecting someone?'

'That's what I told him.'

'Someone who is already a member of this group, who believes the same things he does and lives his life the same way?'

'Yes, that's right. A witness to his final act.'

'And you think we can do that? Turn up and convince him we've been giving him the instructions all the time and we're here to take him away to his dream life?'

'No. Just you. He'll never believe a woman. I know how he thinks.' Harry was shaking his head. 'You said you wanted to get close,' she said. 'That should get you close.'

'And you're okay with your brother getting hurt? He doesn't sound like someone who'll put his hands up and come quietly. You're happy to be complicit in his capture? In his imprisonment?'

'I can't cope with him. I can't keep Alex safe, not for certain. And I think he would hurt me if he ever found out. It's time someone else took control of him.'

'Your messages with Mark? They're on this phone, too?' Harry turned back to Maddie. She appeared distracted, still looking down at the tracker in her open hand.

'They're on there — the red symbol with three yellow dots.'

Harry fumbled over the phone. The home screen had apps lined up as squares. One was a solid red with three yellow dots forming a triangle. He pressed it and a messaging system opened up instantly. There was only one conversation feed. It was labelled X. Harry pressed on it and it opened up to the last few messages. The picture of Rhiannon had been sent fifteen minutes before. The message for him to wait was sent straight back.

'He hasn't replied. How do you know he's waiting?' Harry growled. Michelle shrugged. 'He's listening to me less and less.'

Harry scrolled through the feed. The messages seemed to be never-ending. He tried to absorb what he could. Much of it was repetitive, the language used distinctive. He skipped over the picture of Jack Knight lying out on the road. He handed the phone back to Maddie. Michelle was still sat playing with her hands opposite him.

Harry moved quickly, he grabbed her firmly by one of her wrists and wrenched her backwards. She had no chance to stand up, her chair scraped as she moved and nearly tipped. He dragged her towards the edge of the room.

'WHAT ARE YOU DOING?' Harry pulled out his handcuffs and roughly secured her wrist to a thick radiator. 'WHAT ARE YOU DOING!' she screamed again, 'I'M TRYING TO HELP! IT'S MARK! IT'S MARK YOU NEED!'

'You're under arrest. You have to answer for what you are part of.'

Michelle's chest was rising and falling as she sucked in large gulps, she looked like she was going to scream again, she took in the air but instead of forming words it was expelled in a sigh with words intermingled.

'I was just trying to protect my family.'

'At the expense of all others.' Harry was unrelenting. He wasn't going to give her a way out. She didn't deserve it. He looked at Maddie.

'Are you okay?'

She stared back. 'Yes.' Her voice was more resolute, as if she had rediscovered something within herself.

'I'll get Vince in here to watch her. No one else comes close. We need to handle this carefully. You come with me, but I need you to hold back and stay out of sight. I can't have him seeing you.'

'You're going out there alone?'

'Yes. I'll need you close in case it goes wrong.'

'And you want me backing you up, not Vince?'

'If I told you to stay here, would you?'

'No.' Maddie's expression backed up her words.

'As I thought. Vince is a hothead anyway. I need someone to trust me, to stay back like I've asked. I need the Maddie that follows instructions and is careful. And we need to go now.'

'Okay then.'

'And Maddie . . . how we got here doesn't matter. Not a jot. What we do from now is all that matters, okay?'

Maddie nodded.

Harry threw off his coat. He looked down his front at the red staining on his white shirt. He unbuttoned it and pulled it off.

'Harry?' Maddie's uncertainty was clear.

He ignored her. He strode to the back of the café and through a door that led through to a simple but commercial kitchen. He took a sharp-looking knife from a rack and cut out a stained piece of the shirt. He then paced back through to the café, pulled his jacket back on and zipped it up tight. He held the piece of bloodied shirt as a wad in his left hand. He would tie it on the way.

'Harry, we don't know how much of this is even true. And, say it is, do you really think you can fool him?'

'I don't see any other choice. But we won't fool him like she suggested. He won't fall for that, not for an instant. I need to get close. Pass me her phone.'

Maddie did as she was asked. He typed out a message. The phone made a sound like someone was blowing across the top of a bottle.

'What did you send?'

'Stay close. Call up on air and make sure all other patrols are aware to stay away until they get your signal. And make sure an ambulance is part of the backup. This has the makings of going very wrong.'

'What did you send, Harry?'

'His final task. I'm certain at least some of what she was saying was the truth. That means that the only thing in this world he trusts is this phone.'

'Task? What task?'

'Me.'

CHAPTER 34

The gravel crunched under Harry's feet. The rain had largely stopped. A breeze cut across him carrying a few errant raindrops and squeaked a battered metal sign that clung to the back of the building and announced that *Coke is it!* His jacket was not designed to be worn against the skin and the waxed material was cold and coarse. Still, he pulled it tighter.

The static homes were side by side and the ends of both were presented by his angle of approach. The doors would be on each of their sides. He arced out to the right until he could see the doors. They were halfway up the lengths of the caravans and the door to the left one was open. He glanced back over his shoulder. The door from which he had just left the café was open; he had been sure to wedge it. Maddie might have stepped through it by now and into the cover of outbuildings, old fridges and seemingly random fence panels. It should be easy for her to stay out of sight. He checked his left hand. The bloody rag from his white shirt was tied tightly across his palm. He closed fingers back over it and then thumped on the back of the open door.

The caravan was in darkness. They both were. There were no external lights in this area either. Only the moon and the distant lights from the main road relieved what would have been total darkness. His view through the door was to the back wall and nothing else. Now he was closer, he could see how dilapidated the caravan had become: the door hung at an angle; the once-white walls were yellowed and had a number of thick, black marks smudged into the side; a patch of the ceiling was hanging down; a pane in the far window showed a long crack against the moonlight.

He counted to five in his head and then knocked again, firmer this time, and then listened intently. The sounds were unchanged: the breeze in the trees, the squeak of *Coke is it!* and the occasional drip of rain on something hard. He stepped back from the door a little; he wanted enough space to be able to react.

'Do I have a loyal friend in there?' Harry growled, still watching the doorway intently. 'Or an enemy?' He counted another five before starting up again. 'Time is against us. We need to move. I am to take you to your next phase.' Still nothing. 'You have done well. Few are called . . . this is your calling.' Harry stepped away further, far enough to take in the large window further down and a smaller one at the end. There was no answer. Then the doorway flared with a bright yellow light.

'Enter!' Mark Garner's voice was booming and self-confident, even when conveyed in a single word. Harry knew he couldn't hesitate. He moved to the steps and hauled himself up.

Harry had to squint in the bright light. He had stepped straight into the middle of Garner's living quarters. He could make out kitchen units opposite, a sink with layers of dust by his left hip and a seating area to the other side of it. A bench seat stretched across the left end but much of it was just a wooden carcass with only a couple of battered seat cushions remaining. The carpet was stained a dark brown — heavily. He still couldn't see anybody. A short hallway led away to his right and got progressively darker as it stretched away from him. He could see doors to either side and at the farthest end they hung open like black mouths.

'Where are you, friend?' Harry said. He kept facing to the right.

'Into the light.' The voice boomed from that direction, probably via the left doorway but Harry couldn't be sure. He still couldn't see much. The only light hung on a bare wire from the middle of the ceiling. It was a side-step left — and he took it. Most of the staining on the floor was also directly under the light and he now stood in the middle of it. The floor felt softer here, as if carpeted with sponge. Now he was closer he could see that the staining was more of a red around the edges. There were also red spots on the wall and even on the ceiling. He could feel the heat of the bulb on his head and its brightness meant that his view of the opposite end was now even poorer.

'You're here for me, are you?'

A man stepped out into the corridor. He wore a long, dark coat with the hood up and tight over his head. His face was flushed, his eyes bright and intense. He was the right age to be Garner and the slim build, the coat and the shape the hood made all matched the blurred image on the dashcam footage. His jacket hung open over a white top and black jeans that rucked over boots that had a thick lip running around them.

'You are wise to be cautious,' Harry said, 'but we must move. Your heroic actions have attracted attention. We will move you to safety, somewhere you can regroup. This is a common scenario for us.' Harry had been keeping his hands in his pockets but he took them out and raised them slightly in an open gesture as he spoke. Garner's attention seemed to follow his hand movements and was drawn to Harry's left and the bloodied cotton tied around it.

'You have the wound!' Garner grinned with delight.

'Of course. I made the choice.' Harry repeated a phrase he had seen a number of times in the messages. He was aware that he was quickly running out of stock phrases, though. There hadn't been much time to study the phone message history for long and he wasn't going to stand up to much scrutiny. He needed to move this on. 'We received your last expression. Is she here?'

'I was told to wait. Why?'

'Your expressions have come to the attention of the local police. They may come here at some point. This is not the right place to finish your work. The final act of loyalty is something we need to see and savour. That way there is no doubting you. You have done well. You have achieved much. We seek to witness your final expression.'

'Then take a seat!'

'Not here.' Harry growled, the change in his tone was marked and deliberate. He needed to act like he was in charge.

Garner's smile dropped away and he glanced back into the bedroom from which he had stepped. His hand reached in, a light blinked on inside and made a sharp silhouette of him against the side wall. Harry could see into a section of the room and some of the far wall. There was missing plasterboard from which yawned a mustard-coloured tangle of what would have been insulation. He couldn't see much else. He couldn't see Rhiannon.

'Come and see her. While she is restrained. While she is ready. Come and see how I prepare them!'

Harry stayed still. 'Bring her. You will prepare her again for us all. You will have time and space. Here, we do not.'

'Come see.' Garner's tone changed and was tinged with menace. He didn't believe Harry's facade, not for a second. Harry had to get closer now. He stepped forward, out of the light. He moved down the corridor. The man's right hand was still concealed behind the door. Harry's hands were back in his coat pocket, his right gripped tightly around the solid metal of his baton. As he moved closer the man stepped further into the room. Harry got a flash of someone else's arm further in but Garner hampered his view. He was almost close enough to touch him. The man turned back into the room, his movement just enough for Harry to see in better, to see the side of Rhiannon's face. Her eyes were bulging, her mouth flinching over a piece of rope passing tightly between her jaws. They made eye contact. It was a split second. It was all Harry needed.

The blows came at the same time. The man stepped away from the door and his right arm rose up in a blur of movement, the blade catching the light from the room. Harry's right fist had to swing in an arc. The hall was too narrow to extend the baton, but gripping it in his fist gave his blow extra venom. The knife never reached Harry. Instead the man stumbled backwards, enough for Harry to make it to the edge of the doorway and to see in. Garner looked dazed but he recovered quickly and shifted his weight to where he had a steady base. His face was a snarl but his attention shifted and he turned towards Rhiannon, still holding the knife. She was strung up the same as in the photo, her whole side on show, no means of protecting herself. He lunged towards her. Harry hit out again. This time his baton snapped open in the air. He felt the blow through is forearm, a solid hit across the side of Garner's head and down his back. He roared out as he lost balance and crashed into the far wall. Harry looked over him. He was still holding the knife in his right hand. Harry brought the asp down again on his exposed side as hard as he could. There was another roar of pain. He lifted the baton to strike again.

'HARRY!' Maddie's voice was shrill as it cut through his fog. His baton was still raised but he held it in the air. The man gave a low moan. He didn't look like he was trying to get up. Harry stepped forward, his front foot resting on the knife and trapping the man's fingers at the same time. The man barely reacted. Harry turned to see Maddie fussing over Rhiannon. She was saying something he couldn't make out and talking fast. There was blood on Rhiannon's side and more leaked as he looked. It was a lot. Rhiannon had been fidgeting against her restraints when he walked in. She wasn't now. Her face was down, her eyes still wide but unfocussed. The colour was running from her face.

'She's hurt! Where is she hurt?' Maddie had stepped back, frozen. The blood was now coating Rhiannon's lower half; it looked to be leaking out from everywhere. Harry had a better idea where it was coming from. He lifted his foot and snatched the knife. The end had a film of red that caught in the light as he lifted it to cut through the ropes holding Rhiannon up. It was a thick rope, but it came apart in just a few seconds. Rhiannon dropped towards him and he was able to support her under her shoulders as in an embrace. He was rough and hurried laying her onto the bare floor. He knew there was so little time. He was on his knees but straightened to tear off his belt. Rhiannon was still in tight-fitting running bottoms. He pulled them down. Her white underwear was drenched red. The blood was suddenly unabated, spurting from an ugly gash in the top of her right thigh. It caught him on his neck and his chin, and some into his eyes. He turned away momentarily to gasp. Her leg rose up — someone was lifting it. Harry was now aware of a police uniform next to him, nothing else. He swiped his sleeve over his face and wrapped his belt above the wound then pulled it as tight as he could. It should have hurt like hell but there was barely a reaction from Rhiannon. More officers were in the room, a voice boomed through: Vince's. He was rough-handling the man on the floor. He sat him up. His hands were cuffed behind his back. His bright blue eyes seemed almost backlit as Harry turned to them. He beamed a smile.

'I am part of something now! I have proven worthy! I will be protected!' His voice was filled with glee.

'HARRY!' Someone had been calling his name, now they were yelling. A hand took a firm hold of his shoulder too. He shrugged it off but it was enough to break his attention from Garner. His eyes fell back to Rhiannon's injury. The blood loss might have stopped; it was slower for sure.

'HARRY!' This time he was pulled backwards. 'HARRY! The ambulance is here! Let them through!'

He scrambled backwards, still pulled by his shoulders. Two green uniforms bumped him as they passed. They put holdalls down that they immediately started emptying. Garner was gone. Harry hadn't seen him go. He hadn't seen the room fill with officers either, but now they were everywhere he looked. It was a small room and they all took a step back as the paramedics got to work. Suddenly he couldn't see Rhiannon. The hand pulling his shoulder was gentler, as was the voice in his ear. It was Vince again.

'Come on, boss. Let's get you cleaned up at least.'

Harry allowed himself to be led back down the hall. The rest of the caravan was full of police too. They all fixed on him and he heard a hushed 'Jesus!' as he moved past. He stopped under the light of the living area and looked down at his hands. They were so sticky with blood he could barely part his fingers. It was everywhere.

'Doesn't work!' Vince's was at the dusty sink spinning the taps. 'You okay?'

'Maddie?' Harry spluttered.

'Still in there. She won't leave Rhiannon, boss.'

Harry looked to the doorway at the end of the corridor. A uniformed officer stepped out of the room shaking her head. She ran a hand through her hair, held her hat against her chest and turned her shocked expression to the floor.

'We need everyone out,' Harry said. 'They need room to move. We need everyone OUT!' Heads turned to him and there was an immediate response as officers made for the door. Harry stayed still. Vince did too. 'I don't know how we recover from this — any of us . . . If she . . .' Vince didn't reply. Then there was a shout and the soles of bare feet appeared at the door. Two officers were either side of Rhiannon. She was being carried flat. They bumped and scraped against the doorway. Maddie followed, holding Rhiannon up under her shoulders. A paramedic came next with a bag of fluid above his head so gravity could get it into their fallen colleague. It wouldn't be enough, *surely*? She had lost a lot of blood. It was everywhere, splattered up each of her colleagues and still marking the floor as they moved.

Harry moved out of the way as the procession moved past and out the door then he followed. The rain was back and much heavier. Rhiannon was loaded into an ambulance that had pulled around just a few metres away. Police cars were being hurriedly moved to allow it to get back out. The moving lights from the vehicles sliced up the dark expanse and the thick raindrops. The ambulance pulled away and the rain seemed even harder somehow. Harry turned his face up to it. He rubbed his hands together in it, too. The blood ran off him as he listened to the siren fire up loud. Patrol cars fired up too; they would race ahead to help clear a path. Harry couldn't help but think that it was too little too late. That he had failed, that he could have done something different. He felt a hand back on his shoulder.

'You did good, boss,' Vince said. 'Everything you could.'

'Not good enough.'

'Let's get you cleaned up. Rhiannon's got every chance. You patched her up quick. She'll be alright.'

'And if she isn't?'

Vince sighed. 'You told me something once when I was a lot younger in service. You were telling me off at the time and I thought you were a right miserable bastard. You said don't go building a bridge until you find a river. Hardly original, but you were right.'

'I've always been a pompous shit.' Harry shivered, suddenly aware of water running down his back.

'Oh, I know that! Something else you said to me once, or someone did anyway: a good copper never gets wet. Now look at us stood out here!'

Harry felt a light touch on his shoulder again and he allowed himself to be led away.

CHAPTER 35

Two days later

Maddie remembered the white noise of traffic from the bus depot opposite and the passing traffic from her first visit. The frontage of the Victorian terrace was the same, too, as was the experience when she pressed the doorbell marked *Mills*. Alyssa Mills's dad had been visited on numerous occasions in the previous forty-eight hours. There was an important message about his daughter that needed delivering and it needed to be done face-to-face. Maddie didn't wait long until she was back to leaning on the doorbell. She would stand there all day if she had to. She was certain he was in.

'Keep your eye on the window up there,' Maddie said. She had come out with a uniform officer, someone who had been before and failed to get a response. When Maddie had seen that the message was still outstanding, she had a sudden desire to be the one delivering it. She had been there. She had seen what had happened and part of her felt responsible.

'You lot again!' Maddie turned to where her colleague was leaning back at such an angle that his hat threatened to fall off. 'I don't take visitors! I ain't seen her. If she's in some sort of trouble you need to take it up with her!'

Maddie stepped out from under the porch and Mills's head shifted to her. He was leaning far enough out for her to see his bare arms. She was pretty sure they were sticking out from the same vest he wore last time. His face creased into an instant smile. 'Oh, well . . . Detective Graves, right?'

'Ives. Maddie Ives. I need to come up and speak with you.'

He waved his hands like he was waving her away. His movements were a little clumsy and he tipped towards the window. His right arm shot out to steady himself. 'Well, now, that's different. I know better than to say no to the prettiest police detective in all the forces, now, don't I!' He disappeared as if the building had sucked him back in. It was to push him back out again almost instantly. Maddie just had time to roll her eyes at her colleague before the voice from above was back.

'You ain't gonna nick me, are you?'

'No. That's not why I'm here at all, Mr Mills.'

'Kevin, remember?' He grinned and then he was gone again. It was longer than it should have been before the door opened. Mr Mills's entire outfit appeared to be identical to Maddie's previous visit: the same tracksuit bottoms and the same bare feet that then propelled him up the stairs. Maddie followed him up. As before, the front door to his flat was pushed open. This time he remained standing at least, but the task of looking down and concentrating on his television remote had him swaying. Finally it clicked off and he looked up. 'I figured I'd do it first this time, before you did!' He was still beaming. 'Get you anything?'

'No, thank you. As before, sir, we're here about Alys—'

'Yeah, I ain't seen her. I know she goes away. She's done it before. She goes to a mate's house and she's got an aunt.' His smile was gone. He rubbed the back of his head. He looked embarrassed; his stance was like that of a small boy trying to explain that he had done something bad. 'I drink, you see. My angel, she doesn't like it. She looks after me, but sometimes she takes a break. I get that.

340

She'll be with a mate or with her aunt. I got her address somewhere . . .' His hands plunged into his pockets like he was searching himself.

'We've found Alyssa, Kevin.' Maddie was aware that her colleague reached up to take her hat off in a well-practiced movement. Kevin watched it; his face immediately drained of all colour.

'Oh no, no! Not bad! Not my Alyssa!'

'She was involved in a road traffic incident. I'm sorry, Kevin. She died at the scene.'

And there it was. Maddie had seen this too many times. The human form froze. It was like someone had waved a wand to change them into a waxwork version of themselves. The skin became ashen, the expression unmoving, the eyes opaque. It lasted a few seconds then life seemed to return in the form of a sharp inhalation. He stumbled a little. Maddie reached out. He ignored her. The sofa was behind him and he fell to sit on the arm.

'Died . . .' he whispered. His eyes burst with silent tears. His right hand lifted and just hung in the air. Finally his hand rested under his nose.

'I'm so sorry. Do you have someone that can come here, that can be with you.'

His eyes lifted to hers. 'She was everything, every*one*. No one else . . . they all left me to it. To drink myself to death. I don't blame them . . . She didn't . . .' The hand now squeezed his nose. More tears followed. They were still silent.

Maddie lowered herself to more of a squat, closer to his level. 'I would really like to get someone here. Who's this aunt you talk about? Is that your sister? I could call—'

'You need to leave.' There was suddenly strength in his voice. It wasn't anger — Maddie had seen that enough times when delivering a message like this — it was more like determination. His eyes fell to the floor; they seemed to be searching. She followed his gaze. There were empty bottles of cheap-looking wine and cider under a low table. He bent forward to pull some of them out. He checked their content and threw them to the side of the room in disgust then walked to the kitchen area.

'I'd like to get someone here to be with you!' Maddie called out.

'You need to LEAVE!' This time there was anger, clear anger. Kevin Mills reappeared with two bottles of wine, one in each fist. He swigged at the open one.

'I know this is a shock, but that won't help. You need—'

'I NEED YOU TO LEAVE!'

She could see there was only escalation from here. She held up her palms. 'Of course. But I am so sorry, Kevin. I'd like to come back in a couple of days, maybe. Just to be sure you're doing okay. Is that alright?'

'Doing okay!' He chuckled. His eyes rested on the contents in the bottle in his right fist. He swirled it.

'You'll have questions, when this has all sunk in. I'll sit down with you and we can talk it out.'

His right arm jerked. The sound of the bottle smashing against a far wall made Maddie jump. She hadn't seen that coming. He threw the full bottle too, but this thudded into the carpet and didn't break. He lifted his hands and seemed to be inspecting them closely.

'Questions? I'm terrified of the answers . . . I know I'm part of this, no matter what happened. I pushed her away. All that time I lost, all that time I should have been spending with my girl — being a dad! I saw the way she looked at me. She told me she knew who I was, that it didn't matter, but you can't hide a look. I just kept telling myself that I would be her dad, that there was still time for me to be something she was proud of. But I never will . . . I never will!'

Maddie saw a mobile phone on the counter that divided the living area with the kitchen. She scooped it up.

'What's the name of that aunt? You need your family around you at this time. Is she your sister?'

Kevin nodded. It turned into a shake of the head. 'We don't speak, not for a long time. My fault.'

Maddie was already scrolling through the contacts. There were six. The only female name was *Sandra*. She stepped away. Kevin slumped from the arm of the chair into the battered-looking sofa that seemed to part-swallow him. He was still muttering about how it was his fault. His eyes were down.

Sandra's voice sounded instantly surprised. The conversation was very short.

Maddie squatted back in front of him. 'She'll be here in a few minutes. She asked if there was anything you needed. She sounded genuine.'

He lifted his eyes. 'She was good to me. For a long time. Her patience ran out. Alyssa's never did. My angel . . .' This time, the sobs took him over. Maddie backed away. He slumped onto his side, his head buried in the cushion. Sandra took less than five minutes. Maddie answered some questions. There was no way of flowering them up, of making the truth less harsh. Alyssa Mills was thrown from the back of a lorry by her boyfriend, a man who they now know was under duress at the time and who died too. The man responsible overall was in custody and would never be seeing the outside of a prison cell again — his sister the same. Maddie knew it was scant consolation. She knew it wouldn't be enough for Sandra and she couldn't comprehend the impact on Kevin Mills. And at this moment, neither could he.

Maddie and her colleague backed away. Sandra wrapped herself up in her brother. They sobbed together. It was time to leave. Maddie still had another difficult message to deliver. This was one she had insisted on giving. This one was personal.

CHAPTER 36

Maddie lifted her hand to knock but just rested her knuckles on the cold wood of the door. From Kevin Mills's address in Langthorne she had taken the short journey up the motorway to Ashford, to Hythe Road specifically. Behind this door was a young boy seeking answers, some of which Maddie now had. But Rose would need answers, too, and not just about the boy who was still in her care.

The door yanked open. Maddie hadn't made a sound. Someone must have been waiting for her.

Of course it was Rose. She stepped back from her front door, her bottom lip trapped tightly between her teeth. She raised both hands to rest on her cheeks and her eyes welled. Maddie suddenly felt unprepared for Rose. She surely would have heard bits from the media, an officer seriously injured, fighting for her life even and named as DC Rhiannon Davies. It was a big part of the reason why Maddie had insisted that she be the one to come out and that she do it alone. She knew how close they were. It was only right it was her that told her — and before anyone else.

'She's going to be okay!' Maddie broke into a smile and then welled up herself. It was instant, like a wave that pulsed out from her heart. The embrace was crushing.

Rose took her up with incredible power. Maddie hugged her right back.

'Oh, thank you, God! Thank you, God Almighty! I knew it. I knew it, you know! She's a little fighter that one!'

'She is.'

'Can I see her?'

'She'll certainly want to see you. She's still in hospital. She lost a lot of blood and she's still very weak. They're still monitoring her fluids and they want her much stronger and clear of any risk of infection before they let people see her or she gets out. It won't be long, though.'

Maddie felt Rose shake with a sob. She stepped back. 'Come in! Come in . . . I'll make tea!' The standard British response to news, good or bad: someone had to put a kettle on.

'Great!'

'And you need to speak to our friend?'

'I do.'

'He still hasn't spoken a word to me. I took a call from your lot. They said something about how he just wasn't talking because he'd been told not to or something? They said he might be okay now. Do you think he'll talk to you today? They said you had news about his family?'

'I do. But I spoke to Anna, the psychologist who came here. She's been very good, actually. We may have got off on the wrong foot but she does know her stuff. She's not convinced he will talk. Not straight away. She said he might have found the silence a good way of coping with all this. It may take a while to sink in, but the good thing is, we don't need him to talk to us now. There's no pressure. He can take all the time he needs.'

'Well, that I agree with! I said that to your lot on the phone, I'd like him to stay.'

'Thank you, Rose. We really can't think of anyone better.'

'I said about adoption. Down the line, I mean, if that becomes a need. I don't know what other family he has, but

I'd like him to stay here. I'd like to know he's getting his childhood.'

Maddie beamed. 'I thought you were retired, Rose!'

Rose beamed right back then she leaned forward to take hold of Maddie's shoulders. Her smile dropped away a little. 'I chose to be a parent as my career, love — a mother. You don't retire from that!'

This time, Maddie initiated the hug. Both women's attention was drawn by the creaking of a step. When Maddie looked up she saw a shadow move, then heard footsteps as someone small and light sprinted across the landing.

'I think he's looking forward to seeing you,' Rose said. 'I'll put that kettle on.'

Maddie nodded. She sucked in a final gulp of air and started up the steps. Every one creaked. The lighting was poor, just like it had been for her last visit. The same blind was pulled on the window over the stairs. The window in Alex's room was covered, too. She stopped when she got close enough to see in. Straight away, there was the familiar shape of the boy sat under his duvet. She sat down on the landing.

'Hey, Alex,' she said. She was aware her voice was carrying her tension and she took a moment to gather herself. She couldn't come across as nervous. She had practiced how she could explain what had happened, but her mind was suddenly blank, struggling for a place to start.

'You remember me, right? We've met a couple of times. There's no one else here, okay? So you don't need to worry. I won't come any closer. I just came here to tell you about your brother and sister. Is that okay?'

There was no reaction.

'They're both okay. But you have to come out of there for me to tell you more. I don't even know if you're awake!' She chuckled, she reckoning it sounded more natural. There was still no movement. She chewed on her lip. The message she had practiced was focussed on how his brother and sister were okay, about how they might have made mistakes and how they were in custody, but were still trying to piece it

346

all together. How it might turn out that they hadn't done anything wrong. Now she was sitting in front of him, or at least his outline, she couldn't say it. It didn't seem right, she knew what they had done, they had both made full admissions in their interviews, Mark Garner to the point of boasting. She decided on a change of tact.

'They can't hurt you, Alex. Not anymore.' Her words were almost blurted. She held her breath. There was movement, slow at first. She saw the duvet slither off the upright figure and his face was revealed. The light leaking from behind the curtains was enough for her to see some features at least. His hair was longer than she remembered and it was messed up by static. The last time she had seen him clearly it had been stuck down by a clump of dried blood. He was back to being still and silent, his exposed arms resting in his lap as he wrung his hands.

'We found Michelle first. She told us all about it — all about Mark and how he had got himself involved with some people who were making him do bad things. She told me about your dad, too, Alex.' Maddie paused. The boy's head dropped a little, his frizzy hair pointing towards her. 'About what Mark did. About how you were there. Then Mark told us, too. So you don't need to tell us about that, you don't have to talk about it ever again if you don't want to and no one is going to try and make you. Is that okay?' Maddie waited for longer this time. Alex sniffed. His head was still slumped forward. She chanced movement, rising to her knees and moving to the edge of the room. His head lifted up to her as she dug in her bag. Making sure her movements were slow and deliberate, she pulled out an empty water bottle. She squeezed it gently and it made a crackling sound. She stood it up in the middle of the room and backed away. She stayed kneeling.

'Your dad, Alex . . . We found him, too. I think you probably know that he died. I'm so sorry. But there can be a proper funeral now. I want you to know that it is going to happen. We'll make sure you can go if you want to. I thought you might want to say goodbye . . .' Maddie was starting to struggle now with not getting any reaction. She didn't know if she was making things better or worse. His face was still down; he was still silent.

'I know this is hard. Your family are gone. But Rose, downstairs . . . she really wants you to stay and she really wants it to be for as long as you want. Forever even. You'll be safe here — and so loved! I don't know how you feel about that but Rose . . . she's a wonderful woman. She loves you very much . . .' Maddie heard another sniff. 'Do you think that might be something you would like?'

The boy's head moved so he was looking down towards the bottle in the middle of his floor. He shifted to the edge of the bed, closer to the bottle, still not close enough to touch it. His legs hung over the edge of the bed and he was still slumped forward. She could see the arc in his back. He sniffed again.

'Rhiannon . . . she's a friend of mine. She came to see you. She wanted to come back today. She will come and see you again. When she was younger, she lost her family, too, and she came here. And Rose loved her, too. And, my goodness, she still does! Rhiannon wanted me to tell you that you'll be safe here. She wanted me to remind you that you're not alone, Alex, no matter what you think. And that they can't hurt you.' Maddie spoke out into the room, remembering her conversation with Rhiannon, the concern in her eyes, the sadness in her words when they had talked about this boy.

Suddenly there was movement. The boy had sprung from his bed and he paced towards her. The bottle was kicked over as he moved and it spun against the wall. Maddie was still kneeling. She just had time to raise her arms as the boy made straight for her.

He fell into her, his stick thin arms wrapped around her head at first. She rocked back and the boy reset his grip to hug her midriff. His grip was strong and warm, his head pushed hard into her chest and she could feel his sobs. She steadied herself enough to be able to work her own arms and she hugged him back. She felt herself break, too; the emotion of the past week got the better of them both.

Maddie scrunched her eyes tightly shut. She opened them to the sound of the creaking top step. Rose stood out in the hall.

'Let's start with some sunlight shall we!' Rose said. The hall suddenly erupted in swathes of warm daylight. The boy was still buried in Maddie's chest but he reacted to the light. Blinking and squinting he looked over towards Rose. 'Will you stay then, lad?' Rose beamed. 'You don't have to do anything you don't want to do, but I would love to have you!'

Maddie felt his grip loosen. The boy was looking at her. She smiled and felt a thick tear run down to her lips. She nodded. The boy ran the distance between her and Rose and, judging by her expression, his grip on her was just as tight.

CHAPTER 37

Harry was already sitting on the park bench. He had his back to Maddie as she approached. The sun was bright and carried the warmth of an established spring season. The thick-trunked trees that stood in silent formation on the riverbank were now starting to show their colour on branches that leaned out over the meandering water.

'Hey,' she called out when she was a few steps short. He dipped forward at the sound of her voice, and when he sat back up he was holding two takeaway coffee cups. He held one out for her to take.

'Hey.'

'Now I *am* worried!' Maddie stayed standing at the end of the bench.

'Worried?'

'First you don't show for work, then there's a text asking me to meet you here, but you don't reply to my follow-up questions.'

'And there were a lot of those!' Harry cut in, but his tone was warm, almost jovial.

Maddie relaxed a little. 'What can I say, I'm a detective.'

'So I hear.'

'And now I get here to find you've bought me a coffee.'

You make it sound like I never bought you one before.'

'Never for no good reason.'

She took a seat. The water made a pleasant gurgling sound where it was shallower at the edge. It mingled with the birdcalls and she was almost able to forget that they were in the middle of the busy city of Canterbury. A superstore was visible as a smudge of orange through the branches.

'I checked the system . . . you don't have any annual leave booked this week. It shows you as *in*, actually.'

'Of course you did!'

'I'm a detective.'

'So you said.'

'What's going on, Harry?'

'I got told to stay away for a few days. It's pretty standard.'

'Suspended?' She turned from the nature scene around her to study him. He kept facing forward and her eyes fell on the smudge of scarring across his cheek. She felt her anger rising. The things this man had given for that job and they had *suspended* him!

'No. The boss was quick to tell me it isn't a suspension. The first time he told me I believed him. When he went on to tell me again another two times I started to believe him less.'

'Why would they suspend you?'

'They haven't. Don't forget that. The boss was very insistent. It's standard with this sort of thing apparently. He told me that a lot, too.'

'This sort of thing?' She was incredulous — like their last seven days was in any way *standard*.

'An officer got injured. Seriously injured. I went in alone. I didn't call the area commander or firearms cadre. Knowing what I knew at the time, I should have sent it up the line for other tactical options.'

'Rhiannon would have died. We'd never have got anywhere near her.'

'I agree.'

'The boss doesn't?'

'He didn't say that and he doesn't matter.'

'Did you tell him what you did?'

'What I did?'

'I saw the message you sent on Michelle's phone, Harry. You told Garner that a police officer was going in there to try and fool him. To get close enough to take him out . . . Why would you do that?'

'I saw an opportunity. He was taking orders from that phone . . . *tasks*. I needed to get his attention on me and away from Rhiannon. He was never going to believe I was part of the same thing he was. I couldn't be what he was expecting. I knew he trusted that phone. It was our only chance.'

Maddie failed to suppress a grin. 'You're the cleverest stupid person I've ever met, you know that?'

'She nearly died, Maddie. I can hardly say I'm proud.' The warmth was gone from his voice.

'She didn't, though. I don't see what else would have got that outcome, to be honest. I think you saved her life. And that got you suspended?'

'I'm not suspended, remember?'

'Ah yes, you just can't go to work and you're on full pay.'

'There's more. Another complication.'

Maddie had relaxed a little. She was back to watching two ducks dipping their beaks in the water. Now she stiffened. 'More?'

'Why I wanted to talk to you. I was hard on you. Too hard. And I'm sorry.'

'That's what this is? An apology?'

'Well, no. I mean, that's the apology.' Harry nodded at her cup.

'No it isn't. It's a hot drink.'

'Very good. So, yes, this is an apology. I wanted to say you didn't let anyone down. The whole blundering thing too . . . I shouldn't have said it. We're all blundering through life, truth be told. This wasn't your fault; you shouldn't have to be looking over your shoulder. Mark Garner was the bad man, not you.'

'Okay. I did get lax. I could have done things better. I've learned lessons. I don't need you to say—'

'I wasn't angry with you. I was angry with me. When you went to follow up your lead at the café, I should have come with you . . .'

'You went to Maidstone and had it out with a Probation Officer who wasn't doing his job. It's no—'

'I had no right!' Harry blurted. He came back more measured. 'I didn't . . . I was angry Wootan wasn't going back to prison and I let that guide me. I got nowhere. Then I went to where he lived, I didn't learn, when I called you . . . I should have called you earlier. I know you would have stopped me.'

'Okay. But you didn't. You said yourself, making a mistake can happen, it's only a problem when we don't learn from it.'

'I saw him die, Maddie. And I did nothing. I didn't just sit outside. I barged my way in. And there was a witness. He was there, too, in the flat — with me.' Harry paused. Maddie knew he wasn't finished.

'They found Wootan's body in his flat a couple of days ago. He overdosed. He didn't turn up for an appointment and someone checked his place. They spoke to a few of his associates and someone told a copper that they had seen someone leaving the flat a few days earlier. Old, heavy build, waxed jacket with a scarred face.'

'You were there? In the flat?' Maddie breathed.

'I checked for a pulse. It was weak but it was there.'

Maddie bit down on her lip while she tried to process what she was being told. 'Is that it?'

'What do you mean?'

'Is that all they have? Someone loosely matching your description was at the scene of an overdose? Are they going down the ID route?'

'The point is, I *was* at the scene. Yes he had already overdosed by the time I got there, but I did nothing. I let him die.'

'Is that what you told the boss?'

353

'Of course not!'

'So the ID route then? Are they going to prove you were there?'

'No. This *witness* isn't giving anything official. It's just hearsay.'

'And are they even looking at foul play?'

'They certainly weren't before this witness was located. The report was of someone seen leaving the building, not his specific flat. There's not enough for it to be called as sus.'

'But enough for you to be not suspended.'

'Enough for questions to be asked. If I was ID'd . . .'

'I would nick you for that,' Maddie said.

Harry snorted. 'Of course you would! You're a detective.'

'So I'm told.'

'The boss reckons it'll go away. The scene tells a pretty clear story. Forensics supports that he injected himself with heroin. The toxicology shows it was enough to take down a bear, let alone a recent release from prison whose tolerance may have dropped away if he didn't have access inside.'

'But you lied to me. That's why we're sat on the bench and I had a white coffee waiting and you forgot the sugar?'

Harry tutted. He dug around in his jacket pocket and threw two brown sachets onto Maddie's lap. 'I watched a man die. The first priority of any police officer: protect life and limb. I didn't. I walked away.'

'And does that bother you?'

'No. But I wanted to tell you, I wanted you to know that it's okay for it to bother you.'

'Thanks for your permission, I mean, it doesn't. He was a piece of shit.'

'We don't get to choose.'

'You did.'

Harry sighed. 'I have to live with that. I've been distracted. Wootan . . . my daughter . . . Jarod Logan . . . I couldn't juggle it all. I've not been sleeping well. But that's been for a while.'

'Do you think it will be easier now?'

'I don't know. He's dead. I know that. I thought it would make it instantly better — easier. It didn't.'

'Of course it didn't, Harry. There's a big hole in your life, in all your lives. You can't fill a hole by taking something else away.'

'I know you're right.' He paused and shook his head. 'You know, I stopped using the automatic car the job gave me from the moment I heard Wootan was coming out. My arm still aches — it gives me jip all the time, but I didn't want for him to be out and me still suffering physically from what he did. I just pretended like I wasn't. My arm was aching any time I was in a car. I can't explain why I did that. You think you're someone rational, sensible even. Seems I'm not at all.'

'I can see the logic. It's not irrational, it's defiance. And if there's one thing you're good at . . .'

Harry sighed. 'But the thing that's eating at me the most is how I treated you. I'm going to talk with someone. Not through the job — some bloke my daughter recommends. Some trauma bloke. Maybe I need that.' He shrugged.

Maddie sat back, focussed on the sound of the moving water. A duck eyed them closely as if it was waiting for something to be discarded. 'I've never felt like that before. It was like I suddenly lost all confidence in myself, I could barely think straight. You stepped up though, Harry. Despite all you've had going on, you stepped up and you led us all through it. I look around at who else there is and there's not enough good leaders out there. This thing will blow over. We'll get Rhiannon stitched up and looked after and we can all get back to doing what we do best.'

Harry smacked his lips. His attention seemed to be on the same duck. 'A good leader doesn't smash the confidence of his finest asset just to demonstrate that he can pick up the pieces. I learnt a lesson. That's all I wanted to say.'

'So this is it, then?' Maddie said.

'It?'

'Lack of sleep, a man dragged to his death, a self-harming daughter, a massive injustice, and wearing the blood of your colleague. This is what it takes for you to realise that we all need a little help sometimes? Jesus, Harry, you're not a robot. Stuff like that affects you — how you work, how you deal with other people.'

'Seems you're right.'

'You should know that by now. And you know this is going on the list, right?'

'List?'

'*Things I know about Harry.* This is number four . . . *What it takes to make him crack up.*'

'I'm not cracking up!' Harry's face was stern, but it broke almost instantly into a wide smile with a chuckling accompaniment. 'And if this bloke tells me I am, I just won't go back.'

Maddie laughed harder. 'Classic copper coping mechanism! Bury your head! I'll have to start calling you *Mallard.*'

Harry turned to her, confused. She gestured out towards the river. He followed her gaze, to where the duck now had its head forced under the water, its soaking bottom pointed towards them.

Harry Blaker got the reference instantly. And Maddie reckoned this was the first time she had heard him belly laugh.

THE END

OTHER BOOKS BY CHARLIE GALLAGHER
MADDIE IVES

Book 1: HE IS WATCHING YOU
Book 2: HE WILL KILL YOU
Book 3: HE WILL FIND YOU

LANGTHORNE POLICE SERIES
Book 1: BODILY HARM
Book 2: PANIC BUTTON
Book 3: BLOOD MONEY
Book 4: END GAME

STANDALONES
MISSING
THEN SHE RAN
HER LAST BREATH
RUTHLESS

Don't miss Charlie's next stunning thriller, join our
mailing list:

www.joffebooks.com/contact/

FREE KINDLE BOOKS

Please join our mailing list for free Kindle crime thriller, detective, mystery, romance books and new releases, as well as news on the next book by Charlie Gallagher!

www.joffebooks.com/contact/

Thank you for reading this book. If you enjoyed it please leave feedback on Amazon, and if there is anything we missed or you have a question about then please get in touch. The author and publishing team appreciate your feedback and time reading this book.

Our email is office@joffebooks.com

Follow us on facebook www.facebook.com/joffebooks

We hate typos but sometimes they slip through. Please send any errors you find to corrections@joffebooks.com

We'll get them fixed ASAP. We're very grateful to eagle-eyed readers who take the time to contact us.

Made in the USA
Columbia, SC
06 May 2023